"An engaging sci-fi blend of military and politics ... Fast-paced novel for fans of military science fiction."
– **Mike Resnick**
Hugo & Nebula Award Winning Author

"What a promising first novel from Mike Lynch and Brandon Barr — exciting space battles, convincing characters we can care about, sense of wonder and real heart. If only the space opera I grew up on had been this human."
– **Bruce McAllister**
2007 Hugo Award nominee

"When The Sky Fell's greatest strength is its believable and foreseeable science — you can easily see how our society could evolve into that presented in the book. Fans of military science fiction, with an emphasis on space battles, will enjoy this book immensely."
– **Joshua Palmatier**
author of *The Vacant Throne*

"In war, things can go wrong, and people will react well, or badly. Such is the case in this action-filled, page-turning, epic space battle for the survival of planet Earth. Hang on to your seats!"
– **James C. Glass**
author of the Shanji trilogy
www.sff.net/people/jglass

"Compelling heroes, interesting allies, dastardly villains, wonderful pacing, and lovely descriptions of night skies glimpsed on distant planets. If you love 23rd-century space adventures, *When the Sky Fell* is for you."
– **Kris Stoever**
co-author, *For Spacious Skies: The Uncommon Journey of a Mercury Astronaut*, and daughter of Mercury Astronaut, Scott Carpenter

"Exuberant space opera in the style of the Golden Age of Sci-Fi."
– **Michael Z. Williamson**
author of *Freehold*

SKY CHRONICLES
WHEN THE SKY FELL

by

Mike Lynch & Brandon Barr

HOLLISTON, MASSACHUSETTS

Cover Art by Glenn Kim
First printing, May 2009
10 9 8 7 6 5 4 3 2 1

ISBN # 0-9787782-3-5
ISBN-13 # 978-0-9787782-3-1
LCCN # 2009921816

Silver Leaf Books, LLC
P.O. Box 6460
Holliston, MA 01746
+1-888-823-6450
Visit our web site at www.SilverLeafBooks.com

Brandon's Dedication:
For my wife, my father, and for Gary

Mike's Dedication:
To my wife, Kathleen, for your unwavering support, and believing I
could one day become a published author

Brandon's Acknowledgement:

I want to thank Mr. S, my fifth-grade teacher for sparking in me a fascination for writing, and Dr. Lu, for helping me rediscover that fascination again in college. I want to thank Michael Crichton, and Ray Bradbury, whose stories fanned the flames of my young imagination. Thank you C.S. Lewis, and Cordwainer Smith, for writing science fiction that ministered to my heart, transcending mere escapism.

Mike's Acknowledgement:

I would like to thank Gary Berg and Kevin Lyter for their timely insights and suggestions during the writing of this novel. I would also like to thank Elena Walker for her optimism and encouragement during this arduous process. She helped me believe in myself when I was tempted to quit.

And to Brett Fried, managing editor at Silver Leaf Books, whose faith in us made this whole thing possible. Thank you for your patience, and for answering the hundreds of questions we asked you as you guided us through all the ups and downs. You have our most sincere gratitude.

SKY CHRONICLES

WHEN THE SKY FELL

PROLOGUE

And I looked when He broke the sixth seal, and there was a great Earthquake; and the sun became black as sackcloth made of hair, and the whole moon became like blood; and the stars of the sky fell to the Earth ...
-Revelation 6:12-13

S.F.S. CORONA
0102 PROXIMA MERIDIAN TIME, AUGUST 30, 2217

"I'm beginning to pick up multiple images on my monitor," the RadAR technician cried out.

Commander Yamane kept his place in the command chair, not moving. The Deravans were out there; that he knew. It was just a matter of time before they arrived. He gave his uniform a quick tug. "What's their speed... and how long before they reach the *Lexington?*"

The r-tech's hands fumbled for the information on his console. He turned back. "1.01 stellar velocity, Commander. Their ETA is fifteen minutes."

Yamane glanced at the display on his right. To his horror, dozens of blips had already filled the screen. He turned away, his mind reflexively avoiding what it did not want to acknowledge. The confidence he had in his plan a few short hours before ebbed at the sight so many enemy warships.

Another feeling, almost as powerful as the first, hit him with near perfection. Fear? Panic? No. Irony. Yes, that was it. How else could he describe the very best the enemy had to offer, pitted against a wreck of a ship? He looked up at the main screen. His former command, the *Lexington*, glistened in the distance. Sorrow tugged at Yamane. Images of abandoning ship came crashing into his mind. Both he and his crew had just managed to get to the escape pods before the Deravans closed in for the kill, all but blasting the stellar cruiser out of existence. Now he, however, had turned the tables on them and worked his ship's demise into his advantage. All the hope in the world, however, meant nothing if those power cells hidden in the *Lexington*'s bowels didn't charge up at the precise moment required. Otherwise, the fleet under his command would find itself in a very bad situation. "Come on, girl," he said under his breath. "Don't let me down."

"The Deravans will be in range of the *Lexington* in ten minutes."

Yamane verified their position again. The blips were there, but in even greater numbers than before. "Have all sub-cruisers assume an attack posture. Standby on my mark!"

"Defensive computer protocols have been engaged," C-tech Landis said to Yamane. "All targeting monitors are online. Pulse cannons are at full power."

The commander leaned back in his seat and surveyed the bridge. He tried to gauge the status of his crew. *Will they remember their training when both sides meet in battle?* For that question, Yamane did not have an answer. "Distance to enemy ships?" he asked after glancing at the main screen.

Sitting to the left of the RadAR station, the nav-tech replied, "Sixteen thousand kilometers."

"The Deravans are redeploying their fleet," the r-tech yelled over the sounds of computer systems buzzing around him.

Their overall formation, once a solid and unbroken mass of metal and machines, reorganized itself into three lesser-sized squadrons in a matter of seconds. The efficient manner in which the Deravans executed the maneuver chilled Yamane. "Speed and heading?" he asked.

"Unchanged," the r-tech replied. "They are maintaining their heading toward Mars."

Yamane's ship, the *Corona*, sat behind and a little above the Antaren dreadnoughts. They were laid out in front of her like twelve breech-loaded shells, ready for use at a moment's notice. Located at the highest point of the stellar cruiser was the bridge. And in the middle of the bridge Commander Yamane waited...and worried. The overwhelming numbers at the Deravan's disposal rattled him—and he had good reason to feel as he did. If they tried to take on the enemy one ship at a time, the fighters, dreadnoughts, and destroyers under his command would be sitting ducks against the Deravans' superior guns. But he had learned from past mistakes. They didn't have the firepower to outfight them, but he hoped to outthink them. On this his whole plan rested.

Optimism wrestled against Yamane's fears. *Perhaps we can win this fight with little difficulty after all.* A nice sentiment, but it was a lie. Who was he kidding? A single fear had been haunting him from the beginning—that the Deravans could alter their course at any moment and fly beyond the range of the *Lexington*. And if they did, Yamane would be right back to where he started—taking them on from a position of weakness. On the other hand, the Deravans might also hold their present heading, right into the trap he laid. The odds seemed fifty-fifty, either way.

Doubts crept in. *What if—?* Yamane could not finish so terrible a thought. Shifting uncomfortably in his chair, he stared at their trajectory marked on the r-tech's targeting grid. The enemy armada held firm; they had not changed course. He should have been pleased, but something deep within told him they were taking too much for granted. "Time to intercept?"

"Six minutes, twenty seconds."

Every tick of the clock forced his hand into a direction he didn't want to go. Placing his frontline ships in the line of fire was taking a terrible risk, but keeping the enemy fleet on course had to outweigh all other considerations. Ruthless thinking to be sure, but with the survival of humanity at stake, he felt he had no other alternative.

"Signal Commander Moran," Yamane said to c-tech Landis. "Tell him to prepare for an assault on the Deravan fleet."

Landis spun around. "Sir?" he gasped, his eyes wide. "You want him to do what?"

"You heard me, Lieutenant," the commander barked back. "When the enemy armada flies within ten thousand kilometers of the sub-cruisers' position, they will fire their thrusters and make their course right for them. Then when Moran's fleet is ten kilometers away from the Deravans, they will fire a five-second salvo before circling back, past the *Lexington*. We must ensure the enemy maintains its heading, even if it means risking some of our ships."

Landis shook his head in a knowing way. "Understood, Commander," he smirked. "I'll send the message now."

S.F.S. DRUMMOND
0115 PROXIMA MERIDIAN TIME, AUGUST 30, 2217

In less than a millisecond, decoding algorithms incorporated into the *Drummond*'s transceiver unscrambled Yamane's orders, flashing them across her communication console. "Sir," the c-tech called out, "I am receiving a transmission from the *Corona*. Commander Yamane is giving us the go signal for a direct assault against the Deravan fleet."

Moran brought up his data pad and scrolled down the text. "What are the two distances?"

"Ten and ten."

"Tell him we'll make ourselves big fat targets," he said with a broad grin.

The c-tech offered a weak smile in response and then sent Moran's answer.

Repositioning himself in the command chair, he assessed their tactical situation. There, ahead of him, were hundreds of ships, all positioned equidistant from one another. Moran leaned to his right. "What is the distance between the two fleets?" he asked the r-tech.

Beads of sweat glistened on the tech's forehead. "Twelve thousand kilometers, Commander."

"And their heading?"

The r-tech inputted a set of commands into his console. "Unchanged. They are coming right at us, course—zero-zero-seven."

"Not long now," Moran said, almost in the form of a prayer. "Just a little bit more."

"Deravan ships are now eleven thousand kilometers away."

"Almost there," he whispered.

The distinctive sound of the proximity alarm went off. "Ten thousand kilometers."

Moran stood upright. "Now!" he yelled. "Fire up the main engines."

The c-tech signaled all seven ships waiting in line; their guns poised on those enemy vessels in the line of fire. In an act of unanticipated choreography, the thrusters of every sub-cruiser ignited at the same instant. A flash of brilliant white light demonstrated to the dreadnoughts and cargo barges behind them just how exact their timing had been.

Moran's vessel took the point. Coming up about a thousand meters back, three ships on his starboard side and three on his port, the six other sub-cruisers fanned out like sharpened talons, readying themselves for a quick strike.

The r-tech's attention remained fixed and resolute. Nothing existed for him except the targeting display a few centimeters away. He tracked the enemy's movements, until the proximity alarm just to his left rang out a second time. "We've reached the ten kilometer mark," he said to the commander after turning back.

Moran's face became tight. "All batteries...commence firing!"

A blaze of red and blue plasma bursts shot across the bows of all seven sub-cruisers. Multiple numbers of flashes registered in the distance several moments later, and then—nothing.

"What is their course and speed?" Moran shouted out.

The r-tech verified the results. "Unchanged, sir. Pulse blasts have had no effect."

Moran glanced at the astro-clock. They had just enough time. "Give them a second volley."

"I'm inputting the command now."

Every gunner homed in on his prey, locked on, and then fired. Dozens of energy bolts coursed through the cannon chambers, discharging a fraction of a second later. In a mirror-like repeat of the first salvo, the lethal bursts slammed into the hulls of those ships ten kilometers away, detonating into dazzling fireballs. When the massive bombardment dissipated, the truth became all too evident. Deravan shields had absorbed the full fury of what the sub-cruisers could throw at them. Without exception, every one of their vessels flew through the barrage, undeterred.

"Hard about!" Moran ordered. "One hundred and eighty degrees."

After he entered the command codes into his console, the nav-tech grabbed a hold of two support struts and held on tight. The sub-cruiser's directional thrusters fired on cue. Fighting the forces throwing her forward, the million-ton warship traveling at 0.35 stellar velocity began to buckle. Bulkheads let out deep moans as they contorted under increasing pressure, while deck plates started to pop out of their brackets.

"Commander, we're coming around too fast," the navigator yelled. "She's not going to make it."

"Hang on!" The *Drummond* suddenly lurched over. Everyone on the bridge took hold of whatever was within reach when the sub-cruiser banked hard on her port side.

"Come on, baby," Moran whispered to himself, "don't let me down."

Responding in an almost cognizant way, his ship swung around in a parabolic arc, back towards the *Lexington*.

Moran clutched his data pad tight. "Are the Deravans still pursuing us?"

The r-tech wiped the perspiration from his forehead. "Affirmative, sir. They're holding steady. Course—zero-zero-seven."

S.F.S. CORONA
0119 PROXIMA MERIDIAN TIME, AUGUST 30, 2217

Commander Yamane's ship waited before the crimson disk of Mars. Despite being outgunned by a factor of fifty, he knew they had to be the victors. If not, the enemy armada would snuff out the human race without a second thought. The Deravan's unprovoked attack against Earth had been brutal, savage. Their bombardment of death since that terrible day had brought humanity to the brink of extermination. "Twenty to one," Yamane whispered to himself. Too low. *More like a hundred to one.* He sighed deeply.

"The Deravans will be in range of the *Lexington* in thirty seconds."

Yamane checked the r-tech's monitor for a third time. To his horror, enemy ships encompassed the left side of the display, while shattered remnants of their once proud fleet dotted the right. His attention remained fixed on those barely recognizable derelicts floating in the distance. Would they be joining them? He lifted his eyes. *We'll all know soon enough.*

"The Deravans will be in range in twenty seconds."

Yamane swiveled around in his command chair. His face became hard. "Don't press that button until I give the word," he said to the r-tech, his voice deep.

"Aye, sir," he replied. "Ten more seconds."

Every pair of eyes settled on the main screen. "Five...four...three," the crew mouthed in unison, "two...one...zero." High-pitched alarms rang out from every corner of the bridge.

"The Deravans are now in range!"

Yamane exhaled, paused for a second and then said, "Charge up the cells."

The c-tech's finger came down on that most important of buttons, the one sequencing the final command directive. All three transceivers scrambled the compressed data streams before sending them to the omega band receivers on board the *Lexington*.

A penetrating silence filled the bridge.

"Power signal sent, Commander. They should charge up right about now."

The Deravan fleet, positioned at its closest proximity to the *Lexington*, flew past the stellar cruiser. Every gauge and display tied into the power cells, however, remained at zero. The electro-magnetic field had not formed. Yamane waited for several moments. A feeling of dread crept up on him. Seconds passed, but still no change. Something had gone wrong.

"The signal isn't going out," Landis stammered.

Now dread *and* fear gripped Yamane. "Re-initiate the program and send out the signal again."

Landis inputted the sequence a second time. He looked back, his face pale and glistening. One second turned into two, then four, and then eight. The c-tech's eyes darted back and forth. "I don't understand," he said in a shaky voice. "Power levels are still at zero."

Yamane rushed over to the communication console and singled out the flashing red button amidst a sea of knobs and switches—the one signifying the difference between life and death. Giving it a firm press with the heel of his hand, he forced his attention back up to the main screen. Hope buoyed his expectations. Disaster met him there. They had not stopped the Deravans. Terrible images of what they would soon unleash against Earth flashed before his eyes.

"I've tried everything," Landis complained, "but the signal *still* isn't reaching the cells."

"Try again!" Yamane snapped back with a distant, almost trancelike stare.

Hesitation filled the c-tech's eyes. He started to speak, but re-inputted the directive instead.

Shrill noises came from every speaker on the bridge, providing the dim answer. "The transmitters are working perfectly, but something is blocking the outgoing signal."

Walls, ceiling tiles, deck plates—they all pressed in on Yamane. He responded with slow, deliberate steps away from the main screen. In that one instant, everything seemed lost. There was no backup plan for him or for Moran. The Deravans would hit his ships first, and then attack the rest of the fleet without hesitation. Confusion reigned in his mind. He needed a solution, any solution. None came.

Yamane closed his eyes tight. He hoped it would shake him out of his stupor. It didn't work. He opened them again. The frantic sound of Landis yelling into his headset trailed off into a deep silence. Turning the other way, Yamane became acutely aware that the characteristic noises put out by the ship's instruments were also absent. An undeniable feeling of timelessness seeped over him.

Amidst the darkness and confusion, however, something began to show itself. People and places long since past became clearer as each moment trickled by. Commander Yamane tried to fight the pull back in time, but his desire to return there grew in intensity. Further back he went. Further and further, before the arrival of the Deravans, before the losses they had suffered at Mars, and before the future of humanity hung in the balance.

Then, like a flash of light overwhelming all of his senses, a new reality finally overtook him, too strong to resist...

CHAPTER

1

Lt. Commander Yamane hustled down the walkway, his pace brisk. Major Stan Kershaw kept up with him, stride for stride. They were running late...again. As a person who prided himself on precision and timing in every area in his life, Yamane hated the idea that someone else, even a close friend like Kershaw, could affect his duties in so profound a way. But here he was, late for his third patrol in as many weeks. If things didn't change soon, he would put himself on report.

Yamane caught himself. Despite all his efforts otherwise, he was becoming too rigid, too by-the-book. It bothered him when this happened. It was just another patrol, one of a dozen scheduled to go up that day. If he and Kershaw took off a little past their scheduled departure time, the heavens would not come crashing down on top of them.

Needing a distraction, Yamane found himself staring at a beautiful, darkening amber sky. A middle-aged yellow star hovered a little above the horizon, diminished in size and intensity, given the distance between itself and Titan. The day had almost ended, and many other nighttime stars were already flickering in the distance. Even when the Sun hung high in the mid-afternoon sky, the relative brightness was equivalent to an overcast day on Earth. If it were not for hundreds of light-enhancing satellites ionizing the upper atmosphere, people living in the capital city of

Kalmedia would experience almost perpetual twilight.

"You don't know what you're talking about, Frank," Kershaw objected.

The accusatory statement pulled Yamane out of his refuge of drifting thoughts. He stopped dead in his tracks. "Uh," was all he could get out, followed by a feeble: "I guess—"

"No, you don't guess," Kershaw fired back. His black, wavy hair fluttered back and forth in the wind. "We have just as much right being here as anyone else." He rammed his index finger into Yamane's shoulder patch to better emphasize his point. "Think about it. For over one hundred years, Star Force Command has maintained a consistent policy of outward expansion.

And the planets we've colonized have been nothing more than miserable heaps of dust and rock."

Yamane took in the distant jagged mountains shooting up from the valley floor. Up above them, a shiny object reflected the last bit of light from the waning Sun. He couldn't tell if the ship was coming or going.

Trying a different tactic, Yamane approached their old argument from a new angle. "That's not at all what I'm trying to say. The right to colonize a planet isn't based on whether or not life exists there already. My concern is with the question of Man having a right of to be here in the first place. Who are we that we should claim *any* planet for ourselves?"

A confident grin broke Kershaw's thoughtful gaze. "But you aren't asking a valid question," he replied, as though a pawn had been moved in a game of chess. "When you go back in history, many of our earliest tribes wondered what was beyond the next hill; and then went on over—often with a large contingent of hunters I might add. If there happened to be another tribe on the other side, they resolved their differences, one way or the other. Not many people along the way asked if it should be done. Rather, they fought for what they believed was theirs."

"Again, who's to say either tribe could say this or that piece of land belonged to them. Land is land. It's still going to be here long after we're gone."

"I'll give you that," Kershaw agreed, "but think about what we've been through these past ten years. You remember those planetary leaders who believed Kalmedia could have posed a threat to Earth's security; given the right circumstances. But those fears evaporated overnight when war broke out against the Antaren Empire. After that, no one dared question a need for maintaining a first line of defense here on Titan. Would you just say, 'Hey, this moon belongs to everyone, so go ahead—take it for yourselves?'"

Yamane looked up at the stars again. A stiff breeze from the north had been blowing all day, making the sky particularly clear of dust and clouds. He found the small blue orb circling the middle-aged sun just below the constellation of Cassiopeia. He almost thought he could reach out and touch the planet he called home. "That's my point exactly. You have two groups of people wanting the same thing—territory. Does one side have the right to take it by force?"

"History would say yes. How many peoples and nations have been subjugated by others because they opted not to fight? Again, I go back to Titan. If this base were not here, we would all be speaking Antaren."

Yamane wasn't so convinced. He always believed their fleet of stellar cruisers patrolling the fringes of known space provided a far better defense than a stationary base just outside Kalmedia. "We defeated the Antarens because of you and me, and millions of others who were committed to the fight; not real estate. And now that the war is over, we've managed a peace of sorts between our two peoples. An uneasy peace, to be sure, with suspicions running high on both sides, but they respect our borders, as we do theirs. Your point of view is based on how history has sometimes worked out, not on—"

The sounds of an A-96 Min fighter blasted by them. Haunting in nature, the piercing shrill was unmistakable, rattling a person down to the bones. Even after years of flying, most Star Force ground crews never really got used to the noise a ship's engine could put out.

The pilot angled his ship down, until all three wheels hit the runway hard, filling the air with a multitude of screeching sounds.

"I guess we'll have to settle this matter another day," Yamane concluded. "Duty calls."

A look of disappointment crossed Kershaw's face. Yamane recognized that sulky expression, but winning a philosophical debate paled in comparison to being up there, with the stars. His whole week had been planned around this patrol, and he wasn't about to miss his chance just to appease his friend. Rather than argue, Yamane just spun around and hurried off to the hangar bay.

"Hey, wait up," Kershaw surrendered, and then ran after him.

Upon entering the hangar bay, Yamane noted all fourteen single-seat fighters, seven on one side and seven on the other, parked in their assigned stalls with military precision. Near the front of the bay, Yamane's ship waited for him. His initial inclination had been to climb into the cockpit and roll right onto the tarmac, but he couldn't bring himself to do it, not yet. A ritual needed attending to first, one he had observed since his earliest days in the academy. He wasn't certain if the informal ceremony had been followed out of superstition or habit. Probably a little of both. But he always made it a point of checking over his ship before departing. The mechanics had certainly gone over it with a fine-tooth comb during pre-flight checks, but a trip into space didn't have the same feel if he didn't work the flaps or inspect his fighter himself.

Coming up from behind, Yamane stood before the tail section. Every line and angle came together for him in a significant and profound way. His attention ambled down somewhat. A careful examination of both sets of small, blunted wings, directional thrusters, and the single engine capable of pushing his craft past stellar velocity gave him a sense of limitless freedom. Any chance to go back up there did—every time.

Moving towards the front, Yamane stopped when he faced his ship head on. Two additional fighters parked towards the rear of the hangar caught his eye. Based on their disassembled appearances, they weren't going anywhere. Someone had removed all six turbines from both ships, while parts and tools littered the floor in a haphazard fashion.

"Are you two arguing again?" a mechanic joked after he came from behind a thruster nozzle. Swipes of grease covered his coveralls from top to bottom. "Only reason I know why you'd be this late for another patrol."

Yamane gave the starboard wing a good shake. "I assume she's ready to go up?" he asked.

Kershaw walked up from behind. "Oh, don't worry about him, Sergeant," he said, sarcasm peppering each word. "The lieutenant commander can't wait to get out there and answer the secrets of the universe."

The mechanic let out a restrained laugh before bringing his attention back to the half-repaired nozzle. Finding himself drawn to the same cone-shaped apparatus, Kershaw started rolling up his sleeves, exposing two muscular forearms. "Those crossover valves there need replacing," he offered after a brief examination. "Do you have a modifier wrench handy?"

He had just gotten the housing assembly off when Yamane grabbed his collar and pulled from behind. "You should leave the repairs to the professionals. They know what they're doing."

Kershaw rose to his feet. "But Frank, this will just take a minute."

"We're scheduled for the next patrol, not to put fighters back together."

"I don't know why you always want me flying with you," he replied with that same disappointed look as before. "You know I'm a much better engineer than I am a pilot."

"You don't have to tell me that," Yamane agreed, "but people should find ways of broadening themselves so they aren't stuck in a rut."

Kershaw placed his hands on his hips. "Look who's talking. You've logged in more flying time in the last two months than half the squadron combined."

"Maybe you're right," Yamane countered, "but this will all be a moot point if we don't get out there in the next two minutes. The control tower is waiting for us."

"All right," the major conceded, "but if that fighter is here when we get back, she's all mine."

The mechanic just shook his head, and then resumed his work.

MOFFETT TRACKING STATION, KORIDAN SECTOR
0237 PROXIMA MERIDIAN TIME, AUGUST 17, 2217

Monitor 1 came up negative again. Monitor 2, negative. Ten seconds later, monitor 3 confirmed the results. The tracking computer moved array number 7 to its next pre-programmed position. Once scanned, a single column of numbers popped onto the screen. Monitor 1 came up negative, again. Monitor 2, negative. Ten seconds later, monitor 3 confirmed the results. And on and on the same mind-numbing activity had taken place throughout the night.

Sergeant Morris stared at all nine screens across from him, a blank look on his face, trying his best to remain awake. It had been his tenth double-duty shift in as many days, and he was exhausted. This fact was driven home with the realization that monitoring those same planets in the Rovina system for hours on end had long become a tiresome sight. Most people would feel this way, he reasoned to himself, if they had to do the same monotonous activity for two weeks straight: check an area of space, usually one with little strategic significance, and then move on. The whole thing seemed pointless.

Array number 7 moved over again. Even though the targeted areas were light-years away, the transceiver relayed multiple streams of data in an instant. Morris smiled. In fact, he considered the operational system something of an amusing diversion. Dr. Fredrick Henkle, who had developed the Radial Amplification Resonator fifty years before, created more confusion than anyone he knew. *He must have had a warped sense of humor,* Morris thought. *Why else would he call his creation RadAR?* Confusing name or not, Henkle's invention had revolutionized space travel. At just about any point in the galaxy, an operator could send and receive a signal in a matter of seconds, as though the distance between the two had melted away. From then on, the business of space travel had become a much more practical endeavor. For Morris, however, reaching out to the stars did not give him the personal freedom he thought would be a part of his work. Instead, his duties in the military had become a kind of jail sentence—just him and his keepers, the machines.

Resigned to a purgatory-like existence for the remainder of his shift, Morris picked up another cup of coffee. He couldn't remember if it was his fourth or fifth. As he put in a third packet of sugar, a high-pitched chirp registered on the speaker. He swiveled his chair around. The small, angled display revealed what it had an hour before, a class-M star cluster. Thinking he must be hearing things, Morris reached over and picked up the cream. A beep sounded a second time. He put the cream down and checked the screen again. The same stars appeared, nothing else.

"Those stupid birds are nesting at the arrays again." He picked up his data pad and typed in a memo, "Note to self: Shoo birds away at end of shift."

A high-pitched chirp sounded a third time. The mobile tracker stopped, indicating it had locked onto something. He stared at the screen. Nothing seemed to be different. He rubbed his chin. "Let's see if this works," Morris mumbled to himself. He typed in a series of commands into his console. The booster array signal doubled in strength, increasing picture resolution by almost fifty percent. There, ever so faintly, a hazy image appeared.

"What are you doing all the way out there?" he said under his breath. "Maybe if I tighten the bandwidth." Morris inputted the new directive into his tracking computer. That star cluster, filling just about every square centimeter of the display, moved inward, as though it had collapsed upon itself. Morris' idea was working. There, right before his eyes, the ghost changed itself into a small, fuzzy blip. "Gotcha!" he declared in triumph.

Two rows of analytical computers began to click and whir as they processed a flurry of incoming data. Morris scooted his chair over and studied the numbers. Though broken in spots, the telemetry indicated the object was traveling in a linear direction. "Must be a deep space patrol I forgot about," he concluded. But after accessing flight schedules for that region of space, he found nothing had been scheduled out there for the next two months. *Something's not right about this,* he thought. *Maybe I should contact the duty officer.* Morris switched on the intercom.

"This had better be good," a groggy-sounding voice replied after a lengthy delay.

"Captain Gollanski, this is Sergeant Morris in tracking tower two. I just picked up something unusual on my monitor. I think you should come down here and double-check these findings."

A heavy sigh came through the speaker. "Can it wait until morning?"

"I don't believe so, Captain. Something tells me this might be important."

"You don't believe? That's not much of a—" Gollanski stopped. "I'll be there in a minute," he sighed again. Just as he promised, the duty officer arrived sixty seconds later, on the dot. Draped in a blue flannel robe, he went right up to Morris. "All right, Sergeant," the captain said in a conspicuously gruff manner, "what's so important that couldn't wait until morning?"

Morris swallowed hard. "I've been tracking an unidentified object for the last ten minutes. Telemetry indicates the unknown is coming from sector seven, but we don't have anything scheduled out there until October. I was hoping you might know something about this." The captain, in the midst of a yawn, just shrugged. "Maybe if you see what I'm talking about." He switched the transmission from his console to the one nearest the Captain.

Gollanski rubbed his still-tired eyes. He then bent over and scrutinized the intermittent contact from a closer vantage point. "Preliminary analysis indicates the unknown is traveling in a linear direction," he mumbled to himself. "Are you sure these readings are correct?"

"No doubt about it. I've checked them over three times."

"Sector seven is right at the edge of known space," the captain affirmed. "A transport would need a couple of weeks just to get out there. Has the telemetry indicated what this could be?"

"The object is still too far away. Maybe in an hour or two we can get more accurate data."

"I don't have a good feeling about this." He stood up and stared at the nine screens above. "I think Star Force Command should be informed. Make contact with them right away."

NEW ROANOKE COLONY, BETA CENTAURI
2157 PROXIMA MERIDIAN TIME, AUGUST 10, 2217

Tom Stafford sat on a hill overlooking the desert setting of the Monfort Plains, which had in effect, became his new home. There, down below, he observed twenty temporary shelters set up in two rows of ten, side-by-side. Set inside the shelters, the RadAR shack stood near the middle of the compound. Seven cargo bins placed around it formed a loose circle, and scattered about the camp, various all-terrain vehicles. Except for his fellow settlers, he had not observed any evidence of life elsewhere on the planet, save a seemingly infinite supply of scrub brush growing all over the northern continent.

In his mind's eye, however, their far-flung outpost had already become much more. New Roanoke represented the dreams and aspirations of people who envisioned a better life for themselves and their children. Though the colonists numbered just over a hundred now, perhaps in a few short years the outpost could be the site of a major metropolitan community, with fifty-story buildings lining downtown boulevards, hover ports dotting the landscape, and new cities popping up elsewhere on Beta Centauri.

The collection of shelters below didn't quite measure up to the vision in his mind. And while he would be the first to agree they had a long way to go, the "wild west" aspect of the New Frontier only bolstered his determination. He believed that whatever goals Man set for himself he could fulfill, no matter what the obstacles.

A branch snapped in the distance. Stafford froze. His senses heightened. Unseen rocks tumbled down the darkened embankment. Darting his eyes about, he heard another snap. After crouching down low, he picked up a flashlight lying nearby and grasped it tightly. With his heart thumping, he turned on the light and pointed it into the darkness. His fears subsided when the beam caught a large man with glasses and white beard approaching from below. That description could only fit one person—Jerry Ashby.

"I didn't...mean to...scare you," he gasped between each winded breath. Feeling more at ease, Stafford set the flashlight by his feet again. "I came to tell you the grid will be powered up in five minutes," Ashby said, still breathing hard from his one hundred-meter trek up the steep grade.

"I know," Stafford replied, distance shading his voice. "I just needed a little time alone."

Ashby took in the colony. "Sure is impressive, isn't it?"

Stafford nodded in agreement. "I think New Roanoke is well named. Just as with the colony those English settlers established seven hundred years ago, a whole new future awaits us."

"After the Antares War, I never thought we would see any new settlements in my lifetime. All the ones we had were lost, and no one was so eager to reach out into the unknown again."

A stiff breeze brought a chill to them both. The day had been unusually warm and they were likewise dressed for the weather. But when the blue super giant twelve billion kilometers away crept below the horizon, temperatures dropped fast.

"I think we should get indoors," Stafford suggested.

After feeling the goose bumps on his arms, Ashby quickly agreed.

Because of the sheer drop, the loose, sun-baked clay and dirt made their trip a tricky one. Stafford took a couple of hesitant steps, clomping as he did, and then slid a meter or two before catching his balance. Ashby, slowed by his age and size, approached the descent more cautiously. He tried taking a smaller step before shifting his weight onto the other foot.

Arriving in a cloud of dust and countless small boulders, both men congratulated themselves when they reached the bottom in one piece. Javen Chang, whose turn it was to stand guard that night, powered up the protective grid the instant they stumbled past him. A gentle buzzing noise went from power relay to power relay.

"I've got the next shift in the RadAR shack," Ashby waved. "I'll see you in a few hours."

The name 'RadAR shack' struck Stafford as ironic. Shack was the last name he would give to a building that stretched twenty meters into the sky. The reinforced structure, built out of concrete and steel, easily dwarfed both sets of temporary shelters on either side. But the name somehow stuck, and no one referred to it otherwise.

"Goodnight, Jerry," he waved back and then stopped. Stafford looked at the stars flickering above, and listened. A strong breeze blew past him. A couple of cast iron frying pans hanging on a wire strung between two poles brushed up against each another. The semi-rhythmic dissonant notes drowned out the noise that had first caught his attention. His suspicions eased. *Probably nothing*, he thought, and then continued on his way. Stafford stopped again after taking another half-dozen steps. "Do you hear that?"

Ashby, who had reached the shack doors, also stopped and listened. He scanned the sky above. "Hear what?" he asked after several moments passed.

"Sounds like a low hum...coming from the north end of the canyon."

Ashby looked around. "You must be hearing those energy transformers by the grid."

"No...this sound is different...and it's getting louder."

"I'll go check the scopes inside. Maybe they can tell us if something's out there."

Just as he opened the door, a far-off explosion lit up the night sky. A second or two later, shock waves created by the detonation flew past them, followed by a mild rumbling.

Stafford took a hesitant step forward. "What was that?" he demanded.

Before Ashby could answer, another explosion hit closer to camp. A brilliant yellow and orange plume transformed the night into day for a brief instant, and then faded into darkness. Several families, woken by the noise, came out to see what had happened. Acrid smoke and burning embers met them at their doors. Seconds later, additional explosions detonated all over the compound.

"Get back inside!" Stafford screamed, waving his arms back and forth to get their attention.

A ship of unknown configuration flew overhead in a blink of an eye. The unfamiliar craft targeted a cluster of cargo bins and then fired. Stafford stepped back just as they erupted into crimson balls of light. A blast of superheated air knocked him back a couple of steps. When a second blast landed nearby, he turned and ran in the opposite direction. Trying to keep low, Stafford searched for anything that might provide minimal cover. He caught sight of a person staring at the sky. The person just stood there, frozen.

Three shuttle-sized vessels flew over them both, fired on a pair of temporary shelters, and then disappeared behind a nearby mountain ridge. Stafford took advantage of the opportunity and dashed towards the person standing like a statue in the darkness. "Ashby!" he shouted after recognizing him. "We have to get a message out—before it's too late."

Ashby didn't respond. He just kept his attention fixed on the sky above.

Stafford, realizing his pleas were useless, turned and ran for the RadAR shack. Before he had gone no more than a handful of steps, however, a powerful explosion went off directly behind him. The force of the blast hurled his limp body twenty meters. He struck the ground hard with a thud, and had the wind knocked out of him.

Shaking off the effects of the explosion, Stafford eyed the shack just a stone's throw away. With a force of will almost beyond belief, he scampered to his feet again. The sudden action, accompanied by a terrible ringing in his ears, almost caused him to lose consciousness. *No, I can't be injured*, he willed himself to believe, and then scurried to the other side of the compound. A quick jerk on the outer doors revealed a dimly lit RadAR shack interior. Once inside, Stafford took a split-second to orient himself, and then bolted down a long white corridor. Flying into the control room with almost reckless abandon, he zeroed in on three operators hovering over a pair of consoles. "Have you gotten a message out yet?"

One of them threw down a cipher book in anger. "Neither transmitter is working," he scowled, his voice sharp.

Stafford shot a quick look at both stations. "Not working—why not?"

"The first hit took out our antennas. We did transmit a partial message, but only that we detected some ships on our scopes. The signal went dead after that."

A high-pitched whistle sounded above them. Before Stafford could respond, a massive explosion rocked the RadAR shack. Support beams from above came crashing down, knocking out all but a handful of lights.

Dust and debris filled the control room, followed by an extended period of silence. When he felt it safe enough, Stafford peered out from beneath the computer console he had ducked under. His eyes caught sight of a multi-ton support beam resting on the workstation right above him. The mangled piece of equipment groaned under a weight it had never been designed to support. Thinking quickly, he moved his hand out like a probe, careful to avoid jagged pieces of glass and metal littering the floor. When his index finger bushed past the bent leg of a nearby console, he wrapped his hand around it. Stafford drew in a deep breath and then pulled himself out. Under the flickering of emergency lights, he saw the RadAR console buried under tons of twisted debris. His heart sank. Now there was absolutely no way of getting a message out.

Two more explosions detonated near the building. A wall behind him collapsed into a heap of broken concrete and twisted rebar, filling the control room with even more dust and debris. Stafford wanted to run, to get out while the chance was there, but he couldn't just leave his friends behind. He at least had to try and find them.

As he took a couple of tentative steps forward, a violent coughing fit stopped him in his tracks. Stafford put his sleeve to his mouth, using it to filter out a heavy layer of particulates floating in the air. Then something caught his attention. There, buried underneath tons of concrete and metal, were the men he had spoken with only moments before—all dead. He ground his teeth together. "At least they had a quick end," he thought.

Another hit brought down two smaller girders, slamming them into the concrete foundation below. Stafford realized the RadAR shack was coming undone. If he didn't get out now, the next hit would most likely finish them both off at the same time.

The few surviving emergency lights guided him to a small hole near the south wall. Stafford set his fears aside and scurried through a tangle of wreckage. He found himself outside again. The stars were out now, a pair of moons casting their shadows on the devastation around him. Flames engulfed every building in the camp, both large and small, while thick columns of black smoke billowed up into the heavens. The crackling of multiple fires burned in his ears. He suddenly felt alone.

Two more ships passed by overhead. Stafford took note of their silhouettes against scores of raging fires licking the night sky. He found himself drawn toward the polished, strangely shaped vehicles. They formed a rounded triangle, with appendages flowing out from behind them. It wasn't so much their configuration, but an ominous quality each one possessed. In fact, the very existence of those vessels exuded a frightening darkness—as though some kind of malevolent force was leading Stafford to the edge of an abyss.

Through the fire, a lone figure appeared. His gait remained slow and regulated, unconcerned about what was taking place all around him. "Ashby," Stafford called out.

He stopped. "Is that you, Tom?" he asked in an odd tone, before falling to his knees. Stafford caught him just as he landed on the ground. "Looks like we were wrong. This colony is going to end up like all the others."

Stafford cradled Ashby's head in his arms, rocking him back and forth. "Don't say that...nothing is over until we say it is. We can rebuild ..."

Ashby looked up at his friend, smiled, and then closed his eyes. Stafford felt Ashby's pulse slowing, the last beat dragging out to a standstill. He was gone.

Pain and anger exploded in Stafford. He embraced his dead companion, and began to weep. Another bolt came from the sky and landed near him, but he didn't care. Nothing mattered.

One last blast detonated a short distance away. There was a flash of light and then darkness.

CHAPTER 2

GENERAL COUNCIL CHAMBERS, STAR FORCE COMMAND
0836 PROXIMA MERIDIAN TIME, AUGUST 11, 2217

"How long has it been since that ship's last transmission?" Commodores Hayes asked, his voice amplified by two sets of speakers on both sides of the council chambers.

"About fourteen hours, sir."

"And what was the nature of this transmission?"

"They relayed their speed and location," Colonel Sterfer replied.

"How much time has passed since we first detected the incoming ship?"

"Four days. Sergeant Morris at the Moffett tracking station was the one who sighted the vessel. He informed his commanding officer, who then notified us."

"And how long before it reaches the capital city?"

"Six days—if their velocity and heading remain unchanged."

Seated behind Sterfer in the VIP gallery, a number of high-ranking officers and politicians stirred. They turned towards each other and spoke in hushed voices. About thirty additional junior officers sat behind them, their behavior much more subdued.

"Have there been any other transmissions of significance?"

"Significance?" Sterfer replied. "I'm not sure how to respond."

"The question is straightforward enough," Commodore Hayes stated. "Is there anything else we need to know so a decision regarding the disposition of that ship can be rendered by this body?" He sat back in his overstuffed leather chair behind the elongated, crescent-shaped table and studied the man sitting in front of him. The colonel appeared to be in his fifties, judging by his thinning gray hair. Deliberate in his actions, Sterfer preferred to keep his notes in front of him.

The uneasy seconds ticked by, accompanied by a heavy silence. Hayes could see indecision on Sterfer's face. He was holding back. The commodore did sympathize with him, given the circumstances. The colonel sat alone, pitted against the highest-ranking members of Star Force Command. On his left and right, rows of cameras diligently recorded every detail, both subtle and overt. And sitting behind him in the two-story high, oak-paneled formal meeting room were scores of support personnel scrutinizing the hearings with equal interest.

What weapons did Sterfer have in his arsenal to combat the glare of the spotlight? From what Hayes could see, just two: three rotating fans above, and a glass of water off on his right. An image of David versus Goliath flashed in his mind.

The silence was beginning to grow stale. When a deliberate lack of a response had the potential to jeopardize the outcome of the proceedings, his sympathies were stretched about as far as they could go. "We're waiting, Colonel."

Sterfer frowned first before clearing his throat. "That ship has been sent by a race called the Deravans," he stated. "They have come for the purpose of making contact with us."

Low murmurs filled the council chambers.

Hayes leaned towards his microphone. "You mean to tell me that that ship out there is coming here as a type of emissary?" he asked with a new understanding of why Sterfer had been holding back. If the council permitted the ship's arrival, there were the obvious potential positives: the introduction of new technologies, the eradication of incurable diseases, and the addition of vast repositories of knowledge. If, however, the Deravans had sent that ship as a ploy for making war, namely the annihilation of the human race, then the latter part of the equation no doubt scared Sterfer right to the bones. And as the person responsible for the assessment of such information, all eyes were pointed right at him.

"Yes, sir, that's exactly what I'm saying."

This time, those low murmurs turned into outright talking.

Crack, crack, crack went the gavel in three short, explosive bursts. "I will have order," Senator Garcia objected. Through a direct cause and effect relationship, the voices dropped down by incremental levels every time the sound of the small wooden hammer registered in the chambers. He laid his gavel down in front of him. "Please continue, Commodore Hayes."

The springs underneath Hayes' seat squeaked when he leaned back in his chair. "Thank you, Senator," he replied. "Are we continuing to receive additional messages from the Deravan ship?"

Sterfer shot a quick glance at his notes. "Not at this time, sir. For some unknown reason, they have ceased transmitting."

"Colonel, what are your people doing in light of these unfolding events?"

Sterfer held out his hand and tried to clear his throat. "A moment, please." He picked up the glass and gulped the water down greedily.

The colonel's actions made Hayes feel thirsty, too. The warm, stale air didn't make the situation much better. The purpose of the closed-door hearings was to keep what they discussed from leaking to the press, but having a couple of hundred people cooped up in there all day made it quite hot, almost unbearable. The fans above did help a bit, but the rotating blades mostly circulated the warm air instead of cooling it.

Sterfer finished off his glass of water, but the hot camera lights bearing down on him made his relief short-lived. "When intelligence had been notified about the ship's discovery, we set up a team of specialists so they could track and analyze it. Before their initial transmission, we weren't even sure what we had out there."

"If you weren't certain it was a ship, then why were so many of your people taken off other assignments? It could have ended up being nothing more than a rogue comet?"

Sterfer bristled at the remark. "Because this is standard procedure. The ship came out of nowhere; in a place we barely have a foothold. We had to be sure what we were dealing with."

Hayes pressed the issue and leaned forward again. "And do you have any idea what the point of origin for the Deravan vessel might be?"

"If you trace the ship's path back past the point where we made contact, the trajectory takes it into an uncharted part of the galaxy. So, there's no way to know for sure."

"Excuse me," Admiral Chesterfield interjected. "I have a question." She brushed back a few strands of blonde hair that had slipped down over her eyes. "Can you explain how we can communicate with the Deravans? The odds of them speaking the same language as us must be staggering."

"Standard operating procedure also requires all intercepted messages be tied into the transcoms."

"Transcoms?" Chesterfield asked after she took off her glasses, her tone serious. "What are transcoms?"

"I'm sorry, ma'am," he smiled. "People in my field work with them all the time. I forget it's like speaking Greek to those on the outside." The harsh stare given by Chesterfield indicated she wanted an answer, not an explanation. "That's short for translating computers," he added after clearing his throat. "All incoming messages go through the computers for decoding. While most of this is standard traffic from base to base, we do intercept some classified transmissions from the Antarens on occasion. They have this unusual habit of changing their ciphers about once a year. So, as a means of keeping tabs on them, the transcoms were designed to break new codes with a minimum of information; thus, speeding up the process. They're quite remarkable."

"And that's how you can understand the Deravans' messages?"

"Yes, ma'am, that's correct. It took a couple of days' worth of signals, but the transcoms finally cracked their language."

"Do you believe the appearance of this ship has anything to do with the signal loss at New Roanoke?" she asked, a note of concern in her voice.

"Not at this time," Sterfer replied after a brief pause. "As you know, the New Frontier is a good distance away. The probe we sent won't reach Beta Centauri for another twenty hours."

"Have your people pieced together what they think may have happened there?"

Sterfer paused again. "I'm afraid not. The only thing we know for sure is that their long-range tracking picked up something approaching the planet. There has been nothing from them since. The colony may have only experienced simple transmitter problems. But this Deravan ship could not have been responsible, if that's what you're inferring."

"You sound certain of that," Garcia interrupted, condescension tainting every word.

Sterfer held up his notes. "If you consult this briefing material, you can plainly see the vessel could not have been involved. Unless their technology enables them to be in two different sectors at the same time, what you're asking is physically impossible."

"This is all well and good, but the one issue still before us is what should be done about the Deravan ship," Fleet Admiral Davenport said in a low tone. "Every second we delay means less time to decide a course of action."

"The way I see things," Hayes interrupted, "is that we have one of two choices. Either we do nothing and let that ship arrive, or we destroy it."

"I think you're oversimplifying the issue." Senator Garcia balked, both eyes narrowing.

"I see no other alternative," Commodore Hayes continued, his physical presence enhanced by the power of his voice. "How do we know what their true intentions are? Perhaps the Deravans are a benevolent race, offering us the hand of friendship. But then again, they may have sent the ship as a precursor to something bigger. And by bigger, I mean they may have set their sights on the conquest of humanity."

"I find it difficult to believe a race of intelligent beings coming from such a great distance could see us as a threat to them."

"I believed such notions once," Hayes said with a faraway look, "but after the war against the Antarens, I don't think I ever can again. Even today, they are a ruthless enemy, ready to attack us the moment we drop our guard. When a person experiences this...well, he doesn't offer the hand of trust so openly again."

The senator shook his head. "This situation could not be more different. Just because circumstances happened this way before doesn't mean they will again. We have no evidence to suggest the Deravans' intentions are not honorable. We would be nothing more than criminals if we attacked a race of sentient beings without provocation. I will not condone such an action."

Hayes was about to object when something caught his attention. A man came from the rear of the chambers, every facet of his being brimming with youthful self-confidence. He had slicked-back hair, polished shoes and manicured nails. Hayes had seen him before. When the proceedings started, he had been back up against the wall, sitting on a brown wooden bench. The unknown officer had appeared more or less disinterested in the proceedings, until Sterfer began his testimony. The instant the colonel took his place in the hot seat, the man, for whatever reason, pulled out some papers from his briefcase and tracked the statements made by him.

The young officer stopped just behind the table, extended his right hand as he bent over, and picked up the microphone.

"Captain, what are you doing?" Sterfer asked, surprised by his sudden appearance.

"Don't worry, Colonel," he reassured him. "Everything's under control." He then tapped the microphone with his index finger three times—*plink, plink, plink*—and said, "Please excuse the interruption, ladies and gentlemen, but I think there's a third option we have not yet discussed."

"The council recognizes ..." Garcia's voice trailed off, bemused. He didn't seem to actually know who the person was. "And you are?"

"My name is Captain Reeves," he replied. "I am Colonel Sterfer's assistant."

Garcia gave him a good looking over first. "I assume you have something to add to these proceedings...uh, Captain?"

Reeves held the microphone close. "That vessel is coming whether we like it or not. I suggest we send out a squadron of fighters on an intercept course. After making contact, they can assess the situation up close before taking any action. If the Deravans' intentions are peaceful, we welcome them with open arms. If they are not, then our ships can dispose of the matter—quickly and efficiently."

"Of course," Hayes gasped. The answer had been right in front of him all along.

Garcia swiveled his chair around. He and Hayes spoke. The senator then went to his right and discussed the matter with Admiral Chesterfield. When he had finished, Garcia repositioned himself in his seat and pulled the microphone towards him. "What do you think of the suggestion, Commodore?"

"I think it's an idea worth recommending. I can have a team ready to go by 0600 hours."

"I agree," the senator nodded. "As the head of this council, I am authorizing you to oversee operations personally. Use whatever resources and agencies you may need. Does anyone else have anything they wish to add?" A welcome silence fell over the room. "Then if there are no objections, this hearing is closed." The crack of his gavel echoing off the walls signified the end of the proceedings.

A couple of ideas were already going around in Hayes' head. Sterfer and his associates would continue to monitor the Deravan ship, and analyze any new incoming data. He figured the most strategic location to run such an operation was the Gagarin Star Force located at Titan. But that left the most crucial question remaining. *Who will be the lucky one to make first contact with the Deravans?* A name immediately came to mind—Lt. Commander Frank Yamane. His years of experience made him, in Hayes' estimation, the perfect choice. He glanced at the astro-clock set above a pair of double doors. Time was already running short.

Hayes grabbed his briefcase and hurried out of the council chambers. Intending to return to his office, he ran into a mob of media cameras trying to work their way inside. A pair of frenzied soldiers barely held the crews back, their sheer numbers making it a daunting task at best. But when Hayes stepped into view, they dashed over to him. With his every means of escape blocked off, he soon became overwhelmed by the several dozen reporters shoving microphones into his face and yelling out questions.

Both guards, realizing the commodore's predicament, managed to step in and push the reporters back. Unfazed, the media continued to dog Hayes every step down the hallway. He fired off a flurry of "no comments" every few meters, hoping they might give up and leave. His strategy, however, had the opposite effect. His obvious stonewalling made the news crews that much more determined. They smelled a big story brewing and were determined to stay until they got something out of him, anything.

Despite the news crews hovering around him, the commodore somehow traversed the narrow corridor and reached the elevator doors. After pressing the button, he stood there, biding his time. The lighted numbers counted down to the lobby with a profound slowness.

For the most part, he managed to ignore the barrage of questions thrown at him. Then, even with the noise filling the lobby, one of their queries did manage to get through. "We've had unconfirmed reports that at least one ship of unknown origin, maybe more, is heading right for Saturn. Can you comment on this?"

Hayes tried to figure out who asked the question, but that would have required a miracle. The reporters were still pressing around him jabbering away, while at the same time, waiting for a reply.

Two sets of doors slid open after a bell announced the elevator's arrival. Feeling like a man harried by an unrelenting enemy, he stepped inside; grateful he had been rescued from the chaos.

"Are they a threat to us?" another reporter shouted out. Hayes did not respond.

Even before the doors banged close, the entire press corps made a hasty retreat back to the council chambers. He suspected they were desperate to get some usable quotes for their editors who, if he knew his manager types, would not be satisfied with anything less.

Hayes turned around and faced the front of the elevator. The interior was dingy. Not run-down, but well worn. Probably from decades of use, he surmised.

Looking up, he found the lighted numbers above. He wondered why people did that when they came onto an elevator. The reason didn't matter. The commodore appreciated the fact he had been given a quiet, uninterrupted moment. He had no idea when he would enjoy one again.

ANTARA, HOME PLANET OF THE ANTAREN EMPIRE
DAIETH TIME MINUS THREE

Kel Sen-Ry stepped onto the terrace overlooking the city, his thoughts troubled. Staring down into the valley, he studied the familiar sight. There were thousands of small multi-colored lights dotting the skyline. Many of them were white, while others were blue, joined by reds, greens, yellows, and on and on. Almost every color combination imaginable showed itself, revealing unique hues of radiance and light, and then, as if by magic, replaced by others even more beautiful than before.

Kel Sen-Ry didn't sleep well during the hot summer months. Just like the night before, and the one before that, he stood in his usual place and watched the capital sleep. A warm breeze blew past him. A series of chimes placed throughout his garden rang out, rich and melodious. He enjoyed the song while it lasted, but as soon as the breeze died down, he felt even more alone than before. And still far from being tired. Kel Sen-Ry, minister of the Second Order, official designate of the scribe guild, and confessor of the Martor Province had tried all the usual tricks he could think of to beckon slumber, but his efforts were futile at this point. Nothing would work.

He lifted his eyes. The familiar constellations overhead had always soothed him whenever he felt restless. Their very presence proved order existed in the universe. But tonight he was anxious, and the stars failed to comfort him. He shouldn't have felt this way since he knew of the changes destined to come, but his irrational fears were with him, nonetheless. Kel Sen-Ry figured his feelings stemmed from a need to have the world around him remain unchanged, but reality as he knew it would never be the same again. Many of the priests in his order had tried to explain away the appearance of certain signs since the Terrans withdrew from Antara, but what the Prophets foretold made ignoring the truth all but impossible.

Brushing his thoughts aside, he eyed a pair of galaxy clusters looming near the horizon. The mathematics of how they were created ran through his head, but even they did not provide the solace he needed. The evening sky appeared different somehow. Rather than being a welcome respite, the stars above had become cold...distant.

Kel Sen-Ry turned to go back inside, when a lone star far from the others caught his attention. A powerful sensation pulsed through his body, holding him in place. He couldn't take his eyes off the flickering light above. It almost felt like some other presence had joined him. Strange thoughts filled his head, the foremost of which imparted to him an intuitive understanding. "It has begun," he whispered to himself with an undeniable finality.

He felt alone again, alone and afraid.

Looking about, but seeing nothing, a sense of sadness came over Kel Sen-Ry. He returned to the terrace and stared at the city below. *What will happen to them*, he wondered.

CHAPTER 3

SECTOR THIRTY-THREE
1042 PROXIMA MERIDIAN TIME, AUGUST 11, 2217

The feel of his fighter underneath him was the greatest sensation Yamane ever knew. Miles of wires and circuitry working together, guiding the ten tons of machinery with the flick of a wrist, gave him a sense that anything was possible. Up, down, left, or right. If he chose, he could keep the nose of his ship pointed in one direction and then maintain that course forever. Perhaps one day he might, but today, as long as he could spend some time away from the pressures of his job, so much the better. Life, he thought, seldom worked out that way. It had a nasty habit of striking him when he wasn't looking. *Did these things happen by design or by some cosmic roll of the dice?*

The importance attached to the question faded as the millions of burning suns in the distance drew his attention away from his immediate surroundings. Did the same rules apply to the potentially limitless number of civilizations out there, he wondered, or could humanity be one of the lucky few in a vast, possibly infinite universe? Perhaps, perhaps not, but if it weren't for Man's unquenchable thirst for knowledge, he never would have bothered to stare in wonder at the heavens above those untold centuries ago. Even then, the stars beckoned him. How many times had man, even with his simple knowledge, sat gazing upon the flickering points of lights hanging in the sky, wondering what they were?

Yamane sat and watched a group of star clusters in the distance. He drank in their bluish tint. Traveling at speeds above 1.00 stellar velocity, the visible spectrum became compressed, shifting towards higher wave frequencies. The faster a ship went, the bluer the stars became. For Yamane, it was just a different way of marveling at the striking number of color combinations offered by the universe.

The view reminded him of when he was a young boy lying in a field at night. Falling stars streaked across the sky for hours. He couldn't believe how a meteorite no bigger than a grain of sand could blossom into an object of such intense beauty, and then burn up in a decaying orbit. He wondered what it would be like to watch something like this happen, up close.

What an experience that would be.

Yamane knew he and Kershaw would reach their turn-around point soon. While many of the pilots considered the patrol route from Kalmedia to the edge of the Solar System to be on the mundane side, he relished this time alone, especially when he spent too much time with people. Intense personal interaction left him feeling tired, drained. But get away for a couple of quiet hours, and he felt like a new man.

His arrival at the pre-set coordinates triggered the master alarm. Both sets of speakers on his control panel emitted three short beeps in rapid succession. The action ripped Yamane from his milieu of drifting thoughts. Refocusing his attention back on the targeting grid, he saw that the central display indicated he and Kershaw had reached their fail-safe point. With a loose touch, he grabbed a hold of the control stick. "You still out there, Stan?" he asked in his headset.

"I'm right with you."

"Looks like it's time we head back to the barn." He gave his stick a gentle tug to the left. "I've got the lead." Both fighters banked over on their port sides, changing their heading to zero-one-seven, right for Titan. But just when Yamane had set his sights on the ringed planet in the distance, his radio receiver locked onto an incoming transmission.

"Lt. Commander Yamane, please come in," the voice said. "This is Kalmedia Control."

"Lt. Commander Yamane here," he said into his headset. "Go ahead, Kalmedia Control."

"You are to proceed back to base immediately."

Yamane thought he must have heard the order wrong. "Please repeat, control. We are not scheduled to return for another two hours."

"You have been given new orders. Return to base."

"All right, tower, I'm coming in. Yamane, out."

He switched off his radio in disgust. The traffic controller had not heard it in his voice, but Frank Yamane was angry. He had looked forward to this all week, but someone had to step in and snatch his temporary reprieve from life out of his hand. *Up, down, left or right*, he thought, *but not today*. He switched his radio back on after calming himself. "I assume you heard the order?"

"Loud and clear," Kershaw replied. "What do you think?"

"I can't say for sure, but something's up—and I get the feeling we're in the crosshairs."

"Do you believe there's been an incident with the Antarens?"

Yamane thought long and hard before answering. "I don't think so, but we'll play their little game for now. Stay frosty, though. A lot more may be going on than we realize."

"All right—but if the time comes, you know I'll always cover your back."

"Thanks, but let's not get ahead of ourselves." Yamane scanned the different gauges in front of him, each one designed to indicate the status of his fighter—speed, direction, power output, turbine rotation, and weapons—all at his fingertips. "Increase speed to 1.25 stellar velocity. This should get us home soon enough."

"Roger that. Pushing her to 1.25." Kershaw's fighter shot ahead in a burst of acceleration.

Yamane grabbed the thruster control on his left. Like a master pianist who knew the exact location of each key, he slid the mechanism to the required setting. Vibrations from all three turbines jumped up in an instant. Yamane could do nothing else except try and salvage what he could from the patrol and make the most of the time he had left.

Both fighters corrected their approach as they lined themselves along runway five. Yamane turned a knob just below the radio and reset the second channel for the guidance beacon frequency. Their position from the base popped onto his targeting grid, indicating their respective altitude, distance, and speed.

"Altitude, forty-five kilometers. Twenty thousand kilometers to the runway... speed, twelve hundred kilometers-per-hour."

"This is the control tower. You are to proceed on your present course. Once you have landed, go to hangar bay twelve and wait for further instructions there."

"Acknowledged, tower," Yamane replied as though the peculiar change in orders hadn't taken place. But it had, raising suspicions in his mind.

The two fighters flew into a storm system as they continued their approach. Small droplets of water formed on Yamane's cockpit windows, tapping against them like thousands of little steel pellets. An electrical discharge flashed in the distance, lighting up the night sky for a fraction of a second. A mild buffeting followed soon after. He held the control stick just a little tighter. Doing so lessened the severity of the shaking, but other nearby strikes and swirling pockets of air still made his trip a bumpy one.

As the storm worsened, Yamane leaned forward and activated his night vision display located near the top panel. When his central cockpit window turned orange, the surging clouds and droplets of water slamming into the translucent composite material dissolved into nothingness as the enhanced signal pierced through the darkened billowy masses, showing runway five up ahead as clear as day.

"ETA is three minutes to runway five."

"Copy that. Three minutes to runway five."

Yamane looked up ahead, right where he expected the base to be. "Bingo." He pushed his stick forward, causing the nose of his fighter to level out. Off in the distance, runway lights were already set at green, the final permission code for making a landing. When he pulled back on the throttle, his fighter began to decelerate.

"Fifteen hundred meters to runway," he said into the headset. "Airspeed... one hundred and ninety-five meters-per-second." Yamane then reached over and pressed a solitary blinking button on the control panel. His landing gear came down and locked into position. "One hundred and twenty...contact lights on...touchdown in five seconds."

Lines down the middle of the runway passed underneath almost in a blur. Yamane concentrated on the images right before him, blocking out even the smallest distraction from other sources. He tapped the control stick forward. The nose of his fighter dropped down ever more. "One hundred meters-per-second. Contact in two."

Just as all three wheels hit the runway, Yamane pushed hard on both brake pedals. His fighter fought the forces working against it, pulling to the left. Steering his ship in the opposite direction, she finally stopped about halfway down the runway. After a few moments passed, he gave his thruster control a slight nudge forward. All three turbines responded, pushing the fighter towards the hangar bays.

Number twelve fast approached. Out in front, standing a good twenty meters from the opening, a flagman waited. He was dressed in his distinctive bright orange jumpsuit and goggles, topped off with a white helmet. Two lighted batons were at his side.

When both fighters reached the edge of the tarmac, the flagman started walking backwards, signaling them inside. Just as they edged their way past the gaping maw, he led them towards a pair of pyramid-shaped cones. He held up both batons above his head, forming an "x", after they reached the spot. The flagman then signaled Yamane and Kershaw for an engine shutdown.

A strange silence filled the hangar. Yamane didn't like it. Something was strange about this whole thing since he was ordered back. He took a quick look around. It was only then that he realized his and Kershaw's were the only fighters inside. That in itself was unusual. Earlier in the day, the entire 87th fighter group was parked inside. He'd seen the ships himself. Now they were gone. "What in the world is going on around here?" he asked himself. Yamane decided the time had come to get some answers.

He took off his helmet as the cockpit canopy rose above him. Pushing himself up and out of his seat, he noticed two MP's approaching. Their gait was efficient and direct. He swung both legs over the side and jumped onto the concrete floor below. Kershaw was already waiting by his fighter. His characteristic smirk was gone, replaced with a look of apprehension.

"Lt. Commander Yamane," one of the soldiers said in a distinct monotone, his voice enhanced by the arched ceiling above, "we have orders to escort you two to Commander Federson's office."

Kershaw took a single step forward. "What's going on around here, Corporal?" he demanded. "Why all this secrecy?"

The MP didn't blink. "We weren't given any explanations, sir," he replied, "just our orders." His facial expression barely registered the words. "If you would follow me."

Kershaw was about to object again, when Yamane grabbed him from behind. The major's face grew a distinct shade of red. Yamane gave him a knowing look before speaking. "Like I said when we were on patrol, let's not get ahead of ourselves." He turned and headed for the rear exit. Kershaw stayed right with him, but his expression of concern never wavered.

Two sets of double doors at the far end of the hangar slid open when they entered a hidden scanner's pre-programmed range. Once outside, the two MP's brought Yamane and Kershaw to a staff hover car parked just behind the arched structure. In keeping with the military tradition of blending in with the local surroundings, a muted gray covered the vehicle's exterior, with streaks of black thrown in for good measure.

Both MP's took their places in the front seat, with Yamane and Kershaw in the back. When the engine roared to life with a simple turn of a key, the vehicle jolted away. Yamane, by this time, had prepared himself for almost anything.

The hover car pulled up to the command building just as black clouds blew in, a moment marked by large raindrops striking the roof and windshield. Between them and the front steps, a large white sign stuck out of a patchy green lawn. Bold black letters plastered over a white background spelled out Commander Federson's name.

The MP in the passenger seat jumped out and opened the back door for his passengers. The second MP assumed his place on the front steps of the nondescript facade, facing an uncertain night of rain and thunderclaps.

A clerk was sitting behind the only desk in Federson's outer office. He was a slight man, in his early 30's by Yamane's estimation, balding, with a pair of wire rim glasses resting on his thin nose.

Three empty chairs clung to the wall on his right, though he doubted they would be there long enough to need them. Turning the other way, he didn't see anything else of significance. From all appearances, this was a simple, functional office. He wondered how anyone could work in a place so devoid of any warmth. Given the apparent nature of the personality behind the desk, however, Yamane thought the two might be a good match for each other. The clerk was cold and remote, like the room. Spartan and lacking in originality, like the room. Efficient and functional, just like the room. As he thought before, a good match.

"Is there anything I can do for you, *gentlemen*?" the clerk said with an unmasked tone of contempt in his voice.

Not impressed by his attitude, the MP bent over. "Lt. Commander Yamane and Major

Kershaw are here to see Commander Federson. Can you tell him they've arrived?"

The clerk placed his pen on the desk blotter before pressing the intercom button. "Those two men you wanted to see are here for you, sir." He then looked into the MP's eyes and just stared, the right side of his mouth bent upward slightly in an almost defiant sneer.

"Show them in at once," Federson replied.

The MP took a step to his left and allowed them into the office. Yamane looked back just as the door closed. The clerk had already resumed his work. *If the world ever comes to an end*, he thought, *those are the kind of people who'll survive.*

Federson sat behind a large oak desk, his back to them. With his head cocked, he held up a couple of documents. Just to his left, several shadow boxes filled with medals and citations lined the wall. Over on his right, a number of pictures of officers Yamane didn't recognize were tacked onto the opposite wall. Just below, sitting on a small table, he saw three model sailing ships arranged in a circle. His final analysis: the office was efficient and unassuming, just like the man. These were a few of the qualities those under Federson's command liked about him, though a youthful appearance, aided by his light-brown hair and pencil-thin moustache, didn't hurt either. Gregarious by nature, Yamane often found him engaged in a friendly chat with a new recruit or seeking an opinion from a junior officer regarding some issue. But whenever he requested a meeting in his office, it meant something important had come up.

Federson placed both documents on his desk and signed them. "I'm sorry to bring you in here in this manner," he said with a smile, "but circumstances demanded a certain level of security."

Yamane relaxed a bit. "I understand, sir," he replied, though certain suspicions still lingered.

"There are two men here who have just arrived from Earth," the commander continued. "They have come on a matter which requires the utmost care and secrecy." Yamane had been so intent on confronting the issue at hand that he hadn't even noticed them sitting against the back wall. "This is Colonel Sterfer from intelligence, and Captain Reeves from strategics division." Both of them nodded in reply. "They have been sent by Star Force Command on a matter of vital importance."

Sterfer opened his briefcase and fumbled around for something inside. Finding the file he wanted, he produced a star chart and a page of hand-written notes. The colonel then placed the chart in the image projector just to the left of Federson's desk. After an initial hum, a three-dimensional image appeared in the middle of the room, about a meter off the ground. Sterfer glanced at his notes before he started his presentation. "About a week ago, an operator at the Moffett Tracking Station picked up a mysterious object at the edge of known space. At first, we weren't sure what we had. But after a series of transmissions, intelligence verified they had detected a spacecraft of unknown origin."

Yamane sat upright in his chair, the magnitude of such news catching him completely off guard. He shot a quick look at Kershaw, but his counterpart offered no outward reaction. "I guess that would explain the stepped-up security," he reasoned aloud.

Kershaw crossed his arms and leaned back in his chair. "Have the transcoms deciphered any of the transmissions yet?" he asked.

"Yes, they have," Sterfer replied. He flipped one of the pages over and read the back. "The ship has been sent by a race calling itself the Deravans. They have come with the specific intent of making contact with us."

Yamane's mind reeled. "How long before they arrive?" he asked, hiding his shock.

Sterfer consulted his notes again. "In just under six days. We want you to go out with a squadron of your best pilots and intercept that ship. After you rendezvous with it, you will assess the situation. If you believe they do not pose a threat to us, the squadron will escort it back here to Kalmedia."

Yamane rubbed his chin. "Here? Why bring the vessel to Titan? We're a military installation, not a wing of the diplomatic corps. Shouldn't this fall under their jurisdiction?"

"Star Force Command has taken that into consideration," Federson replied. "But if things get a little hairy, they feel more comfortable having a squadron nearby than an unarmed diplomat."

Yamane sneaked a peek at his watch. "When are we scheduled to depart?"

"At 0630 tomorrow. I want you and your squadron to get a good night's sleep before the mission. Here's a file with all of the information we have received up to this point. I want every piece of data studied and analyzed before tomorrow." The commander picked up a large envelope lying on his desk marked, "CONFIDENTIAL: HIGHEST PRIORITY (12: GAMMA)," and handed it to Yamane.

He examined the packet. "I'll get right on this."

"Because of the sensitivity of what we're involved with, I don't want the pilots told about the mission until tomorrow's briefing. We can't afford to have any leaks. Also, you will be flying under strict radio silence. Except for hourly reports, I want no contact with anyone."

Yamane nodded his head in agreement. "I understand, Commander."

"Good luck to you both," Hayes said, a note of envy in his voice.

Yamane rose from his chair. Facing the door, he began to experience a certain measure of anxiety about the mission. He knew it was irrational. Just pre-flight jitters, he forced himself to believe, and then left the room.

Yamane sat at his desk with the duty records of every pilot in the squadron. For the past couple of hours, he had approached the task of choosing the right ones for the mission with a single-minded determination. But after reading through their records, taking down some notes, and then placing the folder over on his right, all he had to show for his efforts were a sore back, a stiff neck—and some form of mental block. He had filled the first twelve slots without too much trouble, but for some reason, those last two stumped him. His eyes turned upward. They were tired; he was tired.

Believing now might be a good time for a break, similar to the one he had taken a couple of hours ago, he reclined even further back in his chair. The same questions plaguing him then were still plaguing him now, *What criteria should be used for the selection of his team? Should I base my decision on experience or temperament? What about training and flight hours?* He had selected pilots for dangerous missions before, but nothing like this. In the past there had always been something known about the enemy—troop strengths, tactics, even the names of commanding officers at times—but how does one anticipate the unknown?

Yamane stretched both hands outward, tightening every muscle in his body. "One, two, three," he counted, and then released. Rolling his head around in a circle, he caught sight of the opened envelope near the end of his bed. Data files were laying next to it, grouped together in no particular order. He had gone through every bit of information provided by Federson, but it told him what he already knew—a ship of unknown origin would arrive in five days. Nothing more.

Someone knocked on his door. The rapping sound snapped Yamane out of his isolated world of fatigue and frustration. The air around him felt heavy, warm, with a slight smell of perspiration. The person knocked again. "Come in," Yamane called out.

Kershaw strode into the room in a casual fashion, a muted expression on his face. He shot a couple of quick looks around the quarters. "I just thought I would come by to see how you were doing." The major wandered past him.

"Just fine," Yamane bluffed. "Why do you ask?"

Kershaw spun around. "Really," he pounced. "I think I know you a little better than that. Let's face it, that poker face of yours might work with some, but not with me. I know you. Every '*T*' has to be crossed and every '*I*' has to be dotted. Being a perfectionist has its advantages at times, but it also has its disadvantages too—like keeping someone from making a decision. And that someone at this particular moment is Lt. Commander Frank Yah-maw-nee."

Kershaw delighted in over-pronouncing his name, particularly when he was trying to make a point. His stratagem worked. Yamane felt like the Major had caught him. "I guess you do know me too well." He placed his hand on the folder crowning the top of the pile and patted it. "For some reason, I'm having trouble filling the last two slots for tomorrow's mission."

Kershaw wandered over to an opened window on the opposite wall. Deep lines etched his face. "This one is for the record books," he said while staring at the stars shining through the black sky above. "Just think. Even as we speak, a ship of unknown origin is making its way here. Who are the Deravans? Where have they come from? I find the prospect of making contact exciting...and worrisome."

"Maybe this is the reason I'm having difficulty picking the final pilots. Who knows what we'll face out there? There are a whole lot of questions, and not many answers."

Kershaw's demeanor became stiff. "Don't you think this is rather ironic?" he asked while musing to himself with a distant sort of stare.

"What do you mean?"

"We were just arguing about the morality of territorial expansion this afternoon, and here we find ourselves the instruments of the exact same argument."

Yamane tilted his head. "I don't know if I follow."

The major offered a slight smile. "A ship from an unknown part of the galaxy is on its way to make contact with us. Are they saying 'hello,' or are they telling us 'this is our side of the hill,'?"

"Perhaps there's another reason," Yamane suggested. "Maybe they are the ones from the other side of the hill come to see what's on our side."

Kershaw rested his forearm against the window frame. "Kind of puts things in a different perspective. We wrestle with the moral implications of doing something when the initiative is taken by us, but it's a whole lot easier to respond when someone else makes the first move."

Yamane didn't reply. He knew Kershaw was trying to bait him. With what they would soon be facing, it felt out of place.

"Well, I think I should be turning in," the Major offered while rubbing his eyes.

Yamane recognized a tactical retreat when he saw one. Kershaw must have picked up on his reaction. "One other thing." He went back to the list sitting on his desk. From some unknown reason, the decision that had been plaguing him the last couple of hours became quite simple. "Here are the pilots I want at tomorrow's briefing." Yamane made a notation on his data pad, and then tossed it across the room.

The small semitronic device flew right into Kershaw's extended fingers. "Consider it done," he assured him.

"Goodnight, Stan. Thanks for coming by."

He just smiled that crooked smile and left without another word.

Yamane stood up and stretched his arms upward, his hands flared out as he reached for the ceiling. The window caught his attention. He went over to it. Now that the storm had passed, the stars were twinkling brightly in the sky. With Kershaw's words still going around in his head, he thought about what waited for him out there. The moment almost felt like one of those just before a battle. A person wonders if they will "do the right thing" when the time comes. *Only time will tell*, Yamane mused to himself.

Searching the sky, his thoughts stilled. The view reminded him of something—something on the tip of his tongue. The stars twinkled again. Then it came to him. "Twinkle, twinkle, little star," he thought in a child-like way. "How I wonder what you are." Yamane stopped. He knew what they were, but wondered what they would reveal. A deep yawn escaped from him. He eyed his bed just a few meters away, and began to feel tired. His duty, at this point, required he get some sleep.

Just before turning off the light, he reached over and picked up a picture sitting on the nightstand next to his bed. "Liana," he whispered while staring at the photograph. His wife's caressing gaze and radiant smile were meant for him alone. How he wished she were there with him now.

When Yamane put the picture down again, he saw her small gold cross hanging over the frame. Caressing it with his hand, he thought about all the years they had spent together. A deep sigh parted his lips.

He gazed at the warmth of her smile one last time, and then pulled both sets of covers over himself. Yamane hoped he would dream of her that night.

CHAPTER 4

We don't receive wisdom; we must discover it for ourselves after a journey that no one can take us or spare us.

-Proust

GARGARIN STAR FORCE BASE, TITAN
0545 PROXIMA MERIDIAN TIME, AUGUST 12, 2217

Buzz, buzz, buzz. Feeling as though he had just set his head on his soft, downy pillows, the unrelenting beeping of his alarm ripped Yamane out of a deep sleep. Louder and louder the disturbance registered in his ears, the once-dormant neurons firing away as his level of consciousness rose with each passing second. *Buzz, buzz*...he reached over, and with a quick flip of the switch on the side of the clock, quiet filled his room again.

Yamane opened both eyes, narrowly at first, taking in the morning light. The distant sun crested over the horizon. Rays of light came in at a downward angle, illuminating millions of dust particles floating in the air. Those little flecks of dirt floated about here and there as they encountered subtle differences in air pressure. Though most of his room remained in the shadows, a desk and chair by his window lay immersed in a warm, reddish glow, giving both pieces of furniture an ethereal quality.

He let out a deep yawn. Stretching his arms upward, he caught sight of his watch. *0529.* Just enough time for a shower and shave before getting to the briefing room. He threw off his covers. In an instant, the cold air encircled him from all directions and rushed in. Yamane ignored the sudden drop in temperature and hopped out of bed. He grabbed his shaving kit sitting on the top shelf of his closet and a folded towel right next to it. If he was lucky, he just might get to the showers end of the hall before the other pilots.

Five minutes later he had rinsed, shampooed, and rinsed again—like clockwork. He patted himself dry with the towel slung over the shower stall, and then threw on his t-shirt and shorts.

A couple of other pilots stumbled into the showers, still rubbing their tired eyes. Yamane knew the rest were not far behind. He hurried over to the sink and pulled out the can of shaving cream. Twenty seconds of shaking gave the foam just the right consistency. He brought the razor down along the contours of his jaw. Moving the blade this way and that, he finished without a nick. After years of honing and refinement, he could execute his choreographed morning routine in a mere ten minutes—from start to finish.

Yamane pulled out his flight gear from the closet after he returned to his quarters. Every component—thermal suit, pressure suit, flight suit, boots, and gloves—were all put on in their proper order, arranged just so on his bed. He reached down and keyed in the code to activate the power system on the small pad located just above the wrist on his right sleeve. The display went from being a lifeless keeper of information, to one that came alive, glowing in an effervescent sort of way. After the diagnostic program verified the operational status of the suit's internal systems, a cursor appeared in the upper left-hand corner. The flashing marker signified the unit had detected no malfunctions.

He slipped on his thermal suit first, then his pressure suit, followed by his flight suit, boots, and gloves.

Yamane found the space charts and intelligence reports on his desk and tucked them into his flight bag. He then pulled out a small picture of Liana from his nightstand drawer and slipped it into his chest pocket.

Taking in the room as a whole, he looked things over one last time, just to make certain nothing important was left behind. Then it hit him. Yamane had almost forgot his satchel. In the back of his closet, just behind his class-A uniform, he pulled it out, plus a number of Instant Meal Packs, though most pilots just referred to them as I-paks. As he started to put them into his bag, one of the packs caught his eye—BEEF STROGANOFF—a good choice for the trip. *The trip*, he mused. What would they find out there? Yamane caught himself. This was getting him nowhere. Yamane crammed the packet into his satchel. Both he and his squadron would know soon enough.

When he rose to his feet, Yamane caught himself in the mirror. His mind stilled. A single thought coalesced from his subconscious. Yamane knew he might never return. Death had been confronted before on a thousand prior missions, but for some unknown reason, this one seemed different... somehow.

The room felt cold. He suspected his fears were getting the better of him. Yamane closed his eyes tight. For a moment, he relaxed. Then something dark slid behind his lids. It gripped him. Sudden, frightening images flashed in his mind—there one second, gone the next. They were dark creatures, malevolent. Then another presence appeared. He couldn't quite see who or what they were, but these beings had an altogether different feel. Cocooned in rays of light, peace and contentment radiated from them. Those other creatures reacted viscerally with terrible screeching and hissing noises. The animosity they exuded was almost incapacitating. But the beings of light held their ground, and the dark creatures disappeared. The others faded away soon after.

Yamane opened his eyes again. Beads of sweat had collected on his forehead. *Did that just happen?* he wondered. Taking a second look in the mirror, he thought he must have imagined it all. *But it felt so real.* Yamane shook his head. "Just pre-flight jitters," he convinced himself. "Nothing more."

By the time Yamane arrived at the briefing room, Kershaw and the other pilots had already been mustered. He entered from the rear, unnoticed. Making his way down the gentle incline, he heard some of the pilots speculating about the mission. A few of the more boisterous ones boasted of their exaggerated exploits from the past weekend. The rest, Yamane noted, sat alone, lost in their thoughts. He figured they were no doubt feeling an amalgam of conflicting emotions, like what he had experienced just before his first important mission.

The reactions of the pilots now were the same as then—bravado, indifference and fear. Yamane fell decisively into the third camp. In fact, if his memory served him, he had been downright scared. The timing of it all hadn't helped either. He graduated from the Star Force Academy just when the Trans-European Conflict really began to heat up. The prospect of facing the enemy on his first patrol terrified him to no end. He never realized his worst expectations, however, since the mission ended up being nothing more than a long flight there and back. But if they had stumbled on an enemy squadron, he knew he would not be here today. Many of the pilots back then felt the same way at one time or another. Sometimes they were wrong, but more often than not, the sixth sense flex—as the phenomenon became known during the war-- was proven right again and again. Yamane didn't have an explanation for how any of them knew. No one did. But when that particular feeling came over a pilot, a certain facial expression revealed to the world what he already knew—he would not be coming back. Did any of the men here feel the same way?

The instant the pilots became aware he had entered the briefing room they jumped to their feet and snapped to attention. "Commander on deck!" someone barked.

Yamane went from the rear of the rectangular room to the front with long deliberate strides. A podium used for briefings stood near the edge of the stage. Set further back, he saw two flags placed on either side. The one on the left stood in plain view, revealing the distinctive blue and white colors of the Geneva World Government. The Star Force flag positioned on the right rested more in the shadows.

Yamane stepped onto the stage and placed his notes on the podium. The atmosphere in the room was thick, still. A distinctive musty scent also hung in the air. His men, still standing at attention, didn't utter a sound.

"As you were." Yamane's deep voice bounced off the walls, enhanced by the room's natural acoustics.

The sounds of squeaking seats and low murmurs filled the briefing room for several moments.

Yamane produced a star chart from his notes and inserted it into the image projector on his right. Room sensors dimmed the lights as the device came alive. "Good morning, gentlemen," Yamane greeted them warmly. "I hope you all had a good night's sleep. It promises to be your last for a good long while."

A cacophony of groans filled the room.

He came out from behind the podium. "I'm sure many of you don't recognize this quadrant of space," Yamane pointed. "That's because, for the most part, this region is largely unexplored."

"Did you wake us up just so you could bring this to our attention?" one of the pilots joked. The room erupted into laughter. Yamane offered a slight smile, but the micro-expression disappeared almost as quickly as it had appeared. This subtle cue could not have killed the laughter faster if he had tried.

"Now that we have the jokes out of the way, I think we can go on."

Yamane navigated the events of the last six days with the skills of a master storyteller, highlighting only those portions of the report important to the mission, while at the same time not sparing a single relevant detail. When he had reached the end of his notes, to a man, the pilots in that room understood every aspect of the ship's discovery as well as he did.

"Based on the calculations made by Colonel Sterfer," Yamane continued, "this is the approximate point where we should come into contact with the ship. After that...we evaluate."

"What do you mean by evaluate, sir?" a pilot asked.

"I mean just that. We gather all the information we can about the Deravans, and then wait for further orders."

"And what if we can't make contact with the Deravans?"

Yamane studied the pilot first before answering. "That will be a part of the evaluation process."

"And if their intentions are hostile?"

The question floated in the stale air for several moments. "If they are," he finally replied, his face hard, "then we respond in kind." Many of the pilots nodded their heads in silent approval. "If all goes well, we should rendezvous with the Deravan vessel at coordinates one-seven-five in just under forty-five hours...right here in the heart of the Cauldara Sector." He pointed at the spot. "I know this is much further than most of you have flown, but the training you've received has been in preparation for just such a mission. It should be routine all the way."

Yamane approached the edge of the stage, his hands held behind his back. All he could say on an official basis he had said. But because of the obvious risks involved in so dangerous a mission, he felt he owed them an opportunity to speak in an unofficial capacity. "Does anyone else have anything they would like to say? This is your chance for taking off the bars and getting whatever you want off your chest."

The air became still. No one breathed; no one said a word. *The bars stay on.* "The time is now 0620," he said. "I want you in your fighters and ready for take-off in ten minutes. Your flight plans will be transmitted into your navigational computers just before we depart."

"Attention!" Kershaw barked from the front row. Every pilot jumped to his feet in a single, synchronized action. Yamane wished he could have said more. Various expressions on their faces, ranging from concern to outright fear, necessitated he do so. But the clandestine nature of their assignment didn't permit such liberties. Secrecy, above all else, would have to be maintained.

"Dismissed."

As Yamane approached the hangar bay from the south, he heard the sounds of the fighters; first from a distance, and then up close. How could he not? The roar of the engines, sometimes approaching two hundred and fifty decibels, thundered from every corner of the base when a squadron prepared for a flight.

Hurrying past the outer doors, Yamane eyed the fourteen fighters parked inside the massive enclosure. The main load-bearing beam, two meters thick, straddled the length of the roof. On either side, there were two sets of window panels. The retractable shutters adjusted the amount of light, depending on the time of day. Just beyond the windows, smaller support beams curved along the contours of the structure. A number of light fixtures hung down about halfway between the roof and the fighters, positioned over each stall. Rather simple, really. So much so that Yamane often reflected on how little the overall concept had changed over the past three hundred years. It was as if the architects and planners back in the twentieth century had stumbled onto the perfect design, and everyone else since then had just left it at that.

Yamane's ship came into view. His crew chief stood near the front of the hangar, waiting. "Morning, Sergeant Brown," he said after tending to his pre-flight ritual. "Looks like a good day to go up."

The mechanic nodded and then mumbled something under his breath about being in the hangar instead of his bunk. Yamane just grinned before climbing up the ladder slung over the edge of the cockpit and jumping into his seat.

Brown followed him up, still mumbling. Armed with his satchel and flight bag, he handed them off to Yamane, acting like a man who couldn't see them and their fighters gone fast enough.

Yamane stowed his flight bag in an open slot on his right without any problem. His satchel, on the other hand, became a problem. The compartment it was supposed to go into didn't open. He tried the door again. No luck. Impatient, the crew chief began tapping his fingers on the metal hull. The dull, hollow sound somehow pierced through the high-pitched turbine noises made by nearby fighters. Feeling the sting of the chief's gaze, he just dropped his bag between both legs. A tight fit, but sufficient for now.

Yamane sat back against the seat and wiggled his hips back and forth a couple of times.

"Okay, I think I'm ready," he said.

The chief's calloused hands grabbed both metal clasps, and snaked the reinforced nylon straps through two sets of loops, into a pair of locking mechanisms just above his shoulders. *Click...click.* Taking hold of the red tug lines and grabbing them tightly, Brown drew in a deep breath, and then jerked down on the restraints with all of his might. "Now those g-force turns won't knock you around the cockpit."

"A good job, as always," Yamane joked. "I can almost breathe."

The sergeant, still mumbling something under his breath, climbed back down onto the ground.

Yamane focused his attention forward. When he entered the command sequence into the main computer, his actions transferred the lifeless collection of metal and computer programming into a living, breathing organism, capable of pushing him past the speed of light. He considered the relationship between a pilot and his fighter the ultimate combination of man, metal and machinery, all working together in perfect harmony. The ship couldn't operate without the pilot, the pilot couldn't go into space without the ship, and the ship couldn't function without the computer system—all three components working together in a symbiotic relationship, no one part more important than the other.

Brown returned with Yamane's helmet and placed it into his waiting hands. The combination of composites, padding, and plastic felt heavy. Maybe the heaviest it had ever felt. Brown helped him guide the helmet's upper metallic latching ring into the lower one around his neck, creating an airtight seal. Just one procedure remained before Yamane could power up his fighter's main power systems. He keyed several commands into the data pad on his wrist for a static pressure test. The results came back negative—no leaks.

Patting him twice on the helmet before climbing down, Brown grabbed the bottom rung, pushed up with both hands, and unhooked the ladder. By the time he reached a safe distance away, the cockpit canopy had already come down and locked into position.

Yamane made a quick assessment of his ship's operational status. "Forward thrusters are go," he said to himself. "All digital readouts are functioning, fuel is at maximum, weapons arming circuit is go, computers are up and running...all systems show go." He let out a slow, controlled breath, paused for a second, and then entered the code "#H9-A0-L00#" into the keypad at the base of his control panel. A small display marked "engage" started blinking off and on at regular intervals, the action marked by a soft pinging sound. With a simple press of a button, all three turbines awoke from their slumber. A low hum emanated from behind. But as the rotation rate increased, the hum steadily changed into the characteristic rhythmic, pulsing sensation emitted by a Min fighter.

Yamane absorbed the pulses emanating all around him. To him, it felt like his ship was saying she was ready to go up. He turned to his right and made a twirling motion with his index finger. Seargent Brown, who had been waiting a short distance away, ran under the fighter and pulled out the wheel blocks keeping him in place.

"This is Blackhawk One," Yamane said into his headset. "I am ready to taxi."

"Roger, Blackhawk One," the voice on the radio replied. "You are cleared for runway seven."

"Roger tower. Runway seven."

Here goes nothing. With the barest of nudges on the throttle, all three turbines responded without the slightest hesitation; drowning out the sounds of those fighters closest to him.

Dressed in his fluorescent orange jumpsuit and helmet, a flagman appeared out of nowhere. He guided Yamane out of the hangar bay, his actions reflected in the back-and-forth motion of each lighted baton.

When the front wheel of his ship rolled onto the tarmac, the flagman stepped aside and waved Yamane through. The corporal then turned his attention to the next fighter in line. This little dance went on, back and forth, until he had successfully guided all fourteen ships onto the runway.

"This is Blackhawk One, tower," Yamane said into his headset after he assumed his place in the lead position. "We are ready for departure."

"Stand by, Blackhawk One."

The take-off lights, set on the right side of the runway, still showed red. Yamane closed his eyes and soaked in the vibrations from his ship's engines a second time. The oscillating wave pattern soothed him. He opened them again. Up ahead, maybe a hundred meters or so, thousands of skid marks from thousands of landings could be seen as clear as day. So many ships had come down on the runway over the years, it appeared long and black, like someone had taken a brush and painted over the monochromatic gray.

"Blackhawk One, stand by." Yamane shot a look to his right. At that moment, every light changed from red to green. "Permission for take-off has been granted."

He clutched the thruster control with his left hand and the maneuvering stick with his right. With a simple nod to the control tower, Yamane slammed the thruster control forward. Power reserves stored up in all three turbines burst into the thrusters, sending his fighter down the runway like a bullet fired from a rifle.

"Two hundred kilometers-per-hour...two hundred and twenty-five...two hundred and fifty."

Vibrations caused by all three wheels rolling over the irregular surface grew at an exponential rate as his velocity increased. A mixture of trees and buildings, intermittently lining the side, flew by in a blur; their individual shapes no longer distinguishable.

The proximity alarm sounded the instant his fighter reached the required speed of three hundred kilometers per hour. With one sudden jerk, Yamane pulled his maneuvering stick back. The jagged mountains in the distance dropped out of sight, replaced by a cloudy, auburn sky.

"Air speed five hundred and increasing...altitude, one thousand," Yamane said into his headset. His fighter shook a bit when the nose sliced through a couple of air pockets. "Trajectory ..." he glanced down at his display. "We are moving into the corridor...orbit in five minutes."

"We copy you, Blackhawk One," the voice replied. "Our boards show the same."

The higher his fighter climbed into the morning sky, the darker the horizon became. Those first few flickers of starlight caught Yamane's attention. Another star appeared, then another, and another. Soon, the whole sky was filled with stars. When Titan's pull had dropped below fifty percent, the ship's gravitational compensators kicked in, duplicating the effect of normal gravity. The result was so gradual and so real that Yamane often forgot the device existed.

On the central display, he verified the squadron was climbing at a negative thirty-six degree trajectory. They were in the slot. Their course remained unchanged until they reached an altitude of eight kilometers. There, he changed his pitch an additional negative five degrees. At just below sixty kilometers, his fighter finally leveled out and achieved orbit.

Excitement overrode his anxiety as he wondered what they would find out there. "Blackhawk One to tower," Yamane said. "We are at the fail-safe point...awaiting final instructions."

"Roger, Blackhawk One. Your code signal is Tango, Henry, X-ray."

Yamane compared it with the one provided by Commander Federson. His right arm display indicated both sets were a match. Star Force Command had issued the final go code. Feeling hopeful about their chances, he activated the ship's guidance computer. Jumbled numbers and letters flashed across his central monitor in a blur, stopping when their projected course and rendezvous coordinates appeared.

"This is Lt. Commander Yamane," he said into his headset with a low voice, belying no emotion either way. "As you know, we've been given permission to proceed with the mission. On my mark, we will accelerate to 1.01 stellar velocity. The trajectory for our flight has already been programmed into your navigational computers." A flurry of thoughts found their way to the tip of his tongue. So much could be said. So much should be said. He dare not. *Just keep it simple.* "I don't think there's anything more I can say, except good luck. All ships—stand by."

He tightened his grip on the thruster control unit. "Three, two, one... mark!" His fighter shot forward in a burst of acceleration, flying out of sight in a matter of seconds. Feeling as though Commander Federson had sent him into oblivion, Yamane could only guess what would happen next.

CHAPTER 5

GARGARIN STAR FORCE BASE, TITAN
1049 PROXIMA MERIDIAN TIME, AUGUST 12, 2217

Commodore Hayes wasted little time getting off his shuttle and into an awaiting hover car. Colonel Sterfer and Captain Reeves hurried with him. Some bad weather over the Rockies had grounded his ship for several hours. The unexpected setback put him in something of a sour mood. Arriving behind schedule usually didn't bother him so much, but this time was different. Hayes had wanted to meet with Yamane and his squadron before they took off, kind of like a champagne bottle christening a ship before launching it. He could do nothing about the delay, however, and had to accept the fact that he had missed his opportunity.

The driver seemed to sense his mood. He hurried all three officers into the back seat, and then tore off after jumping behind the steering wheel. Making a hard right at the intersection, the sergeant roared down the single lane road in a blaze of dust, breaking numerous speeding laws. After taking another abrupt turn, the command center came up fast—too fast. He was forced to hit the brakes hard, bringing the transport to a screeching halt in a hail of rocks and gravel.

"I'm so sorry, Commodore," the driver apologized several times before he jumped out of the front seat and circled around to the back of the car, the words not coming out fast enough to abate his obvious gaff. He could do nothing else except stand at attention by the open door, his face ashen.

Hayes could have really let the driver have it for bouncing him around like a sack of wheat in a delivery truck, but he decided to let the matter go, reminding himself that chewing out the sergeant would waste valuable time. He just wanted to get inside and meet with Federson.

Without a word, Hayes approached two guards stationed at the main entrance of Command and Control, Sterfer and Reeves not far behind. The building was light brown in color, and lacking in any real detail. So much so, that if it weren't for those guards posted outside, a person could walk right by and miss the command center altogether.

When Hayes reached the top of the granite steps, one of the guards placed his hand on his sidearm, while the other took two steps forward. "Your papers please," he asked, his hand stretched out. The corporal's eyes were steely cold, a look matched by his lifeless expression.

A dumb expression fell on Haye's face. One soldier reaching for his gun, another asking for his papers—it was almost too much to believe. On the other hand, the significance of what they were doing warranted an increase in security. If word got out about the Deravans before Star Force could contain the situation, they could have a full-blown panic on their hands.

The guard scanned Hayes' papers after he produced them from his briefcase. When he came to the commodore's photograph, he stopped. Studying the picture for a couple of moments, he compared it to the man standing before him. The guard appeared satisfied and opened the door. "Go right in, gentlemen," he said after handing the documents back.

"Thank you," they replied in unison.

When both guards resumed their place at the entrance, the door unceremoniously slammed shut with a heavy bang.

White acoustic tiles covered the ceiling, alternating black and white squares dotted the floor, creating a checkerboard pattern, and lining the corridor, were two seemingly endless rows of wooden office doors. A lack of personnel going back and forth suggested they had already left for the day. Hayes thought this a bit odd. It wasn't even noon yet. "Puzzling," he commented to himself, and then continued on his way, faintly aware of the echoing sounds made by his boots in the silent hallway.

When Hayes, Sterfer, and Reeves reached the end of the corridor, it took a sharp turn. Then, in a maze-like fashion, the hallway went left, left, and finally right. More darkened offices.

"This place is closed down tight," Sterfer observed.

Hayes paid the comment little attention. He had just one thing on his mind—the mission.

After making another right turn, the corridor abruptly stopped. A large set of double doors stood before them. Ornate carvings, golden in color, adorned the perimeter, going up one side and down the other. The varied imagery consisted of natural landscapes and intertwining grapevines. Both doors, on the other hand, were simpler in design, appearing as nothing more than smooth, polished surfaces.

They stopped just in front of another guard who had been standing at attention next to the door, his hands held behind his back and his feet set a half-meter apart. Hayes saw him as the perfect embodiment of military precision, sharp and indifferent.

Above the doorway, there were large black letters over a white background:

COMMAND AND CONTROL CENTER

Though the guard didn't move a muscle, his eyes tracked the three until they were right in front of him. "Can you please take out your I.D. cards?" he asked, approximating the same tone and mannerisms of the guard they met outside.

All three officers produced their badges and handed them to the guard. He compared the pictures to their faces. Satisfied they had the proper credentials, he stepped back and pulled out a small card from his left chest pocket. When the encoded magnetic strip passed over a silver panel, a keypad below lit up. He then punched in four different numbers. The small display changed from red to green. Both sets of doors clicked and then slid open. "Right this way, gentlemen."

Hayes, Sterfer, and Reeves fell into the middle of a maelstrom. A dizzying number of personnel were walking about in a sea of computers, consoles, and workstations. The sounds of programs bleating and chirping assaulted the three from every corner of the room. Certain techs dropped off papers and data pads at some stations, and picked up sealed files at others.

A couple of officers rushed past. Heading into the middle of the control room, they disappeared behind a row of analytical computers. Hayes envied them. A social person by nature, he relished the idea of being in the middle of the action—and the action was right in front of him, three steps away. The temptation proved too strong. "I'm going to take a quick look around before checking with Federson. Stick close, and keep your ears open."

Before either of them could respond, Hayes moved right into the flurry of activity. His pulse quickened when a row of displays and tracking computers keyed into Yamane's squadron fell into view. The commodore went to the one closest to him. It happened to be the RadAR tracking console. He leaned forward and placed his hands on the back of an angled chair. Sterfer pulled out a notepad from his pocket and scribbled down a few notes.

"The squadron is traveling at 1.01 stellar velocity," a voice said from behind. A slight hint of annoyance marked each word. "They will link up with Neptune in nine and a half minutes."

Hayes stood upright. Their eyes met.

The r-tech reared back. "Commodore!" he gasped.

"At ease," Hayes said with a comforting smile. "You can have your station back."

"Yes, sir," he replied, his manner hurried. "Thank you, sir."

The lieutenant brushed past Hayes and sat in his chair. Fumbling for the headset, he coughed conspicuously a couple of times.

Hayes looked about the center. "Where's Commander Federson?"

The r-tech pointed at the second level. "He's up there...in the Situation Room."

"You two stay here and get caught up," Hayes said to Sterfer and Reeves amidst the sounds of muffled voices and computer noises. "I want a status report in one hour."

Both of them nodded in reply and then went off in different directions.

"I'm switching over to secondary tracking," the operator said into his headset.

Curiosity got the better of Hayes. He turned back and studied the console display. A small white dot stood opposite a black background. On the right side of the screen, a much larger red dot appeared. Between them, a single yellow line indicated the squadron's planned trajectory. Hayes found the simplicity of what he saw rather amusing. One of the most significant events in human history and the best they could come up with was two circles and a line.

As much as he was enjoying himself, Hayes knew he couldn't stay. Duty called. He pulled himself away from the console and made a beeline for the stairs just past the last row of tracking computers. Skipping every other stair, the commodore reached the second level in short order. *Not bad for a sixty-year-old*, he thought.

Set back a few meters from the top step, the Situation Room doors slid apart from each other the instant he interrupted the sensor beam. Commander Federson, his back facing the commodore at an angle, stood at the far end of the room, studying several printouts.

Once inside, the doors slid closed, quiet as a breath. Hayes watched junior and senior officers bustle about silently below, their conversations cut down by the room's soundproofed glass. The Situation Room, however, created noise of its own. Lined up in two rows on either side of Federson, he heard a cacophony of clicks and beeps emanating from a series of computer consoles.

Hayes remained near the front, unmoving. He then noticed a communications transceiver near the wall on his left. The names of all seven stellar cruisers stood out prominently on the screen, with an accompanying image fixed just below them. Set to the right of each ship, a series of letters, symbols and numbers indicated Federson had already engaged the most sophisticated encryption system ever devised—one with a perfect operational record. If he remembered the sequence right, they were standing by, awaiting further orders. In front of the console, where the angled face leveled off, the cipher index page lay open. At a moment's notice, Federson could give one commander a certain set of instructions, and then give new orders to another without anyone else knowing. Whether for good or bad, he appeared more than ready.

"Seems as though you have things well in hand," Hayes complemented him from behind.

Federson spun around and snapped to attention. Hayes saluted in return. "I'm sorry, Commodore," he apologized, "but I didn't see you standing there." He walked over and extended his hand. The two shook.

"That's all right," Hayes replied, trying to deflect the commander's embarrassment. "You've got a lot going on right now."

Federson gave his uniform a quick tug before adjusting his tie. "How was your trip?"

A cloud formed over the commodore. "Lousy. The weather in the Rockies was pretty bad. They haven't had a storm there all month, and the day I fly over...well, it was just bad timing. I wanted to get here sooner, before Yamane left, but we were held up until the weather cleared."

"You haven't missed too much so far. And if things go as planned, the status of the mission should remain the same, until Yamane rendezvouses with the Deravan ship."

"How are you doing?"

"All right, I guess," he yawned. "I haven't slept much the last couple of days. Getting all the details squared away has been something of a nightmare. But we're holding up. And you?"

"I got in a good few hours between Earth and here. You know how space travel is." His hand mimicked a boat on still water. "Smooth sailing all the way."

The conversation stalled. Catching sight of the transceiver, Hayes placed his hand on top. He rubbed the shiny green finish with a gentle touch, as though he was rubbing a magic lamp. "Do you think we're ready for what we'll meet out there?"

Federson lowered his head before responding. He stared at the names of the stellar cruisers. "I don't know, but I guess we'll find out soon enough."

SECTOR THIRTY-FIVE
1152 PROXIMA MERIDIAN TIME, AUGUST 12, 2217

The planet Neptune loomed off in the distance. Yamane couldn't take his eyes off such a beautiful sight. Ever since he had seen the gaseous giant up close on one of his first patrols, he had been drawn to the hypnotic blue surface of swirling hydrogen, helium and methane gas whipping around the planet in the fastest known winds in the Solar System. Neptune's Great Dark Spot had especially enthralled him. Though the size and location varied over time, the distinctive weather pattern roaming around in the upper atmosphere remained about the same size as Earth. Tracking stations had monitored winds from the centuries-old storm reaching speeds up to 2500 kilometers an hour on many occasions. He wondered how something of such intensity could have lasted so long, unabated.

The proximity alarm blaring in Yamane's ears ripped him out of his milieu of wandering thoughts, forcing him back into the confines of his cockpit. Set in a high-low semi-rhythmic pattern, it indicated they were nearing their first course correction.

"We'll be reaching the burn point in two minutes, people," he said after switching on his radio. "Double-check your directional thruster systems.

Our last burn was a little sloppy."

A procedural check of the targeting display indicated Neptune's gravitational pull was already affecting his fighter. His trajectory was off by two points, and his speed had increased to 1.03 stellar velocity. If they didn't take corrective action soon, the planet's gravity well would pull them down into the atmosphere, burning up in a decaying orbit. The thought of such an encounter held out a certain fascination for him, but not so much where he would do anything about it.

A new sound went off in the cockpit. This one was softer, and much more pleasant. Yamane knew the reason for the second alarm even before he verified the data displayed on the screen. "Point one seven course deviation," Yamane said to himself. "Speed is now at 1.04." Accessing the appropriate command code from the central display, he entered the information into the computer guidance system. His fighter was now on automatic.

When Yamane made a visual confirmation of their position, he was surprised at just how big the gas giant had gotten in so little time. A series of subtle vibrations shook his craft. The engines were already straining against Neptune's gravitational pull. *Our course change won't be long now.* The vibrations increased in intensity, until a muffled explosion sounded from the rear of his ship. A short but powerful burst from the engine came right after, followed by several lesser bursts from the directional thrusters. In an instant, they had broken free from Neptune and gone back to their original course. Yamane checked the velocity gauge. Their speed had also returned to 1.01, just like before. They were safe again...for the moment.

SECTOR THIRTY-SIX
2155 PROXIMA MERIDIAN TIME, AUGUST 12, 2217

The squadron flew the next ten hours without incident. Continually probing the outer reaches of space, they had already traveled far beyond the boundary of the Solar System, denoted by Icarus' orbit some twenty-five billion miles away from the Sun. Whenever Yamane made a trip this far out, he often wondered what Columbus felt like when he left the security of the Portuguese shores, or Leif Erickson, or Magellan, or a hundred other explorers who risked their lives to seek the unknown. A deep-seated sense of loneliness almost always followed. This time was no exception. Rather than give into his feelings of isolation, Yamane focused his attention on the thousands of stars burning in the distance. Some were red giants, while others were white dwarfs. Pulsars, binary stars, and a smattering of ternary systems likewise appeared. Whatever type, they were out there. And between himself and those far-off balls of hydrogen gas, nothing existed, nothing but empty space.

Three successive sharp bleeps indicated the ship's chronometer had counted down to zero. Yamane forgot he had activated the device right after take-off, but the muted chimes declared they were nearing the start of the first sleep cycle. After more than fifteen hours in space, everyone was no doubt feeling drained.

Yamane's nimble fingers worked the radio. "If you check your chronometers, you'll see the time has come for group Alpha to sack out for a while. Set your computers for six-hour intervals. Group Beta will take their turn at 0400 hours."

His speakers hissed and popped. A familiar voice came on. "What about you, Frank?" Kershaw asked. "I'm more than awake. I can take the first watch."

Yamane laughed to himself. "Nice try, but I don't think so. I'll bring my ship around and take yours in tow. Six hours from now, *you* can be in command of the second watch."

A slight pause followed. "You're the boss. But if you change your mind, just let me know."

The radio fell silent.

Yamane checked his tanks. They were fully pressurized. With the simple press of a button, two bursts of helium gas shot out of control nozzle number five, freezing when it touched the near absolute-zero temperature of space. The crystalline particles flickered and sparkled as they floated away, their brief purpose served for the sake of humanity's rendezvous with the Deravans. Yamane's ship responded, turning about on her axis like a spinning top in slow motion. A second controlled burst zeroed out his rotation rate.

Yamane then took hold of the thruster control unit. He curled his fingers around the grip, keeping a light touch before exhaling. Moving it forward just a fraction, all three turbines channeled a bit of thrust into the bell chamber. The relative distance between his ship and Kershaw's began to decrease. "Ten meters...eight meters...six meters," he read aloud. At five meters, he fired a counter-burst with a thruster nozzle located in the aft section of his fighter. His downward motion stopped. "That's got her. Locking it down." The tracking sensor grabbed a hold of Kershaw's fighter behind him, taking his ship in tow. Though most pilots trusted the anti-collision system without question, a person could sleep a little easier knowing his wingman would literally be looking over his shoulder throughout his shift.

GAGARIN STAR FORCE BASE, TITAN
2414 PROXIMA MERIDIAN TIME, AUGUST 12, 2217

Commodore Hayes sat in a chair overlooking the command center below. The excitement he felt at the beginning of the mission had more or less settled into a predictable routine. Many of the technicians still manned their stations, scrutinizing every piece of data appearing on their screens, but other stations, shown by obvious gaps between operators, were empty. He had been watching them off and on all through the day and early evening.

The only real interruptions came at the top of each hour, when Sterfer and Reeves briefed him on the latest update they received from Yamane. As expected, the mission had proceeded without incident. *At least nothing has gone wrong*, he thought, and then knocked on his desk for good luck.

Federson came into the Situation Room and checked the astro-clock posted on the wall above the doors. *2415.* "Yamane's fighters should rendezvous with the Deravan ship in about twenty-eight hours," he said to the commodore.

Hayes let the words settle onto the floor. His mind had already considered the endless possibilities of what might happen once the squadron made contact. One scenario led to another, which led to two more. Any one of his little dramas could be right, or none of them could be. He just wished he could feel a measure of control, but there was none. *Perhaps later*, he thought.

Federson gave the astro-clock a good long look.

Hayes finally acknowledged him with a simple nod. He seemed to need a measure of reassurance. Perhaps they all did. The sounds of all those clattering stations worked their way into his conscious thoughts. Hayes turned back towards the pit. The raw data shown on those screens hadn't indicated much, at least not yet. But if something important did come through, the reactions of the operators below would be a far more accurate indicator than the bleeping of an impersonal machine.

"Twenty-seven hours and fifty-nine minutes."

SECTOR THIRTY-SEVEN
0414 PROXIMA MERIDIAN TIME, AUGUST 13, 2217

At first Yamane felt fine after his shift had ended, more or less awake. But not so many minutes later his eyes were already getting heavy. He had every intention of transferring authority over to Kershaw when the two groups switched over, but something within him just couldn't let go. A deep yawn forced its way out.

Yamane let his head fall back against the headrest. His thoughts, usually well-ordered and disciplined, drifted off into obscurity. His breathing deepened, inhaling and exhaling at slower intervals. The gentle hum of the power systems lulled him away even further. Sleep had almost overtaken him. He could not allow it. He would not allow it.

After sitting up straight again, Yamane came up with a strategy— distraction. If he could focus his mind on a fixed point in the distance, it might make a difference. There were the usual planets and galaxies, of course, cradles of unknown civilizations; but they felt cold, distant. Another yawn forced its way out. Yamane was fighting a losing battle and he knew it. *Pride can be a difficult thing*, he thought. He needed sleep and there was just no getting around it. The half-meter reach between his arrogance and the radio felt more like a mile. After an initial hesitation, his hand bridged the great distance. "Stan, I think I'll sack out for a while. Wake me if anything happens."

"No problem," Kershaw replied. "I'll take good care of your squadron."

Once Yamane surrendered, he descended into sweet slumber. His last conscious recollection was Kershaw coming around and taking the ship in tow...and then darkness.

A person came out of the darkness and ran past him, and then another, and another, and another. Soon hundreds of other faceless people ran past him. In the distance, he could hear Liana call out to him. "Liana," he called back, "where are you?" An explosion went off near her. The brilliant white light almost blinded him as he fell to the ground. He lay there, stunned for a moment. Yamane shook off the effects of the blast and scampered back to his feet. She called to him again. He tried to run to her, but his feet didn't move, as though they were being held down. Using all of his might, his foot slid forward, but just barely. "Hold on, Liana," he wailed. Yamane searched for her through the crowds running past him. She was gone.

CHAPTER 6

SECTOR FORTY-TWO
0342 PROXIMA MERIDIAN TIME, AUGUST 14, 2217

Locked into a tight, but lethal formation, the squadron of fighters under Yamane's command flew into the last vestiges of known space. For the past two days they had moved ever outward, collectively hurtling toward the objective of their mission. One hundred, one thousand, ten thousand kilometers—the vast distances traversed blurred together as each hour passed in the limitless expanse. They had encountered countless numbers of asteroids during their journey; these lone witnesses of when time began came and then tumbled away into the dark cauldron. Seen for an instant, and then gone.

Yamane's squadron pressed on. Another million kilometers traveled, five million, twenty million, until they encountered an unknown gaseous anomaly. The unintended discovery appeared like a solitary beacon of light—the billions of hydrogen particles colliding together, sometimes doing so in a random fashion, while at other times manifesting themselves in perfect synchronization. A mixture of greens and yellows shot across the length of the cloud. The dazzling display could not have been more impressive. But as beautiful as the combination of art and science was, they could not stay, and continued on their journey. The quest, however, took a turn. After the nebula faded away in the distance, his squadron of fighters encountered nothing, nothing but a desert of empty space. The anomaly had not been a beacon, but a doorway into a sea of infinite blackness.

More kilometers passed. Nothing. The hours counted down with equal measure, and still nothing. The stars themselves even gave the impression they stood further away, as though all creation had fled from them. No planets, no interstellar debris, no indication anything out there existed at all. They flew on.

Thirty billion kilometers, forty billion, fifty billion, until, as the prescribed number of hours came and went, the pilots found themselves on the precipice of discovery right in the heart of the Cauldara Sector.

Yamane marked the hours as they passed by. He knew this would make the trip feel twice as long, but it helped occupy his mind. His mind. He couldn't stop thinking about the alien ship. He had asked the same questions about the Deravans a thousand times: who were they, what were they like, why were they coming? There were many questions, but no answers.

He checked their position. His tracking computer had kept them on course, making minute adjustments along the way—a microburst here, a microburst there—but never more than a fraction of a degree. Confirming the data on his targeting grid, he noted the flashing blue triangle superimposed over a solid white line. *Was that ship still out there?* He wished he could have felt better rested. No matter. When the time came, fatigue would be the least of his worries.

0347. Half an hour. Yamane stared at the display for an indeterminate amount of time. The lack of sleep had caught up with him again. He extended both arms as far as they could go in his cramped surroundings. Flexing his muscles helped, as did that small shot of adrenaline released into his bloodstream. He felt awake again.

The cockpit lights started to flash off and on in a frenetic manner. The proximity alarm blared out in three successive bursts—silence—and then three more bursts. A RadAR contact triggered the ship's defensive protocols: weapons, tactical, targeting, the transcom, and long-range communications—all came up in the blink of an eye.

Yamane found the targeting grid. A large blip emerged at the top of the screen, right where he expected the Deravan ship to be. His breathing quickened and at the same time his stomach did a couple of backflips. Additional shots of adrenaline into his bloodstream frayed his nerves even more.

When the analytical computer finished its initial scan, a series of numbers tumbled down the middle of his display, but they passed by so quickly he had a hard time distinguishing one from the other. Then the data stream stopped, replaced with the speed of the unknown RadAR contact. *1.00 stellar velocity.* Yamane compared the information to the last known speed of the Deravan ship. He accessed the file downloaded into his suit's database. Both sets of numbers were identical.

"One down, one to go," he said under his breath.

Yamane reset the display and then keyed in a different set of commands. In an instant, the upper left quadrant of the targeting grid produced the usual jumble of numbers and symbols. And like before, the program stopped on a dime. Confirmed again—the projected trajectory indicated the unknown was heading for Titan. "Got you," he said in triumph.

Every one of the hardships they had faced on the trip faded away in an instant. The deprivation, fatigue, and boredom, they all became unimportant episodes from the past. In their place, Yamane considered the ramifications of what this discovery would mean to the human race. Whatever he said and did from this point on would be recorded for all time. Yamane cleared his head. His thoughts of self-importance were starting to cloud his thinking. He didn't like it. The only thing that mattered was the completion of his mission, nothing more. After that, history could work itself out.

"I have a RadAR contact on my screen," he said into his headset, belying no emotion either way. "Alter heading two-two-five degrees. Our ETA is twenty-five minutes. We will change our squadron orientation into an omega six-clip formation. I repeat, attack pattern omega."

Kershaw acknowledged the order first. With military precision, he brought his ship up to full power, and then positioned himself tight behind Yamane. As the other pilots responded, they mirrored his actions precisely, half moving over to his starboard side, the others to his port, forming a sleeked-back V-shape configuration.

With a passing awareness of the ballet taking place just beyond the confines of his cockpit, Yamane's attention remained fixed on the blip's heading. It was on course, all right, but something struck him as odd. Either the targeting grid had suffered a malfunction, or the image had doubled in size in the past two minutes. "How big can this thing be?" Yamane muttered to himself. *Something must be distorting the signal.* He ran a system-wide diagnostic. The monitors stopped, flashed off and on, and then came up again. Yamane looked down at the targeting grid. To his surprise, the yellow square had grown even larger.

"Sir, I have the object in visual—dead ahead!" one of the pilots shouted on the radio.

Just then, Yamane's instruments went crazy—switching off and on for no apparent reason, as though an invisible pair of hands were flipping switches at will. The turbines accelerated wildly, causing his fighter to lurch forward. Just as Yamane was about to pull the thruster control back, engine power went down to zero. He gripped the maneuvering stick tight, hoping it would get his fighter under control. It had no effect.

When a fighter shot past his bow, Yamane realized the other pilots seemed to be facing the same emergency, their ships likewise moving about to and fro in an erratic fashion. He tried to get them on the radio, but communications were dead as well. Through the jerking and twisting of his ship, Yamane searched for an answer. He came up with just one: they were under attack. Glancing at the pulse cannon arming mechanism, he had no other choice but to take action.

Another sudden jolt struck the ship, snapping his head over like a well-oiled hinge. He grunted when the rim of his helmet struck his chest. Despite his ship pitching this way and that, Yamane somehow reached the arming button in the middle of his display. Power levels went from zero to full power in an instant, capping off at the top of the scale. Yamane didn't know why his weapons were spared, but he could not have been more pleased. His feelings of triumph were short-lived, however. Just to the right of the gauge, the targeting grid remained unchanged. Without the aid of the computer, Yamane would have to target the vessel by line of sight.

With the realization that his ship could shake apart at any second, he grabbed the stick with his right hand and rested his thumb on the firing button. Yamane leaned slightly forward and took aim. Just as he was about to fire, the shaking stopped. His surroundings became quiet, still. He looked about the cockpit. Every system seemed to be operating within normal parameters.

Kershaw came crashing onto the radio. "What was that, Frank?"

Yamane did not respond at first. Instead, he just sat and waited for a moment, collecting his thoughts. "I can't say for certain. Preliminary data is coming through now." He bent closer. "If I'm reading this right, initial analysis suggests we passed through some kind of electro-magnetic field...on the order of one hundred terawatts."

"One hundred terawatts?" Kershaw gasped, sounding impressed. "What could create a field that big?"

Yamane snatched a quick look outside the cockpit window. "Unless my RadAR scope is wrong, it was that Deravan ship."

"My gut's telling me something's not right about this," Kershaw asserted.

Yamane couldn't decide if he agreed with him or not. "What are you getting at?"

There was a noticeable pause before the major replied. "Maybe we should signal Command and Control—see what they advise."

Feeling like his toes had just gotten stepped on, Yamane let his ego do the talking. "This is my mission and my call. Unless I know the squadron is truly in danger, we will proceed as planned."

"All right, Frank," Kershaw backpedaled, "but stay frosty. We could experience round two at any second."

Yamane relaxed his hold on the maneuvering stick somewhat. "Fair enough. From now on, monitoring the Deravan ship will be my explicit responsibility. If anything changes, no matter how insignificant, I'll let you know the moment it does."

"As commanding officer of this mission the call for making such a decision is yours, but just remember one thing—I did warn you. Kershaw, out." Static followed.

Yamane didn't like being harsh with his second-in-command, but the importance of what lay out there far outweighed any concerns raised by one man. His vindication felt weak. Maybe it was far simpler. Maybe he just didn't want anyone else to share in the glory.

His troubled thoughts faded at the sight of the Deravan ship slowly approaching. In the interim, between the "event" and his conversation with Kershaw, it had somehow sneaked up on them. Even at a distance of two thousand kilometers, he noted the size and scale of the alien vessel. To any observer, trained or otherwise, this was not a ship of ordinary creation. In particular, the physical dimensions awed him. He considered the technology required for such a project. "They must be centuries ahead of us," he thought.

Constructed in the configuration of an elongated rectangle, rounded-off edges on all four corners gave the vessel a flattened oval shape. There were no wings or anything else that stood out, suggesting they created the vessel for space travel alone. The hull was likewise devoid of any real detail, except for an occasional window, the largest of which was located near the front. But they were so small the light coming from them looked like pinpoints rather than the panels of a bridge or an observation deck. The hull was shiny bright, almost luminescent, its glow enhanced by three massive engine ports in the rear, like beacons in space.

The sight was mesmerizing, as though it was attempting to summon them closer. Yamane felt the vessel's mysterious spell from the start. The longer he stared at the ship, the more he thought he could see right through it—and it him.

The targeting computer let out two low-toned beeps. The action brought Yamane back into the confines of his cockpit. *Good*, he thought. *Initial scans are complete.* When he activated all three spectral analysis screens, a variety of data streams appeared. Even though the results seemed to be irrefutable, he had a hard time believing them. "Twenty kilometers?" Yamane asked aloud, incredulous. "Twenty kilometers long...four kilometers high...three kilometers wide. Is that possible?" He checked again. The numbers were the same as before. "Well I'll be a—"

A vessel of this magnitude had so much to offer them on the one hand, so much to hide on the other. *Hide...maybe not.* Perhaps, some of her secrets were accessible. He just needed the right kind of key to get at them.

An image of the Deravan ship appeared after he reformatted the central display. The analysis program kicked in, accessing different parts of the visible and invisible spectrum. A subtle shade of white painted over the image. White morphed into a dull blue, and then bright red. Red became yellow, then green, and on and on. Five minutes later, the program stopped. In their place, the analysis offered by the computer blinked off and on at regular intervals, accompanied by the same pinging sound as before: "OVERALL RESULTS: INCONCLUSIVE."

"How can this be?" Yamane asked himself. "The computer must be wrong."

He ran the analysis program again; and just like before, those three same frustrating words appeared, "OVERALL RESULTS: INCONCLUSIVE." Except this time, that pinging sound was now beginning to irritate him.

As the seconds passed, his feelings of annoyance turned into outright frustration. Then he had an idea. Yamane scrolled through volumes of text, until the analysis portion popped onto the screen. "SEVENTEEN UNKNOWN METALS AND COMPOUNDS DETECTED." Followed by, "INTERIOR SCAN: INCONCLUSIVE." He sighed in disbelief. *Whatever secrets lay inside, you Deravans appeared to have gone through a lot of trouble to keep them safely hidden.*

Yamane didn't know what he should do next. Even though it didn't feel like they were in immediate danger, he thought it curious the squadron had been with the ship for almost half an hour, and hadn't been contacted yet. For all he knew, the massive craft could be on automatic. But why build such a large ship, and no crew? No. He couldn't accept such a notion. There was a crew, and they were aware of their arrival; he'd bet his life on it. If true, this meant the same question remained: why hadn't the Deravans made contact? For that, Yamane had no answer.

GAGARIN STAR FORCE BASE, TITAN
0459 PROXIMA MERIDIAN TIME, AUGUST 14, 2217

"We should have heard something by now," Hayes complained, the words dripping off his tongue one acerbic utterance at a time.

Federson's chair popped and creaked when he leaned back in it. "Almost five? Lt. Commander Yamane has sent his reports at the top of each hour without fail. I don't see any reason why this should suddenly change."

Even as his words filled the Situation Room, the transceiver began to click and whine, as it had done every hour on the hour. Hayes recognized those sounds made by multiple semitronic components found within the polished brass casing. He pushed out of his chair and made a beeline right for the source of his hopes...and anxieties.

The machine typed out a string of letters and symbols on the screen. Hayes bent closer, greedily drinking in every decoded piece of data. He turned back to ask Federson a question, but stopped when he saw the pit, as he had grown into the habit of calling the command center, below. Silence descended upon every station, every operator. Hayes could feel the tension ratchet up as the text continued scrolling down the screen. He checked the astro-clock above.

Federson came up from behind, clothed with an expression of guarded optimism. He offered a subtle, yet hopeful nod, before diverting his attention towards the transceiver an arm's length away. Even before the whirrs and beeps stopped, his eyes doubled in size. "They've rendezvoused with the Deravan ship," Federson declared.

In one euphoric moment, the sounds of operators clapping and cheering filled the command center. Others just sat in their chairs wearing large, contented smiles.

Hayes took out a cigar from his chest pocket and held it in front of him. He studied the long brown shape longingly before producing a lighter from the same pocket. Bringing the bright red flame up to the pointed end, he drew in five or six small breaths, before taking one long, satisfying puff. A blend of burning tobacco and congratulations tasted good going past his tongue. He had been saving his Cuban for a special occasion and he could think of none better. Yamane's success meant his success. If he could bring that ship in without incident, Hayes' power base would increase ten-fold, possibly gaining a cabinet position in the Geneva World Government in the process. An appointment at this level meant he could now make the changes he thought long overdue, both in Star Force Command itself, and their overall defensive capabilities.

Ten years ago, the Antarens had caught them unaware—and it had cost the lives of millions of people. He vowed he would never let such a thing happen again.

"Lt. Commander Yamane tried making contact," Federson read from the printout, his tone ebullient. "After repeated attempts, the Deravans haven't yet responded. He's keeping all channels open, in case they do." He looked over his shoulder. "There's more."

Hayes waved his hand in a dismissive manner, and then walked the length of the room, a trail of smoke following behind. He could not have been more pleased. The toughest part of the mission had met with success. After traveling uncounted billions of kilometers, Yamane had found that needle in the haystack. Slipping into his soft leather chair, Hayes took in a long, slow drag. A small measure of disappointment, however, crept up on him not long after. He wished they could have made contact. His place in history would have been assured right then. *It could still happen if matters are handled in the proper way.*

Hayes sat up, suddenly worried. He had given Yamane a wide swath of discretionary freedom when dealing with the Deravan ship. Now he regretted it. The lieutenant commander could act in a rash manner, and very well undermine his plans for the future. Hayes had one trick up his sleeve, however. He had the rank and fortitude to keep that from happening. Tilting his head upward, he called out into the room, "I don't want to take any chances. Have Yamane continue monitoring the ship until further notice. He's to take no action without my expressed permission."

"Of course, sir," Federson replied.

Hayes' anxieties eased. He sat back down in his big, overstuffed chair and enjoyed his cigar.

SECTOR FORTY-ONE
0814 PROXIMA MERIDIAN TIME, AUGUST 14, 2217

Another hour had passed, but still nothing had been heard from the Deravans. The decision to abort the mission rested with him, but Yamane asked himself whether silence was a good enough reason for doing so. Hayes didn't seem to think it was. The commodore's response to the message he sent after making contact was short and to the point, "Maintain flight status." No elaboration, no explanation—just sit tight and wait for them to make the next move. Well, he had. And what did he have to show for all this waiting? Nothing but a sore back and a few short hours of sleep. A person had only so much wait in him, and his had just about run out. Staring at the ship hanging out there several thousand meters away, he figured if they weren't willing to take the first step, then he would.

Yamane reached over and opened the radio. He moved the dial in a clockwise direction, the tuner racing towards the desired setting of 1998 megahertz. He eased up on the knob, stopping only when the precise wavelength appeared. As Yamane stared at the number for several moments, he silently mouthed the speech he had worked on during their journey to the Deravan ship. Just to make certain he had all the words straight in his head, Yamane went through them again. Now he felt ready. All he had to do was draw in a deep breath, open up the circuit, and say it out loud. But just as he began to form the words, a barrier seemed to form between him and the control panel. Yamane fell back against his seat. He just couldn't bring himself to disobey a direct order. Disappointed with himself, he reached over and switched off the radio. That ship was only a couple of thousand meters away, but to him, it might as well be a million. Unless the Deravans decided to signal him, there was nothing he could do except wait. Yamane reached over a second time and re-tuned the transmitter. "You still out there, Major?"

Static sparkled on all four speakers.

He tried again. "Yamane to Major Kershaw. Do you read me?"

"I read you loud and clear," he finally replied. "Sorry for the delay. I was just having a bite from one of my I-paks."

For whatever reason, food didn't sound that appealing right now. Maybe later he would eat. "I was just wondering why the Deravans haven't initiated contact with us yet. Any thoughts?"

"Maybe there's no one at home," Kershaw joked. Yamane let his weak attempt at humor pass. "We assume a ship that big needs a crew, but what if it is automated? Their level of technology might be so advanced the Deravans simply don't need a commander or an engineer to keep the ship running. Maybe we're waiting for a signal that will never come."

Kershaw's last words plunged deep into Yamane, but something deep inside told him otherwise. Even though they hadn't initiated contact yet, he was sure someone was on board that vessel, watching and waiting. "I think the Deravans know we're here," he replied. "They're probably giving us a good look first before they initiate contact."

"What do you think we should do?"

Yamane thought long and hard before answering. "We'll keep the frequency open...and wait." What other choice did he have?

"I was afraid you'd say something like that."

With the development of technologies far beyond the scope of so primitive a species, the Deravans had indeed been monitoring the arrival of Lt. Commander Frank Yamane's squadron. For now, they would maintain strict radio silence. When circumstances warranted doing otherwise, protocols demanded they respond. In the meantime, this stage of the journey gave them the opportunity to complete two important tasks: First, determine if the technologies humanity possessed posed any real threat to their plans, and second, ascertain whether they could be utilized for their own benefit after they had eradicated this latest race.

Yamane and his squadron had more or less assumed a position above the Deravan ship, continuing to shadow the taciturn vessel heading for Titan. Even though nothing had changed since rendezvousing with it three hours before, gazing upon the engineering marvel before them still remained intoxicating. Anyway, that was how Yamane felt about their silent companion. One might feel this way based solely on the graceful manner in which the craft flew, but his reaction went much deeper. He made some mental calculations based on the size and weight of the vessel, trying to determine just how much energy it would take just to move a ship that size, let alone make a journey this long. The numbers he came up with were staggering. Whoever these people were, Yamane thought, they had a thing or two to teach the human race. Awesome was not a word he used much, but in this particular case, the designation was more than appropriate.

His stomach growled. Yamane didn't realize just how hungry he had become. He shouldn't have been surprised since his last meal had been more than sixteen hours ago.

Grabbing hold of the satchel resting between his legs, he took out one of the I-paks. SPAGHETTI AND MEATBALLS. A good choice. He felt like having Italian. Yamane brought the packet up and placed his index finger and thumb on two yellow dots at its base. With an increasing amount of pressure on the area, the two plastic vials nestled inside finally broke. Once the separated chemicals mixed with each other, they begin to react. As temperatures inside the I-pak rose, it began expanding outward, slowly evolving into a brown, rectangular-shaped balloon.

Yamane mixed the contents inside with a few shakes up and down. He then tore off the perforated strip on the top and pulled both sides apart. A puff of steam shot out. His mouth watered when a blended aroma of sauce, spices and seasoned meat filled the cockpit. Plucking the fork off the packet's side, Yamane dug into his awaiting dinner. "Not bad," he thought. "Throw in a little parmesan cheese, and this would be perfect."

The Deravans finished their analysis. As expected, they deemed the technological standing of this latest species inferior to theirs. Humanity posed no threat to their plans. The results reinforced the belief in their own invincibility; even more so now since this ship was a prototype for a new weapons platform, with a far greater explosive yield than anything unleashed before. If the outcome worked out as well as anticipated, they would construct other equally powerful ships and destroy more planets with greater rapidity, thus speeding up projected timelines.

Their analysis had also determined that all resources available within the ten-planet system, natural or otherwise, had no significant uses. This mattered little since humanity's fate had already been decided. Finding no reason to change the parameters of the mission, they would move forward as planned. The time had come to make contact.

Without any warning, a high-pitched whine came over Yamane's receiver. He jumped, gasping loudly. Before he knew what had happened, a whiff of burnt plastic wafted into his nostrils. His pulse rate doubled in an instant. That smell told him his circuits were starting to overheat—and overheat meant...Fire! In an instant, his mind grasped the gravity of the situation.

His eyes darted about, but the reason for the malfunction eluded him. *Blast.* Without a cause or solution in sight, he had but one recourse. With a sense of urgency seldom experienced in his life, Yamane began to deactivate every system within reach. Only after he had neutralized most of them did those pungent smells filling the cockpit slowly dissipate. A sigh of relief passed through his parted lips. Yamane figured he had had only seconds to spare.

His feelings of satisfaction subsided quickly, however. Now that he had shut down all the systems aboard his ship, there would only be enough breathable oxygen for about thirty minutes, forty-five if he didn't move around too much. Yamane could bring the cockpit back to life again, but he would be right back where he started. *Not much of a choice*, he thought. *Death by asphyxiation or death by smoke inhalation?* Either scenario did not hold much appeal for him.

Yamane brought up his hand and flipped the first switch. He braced himself. The targeting grid lit up, went dark for a second, and then appeared the same as before. No smoke or smell. He activated directional thrusters next. Yamane gave the cockpit a sniff. Again, no smoke or smell. A careful examination of the other circuits on his control panel showed it was safe enough to activate them as well. With a flip of a switch here and a press of a button there, he managed to get his ship back up to full power. Yamane should have felt better about the result, but he had a more pressing problem. Why did his fighter almost ignite into a fireball?

He reconfigured the analytical computer. Program after program ran through a vast, almost limitless number of computations, searching for the source of the power surge. Different pictures, equations, and symbols flashed on his screen, until two simple words—1998 megahertz—appeared and disappeared at regular intervals, pinging each time they did.

"Contact!" he blurted out. "They were trying to make contact." His somber mood lifted. This was why he had come, what he waited for. But for whatever reason the transmission had been so badly distorted the receiver could only produce ear-piercing whines. Then he had another thought. *1998 megahertz.* "Of course." The Deravan transmission was so powerful it spilled over into different operational systems. For once, an easy remedy presented itself. He reached over and held the power intake dial with his left hand, the wavelength modulation knob in his right. Turning them both clockwise, the incoming signal fell into a range the receiver could accept.

"... from the planet Derava," an otherworldly voice said, his words short and compelling. "We have come as an envoy to make contact with your people."

Yamane felt ecstatic, relieved. Then a question formed in the back recesses of his mind. How would he respond? What would he ask? Yamane cleared his head. He considered using his prepared speech from before, but for whatever reason, it felt out of place. After giving it some more thought, he considered a different tactic. Simplicity was a strategy he had used well over the years, usually when he found himself in tight spots. This one felt no different. He cleared his throat first before pressing the transmission button. "Greetings to the Deravan people. My name is Lt. Commander Yamane...we have come from the planet Earth. Do you understand me?"

The speakers hissed with static. When Yamane made a slight adjustment to his radio, the noxious sounds pouring through his speakers subsided. "The Deravans are a race which seeks to make contact with others when their existence has become known," the same voice replied, though the tone, voice inflection, and cadence possessed a strange, almost beguiling quality. The articulated words were...different.

"I have come as an official representative of my government to open up a dialogue between our two peoples while we escort your ship to Titan."

Another long pause followed. "We will contact you again upon our arrival," the voice replied, and then nothing.

Yamane stared at the receiver for almost a minute before he accepted the fact that they had terminated communications. Disappointment was not a strong enough word for how he felt. He had hoped to spend his time on the way back discussing differences between each others' societies, their similarities, the reasons the Deravans came, what they ate; or anything else about their way of life for that matter. But just as before, Yamane found his soaring expectations dashed. He wished he could understand the reason for their evasiveness, but only the Deravans could answer such a question. Judging by their apparently terse nature, it didn't seem like they would do so anytime soon.

Yamane found himself staring at the Deravan ship...again. He couldn't help himself, as if doing so might help answer some nagging questions going around in his head. But as long as the Deravans maintained radio silence, he could do little else except sit there and think. He offered a deep sigh. Letting his helmet fall back against the headrest, he considered the ship's construction. In the hours that passed between first contact and now, his feelings of awe had begun to subside. In their place, he saw something new, something cold and lifeless. He had scanned the hull a dozen times already and his readings confirmed an obvious lack of imaginative detail on the surface, almost giving him the impression the Deravans were trying to cover up who they really were. The overall size of that vessel was predatory, frightening.

Yamane caught himself. Perhaps he was overreacting. Nothing they said or did warranted suspicions regarding ulterior motives. Still, though, he couldn't quite shake the notion that something about them ...

Not able to follow through on his misgivings, he looked away. The targeting grid fell into view. Yamane verified their position. Even though he was certain they hadn't deviated from their flight plan, procedures required he make certain they were still on course from time to time. Besides, it gave him something new to think about.

As he had assumed, they were right where they should be. His attention found its way back to the Deravan vessel. He felt cold. Maybe they were all taking a little too much for granted.

CHAPTER
7

GARGARIN STAR FORCE BASE, TITAN
2109 PROXIMA MERIDIAN TIME, AUGUST 15, 2217

Federson studied Yamane's latest update. Text filled the top third of the page. "I just don't get it," he complained. "An alien race sends one of their ships from some distant part of the galaxy, and when we respond in kind, they suddenly clam up. Maybe you can tell me what I'm missing."

Hayes didn't answer at first. He leaned back in his chair and stared at the acoustical ceiling tiles above. He too had wondered why the Deravans had said next to nothing since making contact. So far, the commodore considered the mission a success, but worries about potential setbacks were not far off. Just to allay his own fears, he had already taken corrective steps. He figured it was always preferable to have a back-up plan, just in case. "If it makes you feel any better, I've had Sterfer and Reeves going over every piece of data we've received up to this point. I've ordered them to report here when they finish. Their analysis should make our decision regarding the Deravan ship a little easier."

Even before the last word had slipped out of Hayes' mouth, the automatic doors slid open. Two pairs of feet entered. They possessed a confident, purposeful gait. Hayes looked up and watched Sterfer and Reeves enter. The neutral expressions both of them carried did not offer even a hint of what their analysis might have revealed.

Both men snapped to attention when they reached Hayes' desk. He did not speak until the automatic doors slid shut again, effectively drowning out every bit of noise from outside. "We are reporting as ordered, sir," Sterfer said.

Hayes studied the men standing before him. *Not neutral expressions,* he thought to himself, *but fatigue.* Neither of them looked like they had slept much the past couple of days. He noted their overall disheveled appearance and large bags under their bloodshot eyes. "Thank you for coming in, gentlemen. Please sit down." He pointed at two chairs. "As you know, the Deravan ship will arrive here in less than fifteen hours. And yet, we know just as little about them now as when Yamane first made contact. I'm hoping you can give me something, anything I've missed. Even if you feel it's inconsequential, I want to hear what you have."

Sterfer took the data pad sitting in his lap and placed it on Hayes' desk. "Thank you, Commodore...Commander," he replied, "but after a careful review, I don't think we will be much help. Captain Reeves and I have gone over the reports with a fine-tooth comb, and there just isn't much there. Internal scans, power output readings, spectral analysis, voice analysis, even the message they sent—every test was inconclusive. You could almost say they didn't want us to know more about them than what they have allowed."

"What about you, Captain?" Hayes asked after he offered him a deceptive smile. "Is that your assessment as well?"

Reeves shifted in his chair. For whatever reason, the confidence and bravado exhibited by him in the council chambers seemed to have slipped away. "I'm afraid so," he replied after a short pause.

The meeting had already taken a bad turn, in Hayes' estimation. "I see." He turned back to Sterfer. "And despite this lack of information, can you still offer any recommendations?"

"I do not think I have the proper qualifications for such an assessment. My job is to provide you with an analysis, not to suggest a course of action."

Hayes furrowed his brow. "But I am asking you," he snapped back in an elevated voice. "What do you think we should do?"

Sterfer fidgeted with the data pad, his eyes cast downward. "Well, sir, if you want my honest opinion, I'd say I'm more than a little concerned about the Deravans keeping their ship so well cloaked. And as for their intentions, well, their message was cryptic at best. They have given us just enough to make this operation happen, but not much more. I feel as though we're the fish and they're holding the hook." He sat upright again, his back straight. "The one word coming into my mind over and over again is—caution. Now, from the Deravans' point of view, they may be acting in a reasonable way. But without any more information, I just can't say. That's why I believe we should keep them from entering our Solar System until we better understand who they are and why they have come."

Hayes was pleased he had finally gotten an honest answer. "And you, Captain?"

"I'm afraid I must agree with Colonel Sterfer," Reeves replied without hesitation.

Hayes sat back in his chair. "What about you, Commander?"

Federson leaned forward and placed his forehead into his hands. Both eyes were cast down, though they didn't seem to be looking at anything in particular. "I agree with them, Commodore." He sat up again. "This mission has gone by the book on the one hand, but on the other, nothing has worked out as we had hoped. The Deravans are coming, but why are they coming? They said they want to make contact with us, but since their initial message, there has been little evidence to support this. You've gone through the reports. Why send such a large ship? We can't scan the inside. Are they hiding something?"

Hayes reached his breaking point. "Maybe yes, maybe no," he exploded. "You're not giving me what I need. How can I make a decision unless I have something more than hypothetical scenarios to work with?"

"I understand your frustration," Federson replied, his voice soft, "but a course of action can only be recommended with solid information. And right now, we have almost none."

Hayes exhaled. His hopes for the future, both personally and professionally, were fading fast. Questions had been raised about why the Deravans were coming, and when there was little information to answer those questions, people filled in the gaps themselves. He needed time to think. Perhaps a hasty retreat might be in order. "Thank you, gentlemen," Hayes said without any warning. "You'd better get back to your stations, in case anything new comes through."

Both Sterfer and Reeves turned towards each other first, as if to verify they had heard him correctly before standing up. Offering a salute in unison, they left the room without another word.

Federson also rose from his chair, a troubled expression on his face. "We can't wait much longer, Commodore," he said, almost pleading with him. "Unless Yamane is told otherwise, he'll bring that ship all the way in. And if the Deravans are hiding something, then we might not find out until it's too late."

"I understand your concerns. Taking a cautious approach would be the prudent thing to do, but we are on the forefront of a significant moment in history. I don't want to be the one who let such an opportunity slip away because of fear. I've read the reports." He picked up one of them from his desk and held it up for show. "Several times, in fact...and I come up with many of the same concerns you have. But with this said, the Deravan ship has not acted in a hostile fashion, or done anything of a provocative nature. Therefore...I have decided the Deravans will be allowed to arrive at Titan, just as they requested."

Hayes could tell from Federson's expression he did not agree with him. He placed his hand on Federson's shoulder and smiled. The commander's muscles stiffened.

"But what about—"

"I think I'll be proven right when this is over. Then we'll all have a good laugh and wonder what all the fuss was about." Federson didn't appear so convinced. "Send a message to Yamane. Tell him...tell him to proceed as planned."

"And the people here? What about Kalmedia?"

Hayes brought his hands behind his back and stood upright. "Arrangements have already been made. I intend to implement General Order 24."

His head dropped. "General Order 24? I don't know about this, Commodore."

"I've made up my mind on this one, but I also have an idea which might make you feel better...and I want you to take care of it personally."

SECTOR THIRTY-FIVE
0800 PROXIMA MERIDIAN TIME, AUGUST 16, 2217

Kershaw's chronometer counted down to zero. Three short bleeps followed soon after.

"The time has come to make contact with Kalmedia control," he said to Yamane over the radio. "Commodore Hayes was quite insistent on this point when he signaled yesterday."

"What's the matter, Major?" Yamane replied into his headset, surprised by his friend's impatience. "Can't wait to arrive at Titan and deliver this great big package?"

"To be honest, yes, but what I really want is to get this mission over with so I can pry myself out of this tin can. I don't know if my legs will ever straighten out again."

Yamane chuckled in response before reaching over to re-tune his radio. "This is Blackhawk One. Come in, Kalmedia Control." No reply. "I repeat, this is Blackhawk One. Do you read me?" Again, silence. He checked the bandwidth, but it was set at the right frequency.

"What do you think the problem might be?" Kershaw asked. "Wait a minute. I'm picking up something strange coming from that ship over there."

Yamane turned to the Deravan vessel. "Strange? What do you mean?"

"Power outputs have about doubled since your last scan. I have no way of knowing for sure, but the readings indicate a duplicate power system has been activated."

Yamane eyed the ship with suspicion. "A duplicate power system? Can you lock onto the source?"

"No," Kershaw replied after checking his boards. "Outputs are generalized in nature."

The whole thing didn't sit well with Yamane. He activated the spectral analysis program. The readings appeared on his screen after the computer had completed its computations. "Confirmed, power outputs have almost doubled. If only we knew if this were normal or not."

"If you boost the signal strength by ten percent," Kershaw suggested, "that should pierce through the interference."

"I'm resetting my transmitter now."Yamane opened the frequency and tried again. "This is Blackhawk One. Do you read me, Kalmedia Control?"

"We read you loud and clear, Blackhawk One," sang an excited voice. "Your ETA is fifty-five minutes. We expected your transmission five minutes ago. Are you having any problems?"

"Negative, Kalmedia Control, but there has been a development. The Deravan ship has registered an almost one hundred percent increase in power output. I have tried to determine the reason why, but my analysis has been inconclusive. Do you advise any change of plan?"

"Stand by, Blackhawk One." The receiver fell silent for several long minutes before the c-tech returned. "Follow your present course until you receive further instructions."

"Roger, Kalmedia Control. Blackhawk One, out."

GAGARIN STAR FORCE BASE, TITAN
0846 PROXIMA MERIDIAN TIME, AUGUST 14, 2217

A steady stream of data continued to pour into every monitor, console and recording device in the pit. As a result, the increased level of frenetic activity manifested by the staff were in sharp contrast to the relative calm of a few short hours ago. The primary reason for so dramatic a change centered on a simple reason—the arrival of the Deravan ship.

"Look at her," Hayes said from his station while staring at the unbelievable sight. "The readouts indicated the ship was big, but ..." His fears and anxieties from before had returned.

Federson said nothing at first. He just sat there, staring at the screen, lines of worry etched on his face. "Commodore, I think it might be wise if we scrambled some fighters. If anything should happen, I don't think Lt. Commander Yamane or his men can do much to stop it."

Hayes didn't react; the sounds of "if anything should happen" were spinning around in his head like a paralyzing toxin. He looked down at the screen and stared at it hard. The ship went kilometers in every direction. As though a veil had been lifted from his eyes, the vessel coming towards them suddenly brought a deep-seated fear to his soul. "I've been a fool," he said aloud. "How could I put my own avarice ahead of the people I have sworn to protect?"

"Sir?" Federson asked.

"I don't think one squadron will be enough," he continued. "I want every fighter scrambled, and all defensive batteries manned and ready."

Federson flashed a reassuring smile. "Right away," he replied, and then hurried over to the communication console. In the middle of the control panel, situated just below the monitor, a large red button marked "emergency" stood apart from the others. Over the button sat a clear plastic box, a numbered keypad on top of it. He entered a 5-digit sequence. The box popped up, exposing the emergency button. Federson depressed the raised disk with his thumb.

A cacophony of bells, sirens, and alarms rang out all over the base. "General quarters, general quarters," a mechanized voice repeated again and again. "All personnel report to general quarters."

The instant the klaxons and flashing yellow lights were triggered, pilots from all three fighter groups bolted out of the barracks and into the adjacent flight room. Finding their flight suits hanging in open lockers, they pulled them over their shirts and pants in a matter of seconds, and then ran out the back, pouring into the hangar bay. Most crew chiefs were already waiting, ladders at the ready. The pilots scrambled up the steps and into their respective cockpits.

"All stations report manned and ready," Federson stated after the last defensive battery gave both proper counter-signs. "The 214th and 87th are in the hangars, awaiting final orders. The 99th fighter squadron is going up now. They will assume a protective flight pattern over Kalmedia."

"Kill the alarm," Hayes ordered. "Acknowledge all stations report ready." *Time to put our plan to work.* He looked up at the astro-clock. "Contact Lt. Commander Yamane."

SECTOR THIRTY-THREE
0853 PROXIMA MERIDIAN TIME, AUGUST 14, 2217

"This is Blackhawk One," Yamane replied. "Go ahead, Kalmedia control."

"Abort code: zebra—baker—foxtrot. Your orders are to proceed to sector thirty-two, where your squadron will rendezvous with the *Lexington*. There you will receive further instructions."

Yamane stared at his radio. He must have heard the orders wrong. "This is Blackhawk One," he replied. "Say again. I do not think I heard you correctly."

"I repeat. You and your squadron are to proceed to sector thirty-two, and rendezvous with the *Lexington* on the far side of Saturn."

Yamane's ears burned. He had heard the message right the first time, and hearing it repeated made him angry. For the past four days, he and his men had experienced all kinds of deprivations, taken extended risks, and faced innumerable hazards—just so he could hand the responsibility for the mission over to someone else at the last minute? He was tempted to refuse his new assignment and bring in the Deravan ship anyway, but as unjust as this was, orders were orders. "Roger, Kalmedia Control," he replied, cold and resigned. "Setting course for sector thirty-two."

The Deravan ship reduced speed just after Yamane's squadron fired their thrusters and flew out of range. Establishing a geo-synchronous orbit high above Titan, the immense alien vessel took up a position over the capital city. Kalmedia came to a standstill. People in their hover cars stopped on the roads, and foot traffic stood in place and pondered the sight of so large a craft above them. Even at an altitude of sixty kilometers, the luminescent vessel stood out, its size somewhere between a large star and any one of a dozen larger moons in orbit around Saturn.

Yamane angled his fighter down. The *Lexington* was dead ahead. The dark gray warship appeared ready for a fight: her gun ports were open, the commander had already deployed her porthole shields, and radio transmissions ceased when his squadron flew within fifty-kilometers of the stellar cruiser.

The tracking beacon updated their relative locations at five-second intervals. Yamane called out his position from the ship. At two thousand meters, he lowered the landing gear.

"We've got you in our sights, Blackhawk One," the operator said on the radio. "Reduce speed to two hundred and fifty meters per second."

"Distance...five thousand meters," he replied. "Reducing speed to two hundred and fifty."

"Up two degrees forward motion. Speed...two hundred. Ten seconds to contact."

Yamane grasped the maneuvering stick just a little tighter. "I'm in the slot. Three seconds."

The runway shot underneath Yamane's fighter. As soon as his wheels touched down on the deck he reversed engines, while at the same time hitting his brakes hard. His fighter veered a bit to the left, until he managed to bring it to a complete stop a mere ten meters from the end of the landing bay. Letting out a huge sigh of relief, Yamane nudged his thruster control forward. The fighter started to roll again, right into the nearest stall indicated by a flagman five meters away. Once inside both yellow lines, he indicated an engine shutdown with both lighted batons.

When the canopy lifted up, a blast of cool air rushed in. Yamane removed his helmet and drew in a deep breath. A noxious mixture of engine exhaust and high-octane fumes filled his lungs. Never had anything smelled better in his life. He closed both eyes, drinking in the heavenly combination without reservation. His moment of solitude didn't last long, however. A crewman snapped Yamane back into the present when he slammed a ladder against the metal frame.

Startled, Yamane leaned over and threw his helmet down, and then released both restraints. The metal clasps banged loudly when they tumbled onto two support struts on either side. He tried to push himself up, but after four days in the same position, both legs felt shaky, weak. A second try produced better results. Yamane swung his left leg around first, and then his right. He took great care with each measured step, until both boots made contact with the deck.

A medic appeared out of nowhere. "Health check," he barked, in a way suggesting there would be no way of getting out of it.

Yamane had no time for this. He needed to get to the bridge. "But I—"

"No choice. Regulations."

"All right," he surrendered, "anything to get this done in a hurry."

Under the watchful eye of his terse friend, Yamane went up and down the stall a couple of times. His coordination improved. So did his awareness of the landing bay. Even though it was the same monochromatic gray as all the other ships in the fleet, the walls and ceiling appeared more an amalgam of green and brown, caused by the dozens of bright orange lights along the length and width of the bay.

The medic held out his hand and stopped Yamane in mid-stride. He pulled out a small penlight from his pocket and focused the narrow beam into the lieutenant commander's eyes. Satisfied as to the results, he then placed a small oval-shaped device just below the right ear, making an obligatory check of his pulse and blood pressure. "Heart rate, sixty-two beats per minutes. Blood pressure, one hundred and ten over seventy." The numbers seemed to please the medic. "You're good to go," he declared, "though you might want to find a shower real soon."

Yamane gave him a thumbs-up signal. "Thanks, doc," he said before rushing off to the nearest lift.

Slotted, angled bars, set about a half a meter apart, came together like the bellows of an accordion when he tripped an unseen sensor beam. A quick examination of the interior revealed the control panel was on his right. There were two columns of disks, the top one of which would bring him to the bridge. When Yamane pressed the one marked "B", the gate slammed shut, sending him up in a hurry. As each deck moved past, clattering sounds resonated within the small, rectangular enclosure, stopping only when the ceiling banged into the top of the shaft.

He slid the gate open and hustled down the corridor. Long and narrow by design, the corridor curved to the right. The bridge access way appeared about halfway down. He paused for a second to catch his breath. After tugging on his flight suit, straightening it somewhat, he ran his fingers through his matted hair. "It will have to do."

Yamane stepped onto the bridge, unnoticed. He kept his place in the shadows for a moment, taking in the view before him. Weapons, engineering, power systems, computer control, and analytical computers ringed the outer portion of the bridge in a semi-circular fashion. The remaining stations—navigation, communication and RadAR—were positioned in front of the commander's chair, forming a straight line between him and the main screen. A waist high, semi-circular railing divided both sections. The fence-like structure followed the contours of the bridge; just the way he remembered it.

In the glow of the dim crimson light, Yamane recognized many of the crew, though most of them were far too busy for any kind of informal reunion.

"Welcome aboard," a cheerful voice said from the command chair.

Yamane's eyes narrowed. The officer looked familiar, but he couldn't quite place him. "Thank you, Major ..." he replied while making his way over to the command chair, "... Webster." They shook hands. The two appeared to be about the same age, except that the major was a little shorter than Yamane, and much heavier. He estimated about twenty kilograms, judging by the size of the major's paunch. Yamane's memory finally kicked in. Webster had been his replacement after transferring to the Gargarin Star Force base six months ago. He remembered him as being rather friendly, though a trifle insecure.

Webster continued to smile. Not the most ideal of working relationships, Yamane thought, but as long as his stay on the stellar cruiser was a short one, then Webster and the problem would soon be gone.

"You are ordered to take command of the *Lexington* and rendezvous at Kalmedia at once," he said after stepping aside.

Yamane's eyes widened. "What is this ship doing here? I though you were on a deep space patrol, out in sector fourteen."

"We were, but Commander Federson contacted us twelve hours ago with new orders. He wanted one of our big guns here when the Deravans arrived. So we high-tailed it back here. I can't remember the last time the engines have been pushed at a sustained 1.20. I thought they might shut down a couple of times, but other than a whole lot of shaking and rattling, we're not in bad shape."

This sounded like something Federson would do. He was one of the most pragmatic men Yamane ever knew. Seldom did the commander initiate anything without an alternate plan tucked away in his back pocket.

"Well, let's not disappoint the commander," he said to Webster. "Fire up the main thrusters and make your heading zero-seven-one. Speed...0.55 stellar velocity." He then took his place in the command chair. The symbol of authority felt good, powerful. Yamane's hands found themselves on both armrests. He rubbed them a couple of times for good measure.

The main engines roared back to life, marked by a rhythmic wave sensation pulsing through the ship. The *Lexington* shuddered at first, before settling down again. Saturn's northern pole slowly dropped down out of sight, replaced by a singular, though much smaller, tawny moon in the distance. And above that moon, their destination waited.

When the Deravans achieved orbit, they scanned not only those fighters flying around them a discreet distance away, but also the surface of Titan. Their instruments confirmed what they had already known—this latest species posed no threat to them or the operation. Barring any unforeseen developments, just one thing remained—the implementation of the next and final phase of their plans.

GAGARIN STAR FORCE BASE, TITAN
0902 PROXIMA MERIDIAN TIME, AUGUST 14

While sitting in his chair above the command center, Hayes stared at the cigar in his hand and wondered what would happen next. His confidence waned when five minutes became ten, and then fifteen. He had already sent the pre-recorded message from President Kohler when the Deravan ship assumed orbit above the capital city, but the recording had been met with silence.

Hayes pulled out his lighter and fidgeted with the flip top. Federson, who had been standing behind him the entire time, never took his eyes off the astro-clock.

Suddenly, every speaker, both in the pit and in the Situation Room, crackled with static. An unearthly voice began to speak, "Now that we, the Deravan race, have arrived," the voice said with no discernable emotion, "the disposition of your fate has been decided." The transmission ceased.

A profound measure of unease surrounded the commodore.

Federson spun around, a horrified look on his face. "Is that all there is?" he asked. "Maybe the signal has been blocked by some kind of interference."

"No. Instruments indicate they are no longer transmitting."

"I don't like this. When will the *Lexington* get here?"

S.F.S. LEXINGTON
0903 PROXIMA MERIDIAN TIME, AUGUST 14, 2217

Yamane didn't like it, either. The cryptic message had a sense of foreboding attached to it, as before. "Increase the ship's speed to 0.75 stellar velocity." He went over to the communication console, "Get me Commander Federson."

"Aye, sir," the c-tech replied. He opened the frequency and made contact with the command center.

"This is Commander Federson. Go ahead, *Lexington*."

"Commander—"

Without any warning, a spectacular explosion of immense proportions detonated over the capital city. A white-hot fireball moved outward at an incredible rate of speed, devouring everything in its path. Roughly spherical in shape, the blast wave increased its size a thousand-fold in a matter of seconds, except for a few pockets of super-heated gases accelerating away even faster. As a result, distinctive spindles of plasma energy flared out from the main body in different directions. The light of a thousand suns filled the bridge, blinding anyone looking directly at it.

Before Yamane could react, the shockwave slammed right into the stellar cruiser. The force of the blast rocked the ship over to her side, throwing everyone on the bridge from their stations. Screams of fear and terror filled his ears as various alarms rang out.

The main screen, overloaded by a sudden burst of energy, went dark.

Other consoles throughout the bridge also experienced overloads. Small fires broke out as the systems tried to compensate, but they were overwhelmed in short order as their delicate components either melted or experienced total failure.

The most concentrated portion of the blast wave plowed into the *Lexington*, completely enveloping the hapless vessel. Crewmembers fell onto the deck a second time as the ship listed ten degrees over on her starboard side. Main engines struggled to keep the ship in position, but the prevailing onslaught striking against the hull was too much, carrying the stellar cruiser through the densest parts of Saturn's rings. Small rocks and large boulders alike, trapped in the planet's elliptical plane, smashed into her side. Every one of those sickening sounds registered throughout the bridge with crystal clarity, each hit more sinister than the next.

The *Lexington* twisted and contorted throughout her excruciating ordeal, subsiding only when those forces throwing her headlong into destruction encountered even stronger ones working in the opposite direction. In and odd sort of exchange, Saturn's gravitational pull strengthened its hold on the stellar cruiser as she was carried toward the northern pole. Flying over a sea of frozen methane, the gaseous giant continued to check the *Lexington*'s forward motion, bringing her in at an increasingly slow rate, until she assumed a high, shaky orbit above the planet.

Somehow, though there was no reasonable explanation for it, both the ship and her crew had survived.

CHAPTER
8

SATURN
0910 PROXIMA MERIDIAN TIME, AUGUST 16, 2217

With main power off line, the ship's emergency batteries came on, dimly lighting the bridge. Yamane came to his feet and surveyed the damage. Through smoke and debris, small shafts of light darted about the darkened bridge after some of the crew switched on their portable lights. Beams of various strengths and widths bounced off the walls and deck plates. The dancing shadows cast by them gave the moment a somber tone.

Yamane placed his hand on the back of the command chair. A sweeping light illuminated the control panel for a split-second. In that brief instant, he saw the automatic distress beacon flashing off and on. Despite his fervent hopes otherwise, there was just no way to know if anyone was in a position to pick up the signal, assuming there were any survivors out there.

Stepping over a chair lying on its side, Yamane worked his way over to the navigator's station. He sensed panic and fear all around him. The one thing the crew needed now more than anything else was assurance that everything would be all right. And as commander of the ship, the responsibility for creating this belief rested with him. "Okay people...I want you back at your posts," he bellowed. "Our first priority is getting the bridge up and running again. I need an assessment of how much damage we've suffered. I expect a status report from every station in five minutes, no exceptions." Yamane spun around. "Major. Go down to engineering. Try and find out what shape the engines are in, and when main power will be restored."

Webster tipped his head and then rushed off the bridge.

Yamane turned towards the nav-tech's station. It appeared just as dead as the others nearest his. "What do you think?" he asked him. "Can we get a signal out?"

The navigator shook his head. "No," the lieutenant replied. "Every system was knocked out in the blast—intercom, RadAR, weapons, thrusters— they're all down. I don't know how long before we'll get them operational again."

Yamane looked up and sighed in frustration. They were blind, deaf, and lame. He corrected himself. Their situation was much worse than that. The *Lexington* wasn't a wounded ship—it was a dead ship.

Repairs on the bridge went slowly, far slower than Yamane expected. While poor visibility and stale, dust-filled air complicated matters some, the real culprit lay in what the explosion had wrought. A lucky few stations had suffered only superficial damage, requiring a handful of bypass circuits to get them up and running again. Other consoles and computer boards, however, were in far worse shape. Whole components needed replacing, databases were damaged beyond repair, and a large number of semitronic boards had been fried. No one had to tell the crew how important it was to get those systems on line again. If they didn't make significant progress in the next day or two, everyone on board the *Lexington* could very well be overcome by lethal doses of carbon dioxide, building up after each breath.

Yamane thought he might be getting ahead of himself, but still noted his concerns down on an ever-growing list of repairs. He folded up the sheet and placed it into his shirt pocket. Resigned to their fate, at least for now, he picked up a Turner Wrench lying by his feet and went back to the command chair. Yamane tried the screen again. It remained just as black as before. Fatigue settled over him. He rubbed his tired eyes before going back to the access panel and checking the sequencing circuits for a fifth time. Working in a cramped space for four hours straight without a break had also taken its toll on his tired, aching body.

But as bad as it had been for him, the c-tech didn't seem to be faring much better. His dour expression said more than words ever could. "How close are you to getting communications up again?"

He wiped the sweat from his dirty face. "Not for a while, Commander," he said in a low voice, "but I think I have the intercom operational enough to reach most parts of the ship."

Yamane went over to his station. "Can you raise the engine room?"

"Just a second," he replied after making several adjustments. "Tell me if this works." The c-tech input a coded sequence into his console with a gentle touch, as though the keypad was made of extremely fragile material. The speaker crackled in response. Yamane shook his head. "I'll try another circuit." He cleared the board and entered a different series of commands. "See if it works now."

"This is Lt. Commander Yamane. Can you read me, engine room?"

More static came from both sets of speakers, and then, "Olsen here," a reply came after a good number of seconds went by.

"We need to get the *Lexington* moving," he said with a hint of desperation in his voice. "Any update on estimates made two hours ago?"

"Just a minute, Commander," he replied, annoyance punctuating each word. "Remember, we're still picking up the pieces down here. Primary thermal pulsar generators are down. I don't know if they can be repaired.

The backups are in fair shape, so we can at least maneuver. I think I should have them up in the next couple of hours. Two of the three reactor cores are holding stable, as long as we don't rattle them too much, the coolant system seems to be intact, and directional thrusters are up to eighty percent power."

Yamane looked at the astro-clock. "How long before we can get main power up here?"

Olsen paused. "Maybe in an hour or so," he replied, "if I can create a bypass circuit."

With the threat of asphyxiation looming over their heads, especially with the oxygen scrubbers still inactive, they couldn't wait that long. Yamane needed to get the ship going—now. Then an idea came to him. "Find Major Kershaw. He knows those engines like the back of his hand. He could help you speed up repairs."

Olsen paused a second time. "I'm not sure what you mean. He's been down here with us from the beginning."

Yamane shook his head. "Figures," he replied. "Bridge, out."

"How much longer do I have to wait until the main viewer is working?" Yamane shouted in anger, his patience wearing thin. The technician had promised him an hour ago the screen would be up by now, but he hadn't gotten so much as a crackle since then. He might have been more forgiving if the other stations were in the same state as theirs, but when Olsen finally restored main power to the bridge, repairs had gone much quicker. Except for a couple of glaring exceptions, his was the last essential system not operational.

"I'm re-routing power past the last burned-out circuit," he apologized, "if you can just wait another minute or two."

Yamane backed off. He didn't realize until then just how hard he had been pushing him.

The r-tech placed the tray filled with tools on top of his console and wiped dirt and grease off his hands with a rag. "That should do it," he declared. The tech sat down at his station and flipped a couple of switches. The main screen glowed at first, and then died down. He tried a different code. A mixture of reds, yellows and greens appeared, before fading into black a second time. A look of determination crossed his face. He turned a dial with his left hand, flipped a couple of switches with his right. A blurred view of Saturn came into view. When he pressed a couple of other buttons, the images sharpened after each adjustment, until the screen presented the outside world with perfect clarity.

Yamane's eyes became wide as he rose out of the command chair. He could see nothing except the planet's upper atmosphere. "Our orbit must be decaying." He went over to the RadAR station. "What is our present altitude?"

The r-tech brought up his telemetry display. Nonsensical numbers and symbols cluttered the screen. "Just a minute, Commander." He keyed in a series of commands into his console. Bit by bit, the display began to clear. "We are forty-seven kilometers above the planet." He leaned forward. "Our present rate of decay is...one kilometer-per-minute, and increasing."

Yamane shot a look at the astro-clock. "How much longer before the hull comes into contact with the outer atmosphere?"

His face began to pale. "At this rate, no more than eleven minutes."

They didn't have any time to lose. He went over to his chair and opened the intercom.

"Go ahead, bridge," Olsen replied.

"The *Lexington*'s orbit is decaying. We only have eleven minutes before we burn up. What is the status of our engines?"

"The pulsar generators are only up to twenty-one percent power, but I need a little more time—run a few tests. If we light those engines and they're not balanced, the strain could tear them apart."

"Will it be enough to break out of orbit?" he asked expectantly.

"Yes, but just barely. Although—"

Yamane shot a look at the nav-tech. "Bring the ship about," he ordered, cutting Olsen off. He then assumed his place in the command chair. "Full power."

"Commander," Olsen objected. "We haven't finished crossing the secondary systems over to the primaries. Those two panels are wired together like a Christmas tree. We could lose the whole engine stack."

"There's no time," Yamane snapped back. "You have your orders."

The nav-tech hesitated at first, but an insistent glare from his commanding officer let him know there could only be one response. He inputted the command sequence.

A mournful moan sounded throughout the ship, followed by a host of subtle vibrations. As each second passed, the mild rumbling increased in intensity. Yamane knew that sound. The *Lexington*'s thrusters had fired up, as he hoped. He checked their position on the nav-tech's boards. Despite all three engines putting out maximum thrust, they hadn't budged a single centimeter against the gravitational pull of Saturn. The stellar cruiser was losing.

Yamane swiveled his chair around. He wasn't going to give up this easily. "Can you give me more power?" he demanded from the helm. "Maybe if we use the directional thrusters?"

"I'll try, sir," the nav-tech replied.

The *Lexington* shook more noticeably after he added the thrusters to the mix. Bending metal sounds reverberated through the walls as bulkheads began to succumb to increasing pressure.

"Engines are buckling, Commander," the e-tech called out. "Reactor temperatures are also rising to dangerously high levels. They could go if we don't stop now."

"Can you give me any more?" Yamane yelled over the sounds of all three engines pulsing in his ears.

"The reactors are almost at the red lines now."

He needed more power. There was only one answer. "Disengage safety protocols. Push them

'til they blow, but we have to break out of orbit."

Every pair of eyes turned in his direction. Yamane didn't relent.

"Protocols have been disengaged," the nav-tech called out. "Power levels are now five percent above safety levels."

"Maintain thrust." Yamane placed his hands on the armrests of the command chair and held on tight. "Come on, baby," he said under his breath. "Don't let me down."

Slowly, almost imperceptibly, he caught sight of the stars starting to drift over.

"We're moving," the nav-tech declared, his eyes wide. "Ten meters per second...fifteen...twenty."

The *Lexington*'s thrusters kept pushing against the insidious gravity well fighting to keep her in place, but the higher they rose, the faster they went.

"Our speed is now at 0.11 stellar velocity," the navigator said to Yamane.

"Will it be enough to escape Saturn's pull?"

"I believe so, sir, but not by much."

"Come on. Come on," Yamane begged. "Keep going...just a little bit more."

As though the *Lexington* was somehow cognizant of his plea, a last burst pushed her out of orbit, finally severing Saturn's grip on them.

"We've done it, sir," The nav-tech congratulated. "I don't know how, but we've done it."

Yamane already knew they had succeeded. The vibrations decreasing at a steady rate told him everything he needed to know. "Hard about, one hundred and eighty degrees," he exhaled. "Make your destination Kalmedia." He patted the right armrest with his hand and smiled, "Good girl."

The slow-moving ship circled around in a parabolic arc and headed back for Titan. But when she had completed her course correction, a field of debris came upon them where none had existed before. Irregularly shaped objects tumbled past, strange objects. Some resembled miniature asteroids, while others took on twisted and distorted configurations—grotesque and unrecognizable. What they might have been was anyone's guess, but the closer they came to Saturn's moon, the truth of their origin became much more apparent: a corner of a roof, an intact window frame, half of a RadAR dish, even the wing of a Min fighter floated by.

Yamane watched in chilled silence. "How could this have happened?" he thought, though he already knew the answer. On the right side of the moon, the normally smooth curvature appeared jagged, irregular, as though a giant hand had scooped up part of the surface and carried it away.

More debris floated past. Watching the parade of death go by made Yamane feel sick to his stomach, as though someone had kicked him in the gut.

The *Lexington* approached Titan from its dark side. When the stellar cruiser crested over the moon's edge, sunlight illuminating the other side revealed an unbelievable sight. A subdued red glow replaced the normally brown sky. The further they traveled, the worse the situation became. Up ahead, the Lewis and Clark mountain range came into view, or what was left of it. Instead of seeing the ten thousand meter high peaks reaching up to the heavens, they encountered a range cut cleanly in half. Yamane assumed the hundreds of billions of tons of soil and rock had fallen on the other side, but when the *Lexington* flew over the spot, those mountain peaks were nowhere to be seen. They had simply vanished.

When the battered vessel flew over several more scarred mountain ranges, the reason for their disappearances became all too apparent. There in the valley, where Kalmedia should have been, a crater two hundred kilometers in diameter was all that remained. The once vibrant city, filled with millions of people, was gone.

Yamane felt numb, sick. *Nothing could have survived down there*, he thought, his anger flaring.

"What kind of race could do such a thing?" Kershaw accused from behind. Yamane spun the command chair around, surprised by his sudden appearance. "I had to see what they did for myself," he replied between clenched teeth.

Yamane brought his chair back and faced the r-tech. "Are you getting any readings down there—anything suggesting someone might have survived the blast?"

The lieutenant pressed his headset a bit closer to his ear. "Negative, sir," he replied in a soft voice. "There's a lot of interference below, but I read no power sources at all."

The full impact of what this meant hit Yamane hard. "How about other ships? Some of them must have survived. Maybe a handful were on the far side of Titan when the explosion hit."

The r-tech shook his head. "I've made three sweeps of this sector. My scopes indicate there are no other vessels in the area...above or below."

What the operator said didn't make any sense. There had to be someone out there. Yamane went to the c-tech's station. "Are you picking up anything?"

A reluctant smile appeared on his face, and then faded. "I've sent out a priority one signal several times now, but I haven't gotten a single response."

Every bit of hope drained out of Yamane. His head dropped, both eyes cast downward. He assumed a posture of surrender. "What is our engine status?" he asked Kershaw.

A quizzical look crossed his face. "We're up to twenty-seven percent power. The ship can go almost anywhere you want, but it will take time."

Yamane turned towards the main screen. "Then set a course for Earth."

A dark cloud settled over the major. "What about the Deravans?" he asked in short, angry words. "They're still out there. We can't just let them get away."

Yamane marched right up to him. "There's nothing left to find," he exploded. "Their ship is gone—blown up. They used it to wipe out Kalmedia. Remember those duplicate energy readings we picked up before arriving? Now you know the reason."

Kershaw turned away.

A feeling of regret gnawed on Yamane. He shouldn't have lashed out at his friend like that. "Our first duty demands we get back to Earth as soon as possible so we can report what the Deravans did," he added, his tone soft. "There's nothing else we can do here."

Kershaw spun around. "What do you mean, go back?" he replied sharply. "Look at what they've done." He pointed at the main screen. "There's nothing left."

"I know, but we have a duty—"

"Forget about duty! Everyone down there is dead. We can't just leave as though nothing happened."

"Where do I send the *Lexington*, Major? We don't know where that ship came from. We'll barely make it back to Earth, let alone be able to fly into uncharted space."

Kershaw was about to object again, when he suddenly caught himself. He was wrong, and he knew it. His burning rage had so overwhelmed his senses, that he couldn't accept any other course of action except revenge. "You're right," he admitted, an awkward smile on his face. "My training tells me we can still do something about this, take some kind of action."

"Yes, we can." Yamane went over to the nav-tech's station. "Set a course for Earth."

"Aye, sir, setting a course for Earth. At our top speed, we should arrive in sixteen hours."

"Sixteen hours," he sighed. "Sixteen hours."

When the *Lexington* flew past Earth's only natural moon, Yamane found all six stellar cruisers already in orbit, docked in shipyards above the planet he called home. They were big ships, about the size of an old-fashioned aircraft carrier. Bathed in the Sun's powerful light, the stellar cruisers shone brightly against a canvas of black satin. Approaching them at a slow but steady rate, those rays of luminescence reflecting off dozens of windows and portholes created a kind of sparkling effect. The dazzling light show made them appear like the Star Force crown jewels.

Yamane took his place in the command chair. "We're coming up on our designated berth," he said to the nav-tech. At five thousand meters, reduce speed by one-half. Let's not collide into the moorings because we came in too fast."

"Yes, Commander, reducing speed to one hundred meters-per-second." Directional thrusters fired. The *Lexington's* velocity started to drop. "Fifteen hundred meters until docking," the nav-tech called out. "Eleven hundred." He punched in several more commands into his console. "We are slowing to fifty meters-per-second. Eighteen seconds until contact."

Yamane watched both receiver clamps extend.

"Ten seconds...coming in at twenty meters-per-second." Two more retro-bursts fired. "Retractors out." A series of moorings grabbed hold of latching rings placed along the hull and pulled back, until she rested against the docking port. The *Lexington* shook back and forth a few times before coming to a full and complete stop.

"Zero velocity," the nav-tech declared. "We're locked in."

The bridge breathed a collective sigh of relief. After experiencing the most horrendous ordeal of their lives, they were all glad to be home again; none more so than Commander Yamane. He couldn't have felt a higher level of admiration for his crew than he did at that moment. What he asked of them had been more than any ship's crew should have ever given.

STAR FORCE COMMAND, EARTH
0531 PROXIMA MERIDIAN TIME, AUGUST 17, 2217

When Yamane arrived in the Situation Room, he saw all six commanders already assembled there, waiting for him. At the head of the table, Commodore Harris waited with them. The two had served together five years before when Yamane had been part of his command staff. The commodore was a professional man, through and through. No matter where he was or what he might be doing, Harris always looked his best. He was also a harsh man, expecting officers under his command to deliver their best in every circumstance. If his expectations weren't met, then he let you know it.

Yamane took his place at the far end of a large wooden table and sat in the last empty chair.

A series of carvings dotted the surface along the perimeter. They were tribal in nature, maybe from Indonesia, and the wood—mahogany. The table could not have contrasted with the room more. Up above, he saw smooth white walls, a simple, rectangular shape, and vaulted ceilings. In every way, standard as every other Situation Room at every other Star Force base.

The place itself felt still, almost peaceful, until Yamane felt the piercing stares of all seven pairs of eyes scrutinizing his every move. He imagined what might be on their minds. In many cases, their expressions were more than obvious—curiosity, anger, uncertainty—but others remained a mystery to him. They probably knew something terrible had happened, but not much more. Yamane felt like a keeper of a terrible secret. It saddened him. He wondered what his reaction would have been if their roles were reversed. Either way, the whole thing stunk.

Harris cleared his throat first before speaking. "I wish this could have taken place under better circumstances," he said, "but as of this moment, I am promoting you to the rank of Commander. The *Lexington* is now officially your ship. Congratulations." A forced smile followed.

"Thank you, Commodore," Yamane replied, his voice distant. He should have been happy about his promotion, but the reward for his years of service came at such a terrible price. It paled in comparison with the responsibility of being accountable for hundreds of lives. Crews placed unquestionable trust in their commanding officers — and they expected him to make the correct decision every time. Anything less could mean the difference between life and death. *Life and death.* His throat tightened. Was he the right kind of man for the job? He thought so once, a long time ago. He should have been there for Liana, but ...

"Do you have any recommendations for your second-in-command?" Harris asked. The question brought Yamane back.

"Major Kershaw," he replied after some thought. "I think he's more than qualified for the job."

Harris placed his hand on his chin. "That's two jumps in rank," he replied, "but I guess under the circumstances, I'll let the choice stand...for now."

Harris picked up a data pad in front of him and studied the screen for a moment. He set it back down and focused on the other commanders sitting around the table. "Thank you all for getting here on such short notice. I apologize for all this secrecy, but I'm afraid we find ourselves in a very bad situation." Whatever he was going to say seemed to get stuck in his throat. He sat back in his chair, almost aging right before their eyes. "As you may or may not know, the *Lexington* has just returned from Kalmedia. The commander is here to give his report."

A sustained silence followed.

Yamane searched for just the right words. None came to mind, and so he decided to give it to them straight. "I'm sorry to be the one to tell you, but Kalmedia has been completely destroyed."

Incredulity flashed across their faces, disbelief.

"You cannot be serious," Commander Downey accused. "Is this some kind of joke?"

Yamane looked down at his empty hands. "I have never been more serious in my life. It's all gone—everything."

A dark pall settled on the room. Harris sank into his chair and looked away, seemingly unable to acknowledge their questioning gazes.

After a prolonged period of silence, Commander O'Malley leaned forward. "Who could have done something like this?"

Rather than try couching the truth, Yamane decided he should finish what he had started with complete honesty. "A newly discovered alien race known as the Deravans entered our space two weeks ago. They sent one of their ships, under the auspices of making contact with us. Star Force Command decided a conservative response was the best of all options, and sent a squadron of fighters to intercept it. After making contact, they escorted the ship to Titan. But when the Deravan vessel arrived, it blew up, taking a good part of the moon with it."

Commander Schmidt's facial muscles drew tight. He looked like a tiger ready to strike, "Gone?" He looked about the table. "It seems our duty is clear. We blast their ships back from wherever they came."

"First, we need to create a plan of attack," Harris proposed. "Your ships were recalled at the first sign of trouble. I called this meeting so we can decide our next course of action."

"There have been rumors floating around for the last week about some kind of alien race being discovered, but I didn't put much credence in them. I just thought they were—"

"Unfortunately, in this case, they were true."

Commander Renault sat back in his chair. "How could something of this magnitude happen, and we not hear about it?"

"Twelve hours before the Deravan ship arrived, Star Force Command enacted General Order 24—no unauthorized radio and television broadcasts in or around Kalmedia. Only when they deemed the situation secure were they prepared to announce this to the general population."

"But how could they pull off something of that magnitude?"

"In order to maintain a measure of security, Commodore Hayes had grounded all incoming and outgoing flights on Titan. He also put out a cover story, accusing the Antarens of sending some of their dreadnoughts near our borders so they could tap into our broadcasts for the purposes of gathering intelligence against us. His plan worked out better than we had hoped."

"Even more so than you intended," O'Malley interjected.

Harris furled his brow. "What do you mean?"

"When that Deravan vessel blew itself up, there was already a blackout in effect. So far, the loss of Kalmedia hasn't aroused any suspicions."

The Commodore brought up his data pad and stared at it. "Your assessment is correct. This gives us some time to set up our defenses, get every one of our ships in place in case there are more of those Deravan vessels out there."

Commander Hasan fidgeted with something in his hands. A far off look settled onto his subdued expression. "Have you monitored any other alien activity?"

"When Kalmedia was destroyed, long range tracking for that sector went with it. We're hoping we can use other monitoring stations to compensate for the loss, but there are still some fairly large gaps in our RadAR net."

"We don't know where they've come from," Commander Downey interjected. "The one ship they sent no longer exists. Where do we search for others, if there are others?"

"Until we know more, I think our next step should be defensive in nature," Harris concluded.

"What will this accomplish?" Renault objected, his tone defiant. "We have no evidence there are other Deravan ships in our space."

Harris shook his head. "The destruction of Kalmedia could be a prelude to something bigger. With the gaps we have in our RadAR net, they could fly right through without us even knowing. In the meantime, I propose we position our ships between here and Icarus. If even so much as a microbe enters our Solar System, we'll know it the instant it happens. This should give us some protection for the short term." Harris leaned forward. "Are there any questions?" A prolonged silence followed. "Good. Get back to your ships and await further orders." Harris rose from his chair and hurried out the room.

Yamane sat back and peered upward. His eyes caught sight of the astro-clock above the doorway. For him, right there, right then, time had no meaning. He yawned as his eyelids moved together. Yamane just wanted to climb into a warm bed and get about a year's worth of sleep. Off in the distance, he heard the other commanders leave. An unseen door slid shut.

"Are things as bad as Harris says they are?" Commander O'Malley asked in his usual Irish brogue.

Yamane could hear the apprehension in his voice. He opened both eyes. When he saw the look of pain on O'Malley's face, he knew the emotion went much deeper. "I'm afraid so—even more than you can imagine."

When he turned away with a pained expression, Yamane rose to his feet and grabbed his arm from behind. "Are you all right? Something seems to be bothering you."

His gaze turned downward. "My brother, his wife, and three little ones were living at Kalmedia," he replied, his attention fixed on some distant object. "If what you're saying is true, then they're all gone."

Yamane tried to offer a comforting smile. "There's no way you can know with complete certainty. They might have been away when the Deravans arrived."

O'Malley turned his back to him a second time. "I appreciate what you're trying to do, but we both know it isn't true." He found the astro-clock above. "I need to get back to the *Kennedy*." Yamane could do nothing else except watch him leave the room.

He felt badly for O'Malley, but as cold-hearted as it sounded, this wasn't the time for assessing their losses. They all had a job to do, and needed to focus on the task ahead. If a ship's commander allowed feelings of loss to cloud his judgment, others could pay the price. In times such as these, he believed the only acceptable response for any person was a single-minded determination to defeat the enemy. Feelings like that kept a person alive. And as long as O'Malley and the other commanders remembered that, then mankind had a fighting chance.

Yamane took one last look around the Situation Room before stepping into the base's version of rush-hour traffic. People of all shapes and sizes scurried about in different directions. He tried to work his way through the intermingled flows, but there were simply too many people there at one time.

Rather than face the onslaught, Yamane sidestepped his way to the left. A number of large windows traversing the length of the corridor were a welcome respite from the chaos going on all around him. The sun was still high in the sky, illuminating the hallway, warming it. The sensation felt good. Just below, palm trees swayed back and forth in a warm autumn breeze. Though subtle in nature, the gentle, hypnotic motion drew him in. He could almost hear the sounds of waves crashing onto the shore, a mournful call of a seagull flying past.

Yamane turned to leave for the hangar bay when a series of alarms began to ring out. The distinctive din blared in a rhythmic, high-low pattern, piercing him to the bones. Foot traffic stopped, as though time itself had become frozen. "Red alert—this is a red alert," a baritone voice bellowed. "All personnel to your stations. I repeat, all personnel to battle stations."

Calm descended on the corridor. And then, as though an unseen person had fired a starter's pistol, everyone in the long, narrow hallway tore off in different directions. A mixture of boots clomping and voices yelling further disturbed the already frenetic scene.

"All ships' commanders are ordered to report to the Situation Room. I repeat, all ships' commanders please report back to the Situation Room."

Yamane spun around and threw himself into the melee. Despite a converging tide of personnel working against him, he reached the end of the hallway in short order. He plowed through both sets of double-doors, two other commanders right behind him. Harris, already there, met them inside.

"What's going on, Commodore?" Yamane demanded.

A pained look on Harris' face said it all. "I'm afraid we're in bigger trouble than we first thought," he replied. Pressing a button on his chair, a wall panel opened behind him. A screen descended from the ceiling above, triggering the dimmer switch on every light in the room. "You're looking at a live picture from the Antaqua Tracking Station."

Yamane took a step closer. "I only see a star field."

Harris flipped a switch on the same panel. Over those stars, a targeting display appeared. A curved line marked *Icarus* came up from below and angled off towards the right. Superimposed over that line were hundreds of smaller yellow dots, moving across the display at a steady rate.

The Situation Room pressed in on Yamane. He knew exactly who and what they were. "Do we have a fix on those targets yet?"

Harris paused before replying. "Telemetry indicates they are heading right for Earth."

"This must be the Deravans' main fleet," Renault concluded, his voice sounding certain.

Commander Downey stared hard at the screen suspended above. "How could they have gotten this far without being detected?"

"Doesn't matter now. My only concern is keeping them from getting any closer."

"The first ship was probably sent as a decoy," Yamane hypothesized. "They knew destroying Kalmedia would throw everything into disarray. Then they could swoop in and finish us off."

"How many of them are there?" Commander Schmidt asked. In keeping with his efficient nature, his question was short and too the point.

Harris brought up his data pad and pressed a couple of buttons. "Hard to say at this range," he replied after studying the display. "Initial estimates indicate there could be as many as a thousand."

"A thousand," Hasan gasped. "We won't have sufficient firepower for a fleet that size."

Harris brought the lights up again. ""Given what happened to Titan, we have no choice.

Soon the Deravan armada will pass Pluto, and then arrive here six hours later." He placed his data pad back on the conference table. "Report back to your ships, and prepare to leave orbit."

Yamane didn't have to be told twice. He offered a quick goodbye to O'Malley, and then hurried down the nearly empty corridor. Moving at a speed impossible a few minutes before, he plowed through a pair of doors, and into the hangar bay. A foul smell hit him at once. It was thick, heavy with the fumes of high-octane fuel already pumped into his awaiting fighter. The pungent smell was unmistakable. He often tried to describe the noxious mixture, but the closest he ever came was an unholy alliance of rotten eggs and burning kerosene.

Finding his fighter in the furthermost stall, he shot up the ladder and jumped into the cockpit. *No time for my pre-flight ritual this time*, he thought.

"Control tower," he said into his headset after bringing his fighter up to full power, "this is Blackhawk One. Request permission to taxi onto runway three."

"Roger, Blackhawk One. Proceed to runway three."

"Copy, tower." He grasped the thruster control and inched it forward. All three turbines reacted instantly. Thrust flowed right into the bell chamber. His ship vibrated somewhat at first, but once it started rolling towards the hangar opening, the engines settled down into their distinctive rhythmic patterns.

A flagman appeared from behind the hanger door and ran up to Yamane's ship. He moved both batons in a backwards fashion after each hurried step.

Sunlight filled the cockpit as his ship slipped onto the tarmac. Yamane followed a line of fighters that had rocketed out of an adjacent hangar just ahead of his. He made a beeline right for runway three. Fortunately for him, the others rolled past it and opted for the next one in line.

He slowed his ship down and stopped in front of a huge number three painted at the edge of the tarmac.

The tower must have seen him get into position. A radio operator signaled him at almost the same instant. "Blackhawk One, permission to take off has been granted. Good luck and God speed."

Yamane didn't respond. Instead, he slammed his thruster control forward, sending his fighter down the runway at breakneck speed. When all three wheels left the ground, he knew nothing stood between him and his new command—the *Lexington*. *The Lexington*. He should have been happier about his promotion, but the new rank, he felt, came at too high a price. Maybe one day he would celebrate. Today, however, Yamane wondered if he would still be alive at the end of it.

CHAPTER 9

S.F.S. LEXINGTON
0702 PROXIMA MERIDIAN TIME, AUGUST 17, 2217

The wheels of Yamane's fighter hit the deck, hard. Pumping both brake pedals in quick succession while reversing engines, he stopped a mere five meters from the end of the landing bay. Yamane barely gave the distance any notice. He just banked the maneuvering stick over and turned into the nearest stall. As soon as the canopy lifted up, he unlatched his helmet and popped it off. "Get that ladder up here!" he yelled at the top of his lungs.

A member of the ground crew double-timed it over to Yamane's fighter. He swung the ladder in his arms upward and found both magnetic clamps on his first try. Yamane placed his foot onto the top rung and then jumped down. When his feet hit the deck, he jogged over to the intercom by the lift.

"Commander Yamane to the bridge," he said, his new rank sounding strange in his ears.

"Webster here," he replied. "Go ahead."

"Have the other stellar cruisers left orbit yet?"

"No, but they will soon. Most of the shuttles have already landed on their ships."

"Good. I want the *Lexington* ready to depart as soon as I reach the bridge." Yamane switched off the intercom and stepped into the lift. By the time he arrived, the *Arima* and *Montreal* had already departed, evidenced by their two empty berths.

"How long before we can get underway?" he asked the navigator.

He looked back over his shoulder. "Anytime you say, sir."

"Congratulations, Frank," Kershaw beamed. "We just received the good news."

Yamane spun around, surprised by his friend's unexpected appearance. "What are you doing here? Shouldn't you be in the engine room?"

"Yes, but I couldn't acknowledge a moment like this over the intercom."

Yamane waved off the compliment. "Thanks, Stan, but now's not the time. What is our engine status?"

"No change since you left, but I do have some concerns. I'm not certain how the primary generators will hold up if we get into a real fire-fight."

Yamane went right to the command chair. "I guess we don't have much of a choice." He turned to the nav-tech. "Make your heading one-five-five—the same as the *Arima* and *Montreal*."

"We can match their heading," Kershaw said after he came alongside him, "but we can't keep up with them. The main reactors are still only at thirty-seven percent power levels."

Yamane gave him a piercing glare. Before he opened his mouth, Kershaw anticipated what his intentions were, "I know, I know. I'll see if I can coax anything more from the engines." He offered a quick salute and then hurried off the bridge.

Taking his place in the command chair for the first time as the *Lexington*'s commander, Yamane placed his hands on both armrests. This should have been his moment of triumph, the culmination of a lifetime spent in the military. Instead, he accepted his new position without much fanfare, pressed into service so soon after their terrible ordeal. They had no other alternative. Shipshape or not, Harris expected the entire fleet to go against the incoming Deravan armada. Just how they would defeat a thousand enemy warships heading right for Earth—that was another matter all together.

"Helm," he forced himself to say. "Take us out."

Every tick of the clock brought the *Orion* that much closer. Yamane watched Commodore Harris' ship grow bigger and bigger on the main screen, but he could do nothing about it except count down the distance in his mind. The inevitable outcome had been slow and agonizing for him, especially when he knew the flagship would overtake them in time.

The *Orion* first pulled up alongside, and steadily, gradually, moved off without the *Lexington*. A certain measure of disappointment washed over Yamane when the "event" finally happened. Even though no one could accuse him of being at fault, he still felt like he had let everyone down.

He slunk down in the command chair and ran his fingers through his matted hair. How long had it been since his last shower? Yamane checked the astro-clock above the main screen. Unless anything unexpected happened, they should intercept the Deravan fleet in four hours. Too long. He called Major Webster over to him.

"Yes, Commander?"

"I'm going to get out of this flight suit and into a uniform...maybe get in a shower and shave. You have the bridge until I return."

"She'll be in good hands," Webster replied. "If anything happens, I'll signal you right away."

Yamane ambled down the corridor, lost in thought. At the end of the hallway, near where access panels for the main power lines were located, a lift appeared. He stepped on board and pressed the button. A bell rang once, and then the lift started going down. Clickity-clack. Clickity-clack. Yamane just stood in place, looking up at the numbers counting down. When the lift reached deck five, it came to a stop. He pulled the gate back, and made his way to his new quarters. The somewhat darkened hallway curved to the left, interrupted at regular intervals by overhead lights spaced every five meters. Situated below, at about the same distance, were the crew quarters. Moving past them with a casual indifference, Yamane came to a polished, metallic door. A brass nameplate marked "V.I.P" shone in the light.

When he entered a five-digit code into the locking panel, the door slid open with a mechanical swooshing sound. Yamane stepped inside and examined his new surroundings. Fresh linens and a blanket sat on a bed opposite him. A picture of a sailing vessel hung on the wall above his headboard. He thought it looked like a Yankee Clipper. Just on his left, he saw two pens sitting atop his desk, neatly placed along with a clock, a pad of paper, and a small lamp. The light was on, brightening the gray room somewhat. A computer console rested on an extension arm coming from behind the desk.

After taking a tentative step forward, he noticed two bags sitting on the floor, lying lengthwise alongside the bed. He went over to them before taking in the room a second time. A bit cozy, but functional.

Yamane located the intercom attached to his desk, called the engine room up, and requested Lt. Kershaw meet him at his quarters.

Five minutes later there was a knock at the door.

"Come in."

Kershaw appeared at the door. "Sorry for the delay. I thought you'd be staying in the commander's quarters."

"Those are Commander Federson's, "Yamane replied with a faraway look in his eyes. "I wouldn't feel right about using what should still belong to him."

"I guess I understand," said Kershaw, peering about the room. He gestured towards two pressed and cleaned uniforms in the closet behind Yamane. "Did you know about this?"

Yamane gave them a cursory glance. "I haven't had time to think about much of anything, let alone getting hold of supply and ordering new uniforms."

"Seems as though they run a tight ship around here."

"I think Commander Federson would agree with you, if he were here," Yamane remarked.

Kershaw turned around, his eye twinkling. "Remember the times, Frank, when our old squadron leader would get on your back because of the amount of time you were spending with Liana? He used to say that a pilot shouldn't get involved with women because they were a distraction." Kershaw looked up, as though he was trying to remember something. "What was it he said?

Oh, yes, 'The only good officer is a lone officer.' All the guys thought he was a bit different, especially after we set him up with that dancing girl at Club Midnight."

"How could we have known he would go through with the wedding?" Yamane reminisced.

"I think the coup de grace came that night at dinner when all the guys in our squadron saluted Captain Mitchell with those big shiny rings clipped to their noses. I never saw a guy get so mad."

Yamane burst into laughter. "I haven't thought about that in years," he said after getting hold of himself again. "Makes me wonder how we ever got past the rank of second-lieutenant."

"Me too," Kershaw replied while wiping the tears from his eyes.

"I don't know how you do it, but you always help me see the better side of life."

"I know I do," Kershaw agreed. "How else do you think we've stayed friends all these years?"

Yamane's smile left him. "Speaking of that, there is another matter we should talk about." He placed both arms behind his back. "As you know, Commodore Harris promoted me to the rank of commander—"

Kershaw slapped him on the arm. "I figured he would do that...never had a doubt. As Federson's second-in-command, you were his logical replacement."

"Perhaps, but there is one more thing," he added. "It's the reason I wanted to see you in my quarters. I recommended you as my second."

Kershaw's pallor changed. "Me, a lieutenant commander?" he murmured. "I'm not sure how I should respond."

"Harris approved my request on the spot. I don't think I can do the job half as well without you." Yamane took both insignias off his collar and handed them to Kershaw.

He stared at the shiny gold bars. Light from above reflected off the polished sheen, sparkling into his eyes. "Thank you, Frank. I appreciate your faith in me."

Yamane snapped to attention and gave Kershaw a salute.

Rather than responding in kind, he took a step back, acting as if something frightened him. "I think I had better get back to the engine room and check on repairs."

Yamane began to wonder if he had done something wrong. "I'll signal the bridge and let them know about your change of status."

Kershaw shook his head, though it seemed a half-hearted effort, and turned for the door. When it slid open, he suddenly spun around and offered a salute in return. "Thank you, sir!" he barked like a first year cadet, and then disappeared into the hallway.

When the door closed, Yamane collapsed onto his soft, comfortable bunk.

He began to feel tired. Maybe if he lay there for a few minutes, he could catch his breath. But when both uniforms hanging in the closet caught his attention, his fatigue left him. Time to get cleaned up, he thought, and did just that.

Yamane returned to the bridge after a quick shower and shave.

The c-tech called to him the moment he arrived. "Sir, the *Orion* is making contact with us."

"Put the message on," he replied after taking his place in the command chair.

"This is...ommodore Har...I thought I would...and find out how things going on board the...xington," he said.

Yamane glared at the c-tech.

He held up his hands, shrugging in defense.

"Things are going well here," he bluffed. "We're making steady progress."

"Good. I've already...the other...manders," he added. "... every ship...at Deimos by 0940. I am...the coordinates now." Several seconds later, the information appeared on the r-tech's screen. A printout emerged from a small slit located below the display. The lieutenant brought it over to Yamane.

"Do you think the...xington can make it in time?"

Yamane glanced up at the astro-clock and then checked their position on the nav-tech's display. He did some quick math in his head. They would be cutting it close. "You can count on us, Commodore."

"I'll signal you again...the fleet...reaches Deimos. Harris, out."

Yamane's attention remained fixed on the astro-clock above. They had just two and a half hours before engaging the Deravans in battle. He knew the *Lexington* was still a shaky ship. Just how much pounding could she really take? "Two and a half hours," he thought. "Just two and a half hours."

The fleet approached Deimos, in orbit above Mars. Held in place by the red planet's gravitational pull, the smaller, crater-ridden moon became a temporary refuge for the six stellar cruisers coming up from behind. Twenty-six minutes later, the *Lexington* arrived, taking up a position alongside them.

"How long before the Deravan ships are in position?" Yamane asked the r-tech from his place in the command chair.

He accessed the information on his console. "Enemy fleet will arrive in thirty-two minutes."

"Commander, I am receiving a message from the *Corona*," the c-tech called out.

Yamane swiveled his chair over. "Put her on."

"Glad you can join the party, Commander," Harris joked. Though an unintended slight, the jab dug into Yamane. "If my calculations are correct, Mars should have masked our arrival from the Deravan fleet. If we can maintain the element of surprise, this could make the difference." He paused. "I've already given the other commanders their orders. At 0950, our ships will disperse and head for different staging areas along Mars' elliptical plane. When we attack, this should prevent the Deravans from concentrating their forces. The more we can dilute their firepower, the better our chances. However, since the *Lexington* is at reduced operating efficiency, I'm holding you back in reserve. If any one of our ships gets into trouble, you'll move in to assist. Do you have any questions?"

Yamane shook his head. "No, sir. Seems clear enough."

"Well then, I guess that's it," Harris said, his voice low. "We've reached zero hour, and I can't think of anything else."

"See you on the other side, Commodore," he smiled. "Yamane, out."

He switched off the intercom and brought his attention forward. "Now we sit here and wait," he whispered.

"Sir," the r-tech called out. "The fleet is beginning to break up. They are heading for their rendezvous coordinates."

Yamane spun his chair around. He was just in time to see the *Montreal* and the *Kennedy* fire up their engines and head for the southern pole of Mars. Both the *Gemini* and the *Orion* followed, except they headed for the northern pole. The *Arima* and the *Corona* took up their positions on the opposite sides of the equator, staying just behind the curvature of the red planet.

Now the *Lexington* was alone behind Deimos—waiting for...he looked back over his right shoulder. "Major," he barked. "Send out the order. Put the ship on red alert."

With a single press of a button on his console, every light on the bridge changed to a muted crimson color. He then opened the intercom. "Red alert, red alert," he said, his words short and deliberate. "All crewmembers to their battle stations. This is not a drill. All crews to battle stations."

The c-tech jumped in. "Commodore Harris is signaling the fleet to launch all fighters."

"Send the order."

The first wave of fighters flew out of the inner recesses of the *Lexington*. Once clear of the launch tubes, they executed a three hundred-and-sixty degree tumble roll in perfect synchronization, flying off towards their designated marks five kilometers away.

Before the second wave appeared, Yamane realized just how sweaty his palms had become. He wiped them on both pant legs. These were the moments he hated most, the ones just before a battle. In his mind, a hundred different outcomes came and went in a flash.

When he refocused his attention on the main screen, Yamane noticed the chatter around him steadily decreasing, until he could only hear clicks and beeps from a couple of computer consoles. A few moments later, they too became silent. Then something even stranger happened. A feeling of euphoria came over him. It felt like a covering of peace had descended upon him, and then...a loud buzzing noise suddenly came from the c-tech's station in two short bursts. Commodore Harris had issued the final attack code.

Scattered bursts of white light five kilometers away indicated all fourteen fighter groups and six stellar cruisers sitting behind the crimson disk had fired their thrusters. When they emerged from behind the curvature of the red planet, one thousand Deravan vessels of identical shape and size seemed to fill the heavens. Strangely haunting in their appearance, the polished, tri-angular-shaped ships manifested the deepest black anyone had ever seen.

Yamane observed the more nimble ships shoot ahead of the larger, slower-moving stellar cruisers. When they moved into position and took aim, the leading squadrons fired a hail of red, blue and yellow plasma bursts, blanketing the enemy vessels closest to them. Those targets disappeared behind a curtain of light.

The c-tech turned around. "Sir, the lead squadron reports they have engaged the Deravans." From those words, those simple words, the future of Mankind now hung in the balance. "Just a minute," he added. He bent closer and placed his hand over his left ear in an attempt to block out some ambient noise. "I think we've got a problem here. They report some kind of unknown force has taken over their ships. Power systems are dead and directional thrusters are not operating." He struck the console with his hand. "I've just lost radio contact."

Yamane jumped to his feet. He felt the need to take action, but wasn't sure what it should be.

The c-tech tilted his head, as if he had received another message. After a nod or two, a broad smile appeared. "Whatever the reason for the malfunctions, the fighters' systems have come up again. They are continuing with the attack."

"That's exactly what happened to you," Webster observed from his station. "These ships are much smaller than the one that destroyed Kalmedia, and yet they also put out a dampening field."

Before he could say another word, a squadron of fighters appeared on the main screen. Like a hawk catching sight of a plump rabbit out in the open, the lead pilot banked over hard and honed in on a fresh batch of ships.

"Put the cockpit traffic on the speakers," Yamane ordered. "I want to hear what's going on."

The c-tech retuned the radio frequency.

"Diamond five, where is diamond nine?"

"Watch yourself, green two," the unknown pilot yelled, "you've got one on your tail!"

"Green seven, pick up green two and fly over to that ship at ten o'clock."

"I think I've got him...I got him!" he cried out.

A small burst of pinkish-red light went off in the distance. The bridge burst into cheers. Though this had only been one ship amidst a thousand, nothing could take away the euphoria felt by the crew at their first victory.

"Nice shot, green two," the pilot congratulated.

"It took about twenty hits from me and my wingman before it finally blew."

"STS missiles are armed and locked. Target in range. One and two are away...impact in five seconds." Silence. "That got him."

"Negative," another pilot jumped in. "They only exploded on the surface. I am not picking up any damage."

A flurry of pulse blasts and explosions flashed in the distance. They died down, followed by a dozen others. The Deravans maintained their course and speed without a single shot fired in return. Their lack of a response unsettled Yamane. Either they didn't care or they had something else in mind... something terrible.

"The *Kennedy* is now in firing range," the nav-tech reported.

"Now we'll know if this works," Yamane said under his breath. As he finished his last word, a hail of red, yellow, and green plasma fire poured into the closest enemy ships. Blast after relentless blast came from all forty gun ports, striking their targets with frightening precision. But as the multicolored explosions faded, every single enemy ship emerged unscathed, just like before.

Yamane swallowed hard, unnerved by what he saw. "What is their course and speed?"

Even before the r-tech had a chance to respond, the Deravans began to reorient themselves. Once perfect and formidable in appearance, their formation had broken down, replaced with independent ships moving into different, seemingly haphazard directions.

"Commander!" the nav-tech yelled.

Yamane leaned forward in his chair. "I see them," he replied softly. "Hold your position."

The *Kennedy* circled around and came up from behind. By the time she straightened out, the Deravans had transformed themselves into three smaller formations. Just as the stellar cruiser's cannon batteries were about to fire, several hundred enemy ships unleashed a deadly barrage of their own. Caught off guard by the unexpected tactic, she suffered hit after vicious hit. The vessel rocked over one way from the force of multiple impacts striking her hull, and then another.

"Sir!" the c-tech shouted, "the *Kennedy* is taking heavy fire. They report heavy damage all over the ship. Main thrusters are down and two reactor cores could breach at any time."

Yamane couldn't watch anymore. The time had come for them to act. "Fire up the engines!" he ordered. "Flank speed."

"Aye, Commander. Flank speed."

"Signal the gunners and prepare to fire on the Deravan fleet," Yamane added. "Make your heading one-five-nine."

Mirroring the actions of a weather vane suddenly pushed into a different direction by the wind, the *Lexington* abruptly pivoted around and made her course straight for the *Kennedy*.

Three Min fighters shot past her bow and targeted a cluster of enemy ships. Pulse cannons and STS missiles mercilessly pounded the enemy, coming up on them fast. Their screens absorbed blow after blow at first, but then, quite unexpectedly, the lead Deravan vessel exploded into a ball of crimson light. Yamane's ship flew right through the dying embers.

Pleasure surged through his veins. He had scored a victory for their side. Then he wondered how successful their fleet had been so far. "What effect are we having on the Deravans?"

The r-tech retrieved the information from his console. "Negligible," he replied. "We've managed to destroy just fourteen enemy ships. They appear to have some kind of energy field that protects them from our missiles and cannons."

"Is there any way of counteracting their shields?"

The r-tech was just about to answer when the Deravans unleashed another deadly barrage. Caught off guard by the sudden discharge of weapon's fire, multiple ion bursts struck down a majority of the fighters, vaporizing them in an instant.

The *Arima* came around and tried protecting a squadron of fighters that had somehow survived the melee. The Deravans responded in kind. They turned about and sent multiple blasts down the length of her hull, until they struck the stellar cruiser's engine room. A terrible explosion resulted, obscuring everything else for several heart-wrenching seconds.

Yamane was certain the *Arima* had been destroyed, but when the fireball dimmed, he saw that the ship had somehow survived. With smoke pouring out of her aft section, she tried to maneuver away. Their efforts were commendable, heroic, but Yamane knew the Deravans would finish the stellar cruiser off in short order.

As if cognizant of his every thought, a lone Deravan vessel picked up speed and rammed her on her starboard side, hitting the ship just about dead center. The force of the collision broke the mortally wounded vessel cleanly in half. As both pieces sheared away from each other, people and debris flew out into space with the sudden rush of escaping air. Fires and explosions raged in the affected areas, tearing up the decks and bulkheads. The forward section slowly tumbled away from the aft section, leaving a trail of fire behind.

Yamane could barely mask his shock and dismay as he stared at the screen. "Come on...come on," he pleaded. "Get to the life pods. Get to the life pods."

About halfway down the aft section, between the keel and top deck, small random flashes of light could be seen. Yamane thought more weapons blasts had struck the hull, but as he peered more closely, he realized that some of the crew must have made it to the pods.

He swung the command chair around. "Bring us about," he ordered the nav-tech. "The *Kennedy* can wait until we pick up those survivors."

"Aye, Commander."

With a certain evil predictability, the surrounding Deravan ships changed course and fired on the lifeboats as they emerged from the *Arima*. In a matter of seconds, they were gone.

"It's like shooting fish in a barrel," Yamane said aloud, both to himself and to no one in particular. Then an even more sickening sight met him on the main screen. Already engulfed in flames, the *Arima's* forward section tumbled down into Mars' upper atmosphere. Portions of her hull plating tore away, along with antennas and other equipment on the ship's exterior, showcasing the last gasp of a once-proud vessel in her final death throes.

"Three enemy vessels coming in at three o'clock!" the r-tech cried out.

Yamane swiveled the command chair around. "Give me maximum acceleration," he ordered. "We need some fighting room. Make your course—zero-seven-five—right for the *Kennedy*."

With O'Malley's ship trapped in the middle of a concentrated formation of Deravan vessels, Yamane had no choice but to fly through a gauntlet of enemy fire. Blast after blast slammed into the hull, some at almost point-blank range. The resultant explosions rocked the *Lexington* from one side to the other.

The *Kennedy* fired her weapons in return, but it did little good. Most of her guns were no longer operational, and the stellar cruiser could barely maneuver. She was a sitting duck out there by herself. Yamane knew if they didn't get there soon, he might be too late to save his friend. The Deravans must have sensed this as well. They circled the hapless vessel, firing on her without mercy. The ensuing bursts sliced right through her hull. Both sides paused. The *Kennedy* transformed itself into a huge fireball of red light. When the blast ebbed away, nothing remained.

A shadow crossed Yamane's face. "O'Malley sacrificed himself for the sake of the fleet," he exhaled. "He hoped he could take out as many of the Deravans as possible by destroying his own ship. I don't know if it makes him a hero or a fool."

Nine Deravan ships broke away from the pack and changed their course to an intercept trajectory. Yamane recognized what they were doing. "Hard about—ninety degrees. I want to give them our broad side. Once they're in range, have all batteries fire."

The nav-tech turned back, a skeptical look on his face. "Sir, I don't think the *Lexington* can handle it. We could blow the entire engine stack."

Yamane rose out of his chair. "If you can't obey my orders, I'll find someone else who can."

The navigator nodded in reply and implemented the directive. He reversed engines while simultaneously firing the forward directional thrusters. The maneuver put tremendous stress all along the hull. Distant moans sounded on the bridge. Yamane held on tight as the ship spun around, revealing the length of her hull right to the incoming ships. As those targets came into range, all twenty pulse cannons unleashed a volley of concentrated fire.

They were too late.

"All hands, brace for impact!" the navigator shouted.

As Yamane looked up, time itself seemed to slow, like in the kind of dream where one's legs could barely move. Despite explosions going off all around them, the Deravan ships still approached, but they too appeared to be caught in whatever it was that had affected him. As he turned his head the other way, activity on the bridge likewise slowed. Crewmembers had all but ceased moving, as though they fell in between the ticks of a clock. Yamane tried to call someone, anyone, but no words came out of his mouth. He brought his attention forward again, towards the main screen. The Deravan ship hung there, frozen in time. In one final incredible act, the universe collapsed into the singular spot where he sat. Darkness. Then something remarkable happened. It was as though someone came alongside and brought him back, right to the point where that small piece of time jumped its tracks and gotten stuck.

A pair of Deravan ships plowed right into the *Lexington*, triggering two massive explosions in her lower decks. The stellar cruiser shuddered. When an almost equally powerful explosion rocked the *Lexington* a second time, the vessel rolled over in the opposite direction.

Main power systems faltered, triggering the emergency lights which bathed the bridge in a dull, crimson glow. Yamane heard cries for help echoing through the ship's corridors.

He pushed himself out of the command chair and tried making his way to the engineering station. Coughing loudly and gasping for breath, he realized smoke was wafting up from the lower decks. "Damage report," he shouted to Webster. "How bad were we hit?"

A look of terror crossed his face. "We've lost main power. Engines are down, and—"

Another explosion rocked the damaged vessel. She began to roll over on her port side.

"Hold your stations," Yamane ordered. He spun around. "Can we bring her upright again?"

"Trying, sir," the nav-tech grunted while punching a series of commands into his console.

The *Lexington* did not move. He tried again, but the ship remained ten degrees past vertical. "Controls are not responding. We've suffered too much damage."

A flash of fear grabbed Yamane hard. He turned back to Webster and tried to shake it off. "What about our weapons? Can we get off any shots?"

The major flipped a couple of switches and then pressed a few other buttons in no discernable order. A response was a long time in coming. Yamane began to grow impatient. "Negative," he finally replied. "As far as I can tell, every major power line between here and the engine room has been severed. Also, life support is out, and there are reports of casualties all over the ship."

Yamane couldn't just give up. He had to try something. "How long before the repair teams can get our pulse batteries up again?"

"We don't have that kind of time," Kershaw said grimly from behind.

Yamane spun around. The sight of his blood-soaked uniform met him first. "What are you doing here?"

Though the question had been rhetorical, he answered it anyway. "Those first two took out engineering. I tried getting the generators going again, but they suffered too much damage. I had no choice but to evacuate. Fortunately, we got the wounded out before the coolant pipes ruptured. I tried getting you on the intercom, but it was dead. So I ran up here." Kershaw pointed at the bridge. "There's nothing more we can do, Frank. If we don't leave now, the Deravans will finish us off for sure."

"Does Olsen concur with your assessment?"

Kershaw started to speak, but something seemed to hold him back. He tried again. "Olsen didn't make it," the major stated in a matter-of-fact manner. "We lost him when the shielding plates went."

Yamane hesitated. There had to be a way out of this. He just needed time to think.

Another strong explosion shook the *Lexington*, almost knocking both of them over.

Yamane brushed past Kershaw. "Are there any other ships in the area?" he asked the r-tech. "Maybe they can provide cover."

He shook his head. "I can't say for certain, since I keep losing the signal."

Kershaw grabbed Yamane's arm. "Frank, the *Lexington* is finished. We have to leave now."

"Maybe—"

He jerked him back. "There is no maybe." Kershaw pulled him closer. "You can't win this one. It's over." Three more fusion blasts pounded the hull. The ship listed over just a bit more.

Both men stared at one another.

"Is that the way it is?" Yamane finally asked.

Kershaw shook his head. "I'm afraid so."

Yamane wanted to fight the truth, but his friend was right. It was over. He now had to consider what was best for his crew. "Can we send out a distress signal?" he asked the c-tech.

"I think so, sir, but I'm not sure for how long."

"Contact the *Corona*. Tell Commodore Harris we're abandoning ship."

The ensign shook his head and then sent the message. After a few moments, he looked up at Yamane and said, "Harris will do his best to keep the Deravans at bay, but since most of the fighters have been lost, he can't give us much cover."

Yamane weighed the options in his mind, but there could only be one answer. "What about internal communications? Are they operational?"

After making a quick assessment of his station, the c-tech replied, "Give me one second." With the skill of a master surgeon, he flipped open an access plate on the side of his console. The ensign then flipped a couple of switches so he could bypass some of circuits that appeared to be damaged. When he placed the plate back over the opening, both speakers started to crackle. "That's about as good as I can do."

A dark pall settled on Yamane. "Signal the crew," he said in a distant voice. "Tell them to abandon ship."

The c-tech brought his finger down on a large red button at the base of his console. Alarm bells began to ring, accompanied by flashing yellow lights located on the bridge. "All crew abandon ship," he said into the intercom. "I repeat, all crew abandon ship."

Yamane stood motionless, the reality of losing his first command hitting him like a bolt of lightning out of a clear blue sky. He felt an intense resentment towards the Deravans. What they were doing made no sense, and yet they continued to destroy without provocation...or mercy.

"Commander, we have to leave now."

His gaze fell. "Give the order." Never had Yamane felt more defeated in his life.

"Let's go!" Kershaw barked. The crew immediately abandoned their posts and went to a hatch nestled between the main screen and the e-tech's station. Finding the 'EMERGENCIES ONLY' box in the dark, Kershaw smashed the glass cover, reached in, and pulled a bright red lever. To his relief, the white hatch slid open. He stood at the entrance and hurried each crewmember through.

"Is this everyone?" Yamane asked from the doorway.

Silence.

"Secure the door," he said while stepping inside and taking a seat.

Kershaw grabbed an elongated lever arm in the middle of the emergency door and swung it around in a clockwise direction. The further he rotated the lever, the greater the effort it took to do so, stopping only when it had fully extended every locking bolt.

"Launch the life pod," Yamane said. He suddenly became aware of the fact that these would be his last orders given on board the *Lexington*.

A muffled explosion sounded from behind the pod before it blasted away. Emergency rockets fired as soon as the escape craft cleared the ship. Through the small round window, Yamane saw the *Lexington* fall behind, smoke pouring from her hull. The sight of Deravan ships hovering over his ship like a pack of hungry wolves was simply too much for him. He lowered his head and turned away.

Kershaw didn't move. He just held his place, forcing himself to focus on the heart-wrenching sight.

A moment later, brilliant white light filled the interior of the life pod. The cabin dimmed again shortly afterward, but as darkness settled upon them, Commander Frank Yamane's hopes faded with equal measure. There was still an enemy for him to fight, but he felt, at this point, there was little fight left in him.

CHAPTER

10

MARS

1152 PROXIMA MERIDIAN TIME, AUGUST 17, 2217

"Hold on!" Kershaw shouted. He swung the maneuvering stick over hard, throwing everyone deep into their seats. A flash of light illuminated the interior, followed by a severe thrashing when a blast wave slammed into them. "Those Deravan devils are homing in on us like vultures on carrion." He threw the stick in the opposite direction.

Yamane unlatched his restraints and pulled himself up. "How many of them are out there?"

"Hard to say," Kershaw replied after checking his scopes. "Maybe five or six."

"How about fighters? Do we have any cover?"

A pair of blue pulse flashes flew right past the porthole window at close range, hitting a far-off Deravan vessel. "Yes, but I can't say how long our perimeter can hold those enemy ships back. We have to get on board the *Corona*—now."

Yamane looked down at the targeting grid. He then shot a glance out the window. "We're going to have to take our chances. If we stay out here too much longer, they'll pick us off for sure. No bobbing or weaving. Just plot the straightest course to the *Corona*."

Kershaw looked back over his shoulder. He didn't say a word. Yamane could tell he didn't agree with his strategy, but something from within seemed to override his inclination to disobey. "Here goes nothing," he said under his breath.

A straight line between them and the stellar cruiser appeared on Kershaw's targeting grid. They were coming in low. Another explosion shook the life pod. "We're only going to have one shot at this," he said, his voice hurried. Directional thrusters underneath the pod fired. They went up somewhat, but not enough. The dull metal plating of the *Corona* filled Kershaw's view.

"Pull up!" Yamane shouted.

Kershaw gave the stick a quick jerk. The pod broke through the plane of the cavernous opening. Everyone on board lurched forward when she hit the deck hard. Reverse thrusters fired upon impact. The pod skidded along the runway, spraying millions of sparks into the air, until they stopped a mere five meters from the end of the bay.

Kershaw shut down every system at once and then spun the lever arm clockwise. All seventeen latching clamps retracted, marked by a series of clicks. When the emergency hatch slid upward, everyone threw off their restraints and slipped through the narrow opening. Yamane, in sharp contrast to the others, just stood in place, not moving.

"Frank, we need to go," Kershaw said from the escape hatch.

A sorrowful expression met him back. "I know. It's just that once I leave, then the *Lexington* will really be gone. I've never lost a command before."

"I understand it's a lot to absorb right now, but this is not the time. There are people who are counting on us, and we still have a job to do." He extended his hand. "What do you say?"

Yamane shook his head. "You're right," he replied, resolve infused in his voice. "We can't afford to let our sorrows get to us now. There will be plenty of time for that later."

Kershaw grinned and then pulled him up.

"Stan, I want you to stay with the crew," he said after jumping down onto the flight deck. "Have each person looked over by the medical teams. If they check out, filter them in with the *Corona*'s crew, help fill in some of the gaps."

Kershaw furrowed his brow. "What do you mean?" he asked. "You're not staying?"

"No. I'm going up to the bridge—see if I can assist in operations."

"But Frank—" Before Kershaw could get another word out, Yamane was already heading for the lift. He slammed the gate open and disappeared inside.

Distant sounds of explosions rumbled through the ship as Yamane rushed onto the bridge. He looked for Commodore Harris, but didn't find him. Another officer, presumably the second-in-command, stood just behind the navigator and barked out orders. He was a husky man, tall, who carried a strong sense of his own abilities. When a tech didn't respond fast enough, the officer shouted orders out a second time, loud enough for the whole bridge to hear.

After making another quick sweep of the ship's command center, Yamane wondered why Harris would leave his post at a time like this, unless ...

He approached the officer from behind. "Where is Commodore Harris?"

The man abruptly spun around, "Can't you see I'm busy!" he screamed. "Why don't you ...?" His voice cooled the instant he saw Yamane's rank on his collar.

"What's your name, soldier?"

"Lt. Commander Lee Henthorne—sir."

"I asked you a question, Mr. Henthorne. Where is Commodore Harris?"

He looked Yamane over first before replying, appearing to size him up. "I'm afraid he's dead, sir."

It was like a sudden blow to the head. "Dead," he gasped.

"I'm afraid so."

"What happened?" Yamane asked, but didn't really want to know.

"Just after the commodore ordered you to rendezvous with the *Kennedy*, our primary engines were hit by enemy fire. He left me in command so he could assist with the repairs. I objected, of course, but the commander already made up his mind. One of the engine plates ruptured and he was killed in the blast."

"I'm sorry to hear that. He was a good man."

"I'm sorry too, but I don't have time for this right now, sir." Henthorne went to the command chair. "There are more important things going on at the moment."

He didn't like the way the ship's second-in-command said 'sir.' The tone had a certain air of contempt attached to it.

Yamane closed the gap between the two. "What is the *Corona*'s status?"

Henthorne didn't seem to hear the question, or perhaps he had and just ignored him.

Yamane stepped in front of the belligerent second-in-command, blocking his view of the main screen. "I asked you a question, Lt. Commander. What is the *Corona*'s status?"

Snapping to attention, he replied in a robotic fashion, "Primary thermal pulsar generators are undamaged and our cannons are at ninety-two percent power levels."

"And the Deravan fleet? How many ships lost?"

Henthorne brought up his data pad. "Thirty-seven ships in all. We, on the other hand, have lost one hundred and fifty-two of our fighters and three stellar cruisers."

Yamane turned back to the main screen. "Do any of our ships need assistance right now?" he asked when he realized the gravity of their situation.

"At this point, all our ships need assistance. We are out-manned and out-gunned. I do not think we can survive much longer unless we pull back and regroup. In fact ..." his voice stalled. "We have no chance if we stay here." He turned to the nav-tech. "Back us out, nice and slow. Order the other ships to rendezvous with the *Gemini*. Maybe we can regroup at the Telori Outpost and figure something out."

Run away. Yamane couldn't conceive of such a notion. If they turned tail and ran, Earth wouldn't stand a chance. But what if Henthorne is right? Yamane's mistake had cost him his ship. Could he be making another one by staying to fight? His vision clouded. He closed his eyes. Liana called out to him. His thoughts reached out to her. A dark void met him on the other side.

Then it hit him, like an epiphany that had traversed the corridors of time, uniquely crafted for this one remarkable moment. Something deep down inside told him, demanded of him that he take command. How Yamane knew such a thing, he could not say, but the feeling was irrefutable. And if he ignored the person, the voice, whatever one might call the enigmatic influence, the fate of the human race could very well hang in the balance.

When Yamane opened his eyes again, his attention became resolute and fixed. "Belay that order, Ensign," he countermanded with all the force he could muster. "Now that Commodore Harris is dead, I'm the senior officer aboard this ship."

A dark look came over Henthorne. "But, Commander, the battle is over. If we don't pull back now, then—"

"Article fifty-seven of regulations gives me every right to assume command. We press the attack while there is still a chance of keeping the Deravans from reaching Earth. And as senior officer on board, I am exercising that right."

Henthorne faced Yamane. "I would strongly advise against it."

He did not back down. "If you do not surrender the bridge, I will relieve you of duty."

The threat seemed to catch Henthorne off-guard. He just stood in his place with a look of shock on his face, as though his mind could not quite process someone doing such a thing to him. "Yes, Commander." Henthorne took a single step back and snapped to attention. "Your orders—sir."

"Bring the *Corona* around twenty-seven degrees. Have all batteries bear on the enemy once they are in range." Yamane then assumed his place in the command chair. He felt every pair of eyes on the bridge bearing down on him.

Three Deravan ships turned about and made a course for the *Corona*. They brought their weapons to bear in unison. Multiple hits echoed throughout the wounded vessel. Lights on the bridge flickered off and on a number of times before returning to full strength.

"New course," Yamane ordered, his voice wavering in spots. He looked down at the nav-tech's station. "One-seven-one." The last time he allowed the Deravans to get this close, it had cost him his ship. He vowed he would never repeat the same mistake twice.

Another explosion went off in the distance. Though the ship had been too far away for a visual confirmation, the size of the fireball suggested it had been a big one, perhaps a stellar cruiser. A sick feeling washed over Yamane. He hoped for the best but feared the worst. "Can you tell which one it was?"

he asked the r-tech in a low voice.

"I'm afraid so, Commander. That was the *Orion*."

"We're down to three stellar cruisers," Henthorne said, still at attention. "We must—"

Yamane stared off into space. "How many fighters are still out there?"

"Forty-one."

"That's only three squadrons," Henthorne repeated. "We've barely made a dent in the number of enemy ships destroyed, while ours are being eliminated at will. Harris' plan, though admirable, is not working. If we don't change our method of attack, Earth will be left unprotected."

Yamane shot a look at Henthorne. "You're right," he agreed, albeit reluctantly. "We need to pull back."

"Are you sure your plan is the correct course of action?" he sneered.

Yamane ignored the dig. "Signal the fleet and have them rendezvous at coordinates zero-zero-seven—maximum velocity," he said to the c-tech. "We'll regroup and make our stand there."

He looked at Henthorne and then Yamane. "Aye, Commander—zero-zero-seven."

"But taking the fleet back to Earth is the worst possible decision you can make. I agree we need to regroup, but lead them away from the planet, not to it."

"Take a look at what's going on?" Yamane said while pointing at the main screen. "Those are our men and women dying out there, and the Deravan's heading hasn't changed one iota. Do you think they'll abandon their plans just to follow us?"

Henthorne grabbed Yamane's shoulder. "That's not my concern right now. Stopping them is. And I think your strategy will only make it easier for them to finish what they've started."

He jerked his shoulder back. Never had he been in a situation before where a fellow officer had so openly defied him. Yamane considered his position as the *Corona*'s new commanding officer shaky at best, but if he didn't stand up to his challenge, and right now, the crew might never fully support him. "Mister Henthorne," Yamane said after coming to his feet. "If you cannot follow my orders, then I will find someone else who will."

Both men stared at one another. After what seemed like minutes, he finally replied. "Have all remaining ships rendezvous at our position," Henthorne ordered through clenched teeth. "Once they do, set a course for Earth."

Without another word, Yamane resumed his place in the command chair. He paused while taking in the bridge. Tension and anxiety filled the air. Drawing in a deep breath, he realized that for better or worse, the *Corona* was now his ship.

ANTARA, HOME PLANET OF THE ANTAREN EMPIRE
DAIETH TIME MINUS FOUR

Kel Sen-Ry rose to his feet. He stood before two large doors reaching up to the vaulted ceiling . As soon as they had swung open, Kel Sen-Ry walked into the Council Chambers, his head dipped. The High Council waited.

At the end of the chambers, he reached seven steps. He ascended each one in a slow and deliberate manner. Upon reaching the top, he nodded to his left and then his right, before making a long, slow bow. He stayed in the uncomfortable position for a moment, and then rose up again.

"You may approach," one of the council members, Sul Ren-Ta, said. Kel Sen-Ry took two steps forward and then stopped. "Tell me, my old friend, do you bring news from beyond our borders?"

"I do," he replied. "We have just received the first reports."

"And what do they indicate?"

"As we expected, the Deravans have attacked both the Terran colony on Beta Centauri, and their secondary capital on Titan."

He shifted in his chair. "What is the result of the battle so far?"

Kel Sen-Ry clasped his hands together, his long, flowing robes falling over both of them. "I am afraid the conflict is not going well for the Terrans, just as we also expected."

"Have our military planners made an assessment of their chances?"

"An initial one, based on all available information."

"And what are their projections?"

"The Terrans will make a stand at Earth, but we do not expect they can stop them. Their planet will be destroyed."

A stark silence filled the council chambers.

"Do you believe there will be any survivors?" Sul Ren-Ta asked.

Kel Sen-Ry averted his gaze. "No one can say at this time," he replied in a distant voice, "but we believe it is extremely doubtful. The Terrans have lost four stellar cruisers so far, plus a majority of their fighters."

Another council member rose to his feet. "The question before us is what we do next."

"We do nothing," Din Tru-Ne interjected. "You priests have been telling us that the Deravans will attack the Terrans, defeat their military, and destroy their planet. If you are correct, we've witnessed the fulfillment of these prophecies. Now when they are on the verge of defeat, we rush in and assist them? Where are your prophecies then?"

"Are you saying we should not help them at all? Let them be destroyed?"

"If the prophecies you have extolled for so long are true, then there is no other way. And if we have misinterpreted them, and the Terrans are defeated, our people will still be the benefactors of so great a mistake. Either way, the weight of this humiliating defeat at the hands of the Terrans will finally be lifted off the backs of our people. When this happens, we can think of ourselves as Antarens once again."

"Galidor Din Tru-Ne is correct," Sul Ren-Ta agreed. "If the prophecies are true, then we do nothing. Events must be allowed to unfold on their own, without our assistance—so we know one way or the other." He paused for a moment. "Does anyone else have an objection?" The council chambers heard not a sound.

Kel Sen-Ry took a step forward. "Do you have any instructions for me?" he asked.

"Tell the military they are to do nothing except monitor the course of the battle."

"And the priests?"

"Tell them...tell them they should wait and pray."

2217, AUGUST 17, 2217
1314 PROXIMA MERIDIAN TIME

The three surviving stellar cruisers came up on the moon's dark side. Not far behind, the Deravan fleet closed in on their position. Just as they few past the rim of Earth's ancient satellite, the *Corona*, *Gemini* and *Montreal* began to slow, taking up a position at roughly the midpoint between both celestial bodies, drawing a line in the sand as it were, and waited.

"Commander, we are at the coordinates you designated," Henthorne said with a trace of contempt in his voice. "What are your orders?"

Before he could answer, the c-tech looked back over his shoulder "Sir, I have Star Force Command on the radio, just as you requested."

Yamane swiveled his command chair around. "Good. Pipe it through."

"This is Senator Torres," he said, his voice coming through the armrest speaker.

"Senator, I don't I have to tell you how the battle has gone."

"No, Commander. I've been monitoring your progress. It doesn't look good, does it?"

Yamane paused before answering. "I'm afraid not. We've been forced to regroup at these coordinates. From here we'll make our last stand."

"And if you fail?"

He ignored the question. "I need as many ships as you can spare. Maybe we can still hit them where it hurts."

This time the senator paused before answering. "I'll do everything I can. Good luck, Commander."

"We're going to need all there is. Yamane, out."

He closed the circuit and just sat there, stone-faced. A minute passed. One by one, the eyes of those on the bridge drifted in his direction, silent. They waited with him. Then, without any warning, Yamane rose to his feet and went to the RadAR console. He had to see for himself. All three displays showed hundreds of blips, both large and small, rising up from the Earth's surface. No one had to tell him what each of them represented. Yamane could only imagine how bad things were for everyone below. People everywhere, doing whatever they could to get on any outbound ship—fighting, pleading, bribing—just so they could be among the lucky few who got away. Yesterday, most people were law-abiding citizens who didn't give space flight a second thought. Today, everything was different. The law of the jungle had taken over and they were playing for the highest stakes possible, their very lives.

"Signal the *Gemini* and *Montreal*," he said to the r-tech, his attention transfixed by the images on all three screens. "Have them come alongside our ship. Once they are in position, scramble every fighter and have them take up a position five hundred meters ahead of us. By concentrating our firepower, we might gain the advantage we need to stop them."

The Deravans readied themselves for the final and most important phase of the operation.

Even though they met with a stronger defense than predicted, Earth had not prevented them from reaching their home world. But these considerations had been anticipated long before, and posed no difficulty to the projected outcome. Their fate was decided when contact had first been made, and the results of that decision would soon be realized. And once done, they would be one step closer to achieving what had been denied them uncounted centuries before. The so-called creators had prevented them from taking what was rightfully theirs at the dawn of creation. The depth of their pain and sorrow from that point on was beyond measure. But soon, very soon, it would all be erased.

The proximity alarm at the r-tech's station went off. Yamane pivoted the command chair. "What's going on?" he demanded. "The Deravans can't be in range yet!"

"Commander, I'm picking up Min fighters coming from the surface."

Yamane jumped out of his chair and hurried over to the RadAR station. "How many ships?"

The r-tech's inputted a series of commands on his keyboard. "This can't be right," he muttered to himself. He flipped another switch. "Confirmed." The lieutenant looked up at Yamane. "Star Force Command has only sent two squadrons of fighters. That's all."

Blind fury raced through his mind. "Those fools! Don't they realize—" He caught himself. Despite his feelings otherwise, Yamane knew that it wouldn't do any good to storm all over the bridge, ranting and raving. Star Force Command had made their decision. "How long before the enemy is in range?"

"Three minutes, sir."

Yamane turned towards the main screen. "Signal the fleet. They will attack on my order." He resumed his place in the command chair.

"Commander, enemy fleet is moving into attack formation. They have repositioned themselves into three distinct bodies, just like at Mars."

Yamane glanced at the r-tech's scope and verified the change for himself. "They don't miss a trick," he replied. "Distance."

"Twenty-thousand kilometers."

He readied himself. "Give the order. Have all ships accelerate to 0.40 stellar velocity."

"But Commander," Henthorne protested, "fire control computers cannot lock onto enemy ships at that speed. Cannon crews will have to target them manually."

"I'm aware of that, but I'm also hoping the Deravans have similar problems, and have just as hard a time hitting our ships."

His answer seemed to satisfy Henthorne, for the time being.

Fighter after fighter blasted ahead of the three surviving stellar cruisers and zeroed in on the central Deravan formation. Despite an acceleration rate faster than most pilots were accustomed to, they managed to keep their course fixed and formations tight.

Yamane sat back in his chair and waited. A quick check of the astro-clock confirmed they would engage the enemy in a matter of seconds as he counted down the distance in his mind.

The proximity alarm sounded.

"Deravan fleet now in range."

A barrage of plasma blasts flew right into the heart of the enemy fleet. Red, yellow and green fireballs blossomed before their eyes, and then faded into darkness. As they passed over the three hundred or so ships below them, Yamane realized that just a few gunners had hit their intended targets. Most had missed by a wide margin.

"Bring our ships around one hundred and eighty degrees," he ordered. "Follow the same trajectory and fire at will."

The *Corona*, *Gemini* and *Montreal* banked over on their starboard sides and came around for a second pass. All forty-seven fighters, five thousand meters ahead, tightened their formations. Both groups of ships settled back down into the slot and fired again. But traveling at speeds few gunners were used to when making an attack run, Deravan ships blurred together. They tried compensating, but the results were the same as before—a lot of fireworks, but no ships destroyed.

"Blast," Yamane said in frustration when he realized the results of their second run. He began to wonder if anything could stop those vessels.

He gave the order to come around again for a third pass. Just when the leading squadron of Min fighters targeted the incoming vessels, the Deravans suddenly turned about and unleashed a concentrated burst of their own. Every one of the pilots banked hard in different directions and tried to avoid the deadly blasts. But the lethal volley proved too much. Multiple streams of ion blasts vaporized them in an instant. The fighters were gone before any of them knew what happened.

A second barrage of enemy fire plowed into the hulls of all three stellar cruisers not far behind. The *Gemini* slowed when a series of hits blasted parts of her engine room away. Massive explosions detonated all over the ship.

"We have to maintain fleet integrity," Yamane shouted above the collective noise around him, "or the Deravans will pick the rest of us off for sure."

"The *Gemini* has sustained heavy damage," the c-tech shouted back. "She's slowing to 0.17 stellar velocity."

Yamane hesitated. His plan was already falling apart. If he didn't act soon, what little momentum they did have might be lost. "Signal the *Montreal*. Have Commander Renault match the *Gemini*'s speed. We'll try and form up with her."

Multiple waves of ion bursts again tore into the hull of the *Gemini*. A series of cascading explosions forced her over onto her port side. Yamane shot a glance at the main screen. Additional enemy ships were approaching. "Signal the *Gemini* and the *Montreal*. Have them rendezvous at coordinates one-eight-three. We'll link up and try and make another pass."

Before he could send the message, the *Gemini* signaled them first. "Commander Downey is contacting us," the c-tech said, looking back.

Yamane spun around. "Put him on the speaker."

"... not sure we can take much more of this," he said over the noise of people yelling in the background. "Main engines are gone, I have casualty reports from all over the ship, and a number of fires are burning out of control."

"It's your call, Commander. Are you still maneuverable, or should you abandon ship?" Yamane could barely get the words out, the pain of his own loss still fresh in his mind.

A Deravan ship appeared out of nowhere and fired at *Gemini*'s bridge at nearly point-blank range. The stellar cruiser veered away out of control and plowed into a cluster of enemy vessels not far away. The resultant explosion vaporized everything in the immediate vicinity.

Henthorne came alongside the command chair. "It's over," he declared. "We have to leave now, before our ship and the *Montreal* are lost as well."

Yamane ignored him. "How about the *Montreal*? Is she still maneuverable?"

"Yes, but just barely. When the *Gemini* went, they suffered quite a bit of damage."

The commander sat upright in his chair. "Bring us alongside so we can provide cover."

Another group of Deravan ships came up on her starboard side and sent blast after blast into the weakened hull. The subsequent explosions caused the stellar cruiser to falter. Fewer and fewer pulse cannons fired back as main power diminished.

"Signal Commander Renault. Tell him to fall back to our position."

"There's no time for that," Henthorne objected. "We must get away now, before it's too late." Several hits by the Deravans punctuated his outburst.

Yamane's eyes widened. "How can you suggest such a thing? I will not leave any survivors behind."

A series of flashes registered along the length of the *Montreal*'s hull. Five life pods came into view. Two Deravan ships pounced on them and closed in for the kill. Three Min fighters, however, came out of nowhere and repelled the incoming attackers.

"Sir, another three enemy vessels are heading right for us," the r-tech called out.

Yamane checked the r-tech's screen. "How many life pods have—?"

"Only two so far, Commander."

"Twenty seconds to impact."

"A third pod has just landed."

"Fifteen seconds."

"How long before—"

"Ten seconds." The r-tech cried out, cutting Yamane off.

Yamane dropped his head. "Get us out of here," he ordered. "Flank speed!"

The *Corona* pulled away in a burst of acceleration, leaving the *Montreal* to her fate. Deravan ships fired on the stellar cruiser again and again, until a lone shot struck the defenseless vessel in the aft section and pierced one of her four reactor cores. A spectacular explosion of unparalleled proportions filled the main screen, and then faded into nothing. They were gone.

Unable to watch anymore, Yamane's gaze fell away. "How many fighters do we have left?" he asked while looking down into his empty hands.

"Only five, Commander," the c-tech replied in a hushed tone.

"Recall them immediately." He sat upright in his chair again. "Signal the gunners and tell them to prepare for a final Deravan assault. Maybe we can take a few of them with us."

The r-tech checked his screen. He looked a second time, as though the information didn't make any sense. "There are no enemy vessels in pursuit of us," he finally replied. The r-tech punched in several keys, paused, and then said, "Confirmed. They have all stopped."

Yamane rose out of his chair. "What do you mean they stopped?"

"I mean they just stopped. It's almost as if their ships hit some kind of barrier. I don't know how else I can explain what's happening."

Yamane hurried over to the RadAR station. "Are you sure?"

"I know this sounds strange, but they have tried to force their way through a number of times, and something is stopping them. Wait a minute." He bent closer and scrutinized his display more closely. "The Deravans are giving up. They're resuming their old course—right for Earth."

"Now what do you think they'll do?" Henthorne asked from behind.

Yamane turned back but didn't answer him. "Have the Deravans completely encircled the planet?"

"Yes, sir. They are now locked in geosynchronous orbit."

"Can you tap into any transmissions; something that might show us what's taking place down there."

The c-tech gave an unconscious nod. "That's not a problem, but—"

"Just do it."

The main screen, which had showed the Deravan ships in orbit, changed to a news reporter. A man who appeared to be in his forties was sitting behind his desk and wearing a blue blazer. He gave the appearance of a person who had been told a terrible secret, the depth of which registered on his face. "Since the Deravans have broken through Star Force lines...they are presently in orbit above. Wait a minute." He pressed the tiny receiver in his ear with his finger. "I've just been told we have a live feed from the rooftop of our building. Can you hear me, Jim?" The screen switched to view of the city, though the lack of distinguishing characteristics made it impossible to tell which one it was.

Knowing the name didn't matter, however. It was every city in the world.

Judging by the jerkiness of the picture, the crew didn't appear to be set up when they transferred the video feed to them. A reporter appeared one second, was lost, and then found by the camera again.

"As you can tell," he said, pointing, "the city is in a state of utter chaos. Every road is choked with traffic. At the skyports, private ships are desperately trying to get away before the Deravans arrive." The camera operator pulled back. Two small ships passed overhead before flying out of sight into a bank of clouds. "The billions and billions who are left behind have no choice but to wait. We've had unconfirmed reports that no stellar cruisers have survived the battle, leaving nothing left to stop the Deravans."

The picture they were watching split into two halves. The reporter moved to the left, the studio to the right. "Is there anything else you can see from where you are?" the commentator asked, his voice wavering in places.

"Not at this time...wait a minute. I hear the warning sirens going off." The camera operator panned past him and showed a shot of the entire city. Several explosions went off in the distance. Muffled booms rumbled seconds later. "I'm not certain what just happened," the reporter continued while trying to maintain a measure of professional detachment, "but I can only assume we are being attacked." A second group of explosions sounded off in the distance. "I'm getting something else...pan up, pan up," he said in an excited manner. Just as the camera operator did as he was told, a series of brightly colored plasma discharges rained down from above. He followed the first wave until they hit a ten-story building a few blocks away. "Explosions are going off all around us. Bolt after bolt is hitting every part of the city. It literally looks like pieces of the sky are falling to the ground. I've never seen anything like it. If one of them hits close we won't—oh no!"

The transmission suddenly went dead, the sound of a hissing noise coming from every speaker.

Yamane could do nothing except watch in stunned silence. His home, everything he knew, the Deravans were destroying, one detonation at a time— and he had no way to stop it. "Turn off the main screen," he murmured. "I can't watch anymore."

Henthorne jumped to attention. "What course should we set?" he asked, his eyes cold.

"How can you suggest we even consider leaving?" Yamane snapped back. "We can't just abandon them down there."

He moved closer. "What other choice do we have? Our first priority is survival. If we're dead, then there's no one who can come back to try and rescue survivors."

Yamane felt revulsion for Henthorne and his calculated thinking, almost getting physically sick over the way he could so easily dismiss the loss of billions. He also knew his second-in-command was right, and he hated himself for agreeing with him. But the truth could not be denied, no matter the source. A question then followed. Did a place exist where they could hide? Hide. How could he even conceive of such a notion?

Out of nowhere, like an intuitive flash of insight, a potential choice presented itself. The New Frontier. "The New Frontier just might be the place," Yamane reasoned aloud. "Since most people are unaware of the outpost's existence, it follows then that the Deravans probably don't either." Seemed reasonable. Seemed perfect.

He was about to issue the order when a new thought came to him—as if someone or something else had planted another idea into his mind. How much time would they have before the Deravans came—six months, a year...maybe two? A second thought soon followed. What about supplies? The New Frontier depended on Earth for all but their most basic needs. With no hope of cargo ships making any more runs, his crew could survive there for a while, but where would they go next? Yamane didn't relish the idea of a life looking over his shoulder, wondering if today they had finally been found out. But if he did stay and fight, this meant he needed ships, a lot of them. And if he needed ships, there was really only one place to go. The danger centers in his brain began sounding the alarm. Was he making the right decision? What about before, when he should have been with Liana? Could this be another time when ...? His thoughts trailed off. Yamane considered his decision a second time. Again, his answer came out the same: "Antara."

Rising up out of the command chair, he made his way to the front of the bridge, stopping just short of the main screen. He collected his thoughts first and then turned around to address his crew. They all appeared bewildered.

"I cannot pretend to know what the future may bring, but as long as I have breath, the only thought in my head and my heart is the liberation of Earth. I am certain this is yours as well. This means difficult choices must be made." He paused for a second or two before continuing. "I have no doubt many of you are thinking the New Frontier is our best bet for survival. To be honest, I thought so too—at first. But I believe going there will only buy us time before the Deravans track us down. My experience in the military has taught me the best way of preventing an enemy from attacking is if we destroy them first. In my mind, the only way of making this happen is if we come back with another fleet of ships." He took in the faces of every crewmember on the bridge before continuing. "After giving this careful thought, I have decided we will make our course one-seven-seven—right for Antares."

Every little bit of air was sucked out of the bridge when the crew heard his last, chilling words.

A burst of anger flashed in Henthorne's eyes. "You cannot be serious," he countered. "The New Frontier is our only chance. If we tell the Antarens our fleet has been destroyed, they would sooner see us dead than help us."

Yamane placed his hands behind his back. "I don't trust them either, and I have more reason than you to feel that way, but I am sure I can convince their High Council to support us. Something tells me this is just as much in their best interest as it is ours." He turned and faced the nav-tech. "Set your course for Antares."

Just as he was about to input the command, Henthorne took a hold of his arm from behind and held it back. "I'm sorry, Commander, but that is an order I cannot follow."

"Are you questioning my authority again, Lt. Commander?"

"This mission has absolutely no chance of success. Not only is your order wrong, it is also immoral. And as second-in-command, it is my duty to protect this ship and her crew." Henthorne came alongside the nav-tech. "Helmsman, make your course the New Frontier."

Yamane went around the other side. "Lt. Commander Henthorne," he grunted, "you are hereby relieved of duty."

"No, sir. I'm taking this ship to the New Frontier."

Yamane walked over to his command chair and sat in it. "Call security to the bridge," he ordered. The c-tech did not move. He sat frozen at his station, like a deer caught in the headlights. "Do it!" Yamane yelled after he rose to his feet for emphasis.

The lieutenant coiled back in fear, surprised by his commanding officer's sudden temperament change.

Henthorne's head dropped. Yamane took this as a sign he had backed down and visibly relaxed. Just as he was about to sit back down again, Henthornne suddenly lunged forward and grabbed Yamane around the waist. Caught off guard by the unexpected move, he fell back against the command chair, Henthorne's weight falling on top of him with a loud thud.

The c-tech spun around. "I need security up here, fast!" he shouted into the intercom.

Yamane brought his right arm up and tried to push Henthorne back, but his grip was too strong. He did manage to free his other hand, however, and smacked Henthorne square on the jaw. His head snapped back, causing him to cry out in pain.

Two security officers rushed onto the bridge and immediately jumped into the fray. The first officer grabbed Henthorne's left arm, the other his right. With one jerk, they ripped him off Yamane. He made a threatening move, but the guards held him in place. Only then did Henthorne finally relent.

"Take...him...to his quarters," Yamane ordered between each winded breath. "Keep him there...until further notice."

"Yes, sir," they replied in unison.

Yamane brushed back his hair and straightened his uniform. He went back to his command chair and flipped a switch on the control panel. He calmed himself down first before speaking. "Lt. Commander Kershaw, please report to the bridge."

"Kershaw here. I'm on my way."

Yamane sat down and waited. No one dared to speak. The crew just sat and waited with him.

The instant Kershaw appeared, Yamane rose to his feet. "Reporting as ordered, sir." He looked around. His jovial demeanor became more solemn, more serious. Though he did not say otherwise, he seemed to know something dramatic had happened.

Yamane kept his place. "Lt. Commander Kershaw will take over as second-in-command," he said in a loud, booming voice.

Kershaw appeared bewildered. He turned to his left and then his right. No one else said a word. "Yes, Commander."

"I have ordered the *Corona* to set a course for Antares. Do you concur?"

"Antares?" he asked. Kershaw studied Yamane closely. "If the commander has given an order, then there is no discussion. Antares is our destination."

"Make your course one-seven-seven," Yamane replied without hesitation.

"Setting course, Commander."

Yamane assumed his place in the command chair again, faintly aware of each pair of eyes scrutinizing his every movement. Only then did he realize just how much his heart was still pounding. He had won, but his victory had been a hollow one at best. His feelings were confirmed when the main screen showed the Deravans positioned over the planet like a noose slowly choking the life out of its victim. He could only imagine what they would do next. Such a thought horrified him. Yamane turned away. The realization that he was taking the biggest chance of his life hit him hard. He knew their very survival rested on this decision. The one question going round and round in his head was, Why would a race we defeated in a war ten years before come to our aid? The irony could not have been more poetic. The Antarens had no reason to help, but they were the only hope humanity had left.

CHAPTER
II

S.F.S. CORONA
0854 PROXIMA MERIDIAN TIME, AUGUST 18, 2217

Yamane opened his eyes. He was lying on his bunk. How long have I been here? He found the astro-clock by his desk. 0854. A deep yawn came out of him.

Memories of what the Deravans had done flooded into his conscious thoughts. They almost overwhelmed him. He distracted himself by checking the time again. 0855. He had been asleep for four hours.

As Yamane rubbed his tired eyes, those same feelings from before came flooding back—anger, resentment, sorrow—they were all there, as powerful as ever. The foremost question of "why?" kept bouncing around in his head, but an answer, something that might explain the reason for what the Deravans did, eluded him.

He caught sight of his uniforms hanging in the closet. They appeared distant, lifeless.

Perhaps he was the one who felt distant and lifeless. The view contrasted with dozens of stars shining through the porthole on his right. They were far more appealing than his dark gray quarters. Like so many suns long since dead, he wondered if the universe would cry for humanity if it too passed on, never to see the light of day again.

Someone knocked on his door. The rhythmic rapping sound had a familiarity to it.

"Come in."

Kershaw entered, wearing a crisp, new uniform. Rather than offer Yamane his customary greeting, he went right to the table near his bed and produced a small bottle of whiskey from under his jacket. "I thought you might need some company."

"Where did you get that?" Yamane asked, pointing at the bottle.

"The whiskey?" he smiled slyly. "Oh, I've been carrying my little friend with me for a while now. You never know when you might need something like this for a special occasion. After what we've been through, I think you and I could both use a drink." He yanked the desk drawer open. "Do you have any glasses around here?"

Yamane extended his hand towards the closet. Kershaw grabbed two small glasses near the edge of the shelf. He filled his own about a third of the way, Yamane's a little less. "Bottoms up," the lieutenant commander said, and downed his in one gulp.

Yamane picked up his whiskey and stared at it for a moment. He had never much cared for alcohol, but he also had a hard time saying no to his insistent friend. Holding the glass at eye level, he brought it to his mouth and took a sip. The amber-colored liquid warmed his tongue and throat going down. In one deft motion, he dropped his head back and downed the rest in a single gulp. He slapped the glass on his nightstand and pushed it away. Yamane felt self-conscious, as though he might have done something wrong.

"We still have a long road ahead of us," Kershaw injected into the room. "I just wish I could know how the whole thing will turn out." The commander said nothing. "I guess we finally have an answer for one of life's enduring questions."

Yamane let his head fall back against his soft, downy pillows. "And what's that?"

"The question of our right to be in space—seems as though our alien friends have thought a great deal about this."

"What do you mean?"

Kershaw wandered over to the porthole. "You have a whole galaxy filled with billions of stars, and around those stars circle billions of planets." He turned around and faced Yamane. "No one along the way asks if we should claim them as our own or not. If a planet can support life, we establish a colony. No soul-searching, no questions. We just do it."

"Yes, yes, yes," Yamane said while waving his hand. "We've talked about this before."

Kershaw ignored his dismissive tone. "The Deravans, on the other hand, approach this issue from a very different point of view. They are no doubt aware of these same planets, and yet, they travel who knows how many light-years to go after those ones with people on them. Kind of makes you wonder."

"Wonder? Wonder about what?"

"The facts. Their first ship comes from a distant part of the galaxy. They travel all this way just so they can make war against us. How many planet systems did the Deravans pass just to reach ours? Such an undertaking might appear rather pointless, unless you consider what they've done from their point of view."

Intrigued with Kershaw's hypothesis, Yamane asked, "And what is their point of view?"

"This galaxy isn't big enough for the two of us," he replied colloquially. "As soon as the Deravans become aware of us, they attack. How else can you explain their actions? For them, the purpose of expansion is not for exploration, but destruction. No provocation, no reason; just a primeval response when they become aware of another race's existence." He strode past Yamane, his hands gesturing. "What do the Deravans do when they encounter a hill they have never been to before? Answer—they go over it only when they know someone else is on the other side."

"That's quite a theory, Stan, but it does answer a lot of questions. And if you're right, the importance of our mission becomes that much more apparent."

Kershaw stopped in mid-stride. "Even if I am right, I don't think this will make much of a difference with the Antarens. In fact, they will probably be grateful for what the Deravans did."

"My feelings towards them haven't changed, but I can't let that cloud my judgment, either. Do I believe they could use what happened to their advantage? Yes. Do I think they will? I'm not certain." Yamane picked up his empty glass and stared at it. "Though I suspect they might be more cooperative than you think." The last part caught Kershaw off-guard, and it registered on his face. "By the time the Antares War ended, most of their ships had been destroyed, and their industry lay in ruins. Samaarian pirates had free reign over their outer empire. In short, a power vacuum developed in that quadrant. The only way the Antarens could become self-sufficient again was through our help. But the rebuilding effort took longer than expected."

"Yeah, I know. Boo-hoo for the Antarens. You still haven't told me why they would be inclined to help us."

"After years of occupying their home world, and trillions spent helping to rebuild it, we wanted out. The Antarens also wanted us out. Both sides reached an agreement: we withdraw, but left the fleet of sub-cruisers behind to help keep the peace."

Kershaw turned and faced Yamane. "But that happened a year ago, Frank."

"Without our ships and financial backing, the Antarens could never have established self-rule again. Had we not contributed, Samaarian pirates would have swooped in and attacked those border planets for sure." His face became bright. "This might be enough of a reason for them to help us."

"Sounds reasonable to me, but they're different than us. The way they think and their sense of values are not the same as ours."

"Still," Yamane countered, "what other choice do we have?" He sat back in his chair and sighed deeply. "What other choice do I have?"

Kershaw held up his glass and stared at the last of his drink. "There are always choices."

A distance settled on Yamane. "I could be making the biggest mistake of my life." He looked away. "I don't think I can ever forgive them for what they did, but do I abandon our only hope of survival just because they took away everything from me?" He shook his head. "Maybe I'm just fooling myself."

"We all have our photos, Frank," Kershaw said as he patted his shirt pocket. "You have to stop punishing yourself for what happened to Liana. If you had been there when the raiders attacked, you probably wouldn't be alive today either. Second-guessing yourself about decisions made in the past will only lead you down a darker road. This crew needs you here and now." Kershaw leaned closer. "And for what it's worth, that braid on your shoulder means there's no debate. You issue an order. They obey."

"I appreciate that, but still, I wonder if there's something out there; something that will make everything all right again. I can almost ..."

"You know I'll back you up," Kershaw said with a certain measure of warmth in his voice, "but I am also certain there are members of the crew who feel the same way as Henthorne, and they probably possess unquestioned loyalties to him. Just be sure you don't take too many chances."

Yamane didn't like Kershaw's foreboding tone.

"There's one more thing I wanted to bring up," he added. "Two, actually. They're the reasons I came."

"Oh?"

"First, I think the crew needs a memorial service. They've been through a lot, and haven't had much time to process everything that has happened."

A dark cloud settled over Yamane. "I'm not sure that's such a good idea. I lost Liana ten years ago, but in some ways, it feels as though her death happened only yesterday." He turned away. "How can I stand before everyone and tell them that those who perished at the hands of the Deravans are in a better place now; that all this happened for some greater purpose?"

"The crew really needs this," Kershaw interrupted. "Just like a man with a broken arm, setting the bone is painful, excruciating, but that is the only way it can properly heal."

Yamane saw that all-too-familiar look of determination in Kershaw's eyes. He knew he wasn't going to win this argument. Once his friend made up his mind on something he believed in, nothing would ever change it. Rather than fight an uphill battle, he just surrendered. "What time has the service been scheduled?"

A coy smile appeared. "At 1100 hours, in the aft cargo bay."

"Good. Then we're agreed." He checked the astro-clock. "I guess I should get back to the bridge. Oh yeah, you had something else on your mind?"

"Yes," Kershaw replied, his tone marked with hesitation. "There is one more thing."

Yamane picked up his data pad lying nearby. "Anything, whatever's on your mind."

He bent closer and said in a muted voice, "Lt. Commander Henthorne.

I've been giving this a great deal of thought, and I think you should speak with him."

Yamane stiffened. His blue eyes turned cold. They pierced Kershaw with a deep, penetrating stare. "Why?" he growled. "He's lucky he's not in the brig right now."

"I understand how you feel, but he can still be a valuable asset. I've talked with some of the crew and they hold him in high regard. Evidently, he is a capable and competent officer."

Yamane folded his arms, tight. "I'm sure he is, but how can I trust him again after what he did? If you don't have complete trust in a person you're working with, the whole command structure falls apart. No. I just can't take that chance."

"Your argument works both ways. As I said before, a good portion of the crew believes he is right in wanting to go to the New Frontier. If they think you acted impulsively and removed Henthorne without considering the ramifications, it could affect their ability to trust you as their commander. Please, Frank," he pleaded. "Just hear him out."

Kershaw's point got through. Right now, the one thing he needed more than anything else was allies. The crew might think better of him if he heard the ship's former second-in-command out. "All right, Stan. I'll talk with him after the service. But don't get your hopes up too much. Just because I ask doesn't mean he'll accept."

Kershaw couldn't help but smile. "You won't regret it," he said, and then hurried out the door.

Yamane let the room's silence sink in. He stared out the porthole for a while before getting up and walking over to his closet. Hung on the bar was a new uniform. His hand brushed over his name pinned to the left chest pocket. Yamane had a sense this might be a new starting point for him...one that might ensure humanity would be around tomorrow. He paused and thought about the meaning of the word "tomorrow". What did tomorrow hold? No one really knew the answer to that most important of questions.

Poetic notes from the bugler brought tears to many in attendance. The crew stood at attention before thirty-two caskets in the center of the cargo bay, each with the flag of his or her home country draped on top. On either side, six pairs of columns rose up from the floor. A candle crowned each one, burning brightly in the subdued light. A faint smell of scented wax hung in the air.

Standing further back, apart from the others, a darkened figure waited. When the music stopped, he cleared his voice and then spoke. "As we gaze upon the caskets of our fallen comrades," Yamane declared, his voice strong, "we cannot help but think of so many others who also died: those lost on Earth, Kalmedia, the crews of the *Arima*, the *Lexington*, the *Montreal*, the *Orion*, the *Kennedy*, and the *Gemini*...they all gave their lives in the performance of their duty." He looked up from his speech and scanned the cargo bay. "As I ponder their sacrifice, I wonder why they had to die. These young men and women willingly gave their lives, and their loss has left a hole in our hearts no one can fill. But we must also remember we still have a duty to perform. Their deaths must not be in vain. The enemy is still in our midst and duty demands we must stop him, no matter the cost. This is the task they strove for...and it summons us as well. And in their memories do we pledge ourselves to this goal."

Yamane turned towards Kershaw and offered him a salute. He then spun around and saluted the honor guard waiting in front of him. They snapped to attention. Holding the Star Force flag at a forty-five degree angle, the middle guardsman brought it straight up in one, singular action.

"As we commit these men and women to space, I would like to conclude this service by reading the twenty-third Psalm." Yamane pulled out a small Bible from his jacket pocket and flipped it open to where he had placed a bookmark. He looked down at the words and took them in. He thought about Liana, and the special meaning these verses held for her.

"The Lord is my shepherd, I shall not want," he began after clearing his throat. "He makes me lie down in green pastures; He leads me beside quiet waters. He restores my soul; He guides me in the paths of righteousness for His name's sake. Even though I walk through the valley of the shadow of death, I fear no evil; for Thou art with me; Thy rod and Thy staff they comfort me. Thou dost prepare a table before me in the presence of my enemies; Thou hast anointed my head with oil; My cup overflows. Surely goodness and loving kindness will follow me all the days of my life, and I will dwell in the house of the Lord forever."

Two soldiers, one on either side of the flag bearer, held up their guns, took aim, and fired. A second detachment picked up the first casket and placed it in the airlock. Two more shots sounded in the cargo bay. The detachment moved on to the next casket, until they sent every fallen comrade into the vast unknown of space. A lone bugler, opposite them, played taps. When the first honor guards resumed their place in front of the podium, the bugler stopped, and then placed his instrument at his side.

"Attention!" Yamane yelled, his words resonating off the walls and ceiling. The crew in attendance thrust their arms to their sides the same instant their boots came together.

"Thank you all for coming. You are dismissed."

When members of the crew began to talk with one another and offer their condolences, Yamane took this opportunity to slip out the back of the bay unnoticed. He reappeared on the bridge and went right for the command chair. A faint flicker of amber light flashed in the corner of his eye. Yamane didn't have to look up. He knew exactly what it was. Antares. For him, the red giant had become a personal lifeline, a visible metaphor that represented a chance for survival. And while having the Antaren sun displayed on the screen played no part in their ability to navigate, he wanted it there anyway just so he, and everyone else on the bridge, knew exactly where they were heading.

"Holding at course one-seven-seven," the nav-tech reported. "Speed, 1.01 stellar velocity."

"How long before we reach our destination?"

"Ten days minus two hours, Commander."

"Very good, Ensign. Very good."

Yamane found two guards posted at Henthorne's door when he arrived on E deck. They were standing at attention, their backs against the wall. Another guard stood at a cross-junction further down. Between officiating the memorial service and talking to a mutineer, who wouldn't need a short break?

"Has the prisoner given you any trouble?" he asked, secretly hoping there had been some problems. His decision, then, would be quite easy.

"No, Commander. Not a word."

The answer disappointed him, but rather than reveal his reaction, he tugged on his uniform. I guess I can't put this off any longer. "Open the door."

A guard reached over and pressed the control panel. The door clicked and then slid open. He drew in a deep breath and stepped inside. The door slid shut behind him.

Yamane found Henthorne lying on his bunk, reading a book. He didn't react. His obstinate behavior didn't surprise Yamane in the least. Rather than reveal his intentions too soon, he took in his quarters. A quick examination of them might give him a small insight into his former second-in-command's head. They were devoid of warmth and personality. He saw two citations mounted on the wall above his desk—that was it—no family pictures, nothing that suggested outside interests, or even a personal memento. If Henthorne himself hadn't been in the room, there would be little evidence to suggest anyone actually lived there.

Yamane picked up the only chair in the room and placed it near the end of his bed. Henthorne continued to read his book. "I think there is a matter or two which require clearing up," he opened, offering him an olive branch. This must have been what Henthorne wanted to hear. He placed his book on top of his lap. Several dozen fanned pages fell back on themselves. He crossed his arms and waited in silence. "I don't have to tell you what lies ahead for us. Every crewmember on this ship has an important role, and I need to know I can trust them, without hesitation."

There was a palpable silence between the two.

"I've been giving this a lot of thought, Commander," Henthorne finally replied with a particular forcefulness in his voice. "I'm just as aware of what we're up against, but I also believe we have other options. But that does not mean I'm not a loyal officer."

"I agree," Yamane interrupted. "I've gone over your record. You have already earned advanced degrees in astrophysics and nuclear metallurgy. Your file also shows you to be a capable officer, though there have been some incidents regarding authority issues. You have a streak of independence in you that runs pretty deep. Maybe that's why we clash, because we're alike in too many ways."

Henthorne bristled at the remark. "When I believe a mistake has been made, I say something. It gets me into trouble on occasion, but I stand by my record."

Yamane tipped his head. "I'm prepared to give you a second chance, if you're interested. I may have a job which would be suited to your talents."

The former second-in-command cocked his head over. Both eyes narrowed. "Why are you doing this?" he probed. "I haven't exactly shown myself as being trustworthy. You said so yourself. Trust is what you need from the crew, above all else."

Yamane's defenses went up. Something about him showed he could not be trusted: a word here, a micro-expression on his face, or the cadence of his voice. All unimportant when observed independently of each other, but put them all together, and there were suspicions about what motives existed under his skin. "Though I may not like you," Yamane replied candidly, "I still respect you, and I know what you can do." He bent closer. "And right now, I need all the help I can get."

A steely coldness covered Henthorne's face. "What is it you want from me?"

Yamane scooted his chair closer, hinting at a smirk. "Even if the Antarens give me every ship in their fleet, I fear this will still not be enough. You've seen the results when we tried to use brute force against the Deravans. I need someone who can analyze the data we've collected so a weakness can be found; something I can use that will give us a real advantage." Yamane took out a data pad from his jacket pocket and handed it to Henthorne. "What do you say? I can't think of a better man for the job."

He activated the semitronic device and took a superficial look at the first couple of pages. His eyes moved back and forth as he mouthed the words. Henthorne then looked at Yamane. "I'll need access to the ship's computers."

"Agreed. What I've given you should get you started, but there's still a lot of data to go through. You can use Operations. All of the analytical systems will be at your disposal." He rose from his chair. "I think that should just about cover everything." Yamane had spoken his piece and gotten the answers he wanted, save one. "I just have to know one more thing." He paused for a second and then asked, "Can I trust you?"

Their eyes met. "I swore an oath to serve this crew without hesitation. As long as I have breath in my body, I will do all I can to ensure our survival."

"If you had said anything less, then this conversation would never have officially happened." He turned and left the room.

Henthorne waited for the door to close before putting his book on top of his nightstand. Amidst the sounds of metal coils rubbing against each other, he pushed himself off his bed and put the chair back into its proper place. A sense of orderliness pulsated around him. He took a step back and took in his quarters. Henthorne saw a future of possibilities, and these possibilities centered on himself; a fact reinforced in his mind when he saw himself in the mirror bolted to the wall opposite him. His uniform looked crisp, clean, denoted a certain air of authority. He had never felt more ready to show the crew just what he could do.

With a click and a swish, the door slid open. Henthorne strode out of his room and into the hallway. Those two guards posted by his door were gone. With a quick turn to the left, wearing an expression of personal satisfaction, he became aware of how the outcomes of two days could be so different from each other. Interesting, he thought, before stepping into the lift.

CHAPTER 12

If you hear that a mountain has moved, believe; but if you hear that a man has changed his character, believe it not.
  -Islamic Proverb

S.F.S. CORONA
0117 PROXIMA MERIDIAN TIME, AUGUST 20, 2217

The initial stages of grief had passed. Yamane didn't think it possible in so short a time, but a certain shift for the better had taken place. Crew-members talked about things other than the losses they had suffered, and he even heard a joke now and again. One might even say the crew had taken a collective stand, announcing to the Deravans, "We are no more a defeated people than the *Corona* is a defeated ship."

He took advantage of this opportunity and tried familiarizing himself with his fellow bridge officers. Most were generally cordial, while a few others remained guarded. Yamane understood their reaction. He had been in command for less than a week, and they hadn't quite accepted him as one of their own just yet, with one exception: c-tech Landis. The difference could not have been more profound. He seemed eager to get to know his new commander. In time, others might feel the same way; at least Yamane hoped they would. Only then, he believed, could a crew truly form into a cohesive unit.

A signal came through on the intercom. "Commander Yamane, this is Henthorne in Operations. Can you please come down here? I found something I think you should see."

"I'm on my way," he replied.

Yamane strode into the operations room.

Henthorne leaned on a table between two rows of analytical computers, his attention fixated on a pair of displays. A technician stood behind him. There were two other techs on his right, studying several streams of data scrolling down a different set of monitors. One of them made a notation into his data pad, while his counterpart compared the results to other computations, presumably made earlier that day.

Yamane walked past other consoles and computer stations. The sounds of clicks and beeps filled the air. He stopped and watched a pair of linked terminals with great interest. Multiple equations flashed across the screens for a second or two, followed by a series of graphs and mathematical formulas. They then fed the results into the next console in line.

"There it is again," Henthorne said to the technician on his right. "Those distances coming in and going out are different, but the ratio is the same every time. I think this pretty much confirms my hypothesis. Rerun the program one more time just so we know these numbers are right."

Yamane approached Henthorne. "All right, what have you got?"

"I'll be with you in a moment, Commander," he said while resetting a display. "I want to show you something very interesting."

Yamane moved even closer, getting within a meter or so. He thought being this close to Henthorne might make him feel uncomfortable. In fact, he experienced just the opposite. No anger, no wariness—nothing.

"If you watch from here, I'll go through what I've found so far." After pressing a series of buttons, Henthorne continued. "When your squadron came into contact with the first Deravan vessel, you encountered a force that played havoc with your ships. When our fighters attacked the Deravan fleet, they experienced the exact same thing, but at a much greater distance. The question is, why?" He flipped one last switch. "Log entries made on your return trip to Titan suggest the two most likely causes for this phenomenon are either a dampening field or a weapon. Since this was the logical starting point, I based my analysis on these same suppositions. The results, however, clearly refute your hypothesis. I knew then there had to be a third option. This forced me to start again from scratch. I went through every piece of data, until I found the key. Cross-referencing telemetry from your fighter, and then comparing it to enemy fleet readings, the numbers took me in a whole new direction. Watch the monitor and you'll see for yourself."

Six Deravan ships came into view out of the darkness, approached the screen head-on, and then passed underneath, out of sight. The images froze at that point.

"Now I want you to watch the tape again, but this time, compare those ships' movements with this data stream at the bottom of this display." The images on the screen rewound and started over again. "Notice how peripheral energy readings go up when the fighters approach, and then drop off once they are enveloped by the effect. When you compare these results with your encounter, the range is different, but the ratios are identical. My analysis indicates the source of this effect is simple electro-magnetic energy."

Yamane pondered the significance of his findings.

"This is hardly what you would use for a dampening field or a weapon," Henthorne continued. "There had to be another reason. Then I hit upon the idea of studying the data from an individual fighter rather than the squadron as a whole." He typed a new series of commands into a keypad. "This is telemetry from a ship just before it was destroyed by enemy fire. See the electro-magnetic indicators here, how they change when the fighter passes over? Now watch the readouts when all of the Deravans fire their weapons. The field almost drops to zero, before rising again. There could only be one reason for this. Electro-magnetism is not a by-product of their power source, it is their power source."

Yamane shot a look at Henthorne. "Are you certain of this?"

"No doubt about it. A computer run I made a couple of minutes ago verified my findings."

"Where does this leave us, then?"

"In a very good place," he assured him. "My research also suggests that the reason Deravan shields can deflect our pulse cannons so easily is because the field each ship generates overlaps with every other one in their fleet."

Yamane stood upright again and placed his hands behind his back. "This explains a lot," he reasoned. "Now I understand why they would regroup first before re-initiating an attack. If their ships are too far apart, they become vulnerable."

"If my analysis is correct, and I believe it is, then this is their Achilles heel."

The little wheels in Yamane's head began to turn. "How can we take advantage of this weakness? I mean, is there a way to counteract the electro-magnetic field?"

"The principle is quite simple, really. You just set up an opposite field. This has the effect of neutralizing their power outputs. A positive plus a negative equals zero."

Yamane bit his lip and nodded in a knowing way. Then his look of satisfaction gave way to one more serious in nature. "But can it be this easy? The Deravans seem so powerful, almost unstoppable. Now all we have to do is cancel out the magnetic field of each ship and they become vulnerable. It's almost beyond belief."

Henthorne switched off the display. "What I've shown you is the easy part." He went over to another console and placed his hand on top. "Implementing the plan is the hard part. I don't know if we can generate a counteracting field big enough to affect a fleet that size."

"Well, this at least gives us a starting point."

Henthorne yawned deeply. "Perhaps, but I still have a lot of work ahead of me: calculations, tests, analysis, field strengths, power output readings—the list goes on."

"I think you need some sleep," Yamane suggested. "You look like you're going to drop."

"Maybe you're right." He tried to suppress a second yawn. Without success.

"Report to my ready room at 0900 hours. I think we'll both be thinking with clearer heads after getting some rest. We can go through your analysis then." Just as Yamane headed for the door, he stopped and turned back. "Looks like I put the right man on the job."

Henthorne became still. "That, I already knew."

S.F.S. CORONA
0907 PROXIMA MERIDIAN TIME, AUGUST 20, 2217

Yamane could see Kershaw's frustration level grow by the minute. For most people, the telltale signs usually fell into one of three categories: frequent sighs, a preoccupation with the time, or fidgeting with a small object. In Kershaw's case, number two had been the manifestation of choice. For the past five minutes, he had been circling the oblong table non-stop, his attention never wandering too far from the astro-clock.

Henthorne finally arrived. His demeanor indicated he knew he was late, but his slow, casual manner also suggested a casual indifference about delaying the meeting.

"Glad you could make it," Kershaw said, sarcasm dripping off every word.

"I'm sorry about being late, but a last-minute problem came up."

Yamane suspected he wasn't really sorry, but the issue paled in comparison to the purpose of their meeting. He let the matter go and moved on. "Well then, let's get down to business," he said. Both Kershaw and Henthorne joined him at the table. They sat opposite each other, almost like a showdown. "Our job is a simple one, gentlemen—find a way to defeat the Deravans."

Kershaw picked up his data pad and activated it. "I've gone over your results, and they suggest we only need produce an opposite magnetic field... as simple as that sounds."

"Such a field must have a diameter of at least ninety thousand kilometers," Henthorne said. "The problem, however, lies in finding a generator capable of creating one of this magnitude."

Kershaw sat back in his chair. "Only the Antarens would have the kind of resources we require. If they have enough power cells, we just might generate a field this big."

"I've gone over this particular scenario," Henthorne replied as he shuffled through his notes. He found the needed page and read the bottom paragraph. "Based on power outputs for each cell, we will require two hundred and thirty-two of them. But this is a moot point until we deal with the issue of a conductor. No field can be generated without one."

"Maybe we can use a local generator."

"What do you mean?"

"Equip each of the Antaren ships with one of their own. Rather than produce a large field, we use a local one. You know, disrupt the Deravan ships once they're in range."

Henthorne shuffled through his notes a second time. "I've also gone over this scenario.

Deravan power outputs would only be reduced by thirty-one percent, not enough to make a significant difference."

Yamane leaned back in his chair and stared at the ceiling. The dark gray color stood in stark contrast with the three light fixtures suspended above. "There must be a way."

"The only thing big enough would be a stellar cruiser," Kershaw said, thinking out loud.

The pall over Yamane's mind lifted in an instant. "How about the *Corona*?" he suggested.

"Our systems couldn't handle the increased power flow," Henthorne concluded after he made some computations on his data pad. "They would burn out in a matter of minutes." He sat back and rubbed his chin. "But if you use a ship lost in the battle, this particular problem goes away."

"It would have to be a fairly intact one. Perhaps—"

"I can't believe you would suggest such a thing!" Kershaw exploded without any warning. "They are filled with men and women who gave their lives trying to stop the Deravans. You can't just brush the dead aside simply because it's convenient!" Kershaw held up his data pad and pointed at it. "How can the sacrifice they made be honored when their ships become nothing more than raw materials for Henthorne's science project? Those vessels should be treated as memorials, not piles of scrap metal."

"I've seen officers like you come and go." Henthorne chided in an equally hostile tone, the muscles at the base of his jaw flexing in and out. "This is a life-or-death situation. We don't have the luxury of clinging to some archaic set of values when our survival is at stake."

Yamane leapt to his feet. "Calm down, the two of you," he said in a raised voice. "We don't have time for this pointless bickering. Lt. Commander Henthorne is right. The stakes are too high for us to rule out an option that might offer us a possible solution."

Kershaw sat back in his chair, visibly disgusted.

Yamane regained his composure after glaring both men back into submission. "Now, I think if we take a systematic approach, a suitable candidate could be found."

An hour later, however, they were no closer to a decision than when they started.

"What does this leave us with?" Yamane sighed. Except for the occasional tapping of his fingers, silence filled the room. He stared at them expectantly. Henthorne and Kershaw stared back. Doubts started to creep into his subconscious. "If we don't find a ship, then—"

"The ship you want is the *Lexington*," Kershaw replied almost in a whisper.

"What?" Yamane asked.

"I said, the ship you want is the *Lexington*," he repeated, his voice louder.

Henthorne's eyebrows went up. "But she was destroyed."

"I thought so too, at first. A massive explosion made it appear that the Deravans destroyed her. But when the blast faded, I saw the *Lexington*, still intact. Though a good portion of the aft section had been blasted away, the hull appeared relatively undamaged."

Yamane looked at Kershaw with a deep, penetrating stare; the kind a father presents when his son has let him down. "Why didn't you say anything about this before?"

Kershaw fidgeted with his data pad, careful to avoid eye contact. "I let my personal feelings get in the way. That's why I held back about the *Lexington*—but you now have what you want."

"If the *Lexington* is the ship we will use," Henthorne interrupted, "I'll need time to work out the calculations. Operations should have the data I need." He paused for a moment and then added, "Unless there is anything else?"

"Let me know when you have the results," Yamane replied. Henthorne grabbed his data pad and hurried out of the room. The door slid shut after him. "I sometimes wonder about him," he said in whispered tones. Yamane turned to Kershaw. "Are you going to be all right?"

"Yeah...sure, no problem."

He saw right through the lie.

"That one doesn't work, either," Henthorne said under his breath, frustrated. He tried another set of calculations, but they too came up the same—negative. He threw the measurement converter down in a flash of anger. The semitronic device exploded into hundreds of tiny pieces. "What's the point?"

He stood straight up and stretched. After five hours of work in front of a computer console without so much as a break, his neck and back were just about at the point of collapse. "Maybe I should just turn in and get a fresh start in the morning," he yawned. An array of analyzers caught his eye. His mood turned. "The crew needs me," he said to himself, after a distant memory filtered in from his subconscious. As a child, he had regularly fantasized about the future of humanity in peril, and that he was the only one who could save it. All these years later, here he was, doing just that. Gratification was not a strong enough word. Destiny. Yes, that was a much better one.

"Here are the latest simulations," the technician said when he returned to Operations.

Henthorne scanned through the information. "That's a twelve percent efficiency increase, but I know we can do better. Have the program vary power flows along the main connecting points. This might get us a higher energy output from the cells." He handed the data pad back to him.

The tech slipped the small semitronic device into his pocket. "Even if we do find a way of making this work," he replied, "I don't understand why we would want to go up against the Deravans in the first place. They'll make mincemeat out of the Antarens' ships. I don't know if this suggestion has been made, but has anyone thought about going to the New Frontier?"

Henthorne smiled at the question. "If we returned with only their fleet, you'd be right. But don't forget the sub-cruisers. They'll also be joining our little party."

The technician froze. "Sub-cruisers?" he frowned. "There are no sub-cruisers at Antara."

"Well, maybe not at Antara," Henthorne corrected himself, "but certainly in different parts of the Empire. You know, they were left behind when the occupation ended last year."

"I'm sorry, sir, but you are mistaken. Star Force Command issued new orders a couple of days before we pulled out. Fearing they might be used against us in another war, those ships were reassigned to the Cygnus Base Station."

"Are you sure about this?" Henthorne asked.

"I was on the *Adler* when we withdrew."

Henthorne stared at the console below him. Numbers came and went, but what had once been the essence of his existence, the very thing that had renewed his sense of importance, became meaningless. If the sub-cruisers weren't there, then what was the point? A new realization, even more terrible than the first, invaded his mind. Yamane had lied to him. A deep-seated hatred filled every corpuscle, every fiber of his being. "How could any man do such a thing?" Henthorne snarled. Placing his hands on the table, he eyed various papers and data pads scattered about in front of him. In a fit of rage, he swept them off into oblivion. A dozen data pads bounced off the deck before smashing into the far wall, while a far greater number of technical papers fluttered into the air.

"His concern isn't for us," Henthorne chided while facing the technician, "it's for whatever form of manipulation he could use so we would support him; even if it means sacrificing us along the way." His breathing deepened. "I don't think there's a deeper form of treachery than what he's done to us... and I can't let it go unchallenged."

"Let's say you're right. What can you do about it?"

"Something I should have done before," Henthorne threatened and then stormed out of the room with the most profound feeling of purpose and resolve he had ever known.

Yamane studied the crew from the command chair. He felt they were finally becoming his crew, and he their commander. They had been more personable overall, opening up and talking about people and places from their past during lulls in the shift. This helped him feel more relaxed. And when he relaxed, they relaxed. He couldn't put his finger on a reason for what started the change, but if change was coming, then he gladly embraced it with both arms.

Henthorne bolted onto the bridge in a fury. He spotted Yamane in the command chair, and headed right for him. With a grab and a twist, he spun it around with a sudden, unexpected jerk. Caught off-guard, the action threw Yamane into the armrest.

"Lt. Commander Henthorne, you don't come aboard my bridge in this manner," he objected. "I'll have you removed if you don't explain yourself."

"I just found out there are no sub-cruisers on Antara," he accused. All eyes on the bridge turned towards the pair in unison, stunned by the sudden outburst. "You knew about this, but lied to us anyway."

Yamane's defenses went up. "What are you talking about? You're not making any sense."

"Am I? The sub-cruisers supposedly waiting for us at Antara aren't there. They never have been," he sneered. "You probably figured no one would find out until we got there."

"Is that true, Commander?" the nav-tech asked.

Yamane looked around the bridge. Troubled expressions met him back. Doubts were beginning to fill their minds, and it registered on their faces. "I don't know what Lt. Commander Henthorne has been told, but I assure you, the sub-cruisers are at Antara. I wouldn't lie about something like this."

Henthorne offered three sarcastic claps. "That was beautiful, Commander, but your deception won't work this time." He leaned over and opened the intercom. "Ensign Ivanov, report to the bridge at once." Henthorne issued the order before Yamane could stop him.

"This is Ensign Ivanov. I'm on my way."

"Now we'll all know the truth, Commander."

Yamane's first impulse was to have Henthorne thrown into the brig for insubordination, but decided against it. Suspicions were already floating in the air. If he did anything even remotely construed as being an abuse of his authority, outright rebellion might result. No. If he had any chance of restoring the crew's faith, he would have to face this crisis head-on.

Ivanov rushed onto the bridge, winded. He went right up to Yamane, snapped to attention and saluted. "Ensign Ivanov, reporting as ordered, sir."

"Tell the Commander what you told me," Henthorne demanded.

He looked them both over first before responding. "I told Lt. Commander Henthorne that I was stationed aboard the *Adler* during the occupation of Antara. As you know, all seven sub-cruisers were supposed to remain behind when we withdrew. But at the last minute, there was a change of plans. Instead, they were ordered to the Cygnus Base Station. Halfway during the trip, I took a shuttle to Earth so I could visit my sick father. It's my understanding that demolition teams were waiting to dismantle the sub-cruisers upon their arrival. So there is no possible way they can be at Antara."

Yamane heard murmurs and whispering all around him. He realized the loyalty offered by his crew had begun to waver. "I tell you the truth, I wasn't aware of this. Like you, I believed those ships were at Antara."

"But they're not. There's nothing for us there." Henthorne faced the crew. "I am asking you once more. Will you turn this ship around and head for the New Frontier?"

"But don't you understand," Yamane pleaded, "that will only delay the inevitable. How much time will pass before the Deravans find us? A week? A year? They will stop at nothing until we are wiped out. Our only chance is with the Antarens' help."

"And they'll fight with what? Their pitiful fleet of dreadnoughts was obsolete ten years ago. They cannot stop the Deravans, assuming they help us at all. What you're asking us to do is madness."

Yamane felt as if he were standing on the edge of a precipice. Across from him yawned a tremendous gulf. And on the other side stood the crew. A deadly mixture of fear and betrayal registered in their eyes, their support visibly slipping away.

"Time's up, Commander. What is your decision?"

Yamane crossed his arms. "As long as I am in command of this ship, we are going to Antares."

"Sir, I'm afraid I must agree with Lt. Commander Henthorne," the navtech offered. "The New Frontier is our only chance." Several other officers nodded in agreement.

"Take a good look around the bridge, sir," Henthorne crowed. "This crew will no longer back a plan that will only get us killed." Yamane rose to his feet and gave him the harshest stare he could conjure up. It didn't work. "What do you say? We can do this the easy way or the hard way."

Feeling the crew visibly slip away, Yamane suddenly lunged forward and grabbed Henthorne by the collar. "I can't let you get away with this."

Caught off guard, Henthorne fell back against the rail. They wrestled back and forth, grunting as they did, until Yamane gained the advantage. Henthorne tumbled onto the deck and struck his head against a relay access panel. The blow to the base of his skull dazed him for a second. He shook off its effects and picked himself up again.

Both men squared off against each other, breathing heavily, searching for a weakness. Yamane made a feint to his right and then lunged towards his left. Just as he reached the command chair, Henthorne pulled him away before he could open the intercom. The commander fell onto the deck, hard.

He was about to jump on him again when Landis cold-cocked Henthorne in the jaw. He likewise fell onto the deck.

Two crewmen grabbed Yamane from behind. He tried to pull away, but they were too strong. Henthorne came to his feet, blood dribbling down his chin. He wiped his mouth off and smiled. Landis took another swing at Henthorne, but missed. The r-tech came up from behind and hit him in the head with a casing box from the binary coupling unit. He slumped in the chair before rolling onto the deck, unconscious. Yamane made a move toward Henthorne, but the two officers holding him in place rebuffed his efforts.

"Now there's no one who will come to your aid," Henthorne crowed, triumphant.

"You don't know what you're doing. Heading to the New Frontier will only seal our fate."

Henthorne sauntered over to Yamane and stood over his vanquished foe. "I've had to serve under incompetent men like you for years, and resented it. On the outside I said, 'Yes, sir, please and thank you,' but on the inside, I bided my time, waiting for my opportunity." Henthorne looked around the bridge. "I'd say my patience has finally paid off. And while this isn't exactly the way I envisioned taking command, the *Corona* is now mine."

"What are your orders, sir?" The nav-tech asked.

Yamane stopped resisting when he heard the question. A sudden realization hit him hard—the crew had mutinied against him. It felt as though someone had reached in and torn his heart right out of his chest.

"Take the two of them to the brig."

Three crewmembers went over to Landis. Blood was running down the side of his face. When they jerked him to his feet, he started to regain consciousness. Yamane felt a small measure of relief. Just before the small cadre reached the corridor, he looked back. There, in the command chair, in his chair, sat Henthorne. Yamane had never felt more powerless in his life.

CHAPTER

13

Two members of security brought Yamane and Landis to the brig and shoved them into a cell. As soon as they stumbled inside, one of the guards activated the security screen. Bright yellow lights on both sides of the opening came on, followed by a sustained buzzing sound. With the prisoners secured, both crewmembers left without a word, presumably to report back to the bridge.

Yamane stared at his Spartan surroundings. His mind was still reeling from the unforeseen circumstances that had led to his downfall. He could not understand how the crew could switch their loyalties so easily. Experiencing fear was one thing, but giving in to it, especially when it might very well result in the complete annihilation of the human race, was quite another. A blind man could see it. Yamane caught himself. He also couldn't afford to let his emotions get the better of him. The only way of getting out of this mess would be to keep his head on straight.

Resigned to his fate, at least for the short term, he studied the confines of his imprisonment. There were two sets of bunk beds, each one atop the other, a sink, a toilet and some towels—just enough to keep a person comfortable, but not much more.

Landis started to regain consciousness again. He tried to get to his feet but didn't have the strength. Yamane bent down and helped him over to the sink. He opened the tap just a bit. Channeling some water over Landis' head, the placid flow going down the side of his face washed out the gash. He grabbed a towel lying nearby and pressed it against the wound to stop the bleeding. This seemed to do the trick, at least for the moment. But what Landis really needed was a doctor. Yamane studied his surroundings. What they needed was something that would shift the advantage back in his favor. Until that happened, they probably wouldn't see the inside of a med-lab anytime soon.

"Thank you...Commander," Landis struggled. "I'm feeling a little better."

Yamane patted Landis on the shoulder and helped him onto a bunk. "I should be the one thanking you for what you did up there. It's nice to know I have at least one ally."

Landis did not respond at first. "I'm not sure that I am," he finally said. Yamane felt more than a little puzzled by his answer. "Like Lt. Commander Henthorne," he continued, "I also believe we have a much better chance of survival at the New Frontier."

He wasn't making any sense. Maybe the blow hit him harder than I thought. "I don't understand. You could have been killed for defending me, and yet, you agree with Henthorne?"

"I backed you up for the sake of the crew." Landis stopped and readjusted the bloodstained towel. "I've been having my doubts about him over the last couple of months. I can't say I know the reason, but he's been acting less and less like himself."

"In what way?"

"When I came on board fourteen months ago, I realized pretty quickly that Henthorne was a man who wears his emotions close to the surface. Recently, however, his behavior began to intensify. For instance, when a crewmember didn't answer a question fast enough, he'd really let him have it. Over time, his outbursts worsened. At first I disregarded his little tantrums; people have a bad day now and again, but the flare-ups kept happening over the smallest infractions." Landis winched in pain. He stopped, drew in a couple of short breaths, and then continued. "I asked some of the bridge crew if they noticed any of this, but they didn't think getting involved was such a good idea. The final blow for me came when Commander Harris died. Henthorne stepped in as though nothing had happened. In fact, he even looked pleased. At that moment, I knew something was wrong with him, but I had no way to prove my suspicions. Now I guess it's too late."

Loud grunts and scuffling noises coming from down the corridor interrupted Landis. A couple of loud thumps against the wall suggested the guards were bringing someone against his will.

"Are you crazy?" a voice yelled in the distance. "What's going on around here?"

The same two crewmen as before came from around the corner, pulling and tussling with someone Yamane couldn't see. When both of them brought up their immobilizers, Kershaw suddenly appeared. He held up both hands and grinned. "Move!" one of the guards ordered.

Forcing him over to the cell, the second guard pushed him inside. Kershaw spun around and rushed at the opening. The screen held firm, pushing him back. He was about to try again when Yamane grabbed him from behind. He relented only after his 'escorts' left.

Kershaw spun around. "What's happening, Frank? Has everyone lost their mind?"

Yamane shook his head. "I wish I had an answer for you."

"Who's in command? Why have we been brought here?"

The question was a simple one, but with a complicated answer. Yamane sat back on his bunk. "Lt. Commander Henthorne and most of the bridge crew have mutinied against us."

"Stupid fools—why would they mutiny?" he asked, pacing back and forth like a caged animal.

Rather than sugarcoat the truth, Yamane figured it was best to tell it to him straight. "Because there are no sub-cruisers at Antares."

Kershaw stopped dead in his tracks. "What? What are you talking about?"

"Star Force Command didn't think the Antarens could be trusted and so they changed their minds about the ships."

"How come we never heard about this?" he growled

"I don't know. Doesn't matter now. But what does matter is that we get out of here. Henthorne plans on taking the *Corona* to the New Frontier."

Kershaw turned and faced the cell opening. "I guess that's why he decided to get me out of the way," he hypothesized. "He knew I would never go along with this, no matter what I promised. I could easily sabotage the engines before anyone knew what happened."

"What about other crewmembers? Do you believe any of them could get us out of here?"

Kershaw shook his head. "I don't even think they know what's going on yet. Henthorne is probably putting his people in charge of the vital areas of the ship before announcing what's taken place. Then, no one will be in a position to challenge his authority once this coup is over."

Yamane felt even more imprisoned than before. "I was afraid you'd say something like that."

Henthorne thought he should have experienced at least a little pang of guilt for the way he assumed control of the *Corona*. He didn't. Rather, he saw the inevitability of taking command as his just due. In fact, an intense feeling of satisfaction filled his heart. Could the *Corona* actually be his ship? Was this a dream? Placing his arms on the sides of the command chair, the reality of his new status sunk in. He had wondered over the years what being in command would actually feel like. The experience even surpassed his expectations.

"Sir, I'm receiving a message from the weapons batteries," the new c-tech said. He looked young, no more than twenty-two. "They have been secured."

"Were there any problems?"

"No, sir. The gunners offered no resistance."

"This means the ship is truly mine," Henthorne whispered to himself.

He couldn't help but smile at his sudden turn of fortune. Now, just one last act and his position would be all but secured. There were certain dangers involved, to be sure, but fear could be just the means to garner unquestioned loyalty from the crew. And if he could not elicit loyalty, then he would settle for fear. "Plot a course for the New Frontier," he said to the nav-tech, "Increase speed to 1.20 stellar velocity."

Turning back, the navigator asked, "1.20, sir?"

"You heard me, Lieutenant—1.20."

"But, sir, pushing our engines at that speed might be dangerous. After what they've been through, I don't think this would be a wise course of action."

Henthorne rose out of the command chair in a slow, but deliberate manner. Every pair of eyes followed him as he went around the navigator's station. He stood there, his back to them. The crew waited with bated breath. Then, just when they almost couldn't take the agonizing delay any longer, he spun around. His dark eyes flared out, angry, and the cold grimace he wore on his face shouted his resolve. His appearance would have intimidated anyone staring at him. This was how he wanted them to feel.

"But I think if you just—"

"I don't want any of your opinions," he shrieked. "I am the commander of this ship. You will follow my orders without question. Do you want me to make an example of you as well?"

The nav-tech reared back. "Sir, that won't be necessary, sir."

"We've already wasted enough time going in the wrong direction," he replied, rebuffing the challenge. "As your new commander, I have to set things right. Now carry out my orders!"

"Aye, sir. 1.20 stellar velocity," the nav-tech replied. "Course one-eight-nine."

Antares, positioned in the middle of the screen, shifted over and out of sight. A new star field took its place. A couple of deck plates rattled as vibrations felt throughout the ship increased in intensity.

Believing he had made his point, Henthorne returned to the command chair. Now his position was all but secure.

Yamane leaned back against the wall, scrutinizing his surroundings. "When I was assigned to the *Lexington*, I don't think I ever saw the brig. It probably looked a lot like this one."

"I guess," Kershaw huffed, "though you didn't miss much. A cell is just a cell."

"I know I sent enough crewmembers into them whenever we docked somewhere for shore leave. It never ceased to amaze me how a well-disciplined ship could get into trouble so quickly."

"When you're cooped up in a tin can like this for a couple of months, anyone would get a little stir-crazy, like a couple of cadets I know in their younger days," Kershaw said, reminiscing.

Yamane chuckled to himself. "That was a long time ago."

"Longer than I care to remember. Seems so frivolous now compared to what's going on."

Kershaw let out a deep yawn. He placed his head on his pillow and closed both eyes.

Yamane followed his lead and yawned in response. Within minutes, both men were asleep.

Yamane bolted up. "Liana," he panted, "Where are you?" He looked about, his heart racing. Bed, sink, walls—I'm still in the cell. He breathed in and out several times. It helped.

There, in the quietness of the moment, his fears and anxieties came out from their hidden places. Had he underestimated Henthorne? Could he have prevented the mutiny? And the biggest fear of all, did he make a fatal error in judgment and condemn the human race in the process? Though Yamane had learned to mask such flaws over the years, self-doubt being the most egregious, they often led to mental and psychological paralysis. Such occurrences hadn't been so bad before the war, but since Liana's death... he had begun second-guessing himself. If only he had been with her, she would not have died. Is there anyone out there who could make things right again?

He shunted such thoughts aside. The hour was late and staying up thinking about things no one could do anything about wasn't helping either. Yamane adjusted his pillow and brought his head down just so. A minute later, he was asleep again.

Henthorne rose out of the command chair and took an impromptu stroll around the bridge. He couldn't put his sentiments into words exactly, but they fell in between unqualified rightness and a moral absolute, vindicating his actions. But as much as he relished the concept of his newfound position, the reality of it had taken something of a turn. It had been pretty quiet the last couple of hours and he was bored. For him, there was another reason to check in with the crew. He believed that when a ship's senior officer stood over the shoulder of a tech or an operator from time to time, it was a subtle way of letting him know who was really in charge.

"How are things going, Ensign?" he asked the c-tech.

"Fine, sir. There is nothing new to report at this time."

"Good...good." He wandered over to the r-tech's station. His response was the same.

Without any warning, a muffled explosion sounded throughout the ship, followed by several sharp jolts. Everyone stopped what he or she was doing and looked around. Then a second, more powerful explosion rocked the *Corona*. Lights flickered on and off several times, triggering the alarms. Henthorne made a beeline for his command chair. "Ensign, what just happened?" he demanded.

"Unknown, sir," the c-tech replied. "I'm trying to determine the cause right now."

"I think we may have a problem with the engines," the nav-tech cried out. "Our speed has jumped to 1.22 stellar velocity. Correction, make that 1.23."

Henthorne spun the command chair around. "Well then, slow us down."

The nav-tech inputted several commands into his console. He paused, looked down, and then tried again. "I can't," he replied. "Controls are locked."

"Engine room, what's going on down there?" Henthorne asked after opening the intercom. No response. "Engineering. Come in."

"This is Lt. Walker," he shouted over a cacophony of noises in the background.

"What just happened?"

"I can't say just yet. We're still trying to figure it out down here. I'll report back as soon as I have anything more specific." The intercom became silent.

"The ship is now traveling at 1.24 stellar velocity."

Chaos had broken out in the engine room. Technicians and engineers were scrambling about, desperately trying to reduce the ship's velocity. They engaged overrides, implemented emergency shutdown protocols, and ran computer diagnostic programs. Nothing worked. And to make matters worse, every display indicated the primary systems were operating at normal levels—every engineer's worst nightmare.

"This doesn't make any sense," Walker grumbled. "Nothing's wrong, but we're still speeding up." Lieutenant Moreno tapped him on the shoulder and indicated she knew the source of the problem. They hurried over to the coolant station. A bad feeling began to well up within Walker.

"Take a look at these readouts," she pointed. "Coolant in and around the main reactors has stopped circulating. As a result, temperatures inside those cores are rising."

"Have you tried the overrides?"

"Yes, but they didn't work. I don't think a release valve is stuck, something else—"

"If we don't find a way of controlling those reactors, we could lose the containment fields." Walker hurried over to the next station. "Put the control rods in all the way," he said to the operator. "This should help reduce reaction levels a little, and buy us some time."

"I've already done that," he said, a look of terror on his face, "but with negligible results."

Walker struck the console with his hand. If the control rods weren't behind the unexplained acceleration, then the source of the problem was something more complicated—and complicated meant time-consuming. Judging by the rate at which the temperature in the reactor cores were rising, they would soon run out of what little remained.

"What do you think?" Walker asked Moreno.

"I think pushing the engines caused the coolant pipes to rupture," she reasoned.

Walker ran his fingers through his hair. "If that's true, then the pressure should be dropping."

Moreno glanced at the display. "There must be some kind of blockage."

"Unless we get the circulation going again, there'll be a core meltdown—and we go up like a supernova." He studied the boards. "I think we're in over our heads. I'm going up to the bridge. Maybe Lt. Commander Henthorne might have some answers."

Henthorne could not have been happier when Walker came onto the bridge. If they had been facing a real crisis, he figured the engineer never would have left his post.

"I think we have a huge problem on our hands," Walker said, worry peppering each word.

This was not the news Henthorne hoped he would hear. "All right, let's have it."

"As far as I can tell, there is a problem with the engines' coolant system; some kind of blockage. Without coolant, temperatures in the reactor cores are steadily rising. This is why the ship is accelerating." He glanced at the astro-clock. "If we don't get this under control soon, the engines will explode."

A sinking feeling settled upon Henthorne. "What do you recommend we do?"

"Someone will have to get to the rupture point and repair those damaged pipes."

Henthorne studied Walker closely. He sensed no deception in him. "Is that the score?"

"Unless we can jury-rig a bypass, I'm afraid so."

Henthorne turned and hurried over to the engineer's station. His sweaty palms slid across the smooth, angled surface of the console as he brought up a schematic of the entire ship. Decks, bulkheads and crawl spaces popped onto the screen. He then superimposed the support systems over them. With the use of a multi-directional toggle set at the base of the central display, Henthorne scanned the length of the *Corona* until the aft section appeared. He zoomed in and magnified the area.

"Those coolant pipes here go from the engine room to these outer plasma bypass cables," Walker pointed. "A break could have occurred anywhere along the way."

Henthorne studied the screen. Think...think. An idea came to him. "If we can determine which systems aren't functioning, that might give us a place to start looking."

"That shouldn't be too hard. If you run a self-diagnostic program, those systems that don't comply with the directive should be the ones damaged by both blasts."

Rather than respond, Henthorne inputted a simple compliance program into every system on the ship. In less than a second, dozens of small yellow dots started to appear on the screen.

"I'm not seeing any damage in this area," he said after a random pattern began to emerge.

"Wait a minute," Walker interrupted. "Pause the readout and focus on decks seven, eight, and nine, right above engineering." Henthorne inputted the command. "Take a look at these three indicator lights here. Notice how none of them come up. They form a straight line, from the coolant pipe to the inner hull. Those systems must have been in the path of those explosions."

Henthorne enlarged the image. "Look at all those bulkheads and machinery in the area. The only way of getting to this section is if we cut through the outer hull and work our way inside. I don't think there's any other option." He turned back. "What is our present speed?"

The nav-tech wiped the perspiration from his forehead before replying. "1.27 stellar velocity."

"Have you taken into account the possibility of experiencing bow shocks?" Henthorne asked, concerned. "There's nothing we can do for you if the ship goes through a pocket of inter-stellar gas at this speed. One incident and you're done for."

"I'm aware of that, but we really don't have much of a choice."

"I'll go with you," he offered. "I served as an engineer's assistant when I was assigned to the *Rostov*. Together, we should be able to get those repairs done before the situation gets critical."

Walker blinked a couple of times. "I appreciate that, sir, but if something goes wrong, we can't afford to lose you. Lt. Moreno will go with me. She is more than qualified for this kind of work."

An expression of acquiescence crossed Henthorne's face. "I guess I'm forced to agree with you. Good luck, you don't have much time."

Walker nodded in return and then hurried off the bridge.

Before both engineers entered the airlock, Walker rushed through the safety checklist. EVA procedures would have normally taken ten minutes, but since time was short, he just couldn't go through every step.

"Can you read me?" he said to Moreno on the radio.

She secured the toolbox to the floor before answering. "Loud and clear," she replied, her soft brown eyes showing through her helmet visor.

Walker gave a thumbs-up signal. The operator, standing in front of the control panel outside the airlock, entered a pre-sequence code and then pressed a flashing red button. A large, half-meter thick door started to come down over the opening. Walker and Moreno stood there, waiting. When all four latching mechanisms slid into an equal number of coupling receptors, a deep bang resonated within the octagonal enclosure.

"Oxygen purge in five seconds," the operator said into his headset. A low hissing sound came from every direction. Walker turned and found the atmospheric gauge on his left. The readout, which had started at one atmosphere, counted down. When the indicator reached zero, the hissing stopped.

"Check your system readouts. Do they show any malfunctions?"

Walker held up his right arm and examined the display over his wrist. "I think we're both all right."

"Stand by, I'm going to open the outer airlock."

Both of them rotated clockwise until the hatch stood directly across from them. Bright yellow lights placed at the perimeter of the doorway started to flash off and on at regular intervals. Each of them braced themselves. A second later, the outer door began to move upward. From the bottom of the opening, pinpoints of starlight appeared. The higher the door ascended, the greater the number of stars that shone through.

"This is Walker," he said on the radio, his heart pounding at the sight. "We are ready to exit the airlock." He gently pushed forward with both legs. Around the perimeter, he saw six oval-shaped rings, each one placed there so a person wouldn't float outside by mistake. Walker grabbed hold of the first one within reach and stopped his forward motion. A gentle pull brought him outside. The *Corona*'s dark gray hull went off a good hundred meters' distance. "I'm going on ahead." He activated his multi-directional thruster control unit. Two bursts later, he was gone.

"I'm right behind you," Moreno said. She bent down and released a pair of safety clamps, causing the toolbox to float upward. Allowing it to float up to her hand, she grabbed the large, oversized handle and pushed herself outside. A quick burst turned her clockwise, towards Walker. A long, slow burn later, Moreno had caught up with him.

Their helmet cameras transmitted clear pictures to the main screen. Even though the *Corona* was now traveling at 1.29 stellar velocity, the only real indication they were moving at all was the bluish tint of distant stars. Walker studied them a little more closely. He couldn't remember them being that shade before, but then again, he also couldn't remember traveling this fast before, either. If they didn't repair the damage soon, they would become a whole lot bluer.

"You should be getting close," Henthorne said on the radio. "The area ought to be about twenty meters to your right."

"Confirmed," Moreno said as she moved ahead of Walker. "I see something sticking out of the hull. This must be where both explosions took place."

Walker fired two quick bursts. He began to slow. "The surface has been punctured by three support beams," he observed after getting a closer look. "They are about one meter apart from each other. The joists are essentially straight, with jagged edges. I think we have no choice but to cut through and create an opening."

Moreno handed Walker the tool case. He flipped open the top and pulled out a laser torch strapped to the inside lid. Before igniting the unit, they both pulled down their safety visors. If either one looked at the high intensity beam without protection they would be permanently blinded in an instant.

Walker swung the torch around and set it on the hull. Moreno bent down and entered a five-digit activation code into a mini-control panel on top. Per the unit's pre-programming, a two-second scan revealed the area in question was a hair under three meters in circumference. "Let's make it three meters and call it even," she said to herself.

"What do you think, Lieutenant?" he asked. She nodded in return. "Here goes nothing."

When Walker pressed a flashing yellow ignition switch, a pair of high intensity beams cut right into the outer hull. Sparks immediately began to fly off in different directions, some bouncing off the ship, while others flew directly into space. They looked like thousands of little yellow ricocheting bullets fired in rapid succession. He reminded himself to be careful. A single, momentary contact with a spark, and...POP...your insides were out.

When the cutter completed a circle three meters wide, the internal computer system switched it off.

"We're ready to go in," Walker said into his headset.

"The ship is now traveling at 1.31 stellar velocity," came the reply in their helmet speakers.

"We need to pick up the pace." Moreno bent down and lifted the circular piece of metal. As she pushed upward with all of her might, it floated away and out of sight.

Walker got down on one knee and peered inside. A deep pit of blackness met him. He took out a mini-lamp from his waist belt and shined the light into the hole. "The damage is much more extensive than we thought," he said after surveying the long, dark cavity. "With only three beams sticking out of the hull, I figured it would be minimal. Looks like the explosion created a five-meter wide shaft." He turned his light the other way. "Maybe this is a blessing in disguise. The larger-than-expected radius might make it easier for us to get down there."

"Do you think the gravitational compensators are still functioning?"

"Judging by what I see, I doubt it. I don't think any system in this section is working at all." He came to his feet again. "I'll go first. Just remember to stay away from the edges. There are a lot of torn-up decks down there.

"Did you copy that, bridge? We're going in."

Henthorne did not respond. He just rubbed his hands together and hoped for the best.

Walker activated his maneuvering jets and disappeared inside. Trying to stay as far from the sides of the shaft as possible, he kept his eye on everything coming up from below. The damage was far worse than even he imagined. Support beams and bulkheads were twisted beyond recognition, hatches were fused into place, and power systems had been knocked offline.

"Sir, temperatures in the shaft read one hundred and ten degrees...and climbing."

Walker checked his gauge. "You're right. I didn't realize it had gotten so hot."

"Should we abort?"

"Not unless it becomes a critical issue. Our top priority is getting that coolant flowing again."

They had descended another fifteen meters when Moreno called out a second time. "I believe we're approaching the bottom."

Walker pointed his light right where Moreno indicated. A dull red glow met him at the base of the blast hole. A little further out, towards the sides, he saw a row of joists fused into the deck below. He thought it a miracle the explosion hadn't killed them all.

They stopped a meter above where the coolant pipes should have been. The damage was worse than he had expected. This meant repair would take even longer than he first thought.

"What do you think?" Henthorne asked on the radio.

Walker inspected the area. "From what I can tell, the pipes gave way at this point," he replied, "and metal fragments ripped into these plasma bypass cables. The sudden release of energy was the second explosion we felt. I'm surprised something like this didn't happen sooner, with all the *Corona* has been through."

"Temperatures down here are now one hundred and ninety-five degrees," Moreno interrupted.

A bead of sweat trickled into one of his eyes. The stinging sensation burned. "I feel like I'm being char-broiled."

"Do you think the coolant pipes can be repaired?"

"I guess we really don't have much of a choice. We're getting set up right now."

Walker took out a mini-torch and set up the device near some fused metal beams jutting out in different directions. Jagged razor blades were more like it. No one had to explain to either of them just how easily one of those sharpened edges could slice right through their suits.

Walker pulled down his safety visors and activated the torch. When he freed the first joist, Moreno moved the useless hunk of metal and pushed it out the shaft and into space. He then focused on the next one in line. "We'll stop here after another half meter," he said, "and then widen the other side." She shook her head in agreement.

The white, focused beam of energy sliced through the melted mass without much effort. Moreno tried to lift it up, but the hunk of metal didn't budge. Thinking some unseen conduit or other twisted wreckage must be keeping it place, she moved around to the front so she could get a better grip. But she didn't fare any better there, either. "Come on," she complained. Rather than fight it, Moreno crouched down on one knee and looked underneath. There, she saw three cables fused into the side. "Gotcha," she declared. "Some wires need to be cut first before I can send this off into space."

"No problem." Walker swung the cutter around. "Just give me a moment." He sliced through all three lines in a millisecond.

When Moreno finally pulled the metal mass free, her eyes widened. A stream of fluorescent green plasma poured out one of the cables. "They're still live!" she yelled, "Cut the torch! Cut the—!"

A small explosion rocked the ship...and then nothing.

"Walker!" Henthorne shouted into the intercom. "Come in." Static. "Moreno, please come in. Do you read me?"

The c-tech looked back. "They're gone, sir."

Henthorne stood upright, both fists clenched. Only then did he become aware of every pair of eyes focused in his direction. He felt exposed, naked. "Try again. They might have gotten out." Just as the c-tech lifted his hand, Henthorne countermanded himself. "Belay that order, Ensign." He fell back into the command chair, defeat settling upon him. As the ship's commanding officer, he was responsible for their deaths.

The *Corona* started to shake again. "Our speed has increased to 1.35 stellar velocity," the nav-tech cried out. "She can't take much more of this."

Henthorne needed to regain his composure, and fast. Think, he ordered himself. He looked up. The crew sat at their stations, waiting for him to make a decision. "The life pods," he whispered. No. They would run out of oxygen long before reaching a habitable planet. Think harder. Several other ideas came and went, but after several precious minutes went by, he rejected them too. This left him right where he had started: get the ship under control or die trying. "We'll have to send another team in and repair the damage," he finally said. "Have the computer scan the crews' records."

Webster pivoted his chair around. "Sir?" he asked in a thin, reedy voice.

Henthorne felt himself getting angry. "Bring up every crewmember's biographical information. I need the names of those people who have been trained in demolitions and who also have a working knowledge of the ship's engineering systems."

The e-tech nodded in reply and then accessed every personnel record on file. Amidst the sounds of clicks and whirrs, rows and rows of personal data appeared to the right of each name. After several seconds, two crewmembers topped the list. He bent over and mouthed the words in silence. The realization of who they were pushed him deep into his chair.

Henthorne grew impatient. The task was simple enough, and quick. Five seconds at the most for the computer. Instead, Webster just sat there, a look of reluctance plastered on his face. The delay was wasting time, time they didn't have. "What's taking so long?" he demanded. "Just give me the names."

The e-tech could not put off the inevitable any longer. "After making a detailed search, the computer indicates two candidates: yourself...and Commander Yamane."

It felt like a bomb had just landed in the middle of the bridge, intact. The slightest touch and the device would go off.

Henthorne's throat constricted. "Are you certain?" he wheezed.

"I made two checks. Both lists are identical."

Despite his inclination to lash out in some way, Henthorne sat back in the command chair and thought through the situation. Yamane was the last person he wanted to turn to for help, no matter how critical the situation. Then again, the fate of each crewmember was at stake. As commander of the *Corona*, his primary duty was to the safety of his ship. The word "duty" cut through his mind like a sharpened dagger. The very word forced him into a direction he found personally reprehensible; one he thought he would never go down again. Time, however, had all but run out, leaving no other option. Henthorne choked down the words first before saying them aloud: "Bring Commander Yamane to the bridge."

CHAPTER 14

S.F.S. CORONA
1121 PROXIMA MERIDIAN TIME, AUGUST 22, 2217

Yamane paced back and forth, his mind racing. He tried to think of what might have accounted for the explosions, but nothing came. He even tried to convince himself the problem had probably been a minor one, but increased vibration levels resonating within the walls and deck plates told him otherwise. He knew they were moving much faster than usual—and faster meant they were in trouble.

Quick, heavy footsteps echoed outside their cell.

Yamane stopped, his attention locked onto the corridor. Several pairs of boots approached the brig. He moved towards the opening, as did Kershaw and Landis.

Three crewmembers came around the corner and stopped in front of the opening. They all had immobilizers. "We have orders to bring Commander Yamane to the bridge," the middle crewman said, each word sounding rehearsed.

Looking them over first, Yamane spoke for all three. "What about Lt. Commander Kershaw and C-tech Landis?"

"Only you, Commander."

The direct approach didn't work. Maybe if he tried a different tact. "Can you at least tell me what's wrong with the ship?"

"That's not your concern just now," the crewman snapped back in a rigid tone.

"If you don't know what the problem is, then how do you know they aren't needed?"

"We have our orders—just the Commander." He turned and signaled the crewman standing by the control panel.

When the screen came down, Yamane took a single, cautious step out of his cell. A simple nod brought it back up again, filling the hall with that ever-present buzzing noise.

"Watch your back out there," Kershaw warned from inside the brig.

He offered a half-hearted smile and then disappeared around the corner.

When Yamane arrived on the bridge, he immediately sensed fear and panic all around him. The situation must have been much worse than he had imagined.

Henthorne was over by the engineering station, hunched over the console. He stood up and wiped several beads of sweat off his forehead, trying to present himself as being in control of the situation. Yamane saw right through the deception.

"We don't have much time," Henthorne said, his voice sounding rushed. "The coolant pipes are blocked, which means engine cores are supercritical."

This wasn't bad news—it was catastrophic. Henthorne had taken the ship and transformed it into a flying bomb. Yamane turned towards the nav-tech. "How fast are we moving?"

"1.37 stellar velocity," he replied. "Correction, our speed has now jumped to 1.38."

Henthorne cleared his throat. "Repairing those coolant pipes is the only way we can get the engines under control again. You and I are the only ones who can ..." Henthorne's words fell silent, as though he just couldn't bring himself to say the rest.

Yamane studied the man who had been so self-assured, so cocky a short while ago. Now, he appeared a former shell of himself. "Where are the damaged pipes?"

"They're located on deck three, but the only way we can get at them is through the outer hull."

We? Yamane felt like a sledgehammer just whacked him in the head. "We're going together?"

A flash of anger crossed Henthorne's face. "As unlikely as this sounds, you and I are the most qualified ones for this kind of work. I know we've been at odds with each other since we first met, but—"

"We have a job to do," Yamane said, jumping in. He looked up at the astro-clock. They didn't have time for this bickering. "The longer we talk here means the less time we have to make repairs out there."

"Fine." He turned to the c-tech. "Have the prep teams meet us at airlock five."

Four EVA techs were already waiting with space suits and tools when both men arrived. Without a word, Yamane went over to the first pair of techs and slipped on his suit. He then put his helmet on over his head. One of the techs helped guide the latching rings into place. His suit's power systems came right up. Air from the tanks immediately rushed over his body. The sensation felt good, calming. He brought up his right wrist up and checked the readouts. Several diagnostic programs verified they were operating within specified limits. He hoped they actually were. Otherwise ..."Everything looks good here."

"Mine shows the same," Henthorne said after he donned his suit.

Taking this as his cue, a tech jogged over to the control panel and opened the airlock. Yamane went first—left, right, left, right—his boots clumped. He felt like a toddler who was just learning how to walk. One wrong step and he could tip over onto the deck.

When Henthorne followed him into the airlock, a second crewman brought in a new toolbox filled with equipment needed to make the necessary repairs. He strapped it down onto the deck, and then resumed his place at the controls. When they gave the thumbs-up signal, he pressed the flashing red button on his control panel.

The airlock door began to slide down over the opening.

Henthorne turned and faced the tech in the window. "We are ready for depressurization." The tech nodded in reply and then pressed the flashing green button on the other side of his panel. Air immediately vented into space. Once they were at zero atmospheres, the outer airlock opened. After stepping up to the doorway, he fired his maneuvering jets.

"I've got the tools," Yamane said after he bent down low and released the case by his feet. One short burst from his jets and he found himself outside the ship. Henthorne already had a ten-meter lead. Yamane rotated his body ninety degrees and fired the jets again. The distance between them lessened. As he watched the ship pass by underneath his boots, it made him feel small, insignificant. The *Corona* was a fraction of the size of a planet or nebula, and yet, the stellar cruiser evoked an unparalleled level of awe and respect in him. Her simple lines moving away at subtle angles denoted an understated elegance, like that of a gentle, gliding bird; which at a moment's notice could transform itself into a fiery predator, capable of inflicting a terrifying level of destruction. He often wondered how humanity could create something so devastating on the one hand, and so beautiful on the other.

"I'm coming up on the blast hole now," Henthorne reported. Yamane wished he could be lost in his thoughts a few minutes longer, but there weren't any to spare. "Just make sure you stay in the middle of the shaft. There's a lot of twisted metal around the perimeter. Any one of those serrated edges could slice right through your suit. Also, temperatures inside are two hundred degrees Celsius—residual heat from the blasts. You might want to set your cooling units to their highest settings."

"I'll keep both in mind."

Henthorne fired two quick bursts. Yamane watched him descend into the ship. As he approached the dark, circular opening, the grim view reminded him of a story. His mind raced back to the past. Then it hit him. When he was a little boy, his mother used to read bedtime stories to him at night. Who knows how many he listened to over the years; two thousand, maybe even three? But one stood out above the rest, one from the Bible. Peering into the black hole, the scene was just like how he had envisioned Jonah when the great fish swallowed him up. What seemed like a tragedy became the very means of his survival. Would their "fish" do the same for them?

Yamane felt a rise in temperature the moment he entered the shaft. He brought up his right arm. The climate control gauge had already moved past the twenty degrees Celsius mark. He found the cooling unit on his chest and rotated both dials clockwise. Temperatures in his suit dropped back down to an almost tolerable level.

Henthorne pulled out his light and focused a tight, narrow beam towards the bottom of the shaft. A bright orange glow met him back. "I think we're getting close."

Deck 5 slowly drifted past Yamane, at least what was left of it. Twisted pieces of metal and melted bulkheads revealed the level of devastation had been more than he expected. "There's nothing left," he observed.

When Henthorne reached the bottom, he took a good look around. "Walker and Moreno pretty much cleared the area where the coolant pipes used to be. There's just a little more debris we should cut away before putting in the replacement pipes."

"I had better break out the cutter and get started." He flipped opened the top of the toolbox and unlatched a mini-torch nestled underneath. Positioning himself just above the area, Yamane went right to work. The brilliant white beam sliced through the metal with ease—like the proverbial warm knife through butter.

After he freed each piece, Henthorne collected the floating hunk of metal and sent it through the shaft. One by one, they went up and out. The synchronicity of movement became a kind of dance for the two. Yamane cut, Henthorne removed. Step one, step two.

Yamane pulled the laser cutter away when he finished trimming the surface. "That's about as good as I can do. Get ready to place the micro-charges over the designated areas."

Henthorne didn't respond. Instead, he bent down and opened a small panel on the side of the box. Inside were eight small explosives, each one resembling a shotgun cartridge.

"The *Corona* has now accelerated to 1.46," a voice blared into their helmet speakers. Yamane felt the vibrations under his feet intensify. He knew they didn't have much longer.

"I'm going to set the charges so they can be detonated by remote control." Yamane took out the first replacement pipe. He held the elongated cylinder in his hand. Just a plain ordinary tube, he thought. Probably worth no more than a quick meal at a restaurant, and yet, this simple device no wider than a man's fist became, to them, the most valuable commodity in the universe.

Like a skilled surgeon with a delicate touch, Henthorne placed the charges on one side and then the other. "Okay, all eight are in place."

"I'm on it," Yamane replied. A couple of bursts from his pack brought him around the other side, only centimeters away from the almost white-hot pipes. The heat was almost more than he could bear. Sweat trickled into both eyes, burning them. Despite the pain, he knelt forward and lined up the tube over each charge. Just as he was about to slip both ends over the charges, his hands began to shake. Under normal circumstances, there was little chance the charges would go off once he activated the tripping circuit, but at such close proximity to the heat, he couldn't be certain if the explosive had become unstable or not. One inadvertent tap and they could both be a distant memory.

Get a hold of yourself. You can do this. His little mantra worked. Both hands stopped shaking. He slid the tube right over the charges, pressing both ends against the super-heated surface. "That's it," he said, breathing a sigh of relief. "I'm locking them down."

"I'm getting a signal," Henthorne said. "Finish the other three and let's get out of here."

Yamane went back for the second tube. Positioning it over the charges, he set it in place in half the time. He reached back and grabbed the last two. "This should pick up the pace a little."

Henthorne stepped aside and let Yamane finish. He fitted pipe number three into place, and then number four.

"I'll fuse the connecting points together while you get the gear stowed away," Henthorne said.

"Right."

He held the molecular fuser over the edge of the first pipe. Sweat trickled down the side of his face. Henthorne ignored the distraction. They needed to finish their work and get out of there within the next couple of minutes, or the ship would blow. He activated the unit and brought it over to the first point of contact. In an instant, the tubes bonded with the metallic surface at the molecular level. Henthorne bent over to make certain their weren't any missed spots. If a gap of even the smallest proportion existed, a coolant leak might result. He came down on one knee and checked the other side. "That should do it," he said after finishing the last pipe.

"I've got most of the tools packed up."

Henthorne checked the time. "Leave them behind. We need to get out now. The equipment will only slow us down."

"You're right." Yamane set the box aside and looked up. His portable light showed a clear opening all the way up, no obstructions. "Bridge," he said into his headset. "Is the emergency coolant ready to be pumped in?"

"As soon as you give the word, Commander."

Henthorne switched off the fuser and haphazardly put the tool aside. "Time to go."

Just as he was about to activate his jets, a voice came crashing onto the radio. "Our speed has jumped to 1.50 stellar velocity. The ship will go at any second!"

This was all Yamane needed to hear. He moved into the middle of the shaft and fired one long burst. The decks moved past him at a much faster rate than when he had descended. With a tip of his helmet, he found the stars above. The sight bolstered his hope they just might make it.

"Should we blow the charges now?"

"I don't think we have any choice."

"Are we far enough away?"

"Doesn't matter now. We're out of time." Henthorne looked back down at the replacement pipes. "I'm entering the destruct code now." He brought up his right arm and inputted the sequence into the keypad on his wrist. Eight brilliant white flashes of light went off below in rapid succession.

"Are core temperatures dropping?" Henthorne asked on the radio.

"They're still holding at eighty-seven hundred degrees."

Something wasn't right. After the charges detonated, the coolant should have started flowing again, lowering temperatures in the reactor cores. So far, they hadn't. Then something caught Yamane's attention. One of the connection points seemed to be glowing brighter than the others. He felt a pang of fear. "Stop the coolant flow!" he yelled.

"Are you out of your mind," Henthorne fired back. "The reactor cores are—"

"The left fitting of number two pipe is starting to break down. If we don't do something now, it could go altogether."

Even before his last word dissipated into silence, the fitting gave way. A small focused stream of super-heated coolant shot out of the breach at a forty-five degree angle. Within seconds, the small hole grew even larger.

"No you don't," Yamane said to himself. "I'll go back down there and take care of this, before it burns all the way through."

"Don't be an idiot. You'll get yourself killed. Besides, I was the one who blew it. This is my responsibility." Henthorne fired his jets before Yamane could object. Upon reaching the bottom, he found the abandoned fuser where he had left it. "The hole is still growing in size. I could try and spot-weld it, but I think a patch might be more effective."

Yamane searched the area below. Nothing promising presented itself. "Can you find a flattened piece of metal near you? Anything will do."

Henthrone's eyes darted about. His light shot past a disk-like protrusion near a joist. "I think I may have what we need." He grabbed the torch near his feet and cut right through the exposed piece of metal. Floating towards him in no particular hurry, the oblong-shaped disk bumped into his extended hand. "Perfect," he declared after a brief inspection. "It should fit over the hole without any problem."

The stream of coolant deflected to his right when he set the patch over it. Henthorne spot-welded one side and then moved in a clockwise direction, until the hole was just about sealed. Each pop of the welder reduced the flow at incremental levels. "Almost done. One more should do it." When he leaned over just a bit further to the left, his foot pushed against an unstable beam. The joist gave way and came out from under him. Henthorne tumbled right into the stream's path. Before he could react, the coolant burned a hole into his suit and cut through his right leg like a laser scalpel. "Arrr!" he cried out in pain.

The whole thing felt like a dream. Yamane watched from a distance, but could do nothing to stop it. "I'm coming to get you." He fired his jets and began a quick descent.

"Don't," Henthorne countermanded. "I can still—" He had underestimated the amount of pain he could tolerate, and the intensity level became too much for him. Within a few moments, he lapsed into unconsciousness.

Yamane reached down and pulled Henthorne away from the coolant stream. He, however, wasn't out of danger just yet. Oxygen continued to vent into space where the tear occurred. If he didn't stop it soon, Henthorne would be dead in a matter of seconds.

Yamane brought up his arm and clumsily groped for the emergency repair kit in his top shoulder pocket. He managed to find a self-adhesive patch. After ripping the packet open, he pressed it against the rip on Henthorne's leg.

Chemical compounds immediately bonded with his suit. The leak slowed to a trickle. Yamane then found the oxygen regulator valve next to Henthorne's reserve tank. Turning the knob counter-clockwise increased the flow of air. The lieutenant commander's breathing became more stable, rhythmic.

Yamane had little time to lose. He grabbed the fuser floating nearby and finished Henthorne's work. The joint held firm. "I think the leak has been fused. Pump in the emergency coolant."

"Yes, sir." His voice grew distant. "Get that coolant flowing now." There was a lengthy pause before the c-tech spoke again. "Reactor temperatures are starting to drop...six thousand degrees...fifty-nine hundred...fifty-eight."

"Have a medical team ready at airlock four. Lt. Commander Henthorne has been injured."

"Roger that, Commander. They'll be standing by."

Yamane brought Henthorne upright and held him tight. He winced in pain. A long burn from his thruster unit sent them both through the shaft, and into the infinite void of space. Millions of stars met them on the other side. They never looked more beautiful to Yamane in his life then at that moment. But this was no time to enjoy the scenery. He needed to get to the airlock, and fast.

Ten meters. Twenty meters. Thirty meters. The distanced traveled counted off in Yamane's head. Not much longer, he thought, just stay cool—and don't panic.

He checked Henthorne's condition. His respiration had grown shallow. To make matters worse, his pupils had also become fixed and dilated. The signs were undeniable. Henthorne had gone into shock.

When they arrived at the hatch, Yamane guided him through it. Once inside, the operator closed the outer door. Air began hissing its way inside. At one atmosphere, the inner door opened. A medical team rushed in and lifted Henthorne onto a waiting stretcher. One of the med-techs grabbed a scalpel from an instrument tray and cut the left sleeve off at the shoulder, exposing his ashen arm. Another tech opposite him pulled out an IV and inserted into the needle into a protruding vein. "Ten cc's of sulfamene," he said as they ran down the corridor.

Yamane took off his helmet and leaned back against the airlock door. He stared at a bright light fixture suspended above. A thick layer of sweat covered his face. He tried to wipe it off, but did so clumsily because of the thick, padded glove. The airlock operator, recognizing the difficulty Yamane was having, tossed him a towel.

"That was quite a job you did out there," he said as he helped him with his EVA suit.

Only then did Yamane realize just how much the mission had taken out of him. He felt exhausted. "Is the ship out of danger?"

"Yes, Commander—thanks to you." The tech saluted.

Yamane let his head fall back against the wall. "All part of a day's work."

"You look beat. I think a couple hundred hours of sleep might do you some good."

That's the best idea I've heard all day. "Do you think anyone would mind if I went back to my quarters?"

"I can't think of a soul," the crewman replied.

Yamane envisioned himself on his soft, comfortable bed again. All of his tired, aching joints could hardly wait. But before he could even consider such a self-indulgent luxury, there was one small matter that needed attending to first. "Hold this for me." Yamane handed him his helmet and then scooted down the hallway.

His lift clattered down the decks: ten, nine, eight, seven…until it stopped on the lowest level. A muted bang announced his arrival. He opened the gate almost on an unconscious level and marched down the darkened corridor. After taking two turns to the left and one to the right, he arrived at the brig. Two crewmen stood guard, one beside the next. Wearing an expression of unwavering determination, Yamane came right at them, his eyes focused on the cell just beyond.

Surprised by his unannounced visit, they reached for their side arms. But when the guards realized who he was, they stepped aside and allowed Kershaw's and Landis' release. He didn't say anything to them. He didn't have to. They, like everyone else on board, knew what he had done. How could anyone with even a modicum of appreciation still keep the three of them locked up?

Yamane helped Landis onto the lift. What all three needed was good night's sleep in their own beds. After that, tomorrow would come soon enough. Though no one could guess what might happen next, he at least had the satisfaction of knowing the *Corona* was safe.

Henthorne awoke in a hospital bed. Several medical personnel stood over him when he regained consciousness. He coughed. A glob of phlegm exploded in his mouth. The gooey mass tasted awful. He opened his eyes no wider than two narrow slits. Even then, the intensity of the lights above overwhelmed his unsuspecting retinas. He winced in pain and instinctively turned away. Henthorne tried again, albeit a bit slower this time. Up above, he saw blurry figures on either side of his bed. None of them looked familiar. Lowering his head somewhat, he saw several tubes come out from under the covers. They worked their way to a variety of machines. All of them made dissimilar rhythmic noises. He tried to recall how he had gotten there, but his memory inexplicably failed him. Then a fuzzy picture of himself in an EVA suit flashed in his mind. There had been a crisis of some sort. After that, everything extended back into a black void. His lack of recall made him feel uneasy. He didn't like it.

Henthorne felt some of his strength return, and so he tried to sit up. Fiery pain immediately ripped down his right side, as though someone had plunged a knife into it. He fell back onto the bed, writhing in anguish.

"Nurse, prepare 20 cc's of tylacene for the patient," a voice said from beyond view. "Just hold steady. This should make you feel better."

A nurse rushed over with a dermal injector. She placed the epithelial tip just above the wound and injected him. In an instant, his suffering ended.

"Who are you? What's going on here?" he asked, still uncertain what had taken place.

"I'm Doctor Owens and you're in Med-lab five."

He looked around. "Why am I here?" he demanded.

"You came out of surgery about four hours ago," a different voice replied.

"I know who that is. What's Yamane doing out of his cell?"

"You let me out. Don't you remember?" the commander asked.

"The sedative hasn't completely worn off yet. He'll be a little groggy for a while."

Henthorne looked past his bed. Yamane stood on his left, Dr. Owens on his right. At least he presumed the second person was a doctor, judging by her medical attire: a long white smock and a stethoscope draped around her neck. He thought she looked a little young to be a doctor, though Henthorne figured her long brown hair and the soft highlights around her eyes greatly enhanced her youthful appearance.

"When was I brought here?" Henthorne asked. He hoped the answer might jog his memory.

"About twelve hours ago," Yamane replied. "You and I saved the *Corona*. But just before we finished with the repairs, you burned your leg pretty bad. I got you back just before you bled to death."

"Is that true, doctor?"

"I'm afraid so," she smiled. "This man saved your life."

Henthorne found what they said vaguely familiar. Could Yamane have really saved my life? He pushed such thoughts away, but the memories crept back in, each one more detailed than the last. Bit by bit, the whole unpleasant ordeal—the explosion, the loss of Walker and Moreno, Yamane, and his injury—they all came back to him. Henthorne didn't know if he should feel indignant or grateful. Even with his memory sluggish at best, a strange new emotion bubbled to the surface. He felt guilty, with a little remorse thrown in for good measure. When Yamane brought him back to the airlock, despite lapsing in and out of consciousness, he felt an overwhelming sense of humility. Now Henthorne remembered. Yamane had rescued him from almost-certain death. He hoped the whole ordeal had been a dream, but evidently, he owed his life to the commander. This left him with one inescapable conclusion. He had been wrong about him, the mutiny—everything. Worse yet, his selfish and arrogant ways had almost killed them all. A new emotion crept in, far worse than guilt and remorse. Henthorne felt ashamed.

"What is the status of the *Corona*?" he asked softly.

"We are stopped in space while repair teams work on the pulsar generators," Yamane said. "Despite what they've gone through, the engines are in surprisingly good shape."

"Who is supervising the work?"

"Lt. Commander Kershaw," he replied without the least bit hesitation. "I had him released right after we came on board again. He's been in the engine room ever since."

Henthorne's eyes met every one of those standing over him. "I see. How long before we are under way again?"

"Kershaw estimates the *Corona* should be ready to go within the next couple of hours."

"Good. This will give me a chance...to get some rest," Henthorne said before closing his eyes. A moment later, he was fast asleep.

Standing there beside the doctor, staring down at Henthorne's beleaguered face, Yamane felt like a man without a country. He didn't think it appropriate to return to the bridge. Only one place felt right, felt safe. "I'll be in my quarters, doctor, if you require anything of me."

"I understand, Commander."

He gave Henthorne one last look before leaving the med-lab.

With his head resting comfortably on his pillow, Yamane stared at his photo of Liana. He wished she were with him right now. After everything they had been through, the thought of someone telling him everything was going to be all right proved a strong temptation. Maybe that's exactly what was really happening. Titan, Earth, the mutiny, saving the ship—was a hand guiding him along, making certain he survived? He hadn't thought so before, but after what almost happened to the ship, he wasn't quite sure anymore.

Yamane also thought about the Deravans and the mysterious turn of events that occurred when he had no other choice but to abandon Earth to its fate. They turned to attack the *Corona*, but something held them back, like a kind of invisible force. Could it have been some form of higher intelligence? An unseen power? For the first time since the attack, Yamane opened himself to the possibility that something out there indeed might be orchestrating events for an unknown purpose, and these events somehow involved him.

He heard a knock on the door. Yamane put the picture back in his pocket before answering. "Come in."

When the door opened, Landis stepped inside. He stood in front of Yamane and saluted. "At ease, Lieutenant." Judging by his appearance, it looked like Landis had acquired a new uniform, though he still wore a bandage over his forehead. "What can I do for you?"

"I'm sorry to bother you, Commander," he apologized, "but I wanted to talk to you about something, something important."

Yamane pointed to an empty chair by his desk. "Sit down."

"Thank you, sir." He brought the chair over and placed it by his bed. "I hope I'm not being too presumptuous by asking, but what are your plans for the *Corona*?"

Yamane laughed aloud, caught off-guard by the question. "I'm afraid... I haven't given this much thought since our little ordeal." And that was the truth.

"Well, now might be a good time to think about assuming command again."

The bemused expression on Yamane's face turned serious. "When Lt. Commander Henthorne recovers, we'll probably all end up in the brig again."

Landis leaned forward, a smile on his face. "I'm not so sure. "I've been hearing talk around the ship, and the crew's confidence in him has eroded considerably."

"I appreciate what you are saying, but commanding a ship is more than a personality contest. The person in charge must have complete loyalty from the crew, no matter what. I'm not sure this is even possible after what we've been through. What's to stop them from mutinying again? They did it once. They could do it again."

"The crew knows what you did. When it seemed like we had no chance of getting out of this, you stepped in and did the job. I think they now understand you are our best chance for survival."

He was about to respond when his intercom signaled. "This is Yamane."

"Doctor Owens in med-lab five, Commander. I'm sorry to disturb you, but Lt. Commander Henthorne is asking for you. He insists you get here right away."

"Henthorne?" He looked at Landis. The lieutenant just shrugged. "I'm on my way." He switched off the intercom. "I'll give what you said some thought, but don't expect anything."

Landis nodded in reply before snapping to attention. "Yes, sir, thank you, sir." He saluted and then exited his quarters.

The med-lab door swooshed open. Yamane found Henthorne sitting up, reading a book. As he approached, he thought it looked like the same book Henthorne had been reading when they met in his quarters, before ...

"You look as though you're doing much better," Yamane said out of politeness.

"Thank you," he replied, his voice sounded hoarse.

"Is there anything I can get you?"

"No, no thank you." Henthorne set his book down. "I called you here because I wanted to speak about...about something important."

Yamane's defenses went up. "Go on."

"I've had some time to think things over," he said. Henthorne paused. He leaned over and picked up a glass of water. After a couple of swallows, he continued. "I have come to the conclusion that taking the ship by force was wrong."

His words burned in Yamane's ears, having been the opposite of what he expected. "Go on."

"Earlier today, I checked the ship's logs, and I can see how my actions almost cost the lives of the crew. I have also had to face the fact that if it weren't for you, we would not be having this conversation." He paused a second time. "I think it's safe to say your actions prove you should be in command. I don't think the crew would have much of a problem with what I am going to say next—I must step down as the commander of the *Corona* and give her back to you."

Yamane tensed up, unable to speak at first. Had he heard Henthorne correctly? Was he relinquishing command? Only ten minutes before he had told Landis, in effect, he didn't think this would ever happen. Now, Henthorne was giving the *Corona* back to him—and he found himself wanting her again.

A voice whispered in Yamane's ear, "Antara." He looked around but saw no one. Then, for some unknown reason, his future seemed set. He had but one response. "I accept."

"Good. I've already informed the bridge," Henthorne added. "They're waiting for you now."

Yamane studied the man before him. His anger and resentment were gone, replaced with a look of profound humility. The only other time he ever saw others touched in this way was when they, too, experienced brushes with death. Running headlong into one's own mortality often did that to a person. Henthorne had faced his, and it left him shaken.

"What you did took guts, Lt. Commander. It takes a man with character to admit it when he's wrong."

Henthorne accepted the compliment.

Yamane patted him on the shoulder, and then left the room.

When the lift he had been riding stopped, Yamane drew in a deep breath and then stepped into the future. He moved down the corridor almost as an observer of himself. A myriad of thoughts shot at him. Foremost on his mind was acceptance. Would the crew accept him as their commander again?

Finding himself standing at the edge of the bridge, he wondered how long he had been there—a minute, or two, or five? He stepped inside. The empty command chair stood before him.

"Ah-ten-shun!" someone barked.

The crew stopped what they were doing and jumped to their feet. Yamane saluted in response and approached the command chair. He could almost hear the ship tell him he belonged there.

Like a force too strong to resist, his attention worked its way over to the main screen. To his delight, Antares sat there, right in the middle—right where he had left it.

"As you were," Yamane said. He turned to the e-tech. "What is the ship's status?"

"Lt. Commander Kershaw has already signaled. He said we can resume our journey whenever you give the word."

"Very well. Set a course for the Antaren system. Speed, 1.01 stellar velocity."

"Yes, Commander," the nav-tech replied, his words short and efficient. "1.01 stellar velocity."

Like a sweet song from the distant past, the sounds of the ship's engines filled his ears. Vibrations creeping up from the deck below washed over Yamane. The softer, smaller stars in the background began to change color, shifting into the bluer part of the visible spectrum. Antares, seemingly resistant to such a transformation, wandered away from the center of the screen before correcting itself.

He sneaked a glance at the nav-tech's screen. They had resumed their heading of one-seven-seven, straight for Antara, the home world of the Antaren Empire.

Though Yamane never thought such a thing possible again, he had been given a second chance.

CHAPTER 15

S.F.S. CORONA
1036 PROXIMA MERIDIAN TIME, AUGUST 23, 2217

"Urgh," Kershaw grunted as he tightened down the last shielding plate bolt. The six-sided piece of forged metal would go no further. He leapt off the generator pump and went over to a nearby console. After inputting a ten-digit command code, the re-sequencer started up again. "This should get engine efficiency up a bit."

Control rods on his left, switches in front, and displays on his right. This was where he was master, where he shined. Every dial, hookup and relay had a function, and he understood them all with equal aplomb.

Kershaw stopped and took in the engine room. This was a world he relished. Nothing gratified him more than when he improved the performance of a particular system in some tangible way. He corrected himself: it was not gratification, but challenge. A desire to make something operate more efficiently ran deep in him, always had. At present, his latest adversary had been the aft power generator. After two hours of tireless work, he had finally received a reward for his efforts. "Turbine rates appeared to be holding steady...for now."

He pulled out a folded piece of paper from his grease-stained pocket and drew a line through the twenty-third item on his list. "Now for number twenty-four." This one would be even worse.

Another member of his team tapped him on the shoulder. Kershaw spun around; startled by his unexpected appearance. "I'm sorry, sir," he apologized. "Commander Yamane is signaling you from the bridge."

Kershaw shoved the list into his hand. "Here. Get started on those bypass cables over there. I'll help you when I get back." He then jogged over to the nearest communication console. When he passed his hand over a sensor plate, a pair of transparent barriers, each one standing about three meters high, began to emerge from within the bulkhead. Curving around behind him, the deafening noise created by the ship's engines trickled down to almost nothing when both ends met in the middle. Kershaw pulled out both plugs from his ears. "Go ahead, Commander."

"I thought I'd check in and find out how things are progressing down there."

"Not bad," Kershaw replied. "I'm going through the primary systems, one at a time. As damaged parts are replaced, we're slowly bringing the engines up to full strength. I figure we should be done in a day or so."

"Very good."

A stray thought popped into Kershaw's head. "While I have you on the line, I guess I should mention one more thing. I don't know if this is important, but I thought you should know."

"What is it?"

"Two of my teams have spent the last few hours going over the entire coolant system with a fine-tooth comb. So far, they haven't discovered additional breaks or cracks in the lines. But in the course of their inspections, they did uncover something out of the ordinary."

"Go on," Yamane replied, though his tone sounded more guarded.

"In the spot where those pipes gave way, there are several clusters of plasma cables. I don't have to tell you how much energy flows through those lines. To keep them from coming into contact with each other, the ship's designers doubly reinforced them with tungsten brackets and velthane insulation. Nothing should have budged those cables. Lt. Walker assumed the added coolant pressure, along with a weak point in the pipes, were the reasons they gave way. But if this was the case, the breach should have taken place about twenty meters further down." Kershaw's voice became hushed. "It's almost as if someone or something from outside affected the pipes in an unknown way."

A lengthy pause followed. "Do you think it might have been sabotage?"

That was a word he didn't want to say out loud. "The idea did cross my mind. They're still checking in case something's been missed."

"Keep on it, Stan. Signal me if you find anything, no matter how small."

"You'll be the first," he replied. "Kershaw, out." He put his earplugs back in and then switched off the intercom. When both barriers retracted, every conceivable noise generated in the engine room crashed over him. He picked himself up and hustled over to the bypass cables. Even though they still had a great deal of work to do, Kershaw began to believe they just might arrive at Antara in one piece.

"How long before we reach the territorial buoy?" Yamane asked while scratching his chin. Only then did he realize how sweaty his palms had become. He was feeling anxious. His plan sounded just fine when they were a couple of billion kilometers away, but now that they had arrived, he wasn't so sure. The Antarens were an unpredictable race. No one could say with any certainty just how they would react once their monitors picked up the *Corona* at their border.

"It should come into range any second," the r-tech replied. "Wait a minute—I think the buoy just popped up on my scope."

Yamane came alongside the communication console. "Can you tap in? I want to hear what kind of broadcast it's making."

He accessed the Antaren database. Several thousand coded frequencies went by his display in a blur. The screen froze for a second or two, and then a series of numbers and symbols appeared. "I've got the prefix code. Let me just enter it into the transcom."

A high-pitched whine sounded. He made a couple of adjustments. "... of the Antaren Empire. Any and all ships entering our space are subject to its laws and customs ..."

Yamane went around the console and stood before the main screen, his arms folded. An elliptical-shaped speck approached. "At least we know the Deravans haven't come through here first," he commented to himself." Yamane went back to the command chair. "Kill the signal," he ordered. "How long before we enter Antaren space?"

"Based on the buoy's position...one minute and thirty seconds."

"Should we send a message to the High Council?" Landis asked.

"Not just yet," Yamane answered after thinking it over. "I don't want to give our position away until I know what we're dealing with."

"We will enter Antaren space in thirty seconds."

"Does RadAR show any other ships in the area?"

The r-tech amplified the signal. "Negative, Commander. My scopes have already made two full sweeps. There is nothing in this sector except us and some nearby asteroids."

Yamane didn't have a good feeling about this. It almost seemed too easy. "Keep a sharp eye out. You never know when an Antaren vessel will pop up."

The *Corona* approached the territorial buoy. Suspended in space, in a place of no particular significance, sat a symbol that marked the difference between their past and their future. The marker could have just as easily been ten meters closer or twenty meters further out. But for whatever reason, the Antarens chose that particular spot to be their outermost boundary; and it was at that arbitrary spot that Earth's only surviving stellar cruiser slipped into their space.

In that instant, surrounded by a thousand shining suns, Yamane felt they had passed the toughest test of their lives. Despite every obstacle, every setback, the *Corona* had made it. But they hadn't been welcomed with open arms just yet. There was still the small matter of getting to Antara without being destroyed somewhere along the way.

Yamane leaned forward. "Keep up your regular sweeps of the area. If even so much as a grain of sand is picked up, you let me know."

"Of course, sir."

"Should I order general quarters?" Webster suggested from his station.

Yamane weighed his options carefully. If they assumed a hostile posture, an approaching Antaren ship might presume the worst and open fire. "Not just yet," he replied in a calculated manner, "but—"

Two particle bursts suddenly exploded near their port bow. The concussions were close enough to envelop the stellar cruiser, shaking her with tremendous force both times.

Yamane brought himself out of the command chair. "Where did that come from?" he shouted to the r-tech.

"I have two skyjackets on my screen!" he cried out. "Coming in at 0.53 stellar velocity."

Yamane went over to him. "You didn't answer my question, Lieutenant! Where did those fighters come from?"

The r-tech locked onto the Antaren ships flying past them. His tactical computer extrapolated a position based on their trajectory. A fixed point appeared on the display. "They must have been hiding behind some of the larger asteroids."

"Signal those fighters," Yamane said to Landis. "Tell them to break off their attack."

After taking in a couple of short breaths, Landis engaged the transcom first before sending out the message. Two more shots went past their bow, detonating a mere kilometer away. Both skyjackets circled back and came at the *Corona* again.

Yamane went back to the command chair. He studied the nimble fighters coming at them on the nav-tech's display. Two sets of angled yellow lines painted on streamlined hulls flew past the main screen in a blur. Something didn't feel quite right about their attack. "Bring the ship to a full stop," he ordered.

The nav-tech swiveled his chair around. "Sir?" he asked in a high voice. "If we do, they can pick us apart at will."

"Those skyjackets fired at us twice and missed both times," Yamane snapped back. "If they wanted to hit us, they would have done so by now. No. I think they missed on purpose." He hoped this was the case.

The nav-tech turned back and gave the screen a good long look. "Aye, sir, reducing velocity."

Reverse thrusters fired. As though both opponents were physically connected, the Antarens kept pace with the *Corona*, never getting closer than two thousand meters.

Yamane breathed a sigh of relief, though he suspected his reprieve would not last long. Those skyjackets came for one reason—to hold the *Corona* at bay until reinforcements arrived. He knew the Antarens. This is how they did things. The question was—how long would they have to wait?

Thirty minutes came and went. An hour passed. Two hours went by, and still no word. Each passing minute ratcheted up the crew's nerves that much more. And to make matters worse, both fighters still had their weapons at full power, and pointed right at them.

Yamane never took his eyes off the screen. Their menacing posture alarmed him at first, but over time, he began to relax, figuring their little game of cat and mouse probably wouldn't go on much longer. The Antarens were shrewd and efficient warriors, but as a race, they lacked patience.

A pair of proximity alarms went off. Startled, the r-tech leaned over his display. "Commander, another ship has just entered this sector."

Yamane didn't react. Looks like it's sooner. "Is it another fighter?" he asked.

"Negative, sir. This one is much bigger. Probably a dreadnought."

"They sent that ship to attack us," Webster accused from his station. "We should charge up our pulse cannons and get every available fighter into the launch tubes."

Yamane sat back and placed his fingers on his chin. He had a feeling about their intentions. "Let's not be too hasty," he said, never taking his eyes off the main screen. "We'll let them make the first move."

The r-tech's instincts were right on the mark. The biggest ship in the Antaren arsenal approached them at a slow, steady pace. A massive ship in every respect, she outweighed them by a ratio of three-to-one, and as for firepower, the dreadnought had twice as many guns at her disposal. Marveling at its fearsome appearance, Yamane watched every gun port slide open.

"Commander," Landis called out. "I'm receiving a signal. They're demanding you speak with them at once."

The moment he was dreading had arrived. It was now or never. "Patch it through."

A view of the dreadnought's bridge popped onto the screen. A lone Antaren stood in place, waiting. Others were at their stations, further back. It had been a long time since Yamane was at Antara. He almost forgot what they looked like. Strange, he thought, since humans were so different from them. Their skin was blue, some parts with scales, other parts without, a slight tail came out of their ribbed back, and they all had teeth whiter than any toothpaste company would have you believe. A tight-fitting uniform showed every line, every curve of their muscular bodies. Then there were their eyes. He never quite got used to the way they glowed. No human ever really did.

"I am Subidor Tal Win-Tu," he stated through the transcom. "Why have you entered our space?"

Yamane turned towards Landis and made a slashing gesture across his neck. The transmission went silent.

"Why would they send someone of such high rank?" Webster asked from behind.

Yamane offered his back to the screen. "I don't know, but they're definitely nervous about us being here." He pivoted around and gave Landis a nod.

"According to the treaty between our two peoples, we have open access to one another's territories," Yamane stated. "On what grounds do you deny us entry into your space?"

Two other Antarens came up behind Tal Win-Tu and whispered something into his ear, or at least the approximation of one. Yamane could tell they were not a part of the military. Their clothing was vastly different, almost robe-like. One of them looked right at the screen, studied him for a second or two, and then made a comment. They then took a step back.

"Again, I ask you. Why do you wish to enter Antaren space?"

"I'm afraid I cannot tell you that, Subidor," he replied, his tone soft and apologetic. "What I have to say can only be heard by the High Council."

The second pair of Antarens came into view again.

"Something's got them spooked," Webster said from his station.

"Just keep calm," Yamane whispered back.

"Why must the commander of the *Corona* meet with the High Council?"

"I'm afraid I cannot tell you that, either," Yamane again apologized, "but this is a matter of vital importance for both our peoples."

The two robed Antarens extended their arms and moved them about in an exaggerated manner. It looked like they were trying to convince Tal Win-Tu on a matter they felt passionately about. He seemed to reject them outright. Without any warning, they stopped, turned towards Yamane, and then moved out of view. After a couple of nods, the subidor appeared to back down.

"Here goes," Yamane thought. "This is make-or-break."

"You may enter our space," Tal Win-Tu finally said, though something about his demeanor suggested he spoke with great reluctance. "But if you show the slightest of hostile intentions, your ship will be destroyed."

On that last point, Yamane had no doubt. "We understand, Subidor Tal Win-Tu. Thank you for honoring our request."

The main screen switched back. All three Antaren ships reappeared.

Yamane cleared his throat, only then realizing just how tight it had become. "So much for my skills as a diplomat."

"I should feel better about being escorted into their space," Webster said, "but they're acting strangely, even for Antarens."

Yamane picked up on his suspicions. "Maybe, but we'll just take this one step at a time."

"I hope you know what you're doing. If anything goes wrong, we're all dead."

Webster was right. If their former enemy suspected duplicity on his part, they would almost certainly destroy the stellar cruiser. Yamane was walking on thin ice, and he knew it. "Fire up the main thrusters," he ordered. "Continue on your heading, one-seven-seven—right for Antara."

"The dreadnought and skyjackets are turning about."

"Stay with them. Try to match their course and velocity to the best of your ability. If we maintain a constant distance at all times, they might feel a little better about us being here."

"I'll do my best, sir."

That's all any of us can do, he thought honestly.

Flanked on both sides by the skyjackets, the dreadnought maintained her heading towards

Antara. Sitting one thousand meters back, the nav-tech kept pace. At five-minute intervals, he verified their position, just to make certain the distance between them remained fixed.

"It's strange, Commander," Landis said from his station, "but I'm not picking up anything on my radio."

Yamane sat up. "What do you mean? Are you talking about a malfunction?"

He shook his head. "No, sir. I mean there's nothing out there. The instant we entered Antaren space I should have heard some traffic from a nearby ship or a local planet. It's as if they just up and left." Landis switched the signal from his earpiece to his console speakers. "Here, listen for yourself." Except for an occasional crackle, silence filled the bridge.

Yamane looked back at the main screen. "Are you sure you're on the right frequency?"

"I've gone up and down the band several times, but I keep getting the same result—which is a whole lot of nothing."

"Any idea what this means?"

His attention drifted towards the display in front of him. "This one has me stumped. I've never heard of anything like this before."

Yamane sat back in his chair. The Antarens were by nature a people who kept in constant contact with one another. They regularly checked, re-checked, and then checked again just so there wouldn't be any chance of a misunderstanding. For them to maintain any form of prolonged radio silence was not only unthinkable, but it also went against everything they believed in as a society. Perhaps, Yamane thought, an outside force might be responsible for their aberrant behavior. A cold chill went down his spine. Perhaps, he thought coldly, the Deravans had come here first.

For two hours they made their course straight for the Antaren home world, and in all that time there was not a peep from the speakers. Yamane hoped for the best, but his concerns lingered, never far away. Then, as though they had just emerged from a thick layer of clouds, a faint flicker of light appeared just below Antares. The relative position of their sun had obscured the planet for a time, but as they came closer, the Antaren home world emerged from behind its luminous counterpart.

"Do long range scans indicate anything unusual?" Yamane asked the r-tech.

He checked his scope. "Negative, Commander, nothing out of the ordinary."

Yamane's fears eased somewhat. "Are any ships orbiting the planet?"

"Scans show there are three dreadnoughts equidistant from each other in high orbit."

"Finally," he said, relieved. "Something is the way it should be."

"Sir, Tal Win-Tu is sending a message to the High Council," Landis called out. "He is letting them know who we are and what we want."

Yamane craned his neck, nervous. They were outgunned four ships to one. If the Antarens did not intend to let them get out alive, now would be the best time for them to initiate their plan. "Have they sent a response?"

"Not yet." He bent closer and listened. "Hold on...it's coming through now." He switched the signal over to his speakers.

"Allow the *Corona* to enter orbit," an unknown voice said, his tone deep and penetrating.

"The High Council is awaiting their arrival."

Just like every other message sent between them, it was short and to the point. The news, however, could not have been more welcome.

"The Antarens are signaling us."

Yamane gave his uniform a quick tug. "Put it through."

The auburn-colored planet filling the screen switched over to Tal Win-Tu's ship.

"This is Subidor Tal Win-Tu. You will assume an orbit above Antara. The High Council has been convened for your arrival."

"Understood," Yamane smiled. "I'm looking forward to meeting with them." Maybe he wasn't exactly looking forward to meeting with them, but it was close enough to the truth.

The screen switched back to an image of Antara.

Webster came up and stood alongside Yamane, uncomfortably close. "That seemed a little too easy," he said with an air of foreboding in his voice. "The High Council didn't even question the subidor's request. It was almost as if they've been expecting us. It just doesn't add up."

Yamane didn't want to give in to his fears. "You may be right, but until I see or hear otherwise, we'll assume their offer is genuine. Do you think you can handle the bridge while I'm down there with Lt. Commander Kershaw?"

The question seemed to catch Webster off guard. "I ..." he stammered as his shoulders perked up. "You can count on me, Commander. I won't let you down."

"Good. Prepare to enter orbit."

The major returned to his station and reset both displays.

"Okay people. Let's put on a good show for our hosts," Yamane said to the bridge. "Bring her in nice and slow." He swiveled the command chair in the nav-tech's direction. "I assume directional thrusters are at full power."

"Affirmative, Commander. We are set to enter orbit."

The *Corona*'s bow began to heat up when it came into contact with the planet's upper atmosphere. Shaking mildly at first, the stellar cruiser fell further into Antara's gravity well. Increased levels of friction built up a cocoon of super-heated ionized gases, obscuring Yamane's view of the surface below. Instead of seeing rivers, mountains, canyons, dusty plains, and high altitude clouds in the distance, red, orange and yellow flames flickered upward, filling all but the uppermost portion of the main screen.

"Has the *Corona* begun to level out yet?" he asked the nav-tech.

The navigator held onto both sides of his console when the turbulence became more pronounced. "Negative, Commander," he shouted. "Computer control has not initiated the maneuver...but overrides are standing by."

Decks and bulkheads started to moan. Ionized gases on the screen grew even brighter. When the ship lurched forward, Yamane feared a malfunction might have occurred in the guidance control program. Though it went against his better judgment, he figured they had no other choice but to enter orbit manually. Just as he was about to issue the order, directional thrusters fired, changing their angle of descent at incremental levels.

"0.4," the nav-tech called out. "0.3...0.2. The *Corona* is beginning to slow. Coming in at a negative approach—orbit in five seconds." As the bow leveled out, the dance of light subsided, unveiling a world of beauty and mystery below. The *Corona* had safely attained orbit above Antara.

"Damage report?" Yamane asked.

"My scopes show negative. No damage."

He rose out of the command chair and went over to Webster's station. "Have Lt. Commander Kershaw report to the launch tubes. He and I will be flying to the surface."

CHAPTER 16

ANTARA, HOME PLANET OF THE ANTAREN EMPIRE
0614 PROXIMA MERIDIAN TIME, AUGUST 26, 2217

When Yamane and Kershaw reached the hangar bay, they saw their fighters set in the launch tubes, like two saddled broncos ready to kick down the gates and bust out of their corrals. Maintenance teams finished the last of their pre-flight checks. Flaps, structural integrity, engine seals, program software—they checked them all, and then some.

"Here we go again, Frank," Kershaw said with an edge in his voice, "right into oblivion."

Yamane turned towards him with his hand extended. "See you on the other side," he said, his tone hopeful. Grabbing Kershaw's hand hard, the two shook.

After Yamane pulled back, he climbed into his cockpit. A crewmember came up behind him. "Here's your com badge, sir," he said, handing it to him. "Your receiver has already been tied into the transcoms, so you shouldn't have any problems communicating with the Antarens."

"Thank you, Sergeant," Yamane replied, and then pinned the badge to his chest pocket.

He reached over and powered up his communication systems. Once they were aligned, he activated the rest of his ship's systems—weapons, computer control, RadAR, and guidance. Diagnostic computer programs indicated his fighter was ready for departure. The crew chief gave him a thumbs-up before climbing back down. When another member of the ground team detached the ladder, the sergeant hurried away from the launch tubes and out of sight.

"Test...test. Do you read me, Stan?" Yamane said into his helmet headset.

"Loud and clear."

A rhythmic, pulsing sensation filled the cockpit. "My boards are clear for go, how about yours?"

"Affirmative. All systems show go."

"This is launch control," a voice said on the radio. "You're clear to depart at your discretion."

"Roger, launch control. On my mark, we will fire thrusters in three seconds." Yamane braced himself just as the rim of Antara appeared at the end of the launch tube. Hazy amber light bathed the long, straight tracks, making them appear to be luminescent. He grasped the control with his left hand, the maneuvering stick with his right. "Three...two...one...mark." His fighter shot out of the launch tube like a high-caliber bullet from a barrel of a rifle.

Thrown headlong into the infinite void of space, Yamane nudged his stick forward. When the nose dropped down faster than he anticipated, he jerked the stick back. Better, but his technique was still choppy. No matter, he thought, it would come back to him soon enough.

"How long before we reach the capital city?" Kershaw asked.

Yamane checked his RadAR scope. "If we don't have any problems, in about five minutes," he replied. Not long enough. As soon as his fighter emerged from the inner recesses of the *Corona*, the majesty of the stars affected him deeply, just like always. None of the Antarens would miss him if he took an unplanned excursion for a while, would they? He already knew the answer. There would be no more carefree trips or long patrols for a long time. The Deravans had seen to that.

"This is Surveillance Tracking Station One," an otherworldly voice said on the radio. "Stay on your present course until you reach the central starport. Landing way number three has been prepared for your arrival. We have already fed the coordinates into your targeting arrays."

Yamane accessed the navigational program. Just as the voice promised, their landing coordinates were there, waiting for him. "Confirmed, Tracking Station One. We have received the coordinates. Our ETA is in four minutes."

His right hand clutched two levers atop the starboard control panel, one red and one green.

Two front flaps, represented by an outline of his ship on the central targeting display, lit up. When he pulled both toggles back, his speed started to drop. Yamane looked down the nose of his fighter so he could gauge his descent. Two large clouds shot past. They were similar to those on Earth, with one exception—their color. Antares' ever-present red hue, mixed with the green tint of Antara's upper atmosphere, produced a striking shade of purple he could scarcely describe. As they continued their descent, smaller cloud formations appeared near the horizon. Those at lower elevations tended to be much livelier, often swirling about like pinwheels when a localized microburst crossed their paths. On occasion, tumbling balls of cotton had been said to fill the skies of Antara.

"My scope shows the runway dead ahead."

"Verified," Yamane replied after he corroborated the information on his targeting grid. "We should clear this cloud cover at any moment and sight the base."

Even before he finished his sentence, both fighters emerged from the billowy masses, revealing Tel Shador in all its glory. Yamane felt overwhelmed by the impressive sight. Thousands of buildings, both large and small, glistened in the tawny light. Many of the smooth, metallic surfaces reflected the sun's rays, while others refracted it like a prism. The resulting show of radiance was spectacular.

In the midst of a wide valley lay the city; around it, a series of mountain ranges. Immense peaks rose almost straight up out of the ground like the teeth of some great beast ready to devour its prey. The contrast between the two features could not have been greater. A dark and forbidding atoll of rock somehow existed in the midst of a flat landscape that went in every direction for hundreds of kilometers. Yamane could only wonder what kind of tectonic forces could produce so amazing a geologic formation.

Both fighters lined up along the trajectory provided by the tracking station operator, bringing them right to Tel Shador. A brown, metallic spire flew past Yamane's ship. He turned back at the fleeting sight. The efficiency of the structure, its style and structural motifs, produced a sense of awe in him. Then another went by. The business quarter followed soon after. Over on his left, the more subdued priestly quarter appeared, then the larger, more austere military province. Peppered throughout the city, he saw a host of other towers, until they all fell behind the immediate skyline. Some districts were bigger than others were, though the perceived inequities meant little to the Antarens. Even though they had broken down their society into well-defined classes, they also saw themselves as equals in every respect. Architect, baker, servant, or priest; the distinction made no difference. All the Antarens were one.

"I have the starport in sight," Kershaw declared, "behind that spire."

"I see it. I'm starting the landing cycle now."

Yamane pulled the thruster control back. His fighter began to slow. "Altitude is one thousand meters. We're dropping at a rate of one hundred meters per second." All three wheels came down and locked into position.

Two parallel rows of runway lights shown brilliantly against the dark, looming mountains in the background. As Antares rose higher into sky, turning morning into day, crimson rays found their way through the gaps formed between angled peaks, setting the city of Tel Shador aglow.

"Three hundred meters. Touchdown in six seconds."

Green lights set at regular intervals passed by both fighters as they came closer to the ground.

"Leveling out. Three seconds."

Yamane brought his ship down with a gentle touch. A slight jolt sounded as all three wheels landed on the runway in unison. Pressing hard on the

brakes, his nimble craft decelerated, coming to stop about a dozen or so meters from the end. Not certain where he was supposed to go next, Yamane
took a quick look around. "Where is everyone?" he asked himself. A strange
lack of personnel or hovercars moving about the normally busy base aroused
his suspicions.

Kershaw's fighter pulled up alongside his. He looked both ways before answering. "This is spooky. There aren't any other ships here, ground crews—
nothing. I get the feeling something bad is going to happen, and we're in the
crosshairs."

"I'm beginning to think you may be right," he concluded after another
visual inspection of the base. They were sitting ducks out here in the open.
He eyed the thruster control. They could be up and out of there before the
Antarens knew what happened.

A loud whine burst out of his speakers. Yamane jumped. "The central
starport has been prepared for your arrival," a different voice said. "Follow
the directional lights off the landing way, and they will guide you." His radio
fell quiet.

After a prolonged period of silence, Kershaw asked, "What do you think,
Frank?"

He thought the question over. "I think this scenario has a familiar ring to
it. But as long as we're here, we shouldn't turn down such a gracious invita-
tion."

"Uh-huh."

Yamane moved his thruster control forward. Pitch levels jumped up in
an instant as all three turbines doubled their rotation rate. When he maneu-
vered his fighter back the way it came, an immense, rectangular structure
came into view. The building looked like it could be a hangar, except it stood
six stories higher, and two massive doors covered the opening. He could only
imagine what purpose such a building might serve, since Antaren skyjackets
were about the same size as their Min counterparts.

When the nose of his fighter rolled off the end of runway three, both doors
began to retract, revealing a darkened cavern inside. The gaping maw rising
above heightened Yamane's unease.

He then witnessed something strange. There, about twenty meters ahead,
a circle of self-contained light appeared. No bigger than a soccer ball at first,
it grew in size, until the sphere encompassed an area twice the size of both
fighters combined. Suspended in the air by some unknown means, the ball
of luminosity seemed to beckon them forward. "I guess they want us to park
there," Yamane surmised.

"You're probably right, but stay frosty. We don't know what that thing
is."

Easily slipping into the effervescent glow suspended a couple of meters off
the ground, both ships stopped just within the perimeter of the strange globe.

After Yamane shut down the main power systems, he sneaked a quick look around. As before, they were the only ones there. It left him feeling unsettled. Only then did he realize the amount of light within the hangar was steadily decreasing. He looked back over his shoulder, just in time to see both doors meet in the middle. A deep boom echoed off the walls. They were trapped inside.

With nowhere to go but down, Yamane waited for the canopy to go up. When it stopped, he swung his legs over the side and jumped onto the hangar floor. A lesser but equally sharp bang echoed off the floor.

A pair of boots approached from behind. Yamane spun around in a single, effortless action. Even before he spoke, he could see the shadowed contour of a scowl on Kershaw's face. "This is hardly what I'd call the red carpet treatment." He looked around. "I don't know. I don't have a good feeling about this."

"Try and stay relaxed," Yamane suggested. "There must be a reason for all this."

"Yeah ..."

Yamane looked up. The darkened ceiling above went off into oblivion. If it weren't for the ball of light, the interior of the building would be pitch-black. He heard a noise. Both men froze. "Did you hear that?" he asked. Nothing showed itself. Taking a long, slow look around, Yamane reached down for his sidearm. Then something caught his attention. Off in the distance, a darkened outline stood before a lighted entrance, one that had not been there a moment ago. His eyes narrowed. The figure began to walk towards them. "I'll take care of this," he said.

The Antaren stopped a couple of meters away. He wore a loose, beige-colored robe, covering him from the head down. Around his waist, a sash was double-wrapped and tied off at the ends. He extended both arms in a slow, precise manner. The action caused both oversized sleeves to slide backwards, exposing his blue, scaly hands. "I extend peace and friendship to you," the Antaren said with a slight pause after each word. "My open hands symbolize my open heart as a sign of cooperation and acceptance between us." He bowed forward and then came up again.

An extended period of silence followed.

Yamane realized the Antaren was waiting for a response. "Stan," he whispered. "Now it's our turn. We're supposed to do the same thing."

Kershaw jerked his head over and gave him a look. "Do the same thing?" he asked. "It all seems so pedestrian."

"Stan. Just do it. I'll explain later."

"All right," he surrendered.

Both men bowed, held out their hands and repeated the same greeting. Yamane figured the Antaren must have been satisfied with the manner in which they did it. After they finished, their host pulled his hood back. Both eyes seem to jump off his face. The glow was much more unsettling in person than he remembered. "I am Commander Frank Yamane," he opened, "and this is my second-in-command, Lt. Commander Stan Kershaw."

"I am most pleased to meet the two of you," the Antaren replied. "I am Kel Sen-Ry of the Second Order. I have been sent by the High Council to act as both an interpreter and liaison between our peoples." He pointed towards the lighted doorway. "If you would come with me."

Kershaw put his hand on Yamane's shoulder as if to warn him. He turned back and gave a reassuring nod.

Kel Sen-Ry stepped through the doorway first. To Yamane's surprise, the entrance wasn't an entrance at all, but a small, brightly lit enclosure, about the size of a small elevator. All three fit inside, but just barely. As he had in the hangar, Yamane tried to figure out where the light originated, but like the luminous ball, it seemed to come from everywhere...and nowhere.

Flanked by his two guests, Kel Sen-Ry moved into the middle. He again clasped his hands together. As he angled his head upward, an even brighter beam of light shone down on him. "Skyway number five," he said in whispered tones.

When the light dimmed, Kel Sen-Ry brought his attention forward again. As though he had performed some type of sleight-of-hand, a door materialized out of thin air, covering the entrance. Yamane couldn't feel any movement, though he did get the distinct impression they were now traveling towards some unknown destination.

"It should only take a few moments," the Antaren reassured them.

Kershaw didn't respond. Neither did Yamane.

Then, without any warning, the magic door dematerialized in the same fashion as it had appeared—in the blink of an eye.

"If you will follow me, please," Kel Sen-Ry said as he extended his hand.

Yamane and Kershaw checked with each other first before following their escort outside. What they saw, however, could not have surprised them more. In a matter of seconds, the Antaren had taken them from the outskirts of Tel Shador, to the heart of the capital city. Yamane could do nothing else except look up and be amazed. "Is this the main skyport in the city center?" he asked, dumbfounded.

"Yes," Kel Sen-Ry replied. "From here I will escort you to the council chambers."

The central dome above was immense. It flared outwards a certain distance, and then angled all the way down. Yamane took a step forward and tried to take it all in. The station could easily hold tens of thousands of people at any one time. Along the walls, murals hung between each sculpted column. Many were simple in nature—a pastoral landscape here, an artistic interplay between geometric designs there—while others revealed complex mathematical motifs. The murals contrasted with a host of multi-colored panels straddling the length of the station. Illuminated by Antares above, tinted glass bathed the floor and walls in an almost infinite variety of color combinations. Yamane considered the entire structure an architectural masterpiece. The very place itself seemed to come alive, as if someone had created it just for them. Just for them. The phrase struck a chord in Yamane. Where were the people? He stopped. "Kel Sen-Ry, where are your fellow Antarens? Except for you, we haven't seen anyone else since we landed."

"A hover ship is waiting for us," he replied, belying no emotion either way. "Will you follow me, please?"

Kershaw stepped in between the two. "Commander Yamane asked you a question," he scowled. "We're not going anywhere until we have some answers." He pointed an accusatory finger at Kel Sen-Ry. "Nothing's been right since we entered your space. Where are all the people? And how come the High Council agreed to meet us without knowing the reason why?"

Yamane forced him back. "That's enough, Stan—control yourself. If you cannot act in a respectful manner, then you have no business being here."

He motioned wildly with both hands. "I will not control myself. They're keeping something from us, and I will not take one more step until we get some answers."

The station became quiet. Kershaw stood his ground, as did Kel Sen-Ry. Neither blinked, neither backed down. Then, quite unexpectedly, the Antaren clasped his hands together. Yamane braced himself for the worst. "You will have all of your questions answered soon enough, my impatient friend," he replied without a hint of anger or malice, "but these are matters you must take up with the High Council." Kel Sen-Ry motioned toward the next level. "Now, if you would follow me."

Yamane was in disbelief at what he had just seen and heard. Shock would be more like it. During his previous stay on Antara, he had witnessed Antarens shunned from their class for outbursts nowhere near as loud as what Kershaw had just expressed. Inexplicably, Kel Sen-Ry had absorbed the slight without so much as a comment. What is going on around here?

Kel Sen-Ry headed for several horizontal movers parked at the end of a large, rounded platform. "Our transports are waiting for us on the opposite side of the station. Using them will cut our travel time in half." He stepped on the one nearest him. Yamane and Kershaw followed suit.

Near the front of one end, Yamane saw two squares, slightly raised. Kel Sen-Ry placed his left foot on the left square. Their mover rose up above the ground. He then placed his other foot on the second square. As though some immutable force had formed behind them, their disk shot forward.

They moved at a steady rate of speed down the narrow walkway for a short while, until the mover went up an angled incline, and then down another walkway for several kilometers. When they finally reached their destination, Kel Sen-Ry lifted his right foot, bringing the transport device to a stop.

On the tracks before them, a hover ship waited. He went up to the opened doors and then paused. His hands came out from under his baggy sleeves and extended outward. "From the time of the beginning many years in our past, working toward that great endeavor for which we strive, may this ship grant us safety, so that all may go well for us when we arrive." He moved aside. "Enter, gentlemen."

Yamane looked on ahead just before he climbed aboard. Two parallel rails went up another twenty meters or so. He estimated the hover ship would probably only use half that distance at best. If the pilot was good, he could bring the anti-grav drive to full power after five meters and propel them into any number of skyway lanes in a matter of seconds.

Kershaw stepped inside just after him, followed by Kel Sen-Ry.

When both doors slid closed, Yamane examined the interior. A panel of windows straddled the length of the ceiling above, and along both sides. There were chairs in front and behind, set facing each other. The arrangement appeared comfortable enough, though the hover ship lacked any kind of aesthetic warmth. Antaren designers created it with one specific purpose in mind—to get a person to their destination by the most efficient means possible.

"If you gentlemen will sit down," Kel Sen-Ry suggested. "We are ready to depart." When all three had taken their seats, a low-pitched hum sounded from behind. The station moved past them in silence with the least effort. In a matter of seconds, their ship rose from the tracks and merged into the skyway.

When Antares finally crested the tallest peaks above, every building along the skyline glowed in amber light—almost making the city appear as though it had been set on fire. The mountains thousands of meters above savagely dwarfed the tallest structures the Antarens had created in their long and noble history. Few other sights rivaled it.

"This is amazing," Yamane commented, no longer able to contain himself. "Tel Shador suffered so much damage during the war. And now, look at this." He pointed at a number of edifices moving past them at a distance. "The capital looks almost brand new."

"In a sense, it is," Kel Sen-Ry replied. "Construction teams stripped down every damaged building to its foundations, and built them up again to pre-war conditions."

"This must have been an enormous undertaking."

"The decision resulted in great sacrifices for the Antaren people. Soldiers, priests, carpenters, architects, engineers—everyone joined in the effort. I think the results speak for themselves."

"I remember when construction began. I figured it would take decades before you finished."

A sullen, distant expression appeared on Kel Sen-Ry's face. "The work had to be completed within a certain time frame. There were other considerations. Something ..." his voice fell silent.

Yamane wanted to ask more, but the Antaren looked away.

The hover ship changed directions. They were now heading towards the most prominent building in Tel Shador. The distinctive-looking structure was pyramidal in shape, with the top coming to a point, like a spire.

"Petros Mig-dalah," Kel Sen-Ry declared.

The seat of power for the entire Antaren Empire almost seemed to reach for the sky itself. Unlike the other architectural marvels in the city, the place where the High Council resided had no windows at all, not even one—just a smooth, bronze-colored finish from top to bottom. Yamane could only imagine what lay inside.

When their hover ship made a long, slow turn towards a landing pad, Yamane caught sight of twelve lesser buildings below, plain and ordinary in every respect. But when he peered at them more closely, he saw something unexpected. Water. Not a little, but a lot. Hundreds of millions of liters must have been required to surround the tower and adjacent structures. This obviously represented something important, since the climate of Antara was hot and arid. Why they would use such an important resource for something of a cosmetic nature, he couldn't begin to guess.

The ship slowed. Gentle hums from behind dropped down at incremental levels, until the pilot brought their shuttle down onto a pair of tracks in the middle of a plaza not far from the tower.

Kel Sen-Ry rose from his chair and stepped up to the doors. Yamane expected another ritual before they disembarked, but to his surprise, they opened without any fanfare. A blast of hot air hit them the instant they stepped into the plaza. Yamane looked at the red sun above. He had forgotten just how hot Antares could get.

"This way," Kel Sen-Ry pointed. He walked at a steady but brisk pace towards an arch bridging the gap between the plaza and the other side. As they walked over the top, Yamane scrutinized the lake surrounding them. The mirror-like surface reflected all twelve towers above them with perfect clarity.

On the other side, a series of rather large steps leading to an entrance confronted all three. Set on either side of them, positioned a good distance apart, a pair of burning globes sat atop two enormous pedestals. Flickering streaks of yellow flames licked the air. The polished spheres must have weighed tons, and yet, they hung in the air, suspended a little above each platform.

"You have no idea how beautiful this place is at twilight."

As they went up the steps in subdued silence, Yamane counted them. "Twelve," he thought after they reached the top, "each one probably representing a member of the High Council."

Kel Sen-Ry approached the tower. Yamane and Kershaw looked at one another, as though they needed some kind of mutual reassurance. All that they had hoped and wished for rested on what happened next. Yamane bent backwards so he could better see the top of the tower, but the peak hundreds of meters above was too far out of sight.

With a slow gaze, he followed the lines all the way down, until a large door a few steps away fell into view. Up above, a simple phrase caught his attention. He took a crack at reading it, but the meaning of those words eluded him, since they were symbols he had never seen before.

Just as they were about to cross the threshold, Kel Sen-Ry turned around. "You are about to enter the hall of the High Council," he said with the utmost seriousness. "Conduct yourselves appropriately."

"And how are we supposed to do that?" Kershaw sneered. "No one from Earth has ever addressed the council in person before."

"Follow my words and deeds," Kel Sen-Ry smiled. "The council is aware of your ignorance, but they also expect a certain measure of decorum when in their presence."

"We will do just as you say," Yamane reassured him.

Kel Sen-Ry nodded and then turned around. He gave a slight bow, his hands held upward. "Those who are about to enter give thanks. May we remain contented in all things and keep our humble place before the High Council." Two steps later, all three disappeared inside.

CHAPTER
17

The appointed thing comes at the appointed time in the appointed way.
-Myrtle Reed

PETROS MIG-DALAH
DAIETH TIME MINUS ONE

Darkness.

It took a short while before Yamane's eyes adjusted to the light. Only after he started walking around a bit did he notice just how much cooler it was inside. He welcomed the change.

The interior slowly began to reveal itself. Along the wall, in a circular fashion, intermittent shafts of light shot straight up from the floor—light, dark, light, dark—going all the way up to the ceiling. Yamane was surprised to see figures and scenes suspended above. Like the walls that surrounded them, they too lived in thin slivers of light between the shadows. As he moved more into the middle of the rotunda, Yamane thought he could get a better look. It didn't help. He did notice, however, after looking past these objects, the ceiling was a perfect circle, dome-like in shape. At the base, where the radius met the front entrance, he saw more inscriptions carved into the walls. They were similar to the ones outside.

"Those figures represent significant periods in our history," Kel Sen-Ry said on the other side of the rotunda. "The scene begins here," he pointed, "and goes all the way to the present."

"What does each of them mean?" Kershaw asked.

"Time is the one commodity we have in short supply. Perhaps later, if the opportunity should arise, we can return. But for now we must press on."

Kel Sen-Ry found a small doorway, opposite the entrance. It had been set low, about waist-high. The only way a person could get through was if he crouched down. Kel Sen-Ry went first, followed by Yamane and Kershaw. When all three emerged on the other side, they found themselves at one end of an immense hallway. Simplicity and light replaced the darker, solemn atmosphere of the rotunda. On either side, both walls were spaced much further apart. They started out vertically, like a projectile going straight into the sky, and then tapered in near the top. At about the forty-meter mark, both inward angles collided into each other. The design approximated the hull of a boat flipped upside down. Yamane didn't know about Kershaw, but he felt a sense of deep inner peace here. The feelings inside him seemed to emanate from the walls themselves.

"This place is amazing," Kershaw said, his words echoing off the walls.

As they traveled a little farther through the massive enclosure, Yamane noticed the same contrast between light and dark. He knew it was important, but didn't know why.

Two massive doors met them at the end of the corridor. Like the walls, they assumed a vertical shape most of the way up, both sides tapering in to the top, until an angled point formed its zenith. The hinges alone were twice as big as a full-grown man. Situated between their party and the doors was a short, metallic podium. On top of the podium sat a box. It looked like sheets of dull silver covered the surface. On the sides, written vertically, Yamane saw inscriptions.

Kel Sen-Ry stopped a short distance away from the podium and mumbled a few indiscernible words. Then from underneath his robes, he produced an object of some sort. It was flat, with jagged edges, like a kind of key. He found a narrow slit on the side facing him and inserted it into the opening. After a muted click, an unseen door popped open. Yamane strained to see what was inside, but the darkened interior obscured his view. Kel Sen-Ry reached in and took something out, closed the door, and then turned around. "These strips of cloth will be draped over your shoulders," he said like a teacher instructing his students. "They are reminders of a person's unworthiness to come before the High Council." Yamane and Kershaw examined the long white pieces of shimmering fabric. "They are physical representations of a person's inner being. Death, hatred, and anger—they all emanate from those who are apart from the High Son. That is what these strips symbolize."

"The High Son?" Kershaw asked. "I don't understand."

"There is so much I can say, but time does not permit; so I'll be brief." He looked up. "The dark part of your inner being must be replaced by something new. The High Son made this possible. He transforms a person, makes him new. These cloths represent such a relationship."

Yamane held up his strip. "We don't fully understand what this means, but we will abide by your customs and traditions."

Kershaw offered a nod of affirmation.

This seemed to satisfy Kel Sen-Ry. He walked up to the end of the hallway and bowed three times in quick succession. The immense, multi-ton doors started to move. The moment the leading edges pulled away from each other, dazzling white light burst forth from the other side. Yamane instinctively turned away and covered his eyes.

"Can you see anything?" Kershaw called out.

Yamane lowered his hand. "A little," he squinted. Then he noticed something unexpected. Even though the light filled every corner of the corridor, it did not feel as strong as before. In fact, it felt soft, inviting. He took a chance and opened his eyes all the way, just in time to see Kel Sen-Ry walking inside, his head dipped. A deep inner peace moved Yamane. The longer he stared, the more he felt drawn into the gentle, luminescent glow. He looked right at Kershaw. The anger and resentment manifested by him earlier were gone. Yamane didn't say anything. He didn't have to. They faced each other and gave each other knowing looks before going in together. Both doors swung closed behind them.

The inner chamber was more dazzling than Yamane expected. Light seemingly came from every direction. The place itself emitted a glowing radiance, from the floor under his feet all the way to the top, hundreds of meters above. There were no obvious sources of light; it was as though it existed here and touched the visible world around them. The more he took it in, the more Yamane felt a sense of intense humility. He brought up both ends of his cloth strip and examined them. Now he understood the purpose they served. No one could enter this place and not feel a certain level of unworthiness.

His head dipped, unconsciously. Even the floor below drew him in. Dark greens, light greens, whites and grays danced a dance of infinite combinations and shapes. Then something odd caught his attention. There were no seams. Not one. The entire structure rested on a foundation of cut and polished rock. What the ancient Antarens had accomplished here went far beyond anything he could have imagined. It awed him.

Up ahead, he saw the faint outlines of chairs on an elevated platform. There were two groups, six on one side and six on the other. A small space in the middle created an understated but distinct boundary between the two. Their style of dress further accentuated the division. Those from the military were sitting on his left, wearing uniforms similar to Subidor Tal Win-Tu's. The other group, sitting to his right, wore robes nearly identical to that of Kel Sen-Ry. In front of them were stairs. Yamane counted them in his head. Twelve. It was the number he expected.

"You may approach the High Council," a voice bellowed when all the three of them had arrived at the platform base.

Kel Sen-Ry went first. Yamane and Kershaw followed a discreet distance behind. When they reached the top, the Antaren approached the council. He nodded to his left and then his right before offering a long, slow bow.

"Welcome," a council member said as he motioned them forward.

Kel Sen-Ry, Yamane and Kershaw took several more steps before they stopped a respectful distance away. The moment had a surreal quality about it. Everything Yamane had longed for—desperately needed—had come to be. He also felt terrified. Their future, their past, everything humanity had ever hoped or would hope again, all boiled down to this one moment. It almost felt as though the entire building was pressing down on him. With each passing second, someone added just a little bit more weight. But he had also prepared himself for this. And with preparation came courage. He tried to summon up all that he had.

"Why do you wish to address this body?" the same Antaren asked. The pointed question echoed off every wall in the chamber.

Yamane took a single step forward. He cleared his throat. Here goes, all or nothing. "As you have all no doubt been told, my name is Commander Frank Yamane...and I have come to ask for something, something very important."

"What is this something you seek?" The question hung in the air like a pungent aroma, both sides aware of its presence, but neither group knowing if it should be valued or despised.

"This is rather a long story," Yamane replied. "Perhaps you may understand better if I share with you what brought about our arrival." He drew in a deep breath and started from the beginning. He told them how Sergeant Morris detected the Deravans at the edge of their space. He also told them how he and a squadron of fighters made first contact, how that ship blew itself up shortly after they arrived at Titan, how an armada of additional 1000 Deravan ships destroyed their fleet and then proceeded to Earth, and how they encircled the helpless planet and unleashed a catastrophic attack against his people.

After he had finished, members of the council sat in silence for almost a minute before they turned toward one another. Yamane suddenly felt very exposed, especially in this place. There just wasn't anywhere to hide.

"Your people have suffered much and our sympathies go with you, but what does this have to do with us?"

Yamane figured the best approach was the most direct approach. "If you destroy their fleet, you stop the Deravans."

"Destroy them with what? You have no ships."

Now or never. "I don't, but you do." The council stirred. "I realize this may seem like an impetuous request, but I have given the matter a great deal of thought." More than they would ever know. "The Deravans have come for my world. In time, they will come for yours as well. The only way we can stop them is if we unite. I know the past ten years have been difficult for both our peoples, but I am asking you to put our differences aside for the sake of our future. As I see it, unless we can work together, neither of us will have one much longer."

One of the council members from the military class rose to his feet. The two stood opposite each other. Hope arose within Yamane. "Go back to your Earth," the Antaren said with all the vehemence he could muster.

"Your presence here is a threat to our way of life; maybe even to our very existence."

Yamane's world came crashing down on him. No, it can't be! his mind screamed. He at least hoped there would be a dialogue, some sort of discussion. But his request had been denied before it had even been considered. On the other hand, he hadn't come all this way just so they could refuse his request at the first opportunity. If they wanted to cut him off at the knees, fine. Yamane could just as easily continue the discussion from a lower height. "Do you understand what I am saying? Both our worlds are involved in this."

"You will be silent!" the Antaren soldier bellowed.

Another council member jumped to his feet. "I have belonged to the First Order since before you were promoted to the rank of galidor," he noted. "As the newest member of the High Council, your place is the last."

"Your position is well known to me, Sul Ren-Ta," the galidor replied. "As a minister of the First Order, you embrace the teachings of the Prophets. We in the military rely in strength and might. What you ask is that we abandon our way of life."

The priest's scaly face stiffened. "Galidor Din Tru-Ne, what you object to is not valid, since Commander Yamane has arrived, just as we expected. We have been the guardians of our holy writings since the beginning of our history, and everything they said has taken place with equal measure. Do you now challenge the prophecies because they are a personal threat to you?"

"Galidor Din Tru-Ne is correct. The First Order claims they reveal the meanings of the Prophets, but how do we know they are not mistaken?"

"No one has ever questioned the integrity of the First Order. An accusation of this nature will strip you of your rank and position if the claim goes unproven."

"We will not sit by and allow the destruction of everything we believe in," Din Tru-Ne said while pointing an accusatory finger at Yamane. "He is asking us to go to war for his people, leaving us defenseless."

Yamane found himself lost in the middle of an argument he could barely understand, let alone follow. He had become convinced of one thing, however. Whatever the basis of their argument, it went much deeper than sending their ships to Earth.

"Commander Yamane has come just as the Prophets predicted. Since this is an unmistakable fact, we should adhere to what they say about this man."

Yamane became even more confused. Penned thousands of years ago, how could their sacred writings be connected to him? It didn't make any sense.

"I say we decide now and dispense with this foolishness."

The tide had turned against Yamane. His position had been precarious at best, even before the meeting started, but now he felt this same body had pushed him to the edge of a cliff. One wrong step and he would go over the side. He looked inward, into the past. What he had sought from Henthorne came to mind. The time had come to play his one and only ace.

He took a step forward and cleared his throat a second time. "Excuse me, but there is a way we can stop the Deravans."

Arguments thrown in both directions ceased. One by one, every pair of glowing eyes drifted over in his direction.

"Stop the Deravans? What do you mean by this?"

"A weakness about them has been discovered—one we can exploit."

Kel Sen-Ry turned right at Yamane and stared at him in a way he had never seen an Antaren look before. He appeared genuinely surprised.

"You say you are aware of a weakness. How have you come to know this?"

Yamane offered a heavy sigh. "The cost of such knowledge has come at a terribly high price. But after an extensive examination of all the data, we have determined their ships are powered by simple electro-magnetism." He paused for effect. "This is their weakness. All you have to do to stop them cold is produce an EM field of equal and opposite strength."

Sul Ren-Ta studied him first before responding. "You know this will work?" he asked.

"In principle, yes," Yamane replied. He paused again, and summoned up the last of his dwindling reserves. This is the decisive moment. Stay strong. "In truth—no. At present, we have nothing more than a working theory, but it does fit all the facts."

Sul Ren-Ta rose out of his chair and motioned for Kel Sen-Ry to come forward. Stopping a short distance away, the minister of the First Order spoke with him in whispers. Yamane wished he knew what they were saying. Any advantage would help him at this point.

After Sul Ren-Ta finished speaking, Kel Sen-Ry left the council chambers. Yamane and Kershaw watched him leave, neither of them sure why the Antaren had been sent away.

"I don't understand what's happening." Yamane said to the council after turning back. "Is there something wrong?"

"I have sent for the writings of the Prophets," Sul Ren-Ta replied after he lifted his eyes. "They reside in a special vault above Tel Shador."

"I object," Din Tru-Ne protested in a loud, booming voice. "This Terran is not fit to hear the Prophets. He will never understand them or their meanings."

Sul Ren-Ta walked the length of the platform. "If you do not withdraw your objection, then the council will make an immediate ruling concerning your place here. Choose now what will be done next." He then stopped a short distance from his fellow members. One by one, they rose with him. Though Yamane didn't fully understand what had taken place, he did understand its outcome. The Antaren had been blackballed.

The galidor lowered his head. "I withdraw my objection."

Vindicated, Sul Ren-Ta resumed his place.

After a number of minutes had passed, a door opened on the far side of the chambers. Kel Sen-Ry returned with something resembling a large book. A number of pages stuck out, some more than others. They had yellowed over time, giving Yamane the impression it was very old. The cover was dark and rectangular. Kel Sen-Ry held the book in front of him in a reverent manner, each step taken with the utmost of care.

When he reached the platform, he bowed before the council. Sul Ren-Ta again rose from his chair and went over to him. He mumbled something and then took the sacred writings out of Kel Sen-Ry's outstretched hands. "These sacred words were written at the dawn of our recorded history," he said in an almost prideful manner. "Passed on from one generation to the next, the message found in this book has been preserved without change, without error. The text I have before me is the oldest surviving copy."

In his mind's eye, Yamane could almost see the prophet in some dusty, out-of-the-way place. Hunched over a chair in the corner of a little room, he wrote those most important of words by the dim light of an oil lamp. The quill in his hand scratched out each word, stopping only when he had completed the scroll. Untold centuries later, this same prophet sitting in that room in that out-of-the-way place would touch the life of a man who once called himself...enemy.

Sul Ren-Ta opened the cover and looked at the top page longingly. "I will read three passages, all of which have a direct relationship with the matter at hand." He then placed his finger just under the first letter of the first word. "In order to prepare our people for the final conflict, Antaren society must be divided into different classes. This is a necessary choice so the family lines will be ready at the time of transformation. Many generations will live and die before the appearance of a warrior who is not from our world, but is a part of our people. He must endure many trials on his journey, but this is required for the preparation of his great task. Though he will come to the point of death, he will not be defeated. Through his sacrifice and suffering, he will develop an understanding of his enemy. It is from this knowledge he shall discover their weakness." Sul Ren-Ta spoke louder. "The sword given him to defeat this ancient enemy will be taken away, but a second one will replace the first. The blade must be sharpened and honed over many generations so it will be ready for his arrival."

He flipped a number of pages before stopping. His attention remained fixed, and then said with a booming voice, "Rejoice. I say again, rejoice. The time for shedding your binding ties with the past has come—your traditions. They were a tutor, a teacher for your people to prepare them for the future. Discard the old ways and embrace the new. Antaren will serve Antaren as a single people. And in unity, the prophesied warrior, with his sword in hand, will strike at death, and vanquish a mighty foe. This is the heralding of the age of eternity; not only for Antara but for all peoples far and wide."

Sul Ren-Ta turned to the last page of their sacred text. "All these things offered by the prophets will come to pass only if those who follow them are pure in spirit and heart. The sacrifice of the High Son has made this so. A great temptation will be to obey these actions in deed alone, but you must resist. For if the integrity and character of Antara is found lacking, the evil, which was once thought dead, will rise again, and all creation will succumb to its power."

Sul Ren-Ta closed the book. The words he had just spoken almost seemed to overwhelm him. "What I have read has been debated from the beginning of our recorded history. But since many of these references are vague and rich in symbolism, such an undertaking is difficult at best. As a result, some of the conclusions drawn from them have had catastrophic results." He clasped his hands together. "A sad example, I'm afraid, is the war between our peoples. Certain members of the First Order persuaded the military they had deciphered the intentions of the Prophets. They convinced them the human race was the evil spoken of in these pages. Since the military already regarded you as a threat, it did not take much persuading to gain their support. But as the events of the war began to unfold, we realized we made a terrible mistake. The High Council considered offering surrender terms for a time, but another interpretation would put things in a different light, and war erupted again. This internal dissent went on throughout the conflict, until we were defeated—not by you, but by ourselves. But we have learned from our mistakes, namely, that at the proper time, what the Prophets have spoken about would be lived out before our eyes. I believe everything you have shared with us validates our understanding of them."

Yamane's head was reeling. So much had been said in the last five minutes, he didn't know where to start. He somehow pushed all the confusion in his mind aside, and focused on a single question. "Are you telling me these prophecies written hundreds of years ago foretold the Deravans and their attack against Earth? That's more than I think I can accept."

Sul Ren-Ta's hand slid across the cover of their sacred book. He seemed to draw strength from it. "I can see how this might appear to an outsider, but what I am saying is the truth, one we recognized a year ago. Since then we have channeled all of our energies toward the rebuilding of our fleet. Despite our best efforts, however, it became apparent to us our forces would not be sufficient to win a war of this magnitude. We needed more ships and more men. Then we hit upon an idea: to ask your Star Force for the sub-cruisers. The occupation had ended anyway. We figured they would not object to leaving them behind. With the addition of these vessels, the strength of our fleet might be just enough to prevail against them."

Anger crossed Yamane's face. "You were aware of the Deravans before this, weren't you?"

Sul Ren-Ta looked up. "You are most perceptive, Commander. Yes, we knew about the Deravans before they attacked your world." The words cut through Yamane like a knife. The Antarens could have prevented so much death and destruction, and yet, they had done nothing. He looked around the council chambers. It didn't seem as illuminated as before. "Not long ago, the Haradi were a peaceful people living just beyond the borders of our space. That is, until the Deravans arrived. They attacked and left no trace of their existence. Some of the priests, myself included, suggested the ancient evil spoken about by the Prophets had arrived. Others, however, were not so sure. And so we studied and waited."

"You could have at least warned us," Kershaw accused, his voice deep. "If we were told about this ahead of time, we might have had the means to save millions of lives."

Sul Ren-Ta's gaze fell away. "You do not know how difficult it was for us to watch the destruction of Titan, and the subsequent attack against your world." He collected himself. "When the *Corona* headed for our planet soon after, few doubts remained about your identity. The necessary preparations were made shortly before your arrival."

"And you call yourself an enlightened people?" Kershaw accused after he took a threatening step forward. "I don't care what kind of honor and traditions you hide behind, there is no justification for allowing genocide just so you can keep things in a neat package."

Yamane grabbed him from behind. "Stan, that's enough."

Kershaw's eyes became wide. "They let us get wiped out, and they didn't even care."

"I understand your sense of loss," Sul Ren-Ta said, his head dipped, "but we could not act until the truth became known. If we had intervened too soon, both our races would now be extinct."

Yamane ran his fingers through his hair, trying to make sense of it all. "Prophets, the Haradi, the sword, the abolition of classes—it goes far beyond the realm of belief."

"This is not a matter of belief, but of truth. What the Prophets predicted has come to pass. Commander Frank Yamane, you are the prophesied warrior." The council chambers fell silent. "Our sacred texts leave little room for interpretation of what must be done next. In preparation of your arrival, we have assembled all our dreadnoughts, destroyers, skyjackets, cargo barges and surveillance ships. At present, they are in orbit above."

Din Tru-Ne jumped to his feet. "I cannot permit the fleet be given over to this Terran. How do we know he really is the prophesied warrior? The things he has said just might be a coincidence. If we are wrong, there could be terrible consequences for our people." He spun around and faced the council. "You said so yourself, mistakes were made by the First Order during the war. How do we know you have not made one now?"

Members of the military turned toward one another and nodded their heads in agreement.

"What else can be done?" Sul Ren-Ta asked. "We have already gone through the prophecies point by point, and showed how they have been fulfilled. There is no other way."

Din Tru-Ne's lips curved. "But there is," he grinned. Rising from his chair, he came alongside Sul Ren-Ta. Every pair of eyes scrutinized his subtle, yet fluid movements. "Have you forgotten about the test of character? This will reveal without question if this Terran is the one."

Sul Ren-Ta shot a look at Din Tru-Ne. "Such an ordeal was abandoned centuries ago," he protested. "The High Council of the Tulin Era issued their mandate regarding this matter—any test not specifically referenced by the Prophets cannot be accepted as authoritative, especially when the disposition of a prophecy is in question. This judgment has stood unchallenged to this day."

"Do not lecture me on the history of our people," he snorted. "I am aware of this ruling, but I will not sit by and put our future into the hands of this Terran. If there is a way we can know with absolute certainty, I say we pursue this course of action and let the results speak for themselves."

Members of the High Council discussed the merits of his proposal. Most agreed. A handful did not.

"If we give this Terran the bulk of our ships, what will stop him from using them against us?"

"Should we disregard the prophecies he has fulfilled?"

"Will you stake your life on such a belief?"

"Enough!" Din Tru-Ne yelled. The chambers fell silent. "The time for debate is over. Choose now. But whatever choice is rendered, the consequences, whether good or ill, will be based on what you decided this day; so choose well."

"I too say we must be absolutely certain," another galidor offered. The rest stood up and acknowledged the challenge, save one.

Din Tru-Ne stood a little taller. "We are all agreed," he crowed. "And what is your position?"

Offering a brief pause before continuing, Sul Ren-Ta added. "I will abide by your decision, but with one condition."

"And what is this one condition?"

"If Commander Yamane does pass the test, we will offer him our support without question."

"I find the condition acceptable...assuming he passes."

Sul Ren-Ta went over to where Yamane waited. "The High Council has agreed that you, Commander Yamane, will be given the test of character to ascertain if you are the prophesied one. Know this—this will be the most difficult experience you have even known. We can offer no assistance or guidance at this point. Do you have any questions before we proceed?"

Yamane instantly thought of a million. What did the test entail? How long would it last? What would really happen if he did fail? A lot of questions, but no answers. He needed help. "What do you think, Stan?" he asked in a low whisper.

"Looks as though your back is up against the wall on this one," he replied. "If you don't take the test, the council won't give us their ships. If you do take the test and fail, we also don't get the ships. Either way, we're out of luck."

Yamane looked the council over. "That's how I see it, too."

"He did give you the option of asking some questions."

"I do have a couple in mind, but now I'm not so sure."

He bent closer. "Why not? I figure any assistance is better than none."

"Even though we don't know much about this test of theirs, the one thing they seem particularly concerned about is a person's integrity, not his abilities. If I act in a way that casts a pall over the first part, the council might render a decision before I've even started."

Kershaw nodded his head. "You may be right." He shot a quick look at the Antarens. "This is a tough call, but I'll back you up, no matter what."

"Thanks, Stan," Yamane smiled. "I appreciate that." His fears and doubts ebbed away. Only a single-minded determination remained. He approached the council. They appeared stoic, offering no hint of what they were thinking. "I am ready for the test."

Din Tru-Ne walked the length of the platform in stilted strides, stopping a short distance away from Yamane. "Very well."

Just then, a door behind them started to open. A high-pitched screeching filled the council chambers. Long and sustained were the plaintive wails of three rusty hinges rubbing against each other, as though they were aware of what awaited him. Yamane looked back over his shoulder. He knew the door was meant for him and him alone.

Kershaw extended his hand. "Good luck." Both men shook.

Yamane spun around in pure military fashion. Keeping a precise cadence—left, right, left, right—he counted off each step in his mind. The door continued to swing open until it could go no further. Some dust from the top spilled over the edge. The minute particles sparkled as they fell to the ground.

The closer he came to the darkened opening, the more his perceptions lessened. As though a form of tunnel vision affected his eyesight, the world around him dimmed, with one exception—the rectangular pane of black before him seemed to stand apart from everything else.

His first inclination was to stop and peer inside, but this might make him appear apprehensive, afraid. Whatever the outcome of this test of theirs, the one thing Yamane did not want the Antarens to see was fear.

He just closed his eyes tight and stepped inside without pause or hesitation. The door banged shut behind him.

CHAPTER
18

HIGH COUNCIL CHAMBERS
DAIETH TIME MINUS TWO

Darkness. Yamane stood there, alone. He could see nothing, except a black void.

With his head cocked, the only sounds he heard were his own short, quick breaths. He turned about slowly. Persistent darkness followed him everywhere.

A swirling breeze brushed past. The sensation felt good, calming. His reaction surprised him. Yamane figured wind blowing around in a darkened room might have startled him. Yet, he experienced just the opposite. In fact, he seemed to feel a growing sense of well-being overtake his instinctual fear of the unknown. How can I be enjoying this? he asked himself. Perhaps the breeze wasn't a breeze at all, but some kind of gas affecting his senses.

Without any warning, a flash of light burned his eyes, momentarily blinding him. He stood in place, not moving. That same sense of stillness returned. Then something began to reveal itself. When he fixed his gaze on a distant, hazy object, it began to grow in size and clarity. A dizzying array of colors and shapes seemed to blossom right before his eyes. Yamane began to feel light-headed. When he instinctively reached out for something to hold onto, his hand bumped into an unknown form. He clung to it with all of his strength, as though someone had just thrown him a life preserver.

Another object came into view, and then another, and another. "How can this be?" he asked himself, confused. Rubbing both eyes with the heel of his hands, he opened them again. The same baffling images returned. Yamane knew what they appeared to be, but his mind could not accept them as genuine. If they were, then he could only draw one conclusion—he was home again.

He took a hesitant step towards a nearby wall. Three pictures hung at eye level caught his attention. He bent over and peered at them. "I know these people," he said to himself, as though saying such words made them true. "My family." Is it possible? His guard went up.

The smell of charred wood filled his nose. A quick look around revealed a rocking chair sitting in front of a fireplace. He recognized it immediately. The one hundred-year-old chair had belonged to his uncle before he died. He touched one of the sculpted armrests. The lacquered wood felt real enough.

Other objects registered more on a conscious level: a fishing pole, the table he made in his workshop, the coin collection begun at the age of ten, and most importantly, the coffee mug he brought with him whenever he came home on furlough. The last image stirred his imagination more than the others did. The tradition started out innocently enough. Yamane received the gift from Kershaw on his thirtieth birthday. Not having much use for it, he brought the cup home on his next furlough and intended to leave it there. Liana decided the mug should stay with him. She figured it brought him home alive once it could do so again. How could he refuse such a request? He observed the tradition religiously since then, until her death.

Yamane set the coffee mug down. "But this isn't possible," he reasoned, "If it is, then I must be—"

"Frank? Frank?" a voice called out to him from behind. "Is that you?"

Yamane froze. The hairs on his neck stood on end. He turned around slowly, almost too afraid to embrace the impossible. Then he saw her. His heart leapt into his chest. There, at the bottom of the stairs stood Liana. Can it be true? Her soft blonde hair dangled over her exposed shoulders. Those intoxicating green eyes, alabaster skin, and garnet red lips were exactly as he remembered them. A burst of joy welled inside him until he could no longer contain himself. He rushed over and hugged her with the strength of ten men, refusing to let go. Gazing deeply into her eyes, he kissed her. She resisted at first, surprised by his unexpected expression of emotion, but then surrendered in his arms. He had his precious wife again.

"How can you be here?" he asked softly. "It doesn't matter. You're with me now."

Liana pulled back. She placed her hand on his forehead. "Are you feeling alright?" she asked after raising an eyebrow. "This was what I was hoping for yesterday when your ship docked. Better late than never, I guess."

He hugged her again, even tighter than before.

Liana gave him a funny look, and then asked, "What's gotten into you, Frank? You act as if you haven't seen me for years." She stopped. The corners of her lips edged up into a smile. "I guess your six-month patrol along the Terolli Corridor was rougher than you thought, huh?"

"You know, you're right—wait. Did you say the Terolli Corridor?"

"Yes. Why?"

Yamane looked up. A long-forgotten memory returned. "I was assigned there at the end of the war," he whispered to himself. "That was the last supply route used by the Antarens before we took the key planet in that sector." Yamane paused. Something about the date felt familiar, but he couldn't quite remember. He turned and dashed down the hall to the kitchen.

"Is something the matter, Frank?" Liana asked from behind as she came in.

Yamane shuffled through the morning paper on the table. "Where are you?" he said in short, choppy words. "Sports, business, local, weather, classified." The last page fell onto the tabletop. Three large black letters "STA" met him back. He grabbed the front section and brought it close.

"STAR FORCE TO MAKE FIRST DIRECT ASSAULT AGAINST ANTARA – QUICK VICTORY IS PREDICTED."

His arm fell away. The headline jogged his memory a little. The date was important, but he still couldn't remember why.

Liana stood in the doorway, beaming at him. He held out his arms. She fell into his embrace a third time. The past and the present melted away. They were together again.

He buried himself in the smell of her perfume. It had been so long. "You don't know how hard it's been being away from you," he said, his every word quaking, struggling against an emotional tidal wave.

Liana laid her head on his chest. "Every day you were away became a little more difficult than the one before," she said. "I knew the military would be just as much of a part of my life as yours when we were married, but knowing that doesn't make it any easier. You are gone so much of the time because of the war. I just wish it was over so we can be together, and stay together."

Several silent minutes passed before he relaxed his hold on her. "Why don't we get out for a little while." Yamane couldn't say why, but for some reason he had a sense he needed to be somewhere else. "I think I'll feel better if we stretch our legs, maybe do some shopping."

Liana rose up on her toes. "That's a good idea," she agreed. "The markets will be open for another two hours. I have a few stubs left in my ration book. I'll make your favorite dinner and the two of us can have a quiet night together." She hurried down the hallway.

Yamane couldn't shake that same nagging feeling in the dark recesses of his mind. If only he could remember. The sounds of Liana rustling through the closet upstairs, looking for a coat, made him forget his worries.

"Door lock," she said to the voice panel near where Yamane waited. The door swung closed on its own and clicked twice. Her voice resonating in his ears continued to thrill him.

He went out first and took a good, long look around. He couldn't believe his old neighborhood hadn't changed at all. Those same birch trees in his front yard swayed in the wind, the Kubo twins rode their bikes as usual, slightly rusting street signs at each intersection were still just as rusty, and those same potholes on his street were there too. Everything was just how he remembered it. But Yamane knew this couldn't be possible, could it?

"The next tram is coming," Liana called from further up the street.

He picked up the pace. The streetcar pulled up right in front of them. Most of the passengers getting off were coming home from work. They looked tired, empty. The foremost thought on their minds was escaping into the safety and solitude of their homes. He couldn't blame them. Things went badly for the Star Force when war first broke out. Everyone had suffered a loss of one kind or another. In their homes, however, they could shut out the world, for a while. But these were the lucky ones. They at least had jobs. Most of the factories were nothing more than bombed-out shells. The ones that had escaped destruction not only kept the economy going; they also maintained the flow of arms to the front. But that was then, he caught himself thinking.

The tram stopped just in front of the market district. A mechanized voice announced their arrival. Yamane grabbed Liana's hand when the doors slid open. Even before they had taken their first step, the people behind them surged forward. He pulled her off just before the passengers in the double-wide cars spilled out onto the sidewalk. They both laughed when they realized all those people had nearly trampled them in the melee.

"My hero," she beamed, her green eyes sparkling.

The front entrance of the market burned brightly in the distance. "Come on," Yamane said as he pulled on her arm again, "dinner awaits."

The ironwork grill went up both sides of the entrance and over the top. Just beyond, the market-place was abuzz with activity. Thousands of people hustled and bustled up one aisle and down the next. Everywhere they went—tents, tables, or booths—men and women alike hawked their goods. Whatever a person wanted or needed, he could find it in there, somewhere.

Judging by the size of the crowds, Yamane figured it was probably Monday—delivery day. There were always far more people there when the merchants received a fresh shipment of meats and vegetables. "I almost forgot just how crazy this place could get."

Liana fumbled through her purse. "I'll go across the street and exchange the ration coupons for voucher tickets," she said. "Do you want to come with me?"

"No. I'll wait for you here." She gave him a kiss before running to the other side.

As usual, a line extended from the window and went down the block a good ways. He would never understand why government bureaucrats decided a person needed to exchange coupons for voucher tickets. There was probably a good reason for this, but the logic of it all escaped him.

While he waited, Yamane leaned up against a light pole. The second sun had just slipped past the horizon, creating his favorite time of day—twilight. A number of the nearby lights flickered on. On the other side of the street,

Liana waited patiently in line. She came here almost every week; him, not so much. Yet, Yamane found the spot where he stood familiar. The last time he thought about Liana being here was when he was on board the *Nautilus*. He received a letter from her. In it, she said she only had a few minutes to write. The next tram was coming soon and she wanted to get to the market before it closed.

"Wait a minute," Yamane shuddered. He searched for a discarded newspaper. A tattered remnant of one stuck out of a trash bin. Snatching it out of the dented container, he pulled it up close. "February 11," he gasped. "That was when—" The realization electrified every nerve ending in his body. All the details of that terrible day returned with perfect clarity. He had a five-day pass for that week, but at the last minute, he decided against using it because they were preparing for their first direct assault on Antara. That message from Liana was the last one she sent, before...

A low hum sounded in the distance. Peripheral sounds of people talking fell away into silence. Yamane ran into the street so he could better see the sky. One, five, ten...twelve lights approached from the west. They appeared like luminescent disks at first, but as those ships flew closer, they assumed an attack configuration. They were Antaren. The High Council had somehow brought him to the exact moment when his wife had died.

An ion blast launched into the city by the lead ship scattered the crowds in a thousand different directions, most screaming. Yamane searched for Liana through the throngs, but couldn't spot her. A couple of people collided into him and then ran past. He jumped up on a pedestal at the base of a streetlight, hoping a better vantage point would help. Hundreds of fleeing men, women and children, ran through the streets, but still no Liana. Despite his search, an unexpected thought worked its way into his conscious mind. He had been placed into a position previously denied him. Even though her death had not been his fault, the guilt he carried made him feel as though it was. Had he been here, he might have saved her. Perhaps, he thought quickly, the Antarens are offering me a second chance.

"Liana!" he screamed. "Where are you?" Sounds of people shrieking answered him back. He ran back into the street, hoping to spot her. The next wave of ships fired. With pinpoint accuracy, bolt after bolt struck a row of buildings across from him. Scores of windows shattered, sending broken glass onto the sidewalks below. Yamane ripped off his coat and draped it over his head.

Another explosion hit two other cars no more than ten meters away, which burst into flames. Columns of black smoke began to billow up into the air. Yamane made a mad dash for the other side. "Liana!" he called again. "Where are you?" He looked around, but only saw blurs of people running past. "Liana!"

"Frank," he heard her shout, "I'm over here!"

Yamane looked up. He found her crouched down in the doorway of a nearby building, frantically waving her arms. Two more explosions went off behind him. Now or never, he thought, and then sprinted to the other side. Yamane found himself in her arms again. "Just stay put until this is over. The Antarens will be gone soon." He tried holding her close, but it was difficult because her hands were trembling so badly.

"We can't stay here," she pleaded. "The building could come down on us at any second."

"It's too dangerous. Please, just stay with me." She fought against him. He couldn't understand why she would be so willing to expose herself to danger. That thought triggered another forgotten memory. His mind flashed back to the coroner's report. Witnesses said they saw her in a doorway one minute, and then ran into the street the next. One of the walls from an adjacent building gave way and fell on top of her. They said she never saw it.

"We've got to get away," she asserted. "The explosions are getting closer."

He held onto Liana's arm as tight as he could, so she couldn't run off, but she continued to pull away from him; each time with greater effort. He was suddenly confronted by the inescapable contradiction of losing her again, and knowing she had been dead for ten years. Were the Antarens giving him the chance to prevent her death, or were they waiting to see if he would keep the events of history intact? His mind wrestled with the moral implications of both. Unable to decide, a war between his head and his heart ensued.

Liana looked deep into his eyes. The love he felt for her was almost too much to bear.

His grip on her loosened. She jerked back again. Their hands slipped further apart. Yamane knew from his innermost being she had been fated to die on that terrible day, and no one or nothing could change that. He could act selfishly and save her for himself, but there might also be a terrible consequence if he did. Hundreds, if not thousands of others who had not died before could be lost. In fact, he could very well disrupt, perhaps even alter the outcome of the war. But he loved her. He had her now in his arms. Death could be vanquished.

He gazed upon her one last time. No. Yamane let go, feeling her sleeve run through his hand. "I love you," he whispered, and then she disappeared.

Unable to watch, he turned away and closed his eyes tight. A lone Antaren ship flew overhead. A single blast struck the building across from him. And just as it had happened ten years ago, a wall gave way, landing in the middle of the street. People fled in terror, but he already knew the result. The sounds of the attack and people screaming faded into silence.

A warm, gentle breeze brushed past his face, just like before. Yamane lifted his head. He found himself in the darkened room again. Whatever he had endured, it was now over.

He rose to his feet and straightened his uniform. It was sopping with sweat, and stuck to his skin. A thick layer of perspiration also covered his face.

"Why do you resist me?" a captivating voice called to him with great gentleness.

Yamane spun around, but saw no one. "Who's there?" he called into the darkness.

"Why do you kick against the goads?" the compelling voice spoke a second time.

His eyes darted about. "Is anybody there?" No answer. "Show yourself."

"You are my chosen instrument, appointed as my representative for both your people and theirs. I am sending you to open the eyes of those who follow me."

"Who are you?"

"I am the High Son, whom you resist. I have called you to help them turn from darkness to light. You must suffer for my name's sake, so that one day those who believe will join with the Great Creators and abide with us forever." His voice faded.

Yamane was alone again. What was that voice? It sounded different than the Antarens'. His words were beautiful, mystical. Instead of feeling afraid, he found the voice had calmed him. Not only that, but the lingering questions about what might have been with Liana, and the pain caused by his guilt, they were all gone as well.

Unsure how much time had passed, he became faintly aware of the open doorway ahead. His legs felt weak, as though they had been running for miles. He took a step forward, but the light from the other side made him feel dizzy. He grabbed the door frame and propped himself up against the wall. Light faded into darkness.

Kershaw, realizing his friend was in trouble, bolted off the dais and ran to the other side of the chambers. "It's all right, Frank," he said after putting Yamane's arm over his shoulder. "I've got you." Yamane stared past him. Kershaw tried to get his attention, but he didn't respond. "Frank, can you hear me?" he asked. "Frank!"

After several heart-stopping seconds, Yamane rolled his eyes upward. "Has it gone dark in here?" he groaned. "I can't see anything."

Kel Sen-Ry hurried down the steps. "You must come with me at once." He took the commander by the hand and led him to the far corner of the Council Chambers. Imbedded into the rock was a crudely shaped basin, filled with water. He cupped his hands and scooped in as much as he could. The cool, refreshing liquid dribbled over Yamane's head, most of it running down his face. Something like scales fell from both eyes. After blinking a couple of times, the darkened chambers lightened, and blurry images came into focus. His eyesight returned.

Yamane brought his hands up. "What happened?" he asked after looking upon them, his mind a torrent of conflicting emotions. "What did you do?"

"Our sacred writings tell us the same thing happened to Sop Aul-Us. He had a special encounter with the High Son long ago in the past. But you could not have—"

"I did. A voice called out to me in the darkness. He said I was his chosen instrument."

"Can this be true?" Kel Sen-Ry asked. "This must mean you—"

"And my eyesight?"

"If I hadn't performed this cleansing ritual, your blindness would have been made permanent." Kel Sen-Ry stared into his eyes. "Do not tell the council what you told me just yet," he warned, "until the proper time. Then they will understand." He bowed and then returned to the platform.

Kershaw looked him over, concerned.

"It's okay," Yamane said in a hushed voice after wiping some residual water off his head. "I'm fine now. How long was I in there?"

"Three hours."

"Three hours?" he said to himself, shock registering in his voice. "Are you sure? It felt more like only a few minutes."

"How was it in there? Not too bad, I hope."

"Don't worry about me," Yamane replied. "I'm all right. In fact, I'm better than all right. The Antarens have given me a very special gift." He dipped his hand in the basin again. Water dripped off his fingers. "I think I'm beginning to understand what this is about."

Kershaw studied him close. "Are you sure you're okay? Maybe you should rest a bit longer."

"All in good time. But right now, we have more pressing matters at hand."

Yamane found he could walk under his own power again. The longer he went, the stronger he felt. Both men went up the steps and took their place alongside Kel Sen-Ry. An awkward silence followed.

"Explain your reasons for what you did?" Din Tru-Ne finally asked.

The question surprised Yamane. "You know what took place in there?"

"Except for the end—yes. We, however, are more concerned about why you acted as you did, not what you did."

"I can only say it was the hardest decision I have ever made in my life. No one should ever be put into a position of choosing between the death of a loved one and the lives of strangers."

"We want to know why," he repeated, his tone firm.

"Because I believe things happen for a reason. I don't know if you can understand this, but if I acted selfishly and changed the outcome of the past, even if it meant saving my wife's life, the timeline could have been irreparably damaged. The lives of thousands of people were at stake. I could never take such a chance. You can call me a fool, but I saw no other choice. That's how I see things, and I believe this High Son of yours sees them the same way."

The room stilled, as though a paralyzing force had struck the council. Sul Ren-Ta rose to his feet. "How do you know about him?"

Yamane took a step back, fearing he may have said the wrong thing. Kel Sen-Ry's warning popped back into his head. "He called out to me in the darkness."

"The unaccounted-for part of the test," one of them gasped.

Every council member began turning towards each other and speaking in low tones. Yamane craned his ear over, but he could not make out a single word. When they finished, Din Tru-Ne rose from his chair and walked across the platform. He stopped a short distance away. Yamane braced himself. The Antaren appeared to look Yamane over, as if to convince himself that what he said had been the truth. The two stared at each other. "I give my full support to Sul Ren-Ta's claim that Commander Yamane is the prophesied one." The remainder of the council rose to their feet as a show of support.

"You have done well," Sul Ren-Ta complemented. "You acted as the prophets said the prophesied warrior would. The High Son's appearance has validated this."

"I still don't understand," he replied. "How did I pass your test?"

"Let me begin by saying the grief you felt became my grief, but there could be no other way. Over the centuries, we have studied at great length what the character of the prophesied one would be like. The chief one among these is an attitude of self-sacrifice. This is what the test of character sought above all else. I think the High Son's appearance has confirmed our suspicions. We put you into a place where we would all know, one way or the other."

"You mean I was actually there?"

"In a manner of speaking. Though you never actually left the room, we can access important events from the past. You do not travel back in time, but in a sense, your mind and memories do."

Yamane looked back over his shoulder. "Amazing. The whole experience felt so...real."

"Quite real. And because of what the test has revealed, the High Council grants your request. But before you take command of the fleet, there is one other matter." Sul Ren-Ta approached the periphery of the platform. "This is a subject you have no doubt heard a great deal about, and you may think you know the whole story. But the truth of the matter is that things are never as they seem." As usual, Yamane had no idea what he meant. But if his experiences with the Antarens had taught him anything, he would make his meaning clear soon enough. "Commander, I assume you are aware of what took place at the end of the occupation."

More than Sul Ren-Ta knew, the events of the past few days still fresh in

his mind. "Of course," he answered. "You requested the sub-cruisers be left behind when the occupation ended. Star Force Command agreed at first, but as you know, they changed their minds. Instead, they ordered those ships to the Cygnus Base Station, and scuttled them shortly afterward."

"You would be correct if this indeed had happened." Yamane had a funny feeling about where this was heading. Something big was coming. He could feel it. "The sub-cruisers never arrived at the Cygnus Base Station...and they were never scuttled."

Yamane checked with Kershaw. He just shrugged in reply. "How do you know this?"

"Because we intercepted the sub-cruisers and brought them back here."

"You what?" Yamane gasped.

"How is that possible?" Kershaw asked. "We would have heard something about this."

"Losing seven sub-cruisers is a difficult thing to explain. Our sources in several sensitive positions revealed Star Force Command believed it would be better if they dealt with the matter quietly, rather than face a public scandal. Since the ships were destined for the scrap yard anyway, they just let your people believe their demise had still taken place."

A sober reality swept over Yamane. Surely, the Antarens were not capable of..."If you have the ships, then where are the crews?" He prepared himself for a very hard answer.

"They are all safe," Sul Ren-Ta assured his two nervous guests with a smile. "We have tried to make their stay here as comfortable as possible."

Yamane's worries dissipated. "Here? How much are they aware of?"

"We have elected to say nothing to them at present."

Kershaw's face became beet red. "You mean you hijacked those ships a year ago, held the crews against their wills, and they still don't know why? How could you do such a thing?"

The indignant attitude expressed by Kerahaw seemed to surprise Sul Ren-Ta. "We believed this necessary. The prophecies indicated the Deravans could appear at any time. We had a difficult choice to make, and we made it."

"I suppose you were right, in a sense, but there were other ways this might have been handled."

"Perhaps, but this is not the time for dwelling on the past. The future is the only thing that requires our full and undivided attention. And to the future we pledge ourselves." Sul Ren-Ta's eyes lifted upward. "But a pledge requires proof, and that proof is presently in orbit above."

A knowing look came on Yamane's face. The last missing piece of the puzzle had fallen into place. "That would explain the lack or radio traffic when we entered your space," he reasoned, "and why all your ships had disappeared."

Sul Ren-Ta nodded in agreement. "You are most correct. We recalled the fleet prior to your arrival. Until we were certain why you had come, we placed every ship on the far side of the planet. They are waiting for you to take command."

"But there is still so much we have to discuss," Yamane objected, "battle plans, the number of ships you have, what strategy we will use against the Deravans, and the like."

"I agree. These are important matters—ones that merit discussion. This, however, is not the place for such talks. Kel Sen-Ry will escort you to our underground facilities where we have assembled every senior officer from both fleets. All of your questions can be addressed there."

"Finally, someone here is making some sense," Kershaw said under his breath.

"Before you leave, however, there is one last thing I would like to do," Sul Ren-Ta added. He went over to Yamane and Kershaw and extended his right arm. His oversized sleeve dangled underneath. He grabbed the end of the cuff draped over his fingertips and pulled it back, exposing his hand to the light. "Perhaps this action will make our hope a reality."

Sul Ren-Ta's unexpected gesture of friendship could not have surprised Yamane more. Not once during his previous stay on Antara had he ever touched an Antaren. To do so would have meant putting them through a series of cleansing rituals. Rather than face the unpleasant ordeal, they had always kept their distance. But a council member standing before him had actually put this belief aside. He could not help but be moved.

He extended his hand in return and the two shook. Sul Ren-Ta then stepped to his left and shook Kershaw's hand in the same heartfelt manner. "May the peace of the High Son be with you all...through Him will victory be achieved."

His words seemed to give the council their cue. Without another word, they rose to their feet in unison and exited the chambers through a small door behind the platform. Silence again filed the great hall.

Kershaw came alongside Yamane and placed his hand on his shoulder. "Congratulations—you really pulled it off," he beamed. "I don't know about all this High Son or prophesied warrior stuff, and frankly I don't care, but they believe it, and that's all that matters."

"Shhh," Yamane frowned. He shot a glance at Kel Sen-Ry behind them.

Kershaw caught himself. "Sorry," he whispered. "Just the same, we got far more than what we had hoped for."

"I agree, but now is not the time for patting ourselves on the back. There's still a lot to do, namely, briefing the crews and getting underway." Yamane straightened his uniform. "I think it's time we met the men waiting for us."

CHAPTER
19

PETROS MIG-DALAH
DAIETH TIME MINUS THREE

Yamane, Kershaw, and Kel Sen-Ry hustled down a long, shadowy corridor. At the end of a hallway, about twenty meters ahead, two metallic doors set within the stone masonry emerged out of the darkness. They slid open when the three of them were only a few meters away. The timing had been so perfect they didn't even break their stride until inside. Like the 'elevator' they used before, this one was small, with the same mirrored surfaces on the walls and ceiling.

As he had done before, Kel Sen-Ry stood in the middle, his eyes lifted upward. A beam of light came upon him. "The Operations Center," he said. In a matter of seconds, they had arrived.

Yamane took the initiative and stepped through the opening first. A large room opened up to him on the other side. The walls were high, at least three stories. Except for a gap in the middle, a row of chairs spanned the length of the hall. Behind them, slanting upward, going all the way to the back, were additional rows of chairs. And filling most of those chairs, senior officers from every ship in the fleet sat and waited. Star Force crews predominantly took the seats in the back, while their Antaren counterparts resided from the middle on down. A faint scent of mutual distrust hung in the air.

The instant Yamane stepped into the hall, the eyes and heads of everyone there turned in his general direction. When many of those same Star Force crewmembers recognized who had arrived, they abandoned their seats and rushed down the stepped incline. They completely encircled the pair and bombarded them with questions.

"What's going on around here?" someone demanded.

Another edged his way inside. "Has a deal been cut? Are we going home?"

"Are we leaving now? I don't think I can take this place much longer."

The faces came at Yamane in a blur, until one of them stood out from the rest. The officer stood towards the back, somewhat askew. He looked familiar, but Yamane couldn't quite place him. His thoughts cleared. A name popped into his head.

"Commander Neu?" he asked. The question seemed to mollify the crowd pressing closer. Yamane took advantage of the lull. "Is that you?" A broad smile blossomed on his face. "Don! It is you. I don't believe it—after all these years."

The officer turned towards him. "It's good to see you again, Frank," he lied.

Kershaw knew that voice. The words resonated in his ears like the sound of a tinny piano playing off in the distance. He slowly turned around. Their eyes locked. The anger he felt toward the Antarens paled in comparison with the fury now overriding every other thought in his head. Kershaw approached Neu with slow, deliberate strides. "It's been a long time," he said with contempt dripping off every word.

A knowing look crossed Neu's face. "You're right, it has."

"The last time I saw you, it was at your court-martial."

"Well, maybe this is a portent of better times."

"Under different circumstances perhaps, but these aren't them," Kershaw replied bitterly, his cold blue eyes narrowing.

Yamane forced his way between the two. "That's enough." He pushed them apart. "What happened took place a long time ago. Besides, this isn't where we should be discussing this. We have more important matters before us."

"You're right," Kershaw agreed, "but this isn't settled, as far as I'm concerned."

Yamane took a couple of steps back. "If you would all return to your seats," he yelled above the noise of officers speaking amongst themselves, "then I can start this briefing and answer your questions."

Most of the men surrounding Yamane gave the impression they were reluctant to return to their chairs. But when the senior officers realized the briefing would not begin until they did, they filed back one by one, until the room fell into silence.

The spotlight was on him now. "For those who don't know who I am, my name is Commander Yamane. I have been sent by the High Council to address both sets of crews on a matter of vital importance." A small speaker on the armrest of each chair translated his words into the Antaren language.

"Are you saying we are going on some kind of cooperative mission?" someone asked.

"That is exactly what I'm saying." A number of commanders and subidors shifted in their chairs. A couple of others coughed in a conspicuous manner. Yamane ignored their subtle form of disapproval and continued. "This leads me to my first point. I'm sure you are all wondering, 'why am I here?' Well, I'm not going to sugar-coat the truth for you. We are at war. But unlike all the other wars in our history, this one is for our very existence. I don't have time to give you all the details, but the Antarens have offered their support against a ruthless enemy known as the Deravans." Yamane paused, and then launched into a summary of recent events: Kalmedia, Titan, the battle at Mars, the attack on Earth—all of it. He relayed every detail like a machine, the only way he knew to keep his surging emotions in check.

A commander in the very back row jumped to his feet. "How do we know it wasn't the Antarens who attacked Titan? It makes sense that they intercepted our ships. Getting us out of the way made it easier for them to blow the capital city away."

"Because I was there," Yamane replied. "You'd believe me if you were there too."

"Maybe this is some kind of deception on their part," another commander accused, anger coloring each word. "These Antarens would sooner see us dead than help us."

Kershaw came alongside Yamane. The muscles in his jaw grew tight. "What we faced wasn't a battle," he lashed out. "It was a massacre. Do the Antarens have the ability to destroy entire cities? You heard the commander. Kalmedia's gone. Every major city on Earth—gone."

A sudden pall came over the room, the truth of what he said hitting them all at once.

Yamane thought Kershaw might have overplayed his hand. He appreciated what his second-in-command was trying to do, but the brutal nature of their situation hit the commanders just a little too hard. He needed to instill hope in them again. "We are not down yet," he said. "As I said before, the High Council has agreed to send their entire fleet of warships. Combined with the sub-cruisers, we stand a good chance of defeating the Deravans."

Yamane shifted his attention to the Antarens sitting before him. "I know trust does not come easily between our peoples, but I believe this is the day of change. We must set our suspicions aside and focus on our common enemy." The Antarens responded with cool indifference.

Kershaw came alongside and offered him a nod of encouragement. It helped.

"Before we depart," the commander continued, "there is one other matter I need to address." He looked the Antarens over again. Their demeanor had not changed in the least. "One of my primary responsibilities will be the development of a battle plan against the Deravans. The only way I can do this is if I have some preliminary information regarding your ships." Many of the subidors re-positioned themselves in their chairs. They did not offer a verbal objection, but he suspected this was their way of showing their displeasure. "First thing, how many vessels do you have in your fleet?"

Silence.

Kel Sen-Ry took a decisive step forward. "It is not too difficult a matter for the High Council to replace an insubordinate subidor," he threatened.

"Now answer the question."

One of the Antarens in the front row rose to his feet and stood at attention, his hands clasped together. "There are twelve dreadnoughts, thirty-two destroyers, two hundred and forty skyjackets, one hundred and eighty-seven cargo barges and seventeen surveillance ships," he rattled off efficiently, "plus the seven sub-cruisers and one stellar cruiser." The last part of his statement seemed more like a dig than a recitation of information.

"That's less than the number I expected," Yamane interjected.

"We would have sent more," the subidor replied in a curt manner, "but a small number of ships were held back so we could maintain a minimal defense against Samaarian pirates."

Yamane studied the features of the Antaren. He looked familiar. Then it hit him. Tal Win-Tu. He was the subidor who met them at the border—met them?—Tal Win-Tu had almost destroyed them there.

"I assume your big ships are still using particle disrupters as their main weapons?"

"That is correct. Our dreadnoughts have been outfitted with six batteries, each consisting of ten particle cannons. The destroyers use the same weapons, except they possess thirty per ship. The skyjackets are armed with standard ion blasters. As you know, cargo barges and surveillance ships carry no offensive weapons."

"What about upgrades? The High Council made a reference to this."

"All of our ships have been given an additional two meters of neutronium armor plating. The dreadnoughts have also been installed with the prototype for a new weapon we call the Lambda Wave Generator. Unlike particle disrupters, the lambda wave reaches down into the sub-atomic level and forces an implosion of the nucleus. In effect, the object collapses upon itself when struck by the wave."

Yamane and Kershaw looked at one another. "What success have you had with this new weapon?" the Lt. Commander asked.

"Not as much as we have hoped. Since the weapon is still in the experimental phase, we encountered a number of problems that resulted in the accidental destruction of several ships. But we believe most of the problems have been corrected."

"The lambda wave might be just what we need against the Deravans," Kershaw concluded. "This could give us an edge against their defensive shields."

"That brings me to my next point," Yamane announced. "Our research indicates the Deravans utilize electro-magnetic energy as their main source of power. If we can neutralize them with an opposite EM field, their vessels will be rendered helpless."

"Just how big a field do you intend to create?" one of the subidors asked.

Yamane placed his hands behind his back and stood erect. "Enough to cover a fleet of one thousand ships." The room exploded with the sounds of people conferring with one another. Some shook their heads while others crossed their arms. In either case, the news did not go over well. "Quiet... Quiet, everyone!" he shouted over the noise. "As I said before, we have a plan in the works." Yamane shuffled over to Tal Win-Tu. "Power cells—the big ones. We need two hundred and thirty-two of them. Do you think you can get them on board before departure?"

"The timing might be tight, but I will make every effort."

"Good. Your cooperation has been most helpful. In fact, I believe you can help me do one more thing. During this briefing, I've come to realize just how uninformed I am about Antaren capabilities and protocols. I think it would be a good idea if I had a liaison between your fleet and mine. We obviously have different ways of doing things, and your assistance would be of immense help in minimizing these matters. I was hoping you would take the job."

Tal Win-Tu kept his place. Yamane took his lack of a response as a yes. Not much of a victory, but he would take it. He addressed the crews again. "I realize we are facing a daunting task, but we are also in a position of dictating how and when our attack takes place. Surprise, along with other little tricks up our sleeves, will give us a fighting chance. As important as this is, however, it will not be enough if we cannot put our differences aside and work together. What say you all?" Yamane scanned the room. No one moved. No one said a word.

"Attention!" Kershaw barked.

The crews jumped to their feet in unison.

"We'll depart within the hour. Get your gear and head for the transports."

"Dismissed."

The Antarens immediately left the operations center without attempting any kind of token offer of cooperation. Yamane just shook his head and smiled. The ships' commanders, on the other hand, milled around for a short while before they made their way to the bottom.

"I know you have a lot of questions," Yamane said before any of them had a chance to speak, "but they will have to wait for now."

"Commander, we—"

He offered a look of reassurance. "It's all right. We'll discuss what happened when time permits."

Kel Sen-Ry came from behind him and motioned them towards the corridor.

"Should we go with them?" Kershaw asked as he watched the crews file outside.

"That will not be necessary," the Antaren replied. "Your fighters have been brought here. Just go through the same entrance and proceed to the end of the hallway. Someone will assist you there."

"Thanks for all your help," Yamane said in a mechanical fashion. He looked back. "You coming, Stan?"

"Yeah, I'll be with you in a minute." Yamane turned and disappeared in the hallway.

After he was gone, Kershaw approached Kel Sen-Ry. "I want to apologize for my behavior earlier. I haven't exactly acted very friendly towards you. But I see now you're all right, for an Antaren, that is." He smiled and thrust his arm out. "I know this may be difficult for you, but I would like to shake your hand before we go."

"I only did what was required of me," Kel Sen-Ry said, "but if this is a foreshadowing of things to come, I will not stand in the way." They awkwardly clasped hands and shook. "This is a most curious sensation, but I suppose I may get used to it one day."

"That was almost funny," Kershaw joked. "The next time we meet, I'll help you with your sense of humor."

Yamane watched flight technicians lower both fighters into an Antarian version of a ship's launch tube when he arrived in the underground hangar bay. Unlike the firing system they used, Antarens placed their fighters below deck level.

"Hello, gorgeous," Kershaw declared when he hurried in just behind Yamane. "I can't wait to get up and out of here."

"I'm with you on that," Yamane replied.

From out of nowhere, an Antaren ground team appeared, startling both men by their Houdini-like appearance. The flight crews strapped the pilots in tightly, secured their helmets, checked the flaps of both ships, and fueled them up—all in less than a minute. Kick the tires and check under the hood, and they would have a career at some used hover car lot somewhere on Earth.

The canopy came down over Yamane and locked into place. When he entered the command code into the ship's main computer, his fighter roared back to life. "Do you read me, Stan?" he asked on the radio.

"Loud and clear. Looks good from here."

"Affirmative. I'm firing up the turbines now." He immediately felt the familiar shaking from behind, accompanied by the high-pitched shrill of his main engine. "Every system here shows go," Yamane said over the noise. "How about you?"

"My boards indicate the same. I think we can blast out of here any time we wish."

"Confirmed, Blackhawks One and Two," a voice said on their headsets. "Primary tower indicates you have been cleared for launch at your discretion. Proceed when ready."

"Roger that," he replied. "Lift-off in three seconds, on my mark. Three... two...one...mark." Both fighters shot through the launch tubes and emerged on the far side of Tel Shador. Yamane turned back for one last look. Antares had just pierced through the cloud cover, bathing the city below in soft, tawny light. Seeing the mountains around the city, he thought about the people below. "What will happen to them?" he asked before turning his attention forward again.

Yamane pulled on the stick and changed his angle of ascent. Off in the distance, the first stars revealed themselves.

"You still with me, Stan?" he asked on the radio.

"I'm right behind you. My instruments indicate we will reach orbit in two minutes. Do you have a fix on the *Corona*?"

"Affirmative. Make your course zero-seven-four."

"Roger that—zero-seven-four."

The two pilots kept their trajectory tight. They continued to angle over at a negative five-degree approach, until both fighters leveled out and attained a high orbit above Antara. As they crested over the rim of the planet, Yamane and Kershaw beheld a sight far beyond anyone's expectations. Not only did the *Corona* come into view, but also the entire Antaren fleet positioned behind it.

"Will you look at that," Yamane stammered. "They're all here, just as Sul Ren-Ta promised."

In keeping with Antaren protocol, their biggest ships, the dreadnoughts, took up the first position in line. The sub-cruisers came next, followed by the destroyers, cargo barges, and surveillance ships.

Yamane could not help but think of what these vessels had inflicted against them during the war. The irony of the situation had almost escaped him when he realized they would use them as a tool to save Earth rather than destroy it.

All seven sub-cruisers made their appearance when both fighters flew past the last dreadnought. They were about a quarter as large as their Antaren counterparts, but almost as lethal. Packed to the teeth, he understood why they wanted them so badly.

"This is Commander Yamane," he said into his headset. "Request permission to land."

"Welcome home, Commander," an eager voice on the other end congratulated. "Permission granted. "Proceed to landing bay alpha. I repeat, landing bay alpha."

"Roger, *Corona*."

Yamane altered course and positioned his fighter along the starboard side of his ship. Coming up on the landing bay fast, he edged his stick forward until the wheels hit the deck. He brought his ship to a stop a mere fifteen meters from the crash wall. Never had something so ordinary look so good.

Two crewmembers, ladder in hand, ran up to his fighter. "I don't know how you did it,

Commander," the crew chief yelled after the cockpit canopy lifted, "but the Antarens are coming back with us to Earth,"

Yamane took off his helmet, armed with an expression of stoicism.

"Major Webster is waiting for you on the bridge. He said to tell you well done."

"Thank you, Ensign," the commander replied before heading for the lift.

Yamane felt a kinship with the crew the moment he stepped onto the bridge. It was almost electric. They had changed. Maybe he had been the one who changed—maybe both. He didn't know. What did matter was that they were a crew with a purpose. No. The reason went beyond that. They were a crew with a purpose, and a fighting chance. Perhaps the latter part made the difference.

"Welcome aboard, Commander," Major Webster said, his tone expectant. "The ship can leave whenever you give the order."

Yamane went over to the command chair. "What is the status of the Antaren fleet?"

"Most of the ships have signaled they are ready for departure. Three destroyers and seven cargo barges are experiencing some minor systems failures, but this will not prevent them from leaving on time."

Yamane opened the intercom. "Bridge to engine room."

"Engine room here," Kershaw replied after a short pause. He sounded hurried.

"What do you think, Stan? Is the *Corona* ready to stretch out her legs?"

"They can take whatever you dish out. Just give the word."

"You've got it," he agreed. "Stand by for my signal."

Yamane closed the intercom and came up alongside Landis. "Signal Tal Win-Tu's ship."

"Yes, sir."

"This is Subidor Tal Win-Tu," he replied after a minute had gone by. "I am sorry for the delay, but an unexpected navigational problem distracted me for a moment."

"I understand," Yamane replied. "Things are also a little hectic for us as well, but I am eager to get under way as soon as possible."

"My communications officer informs me we were able to get the power cells loaded faster than anticipated. There is nothing preventing us from departing."

"Excellent. Standby for my signal." He went over to the nav-tech. "Have you plotted a course back to Earth?"

"Yes, Commander. If there are no problems along the way, we should arrive in eighty-four hours."

"Three and a half days," he commented to himself after doing the math in his head. Would the Deravans still be there when the fleet arrived? What about Earth? Did their home even exist? Yamane gave the main screen a good long look. He would have his answers soon enough.

"All the stations have reported in," Webster called out from his post.

Yamane assumed his place in the command chair. He took in the moment. The faces, the sounds, and even the smells were all committed to memory. "Fire up the main engines," he replied. "Take her out nice and slow."

The nav-tech turned back and inputted the command codes into his console. A mild rumbling sounded from behind, followed by a series of irregular vibrations. To Yamane, it was a sweet song. Three and a half days, he thought again. He hoped it would be enough time to get the fleet ready.

When the other ships received their orders, the initial brilliant glow from their engines drowned out the light from Antares. But as each of them blasted out of orbit, the effect gradually diminished.

Yamane studied a faint yellow star in the distance. Their victory may or may not come in three days' time, but right here, right now, he was grateful they still had a fighting chance.

CHAPTER
20

S.F.S. CORONA
1527 PROXIMA MERIDIAN TIME, AUGUST 26, 2217

"Anything yet?" Yamane asked, growing impatient. "Lan Din-Ny should have signaled us five minutes ago."

"No, sir." Landis bent closer. "Wait a minute. Something's coming in. I'm switching over."

"This is Subidor Lan Din-Ny of the destroyer *Ruk-Qia*," the Antaren said on the radio. "Engine repairs are just about complete. We should re-engage the fleet in three hours."

"Confirm the signal," Yamane said to Landis. The news should have pleased him. Instead, he sat back in his chair, his thoughts troubled. They had blasted out of Antara's orbit a few hours ago, and already, a squadron of cargo barges almost collided into another one, and the three destroyers in question had developed engine problems soon after they left orbit. The subidors from each ship convinced Yamane to move on without them since they were confident damage control teams could make repairs in a timely manner. He didn't figure on a timely manner being three hours.

If their problems were this bad now, he wondered, how would they ever make it to Earth? He tried keeping his attitude positive, since the rest of the ships hadn't experienced significant problems, but it was difficult. Yamane reminded himself he had never commanded a fleet this size in his career, and there were bound to be setbacks now and again.

Doctor Owens' voice chimed on the intercom, interrupting his thoughts.

"Yamane here. Go ahead, Doctor."

"I felt I should update you on Lt. Commander Henthorne's progress. Could you please come down here when you have an opportunity?"

A 'no' immediately formed in his mouth, but then he reconsidered. "Maybe a little time away from the bridge will do me some good." Yamane checked the astro-clock. "I'll be there in five minutes." He swiveled the command chair around. "Major Webster, you have the bridge."

When Yamane entered Dr. Owens' office, he found her at her desk, hunched over a data pad. A half-dozen opened medical books lay scattered all around her. On the far wall, three framed diplomas hung over a couple of potted plants sitting on top of a small end table.

"The library computer might help you get the information you need," Yamane suggested after he realized she hadn't heard him arrive.

"Just leave the lab results on the table," Owens replied without looking up. She sat back and rubbed her eyes. Yamane stood in the doorway and smiled, bemused by her failure to recognize him. "I said you can leave the lab results on the table." He didn't respond. After a few seconds, she swiveled her chair around. "Did you—?" Her eyes widened. "I'm sorry, Commander," she apologized. "I thought you were my assistant. I've been waiting for—"

"I know, the latest lab results." Her cheeks grew red. "You called me down here about Henthorne's condition?"

She set her data pad down and gave him her full attention. Yamane didn't take this as a good sign.

"I'm afraid there has been a change in his status since you saw him last," she said, trying to hide some obvious bad news.

Yamane came closer. "What's wrong with him?"

Owens looked at him hard. "We had to amputate his left leg just above the wound," she said, her words sounding heavy. "An infection developed, one I almost didn't catch in time. If I let it go unchecked, it could have threatened his life. I had no other choice but to operate." She drew in a short breath. "He wants to see you."

Shocked by the unexpected news, Yamane just nodded.

Dr. Owens rose out of her chair and led him down a darkened hallway. Yamane noticed her clutching a chart close to her chest, lost in her own thoughts. He wished he could talk about something, anything that might help break the tension, but he knew whatever he offered would come off as superficial. Silence sufficed.

When Yamane entered the recovery room, he saw a wall of white: walls, floor, ceiling, sheets, pillowcases, and beds, the latter going up one side of the room and down the other. At the far end of the med-lab, a nurse stood over a patient. She was dressed in a navy blue smock, uniform and shoes. On the other side of his bed were three IV drips, all placed in a row. There were also several pieces of equipment, some at the foot of the bed, others right next to him, monitoring his pulse rate, blood pressure, and cell count. Except for the high-pitched rhythmic sound of his heartbeat, the room remained quiet.

"Lt. Commander Henthorne is under sedation," Dr. Owens whispered. "He should come out of it at any time."

"I don't understand. He seemed fine after the operation."

She didn't reply.

Yamane approached Henthorne with slow, deliberate steps. He didn't look all that different, though the lieutenant commander's skin did appear a bit ashen.

She bent over and examined his vitals on one of the displays.

"Don't take it too hard, Commander," Henthorne said with a raspy voice as he slowly opened his eyes, a crooked smile on his face. "The doctors here did the best they could."

Yamane stood upright. "How are you feeling?"

He coughed hard a couple of times. "Actually, they tell me I'm pretty lucky. The doctor here saved most of my leg, cutting it just below the knee. Having the joint will make my recuperation somewhat easier. They've already made a cast of the area. I'll start physical therapy once my prosthesis is finished."

Yamane placed his hands at his sides, and them behind his back. No position felt comfortable.

"I don't know what to say," he replied, his tone awkward. "Sounds like they're doing good work here." He knew that came off sounding trite, superficial. "Is there anything you need?" Such a predictable question almost sounded worse.

He tried to speak, but the words didn't come out. Henthorne propped himself a little and cleared his throat. "In fact, there is."

"Name it, whatever you want."

Henthorne brought his elbows back and pushed up. The nurse tried to help, but he rebuffed her efforts with a sneer. "You may not think much of me after all we've been through, but there is one thing I need from you."

Yamane watched him struggle. It was hard to believe this was the same man who ruled absolute not so long ago. "As I said before, I'll do whatever I can."

"Even though I may be slightly incapacitated." Henthorne glanced at his leg. "I can still do my job. Because of the accident, I haven't had the opportunity to finish my calculations. You only have a day or two at most before you send a team to the *Lexington*. Obviously, I can't go, but I can still contribute. You know there's no one else who can do that kind of work better than I can."

"I figured I would take care of this. And besides, I don't think this is the time for—"

"I'm still a part of the crew," he fired back. "Please don't treat me as though I'm not."

Yamane caught a glimpse of the pain Henthorne was experiencing, not only in a physical sense, but psychological as well, the latter probably being much more significant. "What do you think, Doctor?" He asked the question more as a courtesy than in search for the truth. No doctor in his right mind would let someone in his condition near a data pad, let alone put him back on duty.

The semi-present smile on Owens' face disappeared. Her eyes met Yamane's. "If he doesn't exert himself too much, I don't see a problem."

Yamane almost reared back. Since he had met her, Dr. Owens had exhibited a strong concern and protectiveness regarding her patient. Now she seemed to reverse her stance. Something wasn't right about this.

The dark cloud above Henthorne lifted at her words. "Thank you," he smiled.

"I'll have your notes brought here after you get some rest," Yamane said. He hoped the ruse would buy him some time. A little voice in his head told him Dr. Owens was holding back.

"If it's possible, I would prefer Ensign Ivanov as my aide," Henthorne requested.

"I'll make sure you get whatever you need. Just get some rest." Yamane patted the bed.

"That's good advice," the nurse joked, her arms folded like a drill sergeant. "You listen to the doctor. Rest is the best medicine for you right now."

"I'll be on the bridge if you need me." Yamane assumed Dr. Owens would leave with him, but she stayed behind and conferred with a couple of nurses. He stood in the hallway a good ten minutes before she finally headed for the double doors. The wait didn't bother him so much. An apparently cavalier attitude about his condition did. It just didn't make any sense.

Dr. Owens scribbled down some notes on her chart as she walked into the corridor. She went right past Yamane without seeing him.

"Doctor," he called from behind, softly but with authority.

She turned around and acknowledged him, offering no hint she had been surprised by his unexpected appearance. "I thought you already returned to the bridge?"

"I feel like there's something you haven't told me," he accused her as gently as possible. "Is there anything else I should know about Lt. Commander Henthorne?"

She did not respond at first. Based on her facial expressions he could tell she was trying to come up with a nonspecific answer, but years of training in the medical profession were too strong an influence. She just couldn't do it.

"Looks as though you already know the answer to that," she bluffed. Her ploy didn't work. Yamane wasn't buying it. "There is something I've been holding back."

He moved closer. She looked away as an orderly walked past them both. When Yamane took a step back, she visibly relaxed.

"I'm not certain the last surgery has taken care of the problem." She stopped and checked her notes. "His infection is definitely reduced, but we haven't fought it off completely."

"Wouldn't antibiotics work for a problem like this?"

"Under normal circumstances, yes, but this is no ordinary infection. It has the unusual property of mutating every few hours, making the previous antibiotic useless. I've never seen anything like it before. If the infection mutates into a form we cannot treat, it could prove fatal."

"If you're so concerned about his condition, then why did you let him resume his duties again?" Yamane asked, trying to make sense of her reasoning.

She started down the corridor again. "Because I'm not sure it would make much of a difference. He's going through a lot right now. If something makes him feel useful again, it might be better than any medication I can administer."

Yamane stopped her. "But you could be taking a chance with his life."

"I do appreciate your concern for him." She cut herself off when another orderly walked by. "Don't worry, Commander. I told the nurse on duty I want him monitored at all times. If any problems develop, I'll let you know right away."

"I guess you know what's best, Doctor," Yamane conceded and then made a hasty retreat.

"The three Antaren destroyers should rendezvous with the fleet in two and a half hours," Landis said to Yamane when he returned to the bridge. "There is one other thing, however." He hesitated. "It's not a problem, but I find it very strange."

Yamane strolled over to the communication console. "Why don't you let me decide."

Landis re-tuned the frequency, listened for a second, and then pressed a button. "Since we left Antara, I've been picking up these signals. They are on the lower bands and very faint. By the time I try and lock on, the transmissions have ceased."

Yamane looked up at the screen. Two dreadnoughts were in view, along with a handful of destroyers. "Do you have any idea where they might have originated?"

"Not yet, but I'll reign one in sooner or later."

"Monitor the bands for a while and see if anything develops." Yamane returned to his command chair. He sat there, staring at the dreadnoughts. During the war, he had gotten this close to them only a handful of times. Like the sub-cruisers, they were armed to the teeth. They would need every bit of firepower at their disposal if they were to have any chance against the Deravans. The Deravans. He checked the time on the astro clock. 1538. Should be enough time, he thought. "Tie me into Tal Win-Tu's ship."

"Right away, Commander," Landis replied.

As the minutes passed, the 'right away' aspect of Landis' promise became a bad joke. More minutes ticked by. Yamane continued to wait. He held up his data pad. The cursor in the upper left-hand corner of the blue screen flashed off and on at regular intervals.

"This is Subidor Tal Win-Tu," he finally said.

"Subidor, by now I'm sure you had a chance to examine the data we have on the Deravans."

"Yes. When we broke orbit, I accessed the memory systems at my station and have already gone through a good amount. I should have the rest done in a short while."

"Good. Do you think you can bring a team over by 1800 hours? I want to compare notes and begin work on a battle plan."

"I have already written down some preliminary ideas," he replied. "I'll send over what I have now and bring the rest later." A voice in the background interrupted Tal Win-Tu. They exchanged words. Yamane thought he detected the tones of an argument. After a moment of silence, Tal Win-Tu came back on the radio. "My communications officer tells me we can send the transmission any time."

"You may proceed at your discretion." Millions of bits of data flashed across Landis' screen in one short burst even before he finished speaking. Yamane had no way of knowing just how big the file was, but if he knew the Antarens, even a superficial examination of the analysis would probably take a week or more, if he had a week. "Thank you, Subidor. This should help me prepare for our briefing."

"Until then, Commander Yamane. Subidor Tal Win-Tu, out." The screen switched back.

Yamane stared at it for more than a minute before he realized how much time had passed. Going through the numbers in his head, he realized he would need help. Though the strategics division didn't know it yet, they had just been given the most important assignment of their lives.

CHAPTER 21

BOK-NOR
DAIETH TIME MINUS FIVE

The transport aboard the *Bok-Nor* stood ready in the forward launch bay. A thousand points of light shone from the other side of the magnetic doors. A small cadre of Antarens approached the shuttle from behind. His position as their subidor mandated that Tal Win-Tu take the lead. Just before they stepped on board, every one of them stopped. Kel Sen-Ry emerged from the middle and came alongside. Taking a long slow bow, he held out his hands and said, "May this ship grant us safety on our journey so that it may go well for us when we arrive."

When the transport door opened, Tal Win-Tu tried to get on board, but someone grabbed his arm from behind. "Are you sure we are doing the right thing?" Sul Taa-Ni, a look of concern across his face.

"Who am I to challenge the prophets?" Tal Win-Tu replied after he shot a quick look in Kel Sen-Ry's direction. "They have chosen whom they have chosen."

"But these Terrans are a threat to our very existence. We have an opportunity of finishing what the Deravans have started. I say we act."

"That kind of thinking almost ended our way of life," Kel Sen-Ry replied. "Life for our people has been difficult since the war. Without the Terrans' help, the Samaarians would have certainly finished us off."

"What you have said is true, but only after they—"

"I am the subidor of this ship," Tal Win-Tu asserted, "and my orders have come from the High Council. Do you stand in opposition to their will?"

"But Subidor—"

Tal Win-Tu grabbed the hand still clutching his uniform sleeve and brushed it off. He entered the transport without another word.

As soon as he and the others had taken their seats, the transport rose above the tracks and flew through the magnetic doors. The pilot made his course right for the *Corona*.

Tal Win-Tu stared out the port window, lost in thought. He knew his subordinate wasn't alone in his feelings. In some ways, he even agreed with them. When they had faced each other at the territorial buoy, he had sensed a certain measure of self-importance coming from Yamane, not exactly a quality which should be manifested by the prophesied warrior. Tal Win-Tu could think of nothing else except keeping him as far away from Antara as possible. The subidor knew all too well what the prophets had foretold, but he also couldn't bring himself to trust a Terran. It occurred to him then that if the *Corona* were destroyed, the universe might be a better place overall. But at the priests' insistence, he had allowed Yamane's ship entry, albeit reluctantly. The First Order had governed his life for so long, he couldn't find it in his heart to disobey them. With all that said, however, Tal Win-Tu wondered what the results might have been if he had.

Yamane arrived at Strategic Operations just before the Antarens. When both doors slid open, he saw Lt. Robinson and his team already there, sitting on the opposite side of an oval-shaped conference table. Working closely with them for most of the evening, Yamane decided it might be better to have the ranking officer from strategics lead their side of the briefing instead of him. If he had any hope of getting the two sides to listen to each other, he should at least position himself in a neutral role when choosing which battle plan they would use.

On the wall behind them, someone had hung the flags of their representative governments in a crisscross pattern. The colors and stars of the United World Government hung on the left, the blue, white and red of the Antaren Empire hung on the right. Yamane appreciated the psychology involved. Such a symbol had the potential to communicate, the need for working together far better than a set of clumsy words. Around the dark gray meeting room, a number of chairs lined all four walls. Far more than would be needed, he thought.

"Here we are again, gentlemen," Yamane joked. They smiled in return.

He took his place at the head of the table. Positioned an arm's reach away, he saw two identical sets of control panels. Simple in design, they controlled every semitronic device in the room. After pulling his chair up just a bit closer, he noted all eight copies of his team's proposal arrayed in a circular fashion along the perimeter of the tabletop.

The door clicked and then slid open with a soft whoosh. As a sign of respect, Yamane rose to his feet and stood at attention. When the first Antaren stepped inside, Robinson and his team followed suit.

When the Antarens took up the part of the room closest to the door, both sides stood at attention, facing each other. Yamane thought he should say something, but with all of the traditions and protocols Antarens adhered to on a regular basis, he feared he might unknowingly offend his guests.

At the end of the table, almost in the shadows, an Antaren bent forward. Based on his style of dress, he appeared to be from the priestly class. The others repeated his actions. When they stood upright again, Yamane recognized him. Kel Sen-Ry. He could not have been more pleased to see the Antaren he almost considered a friend.

"You have a most impressive ship, Commander," Tal Win-Tu complemented. "Seeing the *Corona* from this perspective helps me believe our efforts will not be in vain."

The show of support felt good. "Thank you, Subidor. You are most generous with your comments." He extended his hand. "As soon as you are seated, we can begin."

Tal Win-Tu offered a slight nod and then sat down opposite Yamane. The three remaining Antarens waited for him to get comfortable before they took their seats. The design of the chairs, while generally accommodating for humans, didn't appear to be so for their guests. Narrower than what they were accustomed to, and without a space for their short tails, they could fit into the seat, but not in a way that they appreciated.

When the room seemed to be ready, Tal Win-Tu extended his hand towards one of his aides. The junior officer took out a polished cylinder from a rectangular box he had been carrying. He placed the device, about the size of a man's forearm, on the table.

"We have gone over the information you sent us just after departure. After a great deal of work, I believe we have come up with an effective strategy against the Deravans."

This time, Tal Win-Tu's aide took out a data pad no wider than a playing card from his chest pocket. When he pressed a green button near the top, the device on the table came to life. The aide then pressed a larger brown button at the base of his pad. An astonishing sight filled Strategic Operations. Floating about two meters above the table, a miniature version of the solar system appeared before their eyes.

Everyone on Robinson's team let out a simultaneous "whoa" at the sight, impressed by the depth of color and detail involved.

The sun, bright and yellow, hovered above the projector, while the ten planets set in various orbits along the elliptical plane moved in a circular fashion relative to each other. For Yamane, the multi-colored rings of Saturn, along with her crater-ridden moons, stood out from the other planets. The brown, yellow and tan bands of Jupiter came in a close second. He tried to get a better look at Earth, but the planet he called home remained hidden in the opposite corner of the room.

"This is quite impressive," Yamane remarked. "Our image projectors are similar to yours, but nowhere near this sophisticated."

Tal Win-Tu ignored the compliment. "Based on the information you have furnished us, this is an exact representation of your solar system as it exists at this moment."

Yamane craned his neck up. "What is the location of our fleet?"

The Antaren aide pressed another button on his data pad. In the adjacent corner, far beyond the orbit of Icarus, a small light sphere appeared.

"If our trajectory and speed are maintained, the fleet will arrive at Earth in a little under seventy-six hours. Several plans of attack were considered before deciding upon the one we believe shows the most promise." He then nodded to the Antaren on his right. "From the beginning, we agreed the two most important elements of our plan are surprise and firepower. If either of these is lacking, then our efforts will be for nothing." A flicker of light flashed in the corner of Yamane's eye. A thin yellow beam extended from the fleet, and made its way to the far corner. The ray looked like a golden bow, soft and shimmering. "Taking into account the position of Neptune in conjunction with the Earth, if the fleet heading for the *Lexington* averages a speed of 1.075 stellar velocity," he said, "we should rendezvous at our destination undetected." The image froze at this point.

Yamane rose from his chair as if hypnotized by the beam suspended above. He looked at the Earth, and then their position outside the solar system. He made some quick calculations in his head. "Looks as though your analysis all works out, the timing and such, but if I am not mistaken, we will travel faster at certain legs of the journey than others."

"You have a good eye, Commander," he complimented. "Yes, if we increase our speed to 1.17 stellar velocity at these two intercept points, three of your planets will line up between our position and Mars, covering our approach. But as you can see in this demonstration, timing is the critical factor." He shifted in his chair. "When our ships arrive at Mars, we break radio silence and give away our position to the Deravans. They will undoubtedly break orbit and make a course right for us. This leads me to my second point." Tal Win-Tu nodded a second time. His aide magnified the image. "If the cargo barges want to have any chance of reaching the *Lexington* before our arrival, they must launch within the next twenty-four hours."

Robinson waved his hand in a dismissive manner. "Aren't you being somewhat optimistic?" he objected. Yamane thought the sound of his nasal voice clashed with the velvet smoothness of the Antaren's. "Lt. Commander Henthorne is still working on his calculations. There is also the matter of preparing ships and crews. We should postpone the operation an additional twelve hours before we even consider sending them."

Yamane tried to gauge the receptivity of everyone in the room. Some nodded in agreement, while others gave no hint what they thought of his plan. "Lt. Robinson is right. We need more time."

"Given the outcome of this first scenario," Tal Win-Tu replied, his voice emotionless, "I would advise against it. I said there would be dangers, and the longer we wait, the greater the risks."

Yamane conceded this point, but as a person who believed multiple solutions existed for every problem, he didn't want to close the door on them just yet. "Go on."

"As I mentioned before, the Deravans will be notified a short time before we reach Mars. When their ships come into range of the *Lexington*, we activate the cells and neutralize them."

"What is your method of attack?" Robinson asked.

"Cargo barges," he declared. "We strip them down to the barest essentials, and then fill them up with as many explosives as they can hold. After the cells immobilize the Deravan armada, we launch our attack, led by those barges. Once they have destroyed their targets, we launch the rest of our ships in a series of waves. I propose we divide our fleet into twelve groups, each one centering on a dreadnought." The projection suspended above changed into a close-up of Mars and the *Lexington*. "Using them as a cornerstone, they will be flanked by two destroyers and twelve skyjackets. This formation will maximize our firepower for each cluster."

Robinson shook his head. "What about the sub-cruisers?" he asked. "Do you propose they just sit there while your ships lead the attack?"

"Our calculations indicate power levels within the cells can only be sustained for thirty minutes," Tal Win-Tu replied. "I estimate the engagement between both fleets will last least three times as long. With this in mind, we will hold back these ships in reserve. If a destroyer or dreadnought gets into trouble, they will be dispatched and offer their support." He then sat back in his chair, finished.

Yamane looked up at the ceiling. Different points from Tal Win Nu's presentation danced in his head. "There is one thing you have not considered," he finally said.

The subidor cast several furtive glances at his data pad. "I do not think I have neglected any important items."

"The assumption you are making is that the Deravans will be at the Earth when we arrive at Mars. How do we know they won't have patrols elsewhere in the solar system?"

"I have taken this into consideration. When the cargo barges destined for the *Lexington* depart, we also send out twelve surveillance ships. Since they will be operating under stealth mode, the Deravans will have a difficult time picking them up on RadAR. Each of these ships will arrive at a pre-set destination that keeps them in contact with our fleet. There, they will be able to track the Deravans anywhere in your solar system."

"I see," Yamane replied, impressed by his thoroughness.

Tal Win-Tu set his data pad down. The image, which had filled the room, disappeared.

"Thank you, Subidor Tal Win-Tu. Now we will hear from Lt. Robinson."

"Thank you, Commander," he nodded. Robinson rose up from his chair and scooted past several Antarens. In the opposite corner of the room, he inserted a data crystal into an image projector set on top of a cart. Just as before, though not as detailed as the Antaren version, an image of the solar system filled the room.

"As you can see by the time index," he began, "this represents our solar system as it stands at this moment." He then took out a pointer from his pocket, and in one deft motion, extended it to its full length. "As we have discussed, the trajectory of our fleet is what makes this entire operation possible. With that said, we would also be taking an undue risk if our ships were expected to sustain 1.17 stellar velocity a good portion of the trip. The added strain increases the likelihood of system overloads and engine shutdowns. Even if we lost just a handful of ships, every one of those losses would tip the battle further in the Deravans' favor."

"Do you not think you are being somewhat hyperbolic in your statements?" Tal Win-Tu asked after he rose out of his chair.

"No—I don't think so," Robinson snapped back. "Three of your destroyers have already experienced engine problems, and at slower speeds." He found his place in his notes again. "The second danger I see in the Antaren plan is flying in a compact formation. We know all too well the disaster that almost resulted from today's incident." Moving the pointer in a snake-like pattern, he continued: "I believe there is a safer way. When we arrive at these coordinates here, we change our course seventeen degrees and head directly for Neptune. The fleet will remain behind the planet for two hours until our orbit lines us up with Saturn. We come around from the backside and fly in at 0.90 stellar velocity. By this time, Earth has slipped behind the Sun. We then make a mad dash for Mars before the planet emerges on the other side. At the appropriate time, we use the surveillance ships Tal Win-Tu spoke of and tip off the Deravans."

"What is your method of attack once we arrive at Mars?" Tal Win-Tu asked.

"We use the sub-cruisers and cargo barges as a feint, to draw out the Deravans," he replied after working his way to the other side of the room. "They will assume this is our main attack fleet. We use them to lure their armada past the *Lexington*. Once the EM field is generated, the rest of our fleet comes from behind Mars and attacks them one group at a time." Robinson paused. "I agree with Tal Win-Tu that we need to concentrate our firepower, but my plan focuses more on keeping our forces together rather than forming smaller clusters and thinning out our reserves."

A single, nagging question kept repeating in Yamane's mind. "What if the Deravans are not at Earth?" he asked. "How does your plan take into account this possibility?"

The question seemed to catch Robinson off guard. He went over to his chair and thumbed through his notes. "I...I guess we could send out false messages; make them think some ships are heading for Earth. They would naturally remain there and wait for out supposed assault."

Every pair of eyes settled on Yamane as he leaned back in his chair. "I give my heart-felt thanks for everyone's hard work. This has been a busy day and you probably wish you had more time to prepare for the briefing. Both of your plans are good ones, each with their own merits." He sat forward again. "Actually, I'm surprised at just how similar they are. This suggests to me that we're on the right track." He found the data pad on the table and picked it up. "But with that said, the one issue we have not addressed is the location of the Deravan fleet. Both plans are based on the assumption they will be at Earth when we arrive, but if they're not, what then? If even one of their ships spots us before we get to Mars, we're sunk."

The room fell silent.

"The only way of making certain the Deravans are where we want them to be is if we provide them with a good reason for being there," Sul Taa-Ni suggested after some thought.

"You're speaking in riddles," Robinson accused.

"Perhaps I am, but the answer need not be complicated." He pointed at Earth. "If the Deravans believe this is our actual destination, they would not dare leave."

Robinson shook his head. "If we sent our fleet there first, and then to Mars, we could lose a lot of ships along the way. This will only weaken our chances."

"I never said anything about sending our ships there. We only need send a small number of cargo barges as a lure, while the rest of the fleet proceeds with the operation."

A light popped on in Yamane's head. "I think I understand what you're saying," he interjected, "but the number of barges we send must be convincing. Otherwise, the Deravans won't buy what we're selling."

"You're taking an unnecessary risk with those ships," Robinson objected. A vein throbbed in the middle of his forehead. "They will be outclassed and outgunned."

"Not necessarily." Yamane accessed the files on his data pad. He scrolled down the information until a picture of a cargo barge appeared. On the right, the specifications for the Antaren ship followed soon after. "While going over the design limits earlier today, it occurred to me they were principally intended for the transportation of heavy loads."

A look of bemusement crossed Tal Win-Tu's face. "Everyone knows this. What of it?"

"Well, what if we stripped them down to the studs? If those barges are made as light as possible, they should be able to outrun their Deravan counterparts."

Tal Win-Tu activated his data pad and inputted several mathematical formulas. "I estimate their top speed to be around 1.71 stellar velocity."

"All well and good, but what about the cargo barges themselves?" Robinson asked. "Their tracking capabilities aren't terribly sophisticated."

"We can use some of the redundant systems from the surveillance ships," Tal Win-Tu suggested. "Installing them should not take too much time."

"I think we're agreed then." Yamane turned his chair toward the Antaren side of the table. "Let me know when you find out how long preparations will take."

"Which one of the two strategies do you plan to put into effect?" Robinson asked, barely masking his impatience.

Yamane held up his data pad. Equations and formulas covered the screen from top to bottom. He then checked the astro-clock above the door. 1901 hours. Doable, but it will be tight. "I shouldn't need more than a couple of hours," he finally replied. "I want to go over the material one more time before making a final decision." He paused and studied the room. "If there are no objections, you can return to your shuttle."

Tal Win-Tu rose to his feet. Until then, he had showed no outward indication of wanting to leave, but the moment Yamane gave him an opening, he grabbed it without hesitation. His assistants, taking his cue, also came to their feet, quietly leaving the table.

When both doors slid open, cool air from the hallway rushed in. Yamane didn't realize just how warm the room had gotten. It felt good. One by one the Antarens filed out, until the last one left Strategic Operations. When both doors slid shut again, Yamane and his team found themselves alone.

Robinson leaned back in his chair and unbuttoned his collar. "Under the circumstances, I think it went as well as could be expected," he commented.

"I'm forced to agree with you," Yamane concurred. "It got a little sticky at a couple of points, but I think they're still with us."

"Perhaps, but sometimes, I'm not so sure." Robinson seemed to catch himself, as though he revealed more than he intended.

"What do you mean?"

The lieutenant just shrugged, and then looked away.

Alarms went off in Yamane's head. "Could you all excuse us, I need to talk with your commanding officer."

Robinson's three aides saluted and then left the room without another word. Both men were now alone.

"If you have a problem with something, I need to know about it now."

Robinson seemed to search for just the right words. "I guess I do have some misgivings about the Antarens. I've asked myself a number of times if we can trust them. In the end, I'm not certain that we can."

"I see," Yamane replied, shaking his head. "Go on."

"Almost half of my family died in the war—killed in several sneak attacks, led by Antaren raiders. I think it would be prudent if we developed a contingency plan, in case they might be planning the same thing again."

Yamane brought his hands up to his eyes and rubbed them. When he brought them down again, it looked as though he had aged a number of years. "Have you ever been stationed on Antara?"

Robinson frowned. "No. Never."

"The Antarens are an interesting lot. In some ways, they are the most rigid and inflexible group of people you would ever meet. On the other hand, they also have a beautiful and rich culture that goes back thousands of years. As societies go, they have a thing or two to teach us. Do you understand what I'm trying to say?" Robinson just shrugged. Yamane tried a different tactic. "Every culture has a way of doing things that seems strange to us. Our tendency is to feel threatened by it. I know I did when I was first stationed on Antara. After a while, though, I got to know some of the people and learned a few things about their culture. In time, they didn't seem quite so bad. I guess you can say their customs and ways of doing things are not wrong, they're just different."

Robinson's eyes fixated on a distant object. "They attacked us once, they can do it again. Going up against the Deravans would be the perfect opportunity for them to blindside us."

"It takes time to appreciate another person's point of view, and an open mind. Wouldn't you agree?"

"I guess I do. But I'm still not sure about their motives."

"I understand your feelings. But if you continue to cling to the past, it will hold you back." Images of Liana flashed in his mind. "Forgiveness is the only way we can be free of it." Yamane sat back in his chair. "Unless anything to the contrary happens, we really should give the Antarens the benefit of the doubt. Do you think you can do that?"

"I—"

The sound of the intercom interrupted him. "Commander Yamane, this is Dr. Owens. Will you please report to Med-lab five?"

"This is Yamane. I'm on my way."

Robinson picked up his notes and rose from the table. "Will there be anything else?"

"Meet me in my quarters at 1945 hours. I think we should go over this data one more time before the final briefing at 2100."

"Yes, sir," he saluted and then left the room.

Yamane wondered just how many others felt the same way as Robinson.

CHAPTER
22

S.F.S. CORONA
1910 PROXIMA MERIDIAN TIME, AUGUST 26, 2217

As Yamane approached the infirmary, he heard a cacophony of voices and mechanical sounds coming from behind a pair of doors. This wasn't a good sign. All those people and medical devices in there meant Henthorne's condition must have taken a turn for the worse.

When both doors slid open, what he saw almost took his breath away. With one exception, every bed in there was gone; replaced by an array of computer systems, data analysis equipment, a targeting display, high-speed computer links, a stack of data pads, and two rows of number crunching consoles. In effect, he had transformed the med-lab into a makeshift situation room.

Off in the corner, Yamane witnessed Henthorne and Dr. Owens arguing about something. She grabbed his wrist. He pulled it away. She tried to grab his wrist again, but with the same outcome. Despite Owens' lack of results, Yamane had to admire her dedication.

"Why did you ask me down here, Doctor?" Yamane asked after he negotiated a minefield of equipment and cables placed around the room.

"Take a look for yourself," she snapped back, strands of her normally neatly-combed hair dangling over her face. "Lt. Commander Henthorne has turned this place into a circus." Owens grabbed a clump of hair and threw it over her shoulder. "I thought maybe you could talk to him."

"Why don't you give us a moment alone," Yamane suggested, a soft tone in his voice. "I'll join you outside when we're finished."

"Don't take too long," she balked. "I should have given him his medication a half hour ago."

Yamane empathized with Owens, but Henthorne's work outweighed his condition, present or future. In fact, her concerns seemed greatly overblown. The man she described at death's door the day before had made a remarkable recovery, almost miraculous.

"You look like you're doing better," he observed after Owens left the med-lab.

"I guess you can say that," he replied. His attention diverted to a data pad in his hands. "It's been up and down, but I do feel better." He made several corrections to the text displayed on the screen. "But you're not here to talk about my health." Henthorne picked up another data pad in his lap and tossed it to Yamane. "I called you in here to let you know I've finished my calculations. We can generate the electro-magnetic field. It will be difficult, but definitely do-able. Everything you need is in there."

Yamane stared down at the screen, dumbfounded. "I don't know what I should say," he replied. "This could not have come at a better time. We are all indebted to your work."

Henthorne scooted himself up. "You still don't understand, do you, Commander?" he sneered. "I didn't do all this because I support your decision—far from it. I still believe taking on the Deravans is a terrible mistake—even with the help of the Antarens." Yamane's face stiffened. "I know...I know. We've been down this road before, but I wanted the truth between us. I did this for me, no one else." He plopped his head on the pillow and closed both eyes. "I don't expect you to understand, but these are my feelings on this matter."

Yamane had thought Henthorne had changed after his near-death experience. He could not have been more wrong. The anger and resentment, they were still there. If anything, his infirmity compounded those dark emotions. Recognizing the hate in his eyes, Yamane saw all too clearly why Henthorne had stepped down; not because he believed someone else could do a better job than him, rather, because he didn't believe himself fit for command, nothing more.

"I'm sorry you still feel this way. Maybe I should just accept the fact that some people will never change."

"I guess so, sir," Henthorne replied and then turned away.

"If I have any questions about this, I'll signal you from my quarters."

"You know where I'll be," he joked. To Yamane, it came off as a bad one.

With nothing left to say, there was nothing more to do but leave. He found Dr. Owens waiting for him outside.

"I'm sorry," she said when he entered the corridor. "I thought Lt. Commander Henthorne might have felt differently about things by now."

"So did I." He looked back over his shoulder. "Whenever we talk, I feel as though I'm being pulled down into his core of hate."

She brought up her clipboard. "Before you go, Commander, I wanted to update you on his condition."

He offered a cursory glance. "He looks as though he's improving well enough."

"I wish this were the case, but his infection has latched onto both kidneys, and the antibiotics are no longer having any effect. I've tried to get him to rest, but you've seen the results. It's as though he has something to prove to me, to you, the world, or maybe himself—I don't know."

Yamane peered into the med-lab a second time. He didn't think such a man could succumb to something as insignificant as an infection. "What are his chances?"

"If things don't change, not good."

"Can you give him something to make him sleep...even if it's only for a few hours?"

"A sedative, even a mild one, might be dangerous. He could lapse into a coma."

"I'm afraid there's nothing I can do, doctor, since this falls under your jurisdiction."

"I know...I know," she nodded while staring at the ground, her ever-present clipboard clutched to her chest. "I simply wanted to let you know where he stood."

"I appreciate all you've done for him," he said, placing his hand on her shoulder. "Let me know if his condition changes. I'll be in my quarters if you need me."

He left the med-lab and jumped onto the lift at the end of the corridor. Yamane felt bad for her. No doctor likes the thought of losing a patient. He wished he could have done more for her; words of comfort or a simple embrace, but the lack of time didn't permit such a luxury.

When the door to Yamane's quarters slid open, Robinson rushed in, winded. "I'm sorry I'm late," he apologized, "but I got here as fast as I could."

Yamane ignored the apology. "Before we get started, I just wanted to let you know that someone else will be joining us."

Except for a simple nod, Robinson didn't react either way.

They waited. Yamane's fingers tapped on the table in rapid succession. One, two, three, four. They tapped again. One, two, three, four. And again after that.

The door slid open. Kershaw came into the room, still wearing his coveralls. Grease covered his face and hands. "Glad you could make the meeting," Yamane joked.

"Just be grateful I'm here," he growled. "I hope this doesn't take too long. I'm in the middle of some crucial repairs with the hyper-static manifolds."

Yamane motioned for his second-in-command to sit down. "I've made a second set of plans for you so you can follow along." He handed a data pad to Kershaw as he took his seat. Bringing the semitronic device close, he scanned through the text.

"I've asked the lieutenant commander here because one of the central components of this operation will be led by him."

Kershaw's head shot up. "What? What are you talking about? My engines—"

"Are in good hands," he smirked. "Wouldn't you agree?"

Kershaw brought his attention back to the data pad. He stopped at about the midway point. "I am troubled by something. As this report indicates, the cornerstone of your proposal rests on the *Lexington*. The only chance we have to destroy a majority of the Deravan fleet is when we generate the electromagnetic field. But if the cells we're carrying don't work, or if the EM field doesn't stop them, we could be in big trouble."

"Is there a question in there somewhere?" Yamane asked.

Kershaw pointed at his pad. "My concern is with who will be in command of the cargo barges. This may seem like easy work—just place the power cell on the ship and go. But believe me, there's a whole lot more involved than that. They'll have to be placed in just the right spot. And don't get me started on the omega band receivers. You'll need someone who is not only familiar with them, but who also has a working knowledge of the *Lexington*'s layout."

Yamane had guided Kershaw right where he wanted him to go. He just hoped he didn't overplay his hand. "This is precisely the reason I wanted you at this briefing," Yamane said, springing his trap. "As you have said yourself, we need an expert working out the technical side of this operation...and you are the obvious choice."

"But I have never commanded this many ships before. And besides, you know I'm a much better engineer than a mission leader."

Steady...Steady. Not too fast or you'll lose him. "I have taken this into consideration. And you're right, someone with more experience in this area should be in command. Once the ships arrive at the *Lexington*, responsibility for the operation will be transferred over to you."

"Sounds reasonable," Kershaw agreed. "Who do you have in mind for the job?"

Yamane braced himself before answering the question. "I've spent a good deal of time on this matter. A number of candidates were considered, but his training and experience make him the obvious choice." He paused, counted to three and then said, "Therefore, I have decided Commander Neu will be placed in command of the barges." Nothing happened. No ranting. No yelling—nothing. Kershaw just sat in his chair, motionless. Yamane didn't know if this was a good sign or not. He would have almost preferred an explosion of emotions, since he could deal with that. But Kershaw's reaction, or lack of one, was a side of his friend he seldom saw. It made him uncomfortable. "Are you all right with this?" he asked, finally breaking the silence.

Kershaw fixed his gaze at some distant object. "You know my feelings about him," he replied, "what he did to my men." His eyes turned cold. "Him, of all people, Frank—why him?"

Yamane felt his pain, but his decision would stand. "I went through the service records of every qualified officer, and his stood out above them all." Kershaw seemed to be somewhere else. "His experience as a pilot, the training he received for stealth operations, and his ability to complete a mission in the most extreme circumstances made him the obvious choice."

"I know you too well, Frank," he said, his eyes narrowing. "You're holding back. I think you at least owe me the whole truth."

Yamane went over to the porthole and stared at a star cluster a trillion kilometers away. "All right, here it is." He turned around. "I respect Commander Neu. He went through a lot after the court dismissed the charges against him. Most officers would have resigned their commissions on the spot rather than face the assumption of guilt by others. I've always admired him for staying in the service when he could have quit. Like you, he has had to live with the consequences of what he did. It's probably been a lot tougher on him than you think."

Kershaw's face darkened. "I hope it has," he growled. The hate in his voice brought a chill down Yamane's spine. "I want him to continue suffering, just as I have." Kershaw pushed his chair back and moved towards the door.

"Making him pay for an error in judgment isn't going to bring any of those pilots back." Yamane paused. "I've often wondered why you have been so relentless in your condemnation of Neu. Why do you hate him so much? Is there something else to all this?"

Kershaw spun around, armed with an expression of defiance. "What are you talking about? You know what happened, what he did."

"The only way any of us can get through the pain of the past is if we meet it, head on."

"Who are you to tell me about facing the truth?" Kershaw attacked. "You can't possibly know how this has been for me." He turned away.

"How can you say that?" Yamane replied, wounded by the accusation. Kershaw knew what the loss of his wife meant to him, what he had gone through. When special services told Yamane that Liana had died in an attack by Antaren raiders, his whole world collapsed. She was everything to him, and they took her away from him in an instant. The grief he felt almost became too much for him, and he almost became lost in it. If it weren't for Kershaw's support, he didn't know how he would have ever crawled out of that deep, dark hole. And now, he was saying this to him?

"You know what really disappoints me, Frank?" he asked, without waiting for an answer. "It's that we're even talking about this. I thought you were a man of your word."

In an act of retaliation, he grabbed Kershaw by the collar. "I think that promise I made was one of the biggest mistakes of my life." Yamane took a step back and stared into his eyes. He hoped his friend might still be in there, somewhere. "Because of that promise, I've helped you keep it all buried deep down for far too long. People say time heals old wounds, but that's a lie. It just teaches us to live with those wounds."

"I don't want to hear any more," Kershaw objected.

When he made for the door, Yamane reached from behind and grabbed his arm. "Until we deal with the past honestly, openly, we can never really heal." He found the suns out of the porthole a second time. They helped him take a moment and collect his thoughts. "The Antarens helped me face my past during the test of character. When I realized I could never change the past, I began to feel a tremendous weight lift off my shoulders. All the guilt I had about Liana's death evaporated. But it didn't stop there. That voice I heard after the test—the one they call the High Son—when he came, I felt he wanted to relieve me of all my burdens. I didn't realize it then, but I do now. The effects of that test have been working on me ever since I left Antara. That voice, too. I feel like it's asking us to make a choice. I don't understand it all yet, but I feel like a new person since I heard those words. I don't know how else to describe what happened in there."

"Stop. Please, Frank."

"You aren't angry with Neu, you're angry with yourself, because of the guilt you feel about the deaths of your pilots." Kershaw froze. "You got drunk the night before the patrol. Rather than owning up to what you did, you claimed you were sick and went to the infirmary. And because you weren't there to prevent what happened, every pilot in your squadron died. Rather than accept the truth, someone else had to be blamed, and that someone was Neu."

"How did you know?" he asked, trying to hide the tears in his eyes.

"I've known from the beginning. I should have said something then, but I made that promise to you."

"Don't you understand? I promised those families I would look out for their sons and daughters. How could I tell all those people the truth at the funeral?"

Yamane placed his hand on Kershaw's shoulder. "There's no way we can go back and change the past, but you can change how it affects you today."

"You're right, I do blame myself for their deaths, but I also blame Neu—and I will never forgive either one of us." He pushed away from Yamane and stormed out of the room.

Yamane stared at the door after it slid shut. What the two of them had said bounced around in his head—the accusations, the apologies—all blurring together. Maybe he had said too much.

Robinson sat in his chair, quiet.

Yamane returned to the table. He rummaged through his notes and found the place where they left off. Wiping the sweat from his upper lip, he cleared his throat. "It's all right, Lieutenant. This goes back a long way...and I'm not sure how it will end."

Not knowing where he should go, Kershaw returned to his quarters. His bed beckoned him from the far side of the room. He went over to it and sat on the side. Leaning forward, he pulled out a picture from his pocket. The black-and-white image had faded over the years. This and a number of creases along the edges made the photograph appear much older than it really was. One by one, he looked at the smiling faces, as he had done thousands of times before. His thoughts raced back to the day he had taken that photograph. It had been unusually warm. The pilots from the 144th fighter group were preparing themselves for their next mission. One of the mechanics had received a camera in the mail from his wife and he was eager to try it out. The squadron obliged him and posed in front of his fighter before take-off.

As Kershaw stared at the picture more deeply, he could almost feel the twin suns shining on him. He unconsciously squinted. Some of the pilots he knew for a short time, while others he had known since their cadet days. The length of time made no difference. When soldiers faced life and death together, they forged a bond that transcended the months and years spent together. You just made sure he covered your back and you covered his.

He looked at the picture again. The warmth of the day stood out above all else. If only I had known, he lamented. It should have been just another routine mission. Instead, it became the last time they ever flew together. Less than a day after he took the picture, they were dead. In times of war, death is an everyday reality every soldier must face sooner or later; and has been since the beginning of time. He accepts it and moves on. But to lose his squadron so senselessly, this Kershaw could never forgive—this tragic mistake he might have prevented.

He folded the picture and slipped it back into his pocket. Flashes of anger burst into his thoughts. Why would Yamane ask me to work with that man?! Kershaw screamed in his mind. He's the one responsible for their deaths. The ugly memories of what his commanding officer had said to him shouted back.

With a deep sigh, Kershaw fell back onto the bed. His arm flopped over his face. He wished he could clear his head, but the feelings welling up within him were too strong—hate, bitterness, resentment—they were all there. He didn't know what he should do. He closed his eyes and thought some more.

"I've met with my officers about the battle plan and I'm signaling you just as I promised."

"I went over the information you requested," Tal Win-Tu said. "Our engineers have determined it will take about two hours to get the cargo barges ready. Several teams are working on them now, as we speak."

"Good," Yamane replied. "How many will you be able to commit?"

Tal Win-Tu appeared to hesitate at the question, demonstrated by the atypical lack of an immediate response. "This is dependent on how many you will need for the *Lexington*. Have your calculations been completed?"

"I have them right here." He brought up his data pad. "Lt. Commander Henthorne estimates we will need seventy-six cells in all. This translates into nineteen cargo barges."

"This is a number higher than we expected," Tal Win-Tu replied, surprise registering in his voice. "This will only leave nine for Earth. Do you believe this is a sufficient number?"

"If this is all we have, then this is the number we send." He set his pad on the desk next to his bed. "How about the surveillance ships? Will they be ready in time?"

"My teams are going over them now, but the work is proceeding slower than expected. Since the war's end, we have needed them to monitor the outer sectors. I don't have to tell you how dangerous those places are. Many of their systems are barely operational."

"What then is your estimate of when they'll be ready to depart?" Yamane asked, a growing sense of anxiety building within. The problems and setbacks he thought they had overcome were back in his face again.

"If nothing else changes, my subordinates tell me by 0130 hours."

"Excellent. I've finished working out the details of my battle plan." He checked the astro-clock. "I guess I'll see you in forty-five minutes."

"Until then, Commander," he replied. "Tal Win-Tu, out."

Yamane let out a huge yawn. He was far too tired to think of EM fields, skyjackets, or any other part of the mission. His body had already sent up the white flag. He threw the notes on the desk, took off his shoes and collapsed on his bed. Just for a minute, he thought. The instant his eyelids closed, he was fast asleep.

CHAPTER
23

S.F.S. CORONA
2048 PROXIMA MERIDIAN TIME, AUGUST 26, 2217

A knock at the door snapped Yamane out of a deep state of slumber. Coming to his senses, he felt as though he had slept for a hundred years. But when he looked at the astro-clock above, he realized he had been there for only an hour. There was a second, more impatient knock at the door.

"Come in," Yamane said after rubbing his eyes. When the door slid open, Kershaw stepped inside. Even after it slid closed again, he remained in his place, expressionless. Yamane felt the tension in the room rise up a couple of notches. He sat up and rubbed his neck. A deep yawn followed soon after. "Why don't you sit down," he suggested, though it probably came off sounding like an order.

Kershaw complied. He brought the chair out from under the desk and set it next to the bed an arm's length from Yamane. The same distant stare, which he had been wearing the entire time, never left.

"I hope you're feeling better," Yamane offered. Kershaw avoided his gaze. Dropping his head just a bit, Yamane took a good look at him. Kershaw appeared as if he had been wrestling with the devil himself. It was hard to tell who had won. His hair was unkempt, both eyes were red and swollen, and the lines on his face were much deeper than normal.

"You doing okay?"

"I suppose," Kershaw finally replied, his voice sounding tired. It seemed difficult for him even to answer such an innocuous question, but it had been a start. "I'm sorry about what happened earlier."

Yamane relaxed as he shook his head in agreement. "So am I. I wish I didn't have to say the things I said, but you needed to hear it."

"I know. Why do you think I reacted so strongly? What you were saying was the truth and I couldn't handle it." He offered a faint smile. "We've been through a lot over the years, and I couldn't bear the thought of anything coming between us."

Yamane leaned closer. "I agree. Besides, I'd get bored quick if you weren't around. Might take a while before I found someone else I could beat in a debate."

The corner of Kershaw's lips moved up, forming into a smirk.

"I realize what I've asked from you is difficult, but I can think of no one better." Yamane's demeanor became serious. An unspoken question existed between the two; one both knew was there, but hadn't been broached yet. "With that said, I have to know now. Can you set your feud with Neu aside or should I offer the job to someone else?"

Kershaw's attention locked onto Yamane's data pad sitting on his desk. "If the fault of what happened rests with him, then it also rests with me." He looked at his commanding officer. "Could I have saved my men if I had been there? I don't know; probably never will. But there is one thing I do know." He rose to his feet and stood at attention. "Even though this is probably the hardest thing you have ever asked of me, sir, I would say yes, I can put my feelings aside and get those cells on board the *Lexington*."

Yamane had never felt more proud of his old friend. "I know this can't have been an easy decision, but with everything riding on getting there and back undetected, I wouldn't feel nearly as confident of our chances of success without you helping in a crucial way."

The compliment seemed to make Kershaw uncomfortable. "I should get going. I need time to go over the personnel records and get my team set up." He shot a glance at the astro-clock. "When are the barges scheduled to depart?"

"Unless anything changes, 2100 hours."

"2100 hours," he whispered. Yamane could almost see the wheels turning in his head. "It will be a bit tight, but what else around here isn't?" He extended his hand. "See you on the other side."

"You too," he replied as they shook. There were a hundred other things left unsaid—important matters, memories of a lifetime ago, and what the next day would bring—but they both had duties to perform, and neither could put them off any longer.

Kershaw took a step back and then disappeared into the corridor.

Yamane suddenly felt alone. Lost. Would his plan work or was he bringing them to ruin? If only Commander Federson or Commodore Hayes were there with him right now. He sure could use their help. "What would you do?" he asked the room.

A warm presence descended upon him from out of nowhere. He felt accepted, embraced. The fears, like shadows exposed to the light, fled from every corner. In an instant, he found himself back in the council chambers, right where he heard that voice, the same voice that gave him his charge. The doubts in his mind dissipated. "Time to go," he said.

Yamane strode into Strategic Operations with a single-minded determination he had not experienced in a long time. Both teams were there, waiting for him. Members of the Star Force sat on one side of the table,

Antarens on the other. After setting his notes down, he cleared his throat, and then said, "Thank you all for being so prompt. I know it's a bit crowded in here, but I think having everyone here at the same will streamline the process." Yamane could not have understated the obvious more. It wasn't a little bit crowded, but a lot crowded. Antarens and humans were practically crammed together, not only around the perimeter, but the table as well. "Barring any problems, this shouldn't take too long."

He pulled his notes closer after sitting down, and skimmed through the top page. "Now, if you activate your data pads, you will find the specifics for the mission have already been downloaded into them. Drawing on my chess-playing experience, the file you are looking for is entitled Operation: *Lexington* Gambit. I want every person in the fleet to have a basic understanding of this plan. By the time the Deravans arrive, I expect our people to know every part of it, forwards and backwards. Anything less would not befit my role as the prophesied one."

Every Antaren in the room nodded in agreement. The commanders, on the other hand, turned toward each other, looking confused.

"Chess, sir?" one of them asked. "What does this have to do with the operation?"

Yamane pushed his notes aside. He agreed. A clarification was in order. "A gambit move is an important tactic used in chess. A player can sometimes gain an advantage against his opponent by sacrificing one of his pieces at a key moment. What we are doing with the *Lexington* is no different. Her sacrifice will give us the advantage we need against the Deravans." His answer seemed to satisfy everyone in the room.

"Now we can get down to business." Yamane pressed a flashing red button near the top of the control panel. The overhead lights dimmed down to half strength. The action likewise triggered the image projector positioned in the far corner of the room. A large blue planet materialized over the conference table. Positioned above the cloud-laden atmosphere, one thousand Deravan ships fired on the surface. Yamane took a pointer from his pocket and rose out of his chair. "This is what those on Earth have faced since we left," he said as he walked around the room, one slow stride after another. "The best way of defeating your enemy is by learning to think like him, understanding his tactics. This thought process, combined with the recommendations you made earlier, are the basis for my plan."

Yamane changed the image when he had come full circle. The entire solar system shrank in size. "The time scale I have used is ten seconds for every hour." He brought up his pointer. "Now you will notice three smaller lines pulling away from the bigger one. This blue line represents the first group of cargo barges heading for the *Lexington*, the white line is the surveillance ships, and this third red line represents the group of decoy cargo barges heading for Earth." He stopped in mid-stride and looked at Tal Win-Tu. "Will your ships still be ready by 0130 hours?"

He stared at his data pad, both glowing eyes focused on something a million kilometers away. "I am sorry," he apologized. "I was figuring something out in my head." He sat back in his chair. "Yes. My subordinates tell me preparations will be completed by then."

"Good." Yamane refocused his attention on the images above. "Now for the barges slated for the *Lexington*. I thought it best if my people were in command of this part of the mission."

"I agree," Tal Win-Tu replied. "They have operational and technical knowledge of your ship we do not possess."

Yamane drew strength from the subidor's show of support. "Commander Neu will be in charge of this phase of the operation. If his ships maintain 1.02 stellar velocity along this trajectory, he should slip in unobserved."

The news immediately registered on his face. "Me, sir?" Neu asked, his eyes wide.

"You're the right man for the job, hands down," Yamane congratulated. He wished he could have offered him more, a small payment of compensation after all those terrible years, but it would have to suffice.

"Thank you, Commander," he replied, still a little bewildered. "Will I also supervise transferring the power cells? I do have some familiarity with them, but not enough to consider myself an expert."

Here goes round two. "I agree. This is why Lt. Commander Kershaw will be your second-in-command. Once you arrive, he will oversee operations on board the *Lexington*."

Neu seemed to slink back in his chair. "But, sir," he objected, "there must be someone else who would be better suited. The two of us working together might cause some...difficulties."

Yamane felt the momentum he enjoyed a minute ago grind to a halt. If he didn't regain the initiative now, who knew how long it would take to get back on track? "You think I'm making a mistake. Under normal circumstances, maybe, but this is hardly what I would call normal. We are fighting for our very lives, and the needs of the mission are far more important than your past with Lt. Commander Kershaw. He has already agreed to set his differences aside for now. Will you do the same?"

Neu hesitated. Yamane could sense the conflict raging within him. A clenched jaw and a fiery intensity in his eyes indicated just how strong his feelings were on the matter. Then, as though the internal war came to a sudden end, he visibly relaxed. "You're right, Commander," Neu replied in guarded tones. "We can't let the mistakes of the past distract us from the present. I will be ready to go whenever you give the word."

Then something extraordinary happened. To Yamane, it looked like a kind of transformation took place in the commander. Long buried under years of self-recrimination, the old Neu began to reassert himself again. Not all at once, like someone flipping on a switch, but slowly, gradually, his long-lost confidence had been reborn—and was gaining strength by the second.

"Consult with Lt. Commander Kershaw," Yamane added. "He's picking the men for his team even as we speak. You are to meet in the starboard landing bay no later than 0115 hours."

"That's cutting it a bit close, but I think I can handle it."

"Good. Now we can proceed with the rest of the briefing."

Yamane shifted his attention back to the room and resumed the briefing. "We will continue on our course until reaching the fail-safe point here." The line then took a sharp turn to the left. "Traveling under absolute radio silence for the next four hours, we will rendezvous with Neptune. The planet will conceal our presence from Earth, until it slips behind the Sun's *Corona* seven hours later. We then fly to Mars at 0.953 stellar velocity, getting there just as it reappears on the other side. By this time, Commander Neu and Lt. Commander Kershaw should have completed their mission, and are heading back to the fleet. This is where the surveillance ships come in. They will signal the Deravans when we are one hour away from Mars."

"What about the cargo barges you sent to Earth?" an Antaren interrupted. "How do you propose we get them out of there?"

His question appeared harmless enough at first, but the more Yamane thought about it, the more he realized the intent of his inquiry. A comrade in arms had concerns about the survivability of fellow soldiers sent into harm's way. Maybe it was simpler than that. Maybe the subidor knew some of the crews and he was worried they might never return.

"I know how troubling this might be for you," Yamane replied, "but we must ensure every Deravan ship is at Earth before the fleet arrives. If this means sacrificing some of our own vessels to guarantee this result, then I'd say it's a fair exchange." The answer was harsh, inflexible, but the course set before them gave him no other alternative. "If all goes well, both fleets will arrive at the *Lexington* at the same time. We then charge up the cells and immobilize their fleet."

"Is this when you plan to initiate our attack against the Deravans?"

Yamane scooted past several Antarens and went over to the projector. The scene above them morphed into a close-up of the stellar cruiser. "Yes. All one hundred and fifty-nine cargo barges will be launched at this point. Their collective firepower should destroy about two-thirds of the Deravan armada. When power in the cells is exhausted, it will be up to us to finish the job." Yamane placed his pointer on the table in front of him. "Are there any questions?"

"What about the remaining skyjackets, destroyers and sub-cruisers?" one of the Antarens asked. "It looks as though you are holding back a number of ships, especially yours."

Yamane did not like his accusational tone, but he understood it. "Ships will be lost during the battle. There is no getting around this. My intent is to keep some in the rear area as reserves. When the Deravans damage or destroy one of our vessels, another will take its place. It is absolutely imperative we maintain our plan of attack as long as possible."

Tal Win-Tu rose out of his chair without any warning. He looked everyone over first before speaking. He appeared to have something important to say. "This is a complicated operation, with many places where a great deal can go wrong. Anticipating the future is always a difficult proposition, but as I listened to Commander Yamane's words, I could see in my mind the prophesied warrior standing before me. This leaves me with but one option. We must back your plan without hesitation. Only this way can Antarens and Terrans work together."

His vote of confidence was unexpected, but most welcome. Tal Win-Tu could have just as easily challenged his authority—bringing undue disorder and acrimony into the process. Instead, Yamane found himself in a greatly enhanced position. He capitalized on the currency offered him. "I want all of you to return to your ships and study the operation until every detail has been burned into your minds. The better prepared we are now, the better our chances later." He looked the room over. "Is there anything else?" Subidors and commanders alike turned towards another, but no one raised their hand or asked a question.

"Attention!" Neu barked. Everyone in the room jumped to their feet and stood at attention.

"Dismissed."

Tal Win-Tu took his leave and hurried out of Strategic Operations. His fellow Antarens followed suit and disappeared into the corridor—silent, determined, and committed.

The commanders, on the other hand, did not seem to be in a hurry to leave. They milled about for an indeterminate amount of time, some engaged in conversations, while others stood in place, alone. Yamane did not have an immediate sense they were stalling, but the longer they lingered, the more he began to suspect their delay was intentional.

"Is there something on your minds?" he asked, his curiosity finally getting the better of him.

Commander Baker gave his uniform a quick tug. His two-meter tall frame and wide shoulders parted the other commanders standing before him. He seemed too confident, too well-rehearsed. Yamane knew something big was coming. "We all talked about this in the landing bay, and none of us is going anywhere until we have some answers."

Yamane might have been premature in his assessment about their support of his operation. "All right, I'll try and answer your questions. Hopefully I can put all your fears to rest." Could they all be against my plan? Could they be against me?

"You've already told us a part of the story, but we need to know a couple of things." Yamane shot several furtive glances around the room, trying to determine what might be on their minds. "On more than one occasion you have referred to yourself as this prophesied warrior, as though the Antarens had anticipated your arrival. You don't actually believe this, do you?"

The question was straightforward and too the point. Yamane knew he had to answer it well, or..."I wish I had time to explain this in greater detail," he sighed. "But since I don't—yes—they believe I am that warrior." Some of the commanders snickered aloud. Others stood silent, listening, though Yamane could tell from their expressions they didn't believe him either. "I know this sounds crazy. Even I thought so at first, but what they said makes sense. Their prophets predicted the arrival of the Deravans. They also said this warrior would come and unite both peoples into one. Look around you and think about what Subidor Tal Win-Tu said. I believe this is a fulfillment of those prophecies."

Commander Nikolovich frowned. "Do you actually believe what you are saying?" he asked in a thick accent. "We've had a number of conversations regarding this matter, and frankly, we're concerned." Some of the commanders nodded in agreement.

Yamane's eyes closed halfway, focusing on Nikolovich like two laser beams locked onto a target. "The Antarens believe this and I believe this. I know this doesn't sound logical, but truth is not often a logical entity."

Nikolovich turned to his left and then his right, as though he sought support from the others around him. "What you're saying is more than a little unbelievable. Do you think we should put our faith in someone who believes all this, how you say—mumbo jumbo?"

A veil of silence descended on the room for several moments. Yamane used the pause to his advantage, and made eye contact with every commander in the room. "I don't care if you believe I'm the prophesied warrior, or the tooth fairy for that matter," he finally replied. "The only thing I care about is defeating the Deravans. After that, you can think whatever you want. But I have to know right now, are you with me or against me?"

An even more penetrating silence filled the room. No one moved, no one said a word. Yamane feared he might have said too much.

Nikolovich snapped to attention. "Thank you, Commander," he quipped like a first year cadet.

"But if you will excuse me, I must return to the *Rostov* and go over the operation."

Every muscle in Yamane's body relaxed.

Commander Moran likewise snapped to attention. "Thank you, sir. Permission to disembark?"

"Permission granted."

Taking their cue from the first two commanders, the others did the same. One by one, they saluted, spun around, and left the room. In a matter of moments, Yamane found himself alone in Strategic Operations. He fell back into his chair and closed both eyes, relieved. His mind began to drift. Soon, he found himself on an empty beach of white sand and palm trees. A soft, warm breeze blew against his face. He could almost hear the sound of the waves lapping onto the shore. A flash of light caught his eye. Yamane went over to the oddly shaped object. A beautiful conch shell lay half-buried in the sand. When he kneeled down to pick it up, a voice called to him from a far off place. "Commander Yamane." His vision faded. Yamane opened his eyes again. Finding himself still in Strategic Operations, he heard the voice a second time.

"Bridge to Commander Yamane. Please come in."

The pull of the beach tugged at him from behind. He closed his eyes again, hoping to return, but it was a half-hearted attempt at best. The picture in his mind was gone.

"Yamane here," he replied after pressing the blinking green button.

"This is Major Webster, Commander. There are two things, actually. First, Dr. Owens from Med-lab five just signaled. She said she needs you there right away. Second, another matter has come up. Can you come to the bridge after you meet with her?"

"I'm on my way. Yamane, out." He clumsily picked up his notes and headed for the door. Just before entering the corridor, he looked back, taking in the dying embers of a carefree moment. Feeling the warmth of the sun's embrace on his face, he headed for the lift.

A lack of noise coming from the infirmary was the first thing he noticed after both doors flew open. Looking about, he realized no one was there. "Strange," he commented to himself. Just a few hours ago, all kinds of clicking and bleeping monitors filled the med-lab; and now—nothing.

An adjoining office caught his eye. Someone had left the light on. For some reason, he felt drawn towards it. A wall of files met him inside, all color-coded: reds, blues, oranges, yellows, and greens. They started on the floor at one end and went up to the ceiling on the other. Over on his right, near the end of the office, he saw a lone desk. In front of that desk sat someone in a white lab coat.

"Excuse me," he said, "Where's—?"

Dr. Owens turned around, startled by his abrupt appearance. "Commander."

"What's going on around here?" he asked as he approached her. "The med-lab is empty. Where's your patient?"

She looked up, her soft blue eyes meeting him first. She pushed her chair back and stood uncomfortably close. "There's no good way to say this, and so I'll just come out with it." Dr. Owens drew in a deep breath. "I'm afraid Lt. Commander Henthorne is dead."

Dead? Shock registered throughout his body. "How? When?" It was all he could get out.

"It happened right at 2100 hours, almost to the second. Just as the time ticked down, he stared at the astro-clock; as though he knew something, something he couldn't possibly know. Holding up his data pad one last time, he turned it off, and then closed his eyes. I thought he was just falling asleep, but his heart rate dropped down, setting off the alarm...and that was it."

Yamane looked at the astro-clock above her desk. The relevance of the time did not escape his attention. Like an immutable force pulling on him, he went to Henthorne's empty bed. Someone had already removed the sheets and pillows, leaving only an exposed mattress. "You said his work might help him recover."

She reeled back at the accusation. "If he had followed my instructions, there might have been a chance, but Lt. Commander Henthorne kept pushing himself. Refusing to eat, barely getting any sleep—those stresses finally took their toll."

Yamane placed his hand on the cold, rolled steel headboard.

She walked around the other side and looked down. "He appeared to be a man competing against something. He may have directed his struggle at you, but I think it went much deeper, almost as though he were really at war with himself. I got the sense he felt that if he finished his calculations, he would have beaten you in some way. Finishing his work, however, depleted his strength. In the end, Henthorne's immune system could no longer fight the infection. But I don't think he cared much about that. Only finishing what he believed was his great triumph did. That's when he permitted himself to stop."

Yamane tightened his grip on the headboard. "It's interesting," he observed. "We were at odds with each other from the beginning, and yet, if he hadn't finished his calculations and given me what I needed, I never could have developed a plan against the Deravans. How do you reconcile these contradictions?"

Owens' hand brushed past his. Intentional. Her touch felt good. "I don't think we'll ever have an answer."

"Now that he's gone, I feel like I have lost a part of myself. Kind of a strange reaction, don't you think?"

She moved even closer. "Maybe it's better if we focus on the contributions he made. He had some deep-rooted demons in his life, and they were partly responsible for ending it, but this doesn't mean we can't remember the positive. From what I understand, he was a good officer."

"I suppose you're right," Yamane agreed. Her warm, inviting eyes welcomed him, drew him in. No other words came to mind. He just stared.

"Is there anything else I can do?" she asked, stepping close to him.

He couldn't hold back any longer. Yamane stepped towards her, sliding his hand around her back. She was waiting. The two embraced and held each other close. He drank her in like a man dying of thirst. It had been a long time since he permitted himself to feel this way about anyone. Not since... he pulled back. Guilt racked him, as though he had somehow betrayed the memory of his beloved wife. The distance between them increased. "I...I... Thank you, Doctor," he said awkwardly.

She took a step forward. "Janice. It's Janice," she said, acting hurt, as though Yamane should have known to call her by her first name. Then she looked at him funny. "Thank you—for what?"

"Just for all you've done...Janice," he replied warmly, and then made his escape.

CHAPTER
24

Yamane shuffled onto the bridge, still clutching the notes from his briefing. He felt tired, defeated—guilty. How many more men have to die, he thought, before the Deravans get their way?

The crew paid him little attention. He didn't mind so much. His command chair was the only thing in view; and in it sat Webster. "Why was I needed on the bridge?" he asked him in a curt and direct manner. His thoughts went back to Henthorne.

Webster picked up the data pad in his lap and scrolled down the screen. He stopped at the required entry. "About fifteen minutes ago we received a transmission from the Antarens. They said seven of their cargo barges have developed engine problems. In time, they will go critical. No chance of repair, I'm afraid."

Yamane snatched the data pad from his hands and read the transcribed message for himself. He handed it back to Webster after scrutinizing the fleet on the main screen. "I thought the Antarens maintained their ships better than that."

"It would seem some of them don't."

"Why can't we catch a break?" he asked in frustration.

Webster rose from the command chair and stepped aside. Yamane fell into his seat, a distant stare on his face. He sat there, just looking at the screen, saying something to himself. Webster was about to resume his post when Yamane called him back. "How much open space do we have in the main cargo bay?"

"Sir?"

"Open space. How much do we have?"

"I don't know, let me check." He went over to his station and accessed the *Corona*'s schematics. A three-dimensional image popped up on his screen. On the left side of the display, a summation of the ship's manifest scrolled down. On the right side, the database included the location of each item, along with its description and tag number. "There is just over two hundred thousand cubic meters of space," he called out.

Yamane made some calculations in his head. "Seven barges," he whispered to himself. "A bit tight but sufficient." He came alongside the c-tech. "Signal the Antarens and have those vessels rendezvous at our position. We can offload everything in their bays and store it on our ship."

Landis looked up at him. "Brought on board, sir? I don't understand."

"Those barges can't be saved, but what they're carrying can. We send out a tether to the first one in line, transfer their cargo into a holding bay, and then work our way down, until they've all been cleared."

"How much should I slow the *Corona*?" the nav-tech asked. "To 0.50...0.60?"

Yamane studied the ships on the main screen. "No change," he replied softly. "We'll maintain our course and speed."

The nav-tech jerked his head over. "But, Commander," he protested. "Safety protocols require we drop below 0.75 stellar velocity. Transporting cargo at this speed will be dangerous. Those barges will be no more than twenty-five meters off our port side. I don't have to tell you what will happen if we experience any bow shocks. I don't think the Antaren pilots can handle that kind of precision flying."

Yamane fixed his gaze on the nav-tech. "I've just lost a good officer because of the Deravans. How long can those survivors on Earth hold out? Enough people have died there already." He turned his back to the screen. His answer was harsh, and he regretted saying it. "I'm sorry, Lieutenant. I know you're just doing your job, but every second we delay could mean the difference for thousands of lives back at home."

"If only those ships were smaller. We could have brought them into the landing bay."

"I agree, but unfortunately, they're not." Yamane returned to the command chair. "This brings us back to where we started." He fixed his gaze on the main screen. "Signal the *Bok-Nor*. Get Subidor Tal Win-Tu on the line."

"Yes, sir," Landis replied, his reply sharp.

While Yamane waited, he gave himself permission to stop thinking about Henthorne's death.

"This is Subidor Tal Win-Tu," he said on the speaker. "Go ahead, Commander."

"Subidor, I have been advised as to your situation concerning the seven cargo barges. Even though there's nothing we can do for the ships, we can still save their cargo. I think it would be best if we offloaded them while in flight. Since timing is crucial to the operation, this will minimize the chance of falling behind schedule."

He heard a voice in the background, but couldn't make out the words. The conversation went on for a good couple of minutes before he got a reply. "I have just given the order. The first cargo barge should reach you shortly."

"Good. We'll be standing by." He then went over to the engineering station. "Signal Captain Deniker. Have his teams prepare for emergency transport."

"Yes, Commander—right away."

Alarms rang out in the forward cargo bay. Work crews going about their assigned tasks in the vast, warehouse-sized enclosure five decks high stopped what they were doing. "This is a priority one message," a voice boomed on loud speakers amidst dozens of thirty-meter high shelving units. "All personnel prepare for emergency transport. I repeat, prepare for emergency transport."

They literally dropped what they were doing and came running to the long yellow line bridging the distance from one end of the outer door to the other. Some had to dart around cargo loaders, while others hurdled over parts and equipment strewn about the deck.

On the other side of the line, Captain Deniker waited. He strolled back and forth in front of the enormous, rectangular-shaped cargo door. His harsh nature was matched by his appearance: uniform, always pressed and creased; his hair, never a strand out of place; and his manner, precise and efficient.

He scrutinized all three teams standing before him. His unflinching expression and cold penetrating stare intimidated everyone under his command; something he reveled in on a regular basis. "I've just been told that there are seven cargo barges heading for the *Corona*," Deniker barked in his typically boisterous fashion. "We have five minutes to prepare for their arrival. And because Commander Yamane knows how well I've trained you, he has elected not to drop below stellar velocity. This is going to be a real shake-and-bake operation."

The crews responded with the sounds of mixed groans. Deniker stopped in mid-stride. Turning right, he stood toe-to-toe with one of the men under his command. "Do you have a problem with this, soldier?" he bellowed.

"Sir, no, sir!" the supply tech barked back.

"What about you, Bryers? Are you afraid of a little bow shock?"

"Sir, no, sir!" he screeched.

Deniker resumed his slow, purposeful gait. At the end of the line, he spun around and went back the other way. "I get the feeling you don't think much of the way I do things around here."

"Sir, no complaints, sir!"

A half-hearted smile formed on his face. "You don't know how much that warms my heart," he chided. "Some people might think I'm being too hard on you; that we should please ask Commander Yamane to slow down the ship so it won't upset our sensitive stomachs. I would hate to think I was being inconsiderate."

"Sir, no, sir!" The teams replied in unison.

"That's what I want to hear." Deniker pointed to the edge of the bay. "Now, I want team A to prepare for cargo transport. Team B will send out the lines and link up with the barges. Team C will be on fire control." He stopped and looked the crews over. "Are there any questions? Good," he said before any of them could think of one. "What are you waiting for? Let's move it."

All three teams bolted from the yellow line and ran to the stations they had been assigned.

Deniker walked over to the control panel just to the left of the outer door in no particular hurry. There, he accessed the master control program. With a delicate touch, he took hold of the joystick in the middle of the panel and moved it forward. His station rose about a quarter of the way to the top. All six displays in front of him flickered to life as he pressed certain knobs and switches. Below each of them were toggles for up, down, left, and right. He gave them a quick check. The six cameras mirrored his actions precisely.

"This is your captain speaking—doing a communications check," he said after strapping on his headset. "How do you read me?"

"Loud and clear," the leaders of all three teams responded in unison.

"All right then. I am entering the final code. Stand by."

Yellow warning lights located along the perimeter of the outer door started to flash off and on, followed by the sound of an automated voice indicating it would soon be opening. Two cylindrical locks at the far end started to retract. A high-pitched motor whirred incessantly, stopping when the locks could go no further. Then a second, more powerful motor kicked in. When the seal broke, the massive door started to move along the length of the hull. The opening, just a sliver a first, steadily grew in size, revealing a tantalizing view of stars and ships in the distance. The only thing that stood between the teams and the vacuum of space was a single millimeter of binary magnetic shielding.

All three pilots jumped into their respective cargo containers and strapped themselves inside.

"Team C, get those tow cables locked into place," Deniker ordered. "Remember, when you're approaching the cargo barges, keep a distance of at least three meters between you, or your lines will get crossed."

Members of team B ran up to the containers from behind. They flipped up three small panels on the deck just below the skids, and then reached in and pulled out three, tightly wound cables; hooking them onto the undercarriages. Once they locked the cables into place, the techs backed up and took up positions near their emergency equipment.

"All crews, standby," Deniker said on his headset. "The first barge will arrive in one minute."

The pilots strained to see the incoming ship, but it was still out of view.

Deniker got a fix on his position once it had entered the limited range of his tracking console. A single blip steadily made its way towards the center. "Stand by," he repeated.

Team A readied itself.

"Cargo barge one, bring your ship closer another twenty meters." The pilot fired two directional bursts. "Fifteen meters...twelve meters. Almost there." Another burst slowed the vessel. "Five meters...two meters. You're in position. Prepare to receive transport crews."

"Affirmative," the voice replied.

Deniker monitored the ship on his display. A sea of bluish stars shone behind it. If the *Corona's* bow sliced through a gaseous cloud or other concentration of interstellar debris at this speed, the ensuing bow shock could do some serious damage. No matter, he thought, nothing we can do about it now, anyway. He reconfigured his screen, setting vertical and horizontal white lines over the binary magnetic shielding. Manipulating the field into a boxlike configuration, the effect enveloped those carriages waiting in line. Air pressure within the temporary cube nearly doubled. All three pilots indicated they were ready after a couple of jerks on their safety harnesses and a quick thumbs-up.

Deniker brought his finger down on the flashing red light at the base of his display. When the forward portion of the magnetic field collapsed, escaping air pushed all three carriages out into space. The moment they cleared the cargo bay, the pilots fired their maneuvering jets, bringing their transports under control.

Two Antarens in EVA suits stood in the aft section of the barge, both doors fully retracted.

"Slowing...five meters," the lead pilot said into his headset. He fired one short burst. The front edge of the carriage slowed before gliding onto the aft deck. "That's it."

A minimal amount of gravity caused the safety harness to drift downward when the operator pressed the release. He pushed himself out of the cage and floated over to the front part of the carriage. Nestled under a protective grate, he took hold of the transport cable. Activating the motorized pulley system, the pilot negotiated a maze of stacked bins and storage containers in the rear of the barge. When a couple of particularly large canisters passed by on the right, the back wall appeared. Set in the middle, about waist-high, seven large rings attached to a flattened metal beam fell into view. The pilot looped his cable through the middle one and then clamped both ends tight. "This should hold the lines." He signaled the other two carriages waiting a short distance away. In a matter of minutes, they were ready to begin transporting their cargo. "I think we're set up over here," he said to Deniker on the radio.

"All right, Ensign," he chided. "Start getting those shipments to the cargo bay. Team B has been waiting for two minutes already."

"Yes, sir," Jones said under his breath. He followed the middle cable back to his transport. "We'll start with the smaller bins first, and then work our way to the big stuff in the back." All three Antarens nodded in return.

They formed themselves into two groups of three. One group grabbed cylinders and boxes, while the other two combined their strength and focused on the bigger, more cumbersome bins.

When they had loaded up his carriage to the brim, Jones himself strapped inside the cage, and zipped across the twenty-five meter gap between both ships, right into the awaiting arms of team B. Upon landing, they set about getting the shipment unloaded as quickly as possible.

Jones returned to the aft section of the barge just as members of his team loaded the last few containers onto the other transports. When the ship suddenly decelerated, the Antarens lost their balance and slammed into a nearby wall.

"Is everyone there all right?" Deniker yelled on the radio, losing his characteristic cool.

"That was close," Jones observed. "We took a bit of a hit, but I think we're okay."

"Finish up with that barge before we encounter another bow shock."

"Yeah, yeah, yeah." He took a step back. Just outside, about fifty meters away, he saw the next barge in line, waiting for its turn.

"I think we're done here," Jones concluded after he scanned the open space. "Detach the cables and get that shipment over to the *Corona*."

The barge decelerated again, but not as severely as before.

Team B stood ready. As each carriage came aboard the *Corona*, Deniker opened the temporary barrier. With short directional bursts, the pilots landed on their assigned spots. Forming a line of sorts, the crews grabbed boxes and bins with reckless abandon, throwing them into nearby carts.

When Jones' barge blasted away, his carriage flew over to the next ship. Several back-and-forth excursions later, he and his partners had all but delivered the last of the cargo to the *Corona*.

"We're ready to send the final shipment. When you give the word, I'll detach the cables."

"Do it," Deniker replied, short and to the point. "Just get off that barge."

Jones grabbed the locking mechanism and pulled out both holding pins. When the clamps released, his assistant reeled in the line and secured it to the undercarriage.

"You two get your cables detached," Jones said between winded breaths. All that heavy lifting had begun to take its toll on him. "I'll head back to the bay and wait for you there."

Just as he pushed off the deck, another bow shock struck the cargo barge dead on. Unlike the first two collisions, this one overcame the ship's directional stabilizers. The vessel started to list over onto her port side. The Antaren pilot tried to compensate, but the force of impact knocked his power systems offline. Every light in the bay went dark for a few moments before emergency systems kicked in.

In an effort to stay on his feet, Jones clung to the latching ring. He instinctively looked out the back of the barge. To his horror, he saw the *Corona* coming up on him fast. "We have to detach the cables before it's too late!" he yelled into his headset.

At the worst of all possible moments, the stellar cruiser's bow plowed right through another ionized pocket of interstellar gas. The resultant wake slammed into the nearby cargo barge, pitching it over even further. All three cables went taut. Holding the ship in place under great stress, one of the lines gave way. It recoiled back right where Jones was standing. He ducked just in time. The line the width of a man's arm sliced right through the side of the bay, right where his head had been a second before.

"Can you get to your carriages?" Jones asked the other pilots.

"Don't wait for us, Lieutenant," one of them answered. "We can make it back."

Jones flashed a smile at them. He then eyed his transport a few meters away. Just as he was about to make his way towards it, the barge unexpectedly lurched downward. Both he and it slammed into the rear bulkhead. He shook off the effects of the collision and climbed into the cage. When he blasted his carriage off the deck, he saw a burst of white light in the corner of his eye. A large part of the barge flew off at an odd angle. Then another shock wave slammed into the barge. Several pockets of compressed gases easily overtook his fragile craft.

Yamane stared at the main screen. His breathing quickened. "I was doing this for those on Earth," he muttered under his breath. Mathematical equations danced around in his head. He had figured there was almost no chance of encountering a hydrogen cloud in this sector. Unfortunately, his gamble had not paid off, and it had cost the lives of a cargo barge crew and three transport teams. "Maybe Henthorne had been right all along. Maybe ..." Yamane turned away. How long will this go on?

One by one, the crew turned towards him in silence.

"Lieutenant, offer our condolences to the Antarens."

"Yes, Commander." Just as he was about to send the message, he stopped. Bending forward, the corners of his lips turned upward. When Landis flipped a switch on his console, an unexpected transmission interrupted the dour atmosphere on the bridge. "We are alive. I repeat. We are all alive."

"Sir, there's a small object off our port side," the r-tech said after double-checking his display. "The signal is originating from that location."

Yamane jumped to his feet. The sounds of his heart pumping in his chest drowned out the collective noises made by the bridge. "Lock onto the source. I want to see it."

The image switched from a cluster of stars to a rectangular-shaped object. Yamane peered at the shape, his hopes buoyed.

The r-tech verified the image on his scope. "Confirmed," his said. "The bridge from the barge must have jettisoned just after the bow shock plowed into it."

"Well I'll be," Yamane said. "Send out a Min fighter and have the bridge towed into the landing bay."

"With pleasure, Commander."

Not so bad after all, Yamane thought, relieved beyond description.

Jones tumbled away out of control, away from the other ships. Alarms blared in his helmet speakers as stars spun around him in a tumult. If he didn't do something soon, he would be lost in space—forever. Then an idea hit him. He reached over to a large red button under a plate of safety glass. Pushing down on it with all of his might, the directional thrusters fired in unison. The activated gyroscopes slowly brought the transport under control, and out of danger.

Battered and barely functional, Jones steered his carriage back to the cargo bay. He made sure to avoid small pieces of debris flying past him.

"Captain," he said on the radio, "permission to come aboard."

"I don't know how you did it, Jones," Deniker complemented, "but welcome back."

"My targeting display is all smashed up, so I'm not certain just how far out I am."

"I've got you on my screen. Just hold your course and you'll land in no time. There will be a couple of friends waiting for you when you do."

The carriage slipped onto the deck of the landing bay, skidding slightly before coming to a stop. Deniker immediately reconfigured the magnetic shield. Sliding horizontally along the hull, the massive outer door retracted into the opening, creating an airtight seal.

Jones pried himself out of the cage. He took a couple of steps back and looked his carriage over. His transport had taken quite a pummeling, but she was still intact. He placed his hand on a support bar and patted her several times. "You did real good."

"Break time's over," Deniker bellowed from his station. "We've still got a lot of work to do."

With the last of his gear stowed, Kershaw zipped up his bag. He had been dreading the operation from the outset. The one strike against him was big—Commander Neu. This was a name from his past he never wanted uttered again, and yet, here he was, about to embrace him with both arms.

He picked up his bag and scanned the room. Conflicting ideas and emotions swirled around in his mind. How could he abandon the ship's engines at a time like this? There was so much left undone. Then, out of nowhere, a strange sensation of contentment floated down on top of him. Resolve replaced the anguish bubbling inside of Kershaw. An explanation eluded him, but he embraced his newfound perception of the mission. When he came to his senses again, he realized he was running late. Kershaw grabbed his flightbag and his satchel and headed out the door, straight for the landing bay.

The gate slid open amidst the sounds of pilots and technical teams mingling about the flight deck, waiting to board their ships. Loaders were getting the last pieces of equipment on board the transports. The smell of exhaust hung heavy in the air.

"Commander on deck!" someone yelled as Neu arrived. He strutted confidently into the general area where the crews had more or less congregated. Two officers Kershaw didn't know followed close behind. Time melted away, as if it was ten years ago. Nothing had changed in the interim. Neu was still the same cocky and self-assured man he remembered. A bad taste formed in Kershaw's mouth.

"I want every team member over here so I can address you before we leave," Neu bellowed, his voice deep.

The pilots and technical team inched their way closer, forming a loose semi-circle around him. Kershaw stayed over to the side. He could not have been more conspicuous in his actions.

"We will be boarding our assigned ships in the next couple of minutes. Group up by teams so you will all be together. In the meantime, check your gear; make certain nothing has been forgotten." He took two steps down the line and then added, "This is a dangerous mission, but we are the vital key that either brings success or failure. I know you will all execute your duty without hesitation. Make me proud." He eyed every man and woman. "Dismissed."

The crews broke ranks and headed for their assigned ships. Neu, on the other hand, went over to where Kershaw waited. "Is everything ready?" he asked.

"As much as can be hoped for," Kershaw replied in a brusque fashion.

"Good. You should get loaded up. Your men are waiting for you."

"Whatever you say, Commander," he sneered and then brushed past him.

Neu gave Kershaw a good long look before hurrying over to the transports. "All your gear should be stowed away," he yelled over the sounds of engines roaring to life. "I want three lines, each one behind your assigned ship."

When the airlock door slid open, the crews started boarding. Neu went up and down the lines, helping them along. "Move it, soldier!" he barked. "Come on, double time. The clock is ticking, and we have a schedule to keep."

"The landing bay operator is asking for the final clearance code," the r-tech said to Yamane after he confirmed their status from his station.

He checked the time. 0129. They were right on schedule. "Give him permission to launch."

The r-tech switched views on the main screen, just in time to see the first Antaren transport flying out of the landing bay. The next one followed right after. In time, every one had safely disembarked, heading right for the cargo barges waiting three kilometers away.

"Five minutes until launch, Commander," the r-tech called out.

Yamane looked down at the light blinking on his display. With the entire operation downloaded into the main computer, the transceivers would soon send a signal to the awaiting ships, setting each of their master control programs in motion.

"Three minutes until launch."

The bridge became deathly silent.

After the transports transferred the crews to their awaiting ships, every set of docking rings retracted and pulled away from the barges. Not far away, the nine additional barges slated to go to Earth likewise waited, along with the surveillance ships. Even though Yamane's attention remained fixed on the main screen, he never took his finger off the final sequencing button.

"One minute to launch."

Yamane drew in an unconscious breath, and then activated the program. The astro-clock above began to count down from sixty seconds. "Signal the fleet. Tell them we're on automatic."

Landis nodded in return.

"Thirty seconds."

"RadAR screen shows all clear."

"Twenty seconds."

"All systems functioning as expected."

"Fifteen seconds."

Yamane looked at the console readout as the program sequence initiated the next series of transmission codes. "Ten seconds. Stand by on my mark."

"The boards are clear. All circuits indicate green. Launch is go."

"Three...two...one...mark." All three groups of ships fired their thrusters and accelerated away from the fleet. The sounds of spontaneous yelling and enthusiastic applause exploded on the bridge.

Glowing white light from every engine port produced a light show of unparalleled magnificence. Streams of exhaust blazoned across the screen like nimble fingers of light. Then, in an act of unanticipated choreography, they broke away from each other and headed toward very different destinations.

The bridge watched as all three bodies continued flying further out of view. It was as if the longer they could see the flickering lights, the better their chances for success. Their reaction made no sense logically, but it felt true.

Yamane wished he could relish the sweetness of the moment just a bit longer, but with so many other aspects of the operation still demanding his attention, he needed to get his thoughts back in order. The fleet would reach the first of several course corrections in a few hours. Then there were the hundreds of other decisions required of him along the way. With the fate of humanity hanging in the balance, he figured the decision quotient had been increased by a factor of ten. He corrected himself. "No. More like a thousand."

CHAPTER

25

DEK-PAR
DAIETH TIME PLUS FOUR

Carrying his gear up and down the corridor several times, Kershaw finally stopped right where he was. He took note of the darkened hallway and strange smells emanating all around him. A huge sigh followed. He dropped his bags and sat down in frustration. Because the cells and support equipment had taken up almost all of the free space in the cargo bay, extra supplies had to be stacked wherever an open spot existed, tucked away in some dark nook or cranny. Kershaw knew ahead of time it would be a tight fit, but he didn't expect the situation to be this bad.

"What have I gotten myself into?" he wondered aloud.

But as bad as the corridors had been, the limited space was nothing compared to the sleeping quarters. He had already checked a number of them. What had originally been designed to hold four occupants were housing double that amount, and in some cases, triple.

He heard several people coming from around the corner. Not wanting anyone seeing him in this state, he quickly unzipped his bag and pretended to look for something. They walked by, barely giving him any notice. When the three disappeared around the corner, he stopped his little charade.

"There you are," Subidor Tul Lan-Ro declared after appearing out of nowhere. "I've been looking all over the *Dek-Par* for you." He stopped and surveyed the stacked containers in the corridor. "As much as possible, that is. I guess you would consider her a small ship."

"I was just going through my bags and checking some equipment," Kershaw lied. "Semitronic instruments are extremely sensitive, you know."

"Interesting," he replied with a certain lilt in his voice. "Well in any case, since we are both here, I can escort you to your quarters. It is not much, but what I have is at your disposal."

"I appreciate that," he replied. Tul Lan-Ro would never know how much.

Kershaw picked up his bags and followed him to his new housing. The Antaren's joyful disposition had been a stark contrast to the muted colors all around them. He didn't know why, but they seemed to favor the darkest ones: grays, blues and browns. An overall lack of lighting made the effect even more pronounced. At a number of points during their brief excursion, usually at right-angle turns, he almost couldn't see his hand in front of his face. No matter, he thought. Tul Lan-Ro seemed to know where he was going.

The Antaren stopped in front of an unmarked hatch after they rounded a corner. He extended his right hand and waved it over a gold-colored plate placed just beyond the perimeter of the doorway.

"Open sesame," Kershaw mused to himself. And as with Ali Baba and his forty thieves, the door slid open.

"You may put your bags down anywhere you wish," he said, motioning him inside.

Kershaw took tentative steps forward. He wasn't the kind of person who just went into someone's room and treated it as if it were his own. He at least wanted to establish a level of respect with his host first before doing so. Then he could trash it to his heart's desire.

Taking a quick look around, he was surprised to find the subidor's quarters remarkably similar to his own, except for the size. The room appeared about half as large. This didn't surprise him though—smaller ship, smaller room.

Across from him, about a meter away, was a bed. The walls were bare, no portholes, and the same dour color as the corridors. Next to him, near his knees, a strange-looking device sat humming. Kershaw could only guess what purpose it served. A single light lit the room from above, but only dimly. A makeshift cot had been set up, with a thin green blanket and small pillow resting on top. It wasn't exactly up to specifications, but at least he would be comfortable.

"You can see I have gone far as a subidor," he declared while walking around his quarters. "Not too bad, if I do say so myself."

Kershaw produced a fake grin. "You must be proud."

"Subidor Tul Lan-Ro," an unknown voice called. Kershaw looked around, but couldn't see where the sound came from. "You are needed on the bridge. Please report there right away."

"I will return as soon as I can and help you get acquainted with the ship," he said, almost hinting at a smile. "In the meantime, you can put your things away and get comfortable." The door slid open. In the blink of an eye, he was gone.

S.F.S. CORONA
2101 PROXIMA MERIDIAN TIME, AUGUST 27, 2217

"How long before we reach the coordinates for our course change?" Yamane asked after wiping the sweat off his hands. He paced back and forth on the bridge, nervous.

"Five minutes and twelve seconds."

"Have the ships in the fleet signaled they are prepared to make the change?"

"Yes, Commander."

"RadAR. Anything ahead of us?"

"Negative. My scope shows all clear."

Yamane stopped and stared at the main screen. The course correction could not come soon enough. "I want a message sent out to all ships in the fleet. We will now be operating under stealth mode—no radio transmissions or active RadAR sweeps of any kind until we reach Neptune. I don't want to take a chance on the Deravans picking us up."

"Yes, sir. I'll send the order now."

Yamane returned to the command chair. The techs in front of him monitored the ship's engine output and life support from their stations. A failure in any one of these or a hundred other systems might put the ship in danger. So far, they had been fortunate. "Time?" he asked

"Two minutes."

He glanced at the display by his armrest. Commands and protocols scrolled down the screen in sequential order. Even though every decision rested on his shoulders alone, it felt good having a pre-determined directive already in place, just in case.

Landis bobbed his head up and down after each ship responded. "The fleet has confirmed your last order, Commander," he said to Yamane.

"Prepare for course correction," he said, and then sat back down in the command chair.

"One minute."

Thousands of stars appeared like white flecks over a canvas of black on the main screen. Yamane focused on a cluster of larger ones near the center. Any time now, he thought. Even before the words faded from his mind, they started drifting over; slowly at first, but then picked up speed. He checked the astro-clock. Right to the second.

"Computers are initiating the course correction."

Yamane took a quick look at the r-tech's console. "Are the other ships still with us?" he asked.

Mechanical beeps and clicks preceded the r-tech's response. "Yes, Commander. Fleet integrity is holding firm."

Drawing in a long, steady breath, Yamane closed both eyes. His nervous thoughts calmed. Even though this had only been a simple course correction, the potential for an "event" still ran high. And the way their luck was going, a major systems failure or another collision seemed a likely outcome.

"Rear view," he ordered, still needing a small measure of reassurance. The main screen changed to a view of the fleet behind them. Coming around in a slight parabolic arc, every ship maintained the same distance from each other, as though they were all physically connected. "What is our new trajectory?"

The nav-tech pressed a pair of buttons before giving his answer. "My instruments indicate we are heading directly for Neptune. Point one-five deviation."

The master control program clicked off another command, bringing up the next one in line. Yamane sat back in his chair. One down, four hundred and sixty-two to go. He sighed deeply.

DEK-PAR
DAIETH TIME PLUS FIVE

Kershaw stumbled over another box in the corridor. "Ow," he blurted out as shooting pains went up his shin. He gently rubbed his bruised leg for a second before heading down the main corridor again. A closed hatch appeared. If he read his Antaren right, the cargo bay resided on the other side. He must have tripped an unseen sensor, as the door slid open when he came within a couple of meters of it. Lights flickered on when he entered the bay. Crates, cylinders, boxes, canisters and containers were stacked from floor to ceiling; and down the middle, a narrow walkway barely existed, just big enough for a single person to slip through.

Kershaw drew in a deep breath of cool, musty air. "Those power cells could be in any one of these containers," he muttered to himself. Activating the data pad in hand, the ship's manifest popped onto the screen, followed by a three-dimensional image of his surroundings. "Another five meters this way."

He squeezed past two boxes, both about waist high. Several large metal bins sat in an area by themselves. He figured they had to be them. A quick search of the area revealed Antaren markings on the tops of each container. When Kershaw peered more closely, he realized someone had translated the phrases into English. Bingo. He popped open one of the sides. Much to his relief, the control panel was facing outward in his direction.

He accessed the startup procedures from his data pad. A list of instructions scrolled down the screen. "Now this is a better way of spending one's time," he said aloud, "better than sitting on my cot and doing a whole lot of nothing."

Kershaw entered a five-digit command code. The panel lit up, followed by a low hum. In the upper left-hand corner, a set of options appeared.

"Who's in here?" a voice called from behind.

The person sounded familiar. Kershaw rose to his feet as a shadowy figure approached. Even in the dark, he recognized that cocky disposition. "Commander Neu," Kershaw said with a certain measure of contempt. This was the last person he wanted to see.

"I've been looking for you all over the ship," Neu said after he had negotiated the last box. "Figures I would find you in here. You always were something of a techno-hound."

"Looks like you found me," he replied, his tone indifferent.

"I've just come from the bridge. We are heading for the *Lexington* as planned."

"Uh-huh."

"Those RadAR scanners from the surveillance ships are working perfectly," Neu added. "Forward sweeps have been negative, no Deravan ships in this sector, so far."

Kershaw said nothing.

Neu slid past a canister by his foot. "Is there anything I can help you with here?" he offered. "I spent a couple of years on Antara, and could give you some insight into how they do things."

Kershaw just couldn't take any more of this banal conversation. "Let's get one thing straight," he attacked. "The only reason I'm here is because Commander Yamane asked me. I don't want your help. I don't need your help—got it?"

Reacting as though he had collided into an invisible barrier, Neu stopped right in his tracks. "You will not address a superior officer in that manner," he fired back. "I am still in command of this mission, and you will show me the proper respect."

Kershaw drove his finger into Neu's chest. "You don't deserve command. If I'd had my way, you would have been court-martialed ten years ago."

"So that's how it is between us," Neu replied, his eyes narrowing. "Well let me tell you one thing, I've had to live with that mistake every day of my life. There have been a lot of sleepless nights since then." He stopped and looked up. "You know what the worst part of this whole thing is?" Kershaw didn't respond, nor did he care to. "I've gone through the incident round and round in my head more times than I can remember, and in the end, I would not have done anything different. Sometimes, these things happen in war."

Kershaw drew close. "If you didn't do anything wrong, then why is my squadron dead?"

The dagger drove deep into Neu. "I'm sorry you feel that way, but neither of us can change the past."

Kershaw moved back a couple of steps. "I guess you and I can agree on something."

"Your only concern is those power cells. Other than that, you do whatever you want." Neu left the cargo bay without another word.

S.F.S. CORONA

2213 PROXIMA MERIDIAN TIME, AUGUST 27, 2217

"Incoming message from the *Bok-Nor*," Landis said from his station.

Yamane swiveled the command chair around. Worry flashed in his eyes. He figured the only reason someone would violate his standing order of maintaining radio silence was because some kind of emergency had arisen. "Who is it?"

"Tal Win-Tu. He says it's urgent."

"Put him on."

The main screen immediately switched over from a shot of the stars to the bridge of his ship.

"I am sorry to break radio silence, Commander Yamane," he said in a rushed manner," but there is something important we should discuss before it is too late."

"Make it quick Subidor, so we can clear this channel."

"I have discovered a major flaw in your plan, one that might jeopardize the entire operation."

Yamane clutched his data pad close. Tal Win-Tu must be mistaken. He had gone through the sequence of events so many times he didn't think it possible something important had been missed. "What part of the operation are you referring to?"

"If you look on page nine, paragraph two, the part where we send the cargo barges against the Deravan armada ..."

Yamane accessed the file. "That's correct. They will initiate the attack against the Deravans after the EM field has been generated." He fixed his gaze on Tal Win-Tu.

The subidor almost appeared annoyed. "I am not disputing this point. The problem is with the ships themselves. They are operational only if a crew is on the bridge. Those barges cannot be piloted by remote control."

Yamane re-read the second paragraph. Tal Win-Tu was right. A sinking feeling overtook him. "How could I have missed something so obvious?" he groused, disappointed with himself.

"Do not blame yourself. I doubt if you have even heard of the incident at the Mensari launch platform. Since that tragic accident, we re-designed our ships so no one could pilot them by remote. I wished I had discovered this part of your plan sooner."

Yamane's hand fell to his side. "This leaves us in a bad spot. Without them, I don't see how we will bring about an adequate level of destruction against the Deravans."

"I am disappointed as well, but there are always alternatives."

Yamane scrolled through the operation, hoping an idea might jump out at him. None did. This left him right where they started. He needed those barges. On the other hand, he couldn't very well send those crews to their deaths. There had been enough of that already. Then, like a lightening bolt flashing in the sky, a memory appeared in his mind; disjointed at first, but definitely there.

He snapped his fingers several times. "Come on, you know it's still in there," he said to himself.

"What is it Commander Yamane?" Tal Win-Tu asked, concerned. "Are you alright?"

"The bow shocks from earlier today," he processed aloud.

"You mean the collisions between those two cargo barges?"

"Yes," he said. "The bridges. Do you remember what they did?"

"Of course," the subidor replied. "They jettisoned just before the ships exploded." The impact of what he said registered on his face. "Now I understand what you are getting at. We send out the cargo barges with a minimal crew. Just before they ram the Deravan ships, they jettison the bridge and fly away, unharmed."

"I know it's a risk for them, but I think this might be our best option."

"You may be right, Commander Yamane. I will have my specialists work on the problem."

"Signal me with your results when we reach Neptune. Yamane, out."

DEK-PAR
DAIETH TIME PLUS SEVEN

Kershaw stared past three large windowpanes on the bridge of Tul Lan-Ro's ship, lost in thought. Fanning out on either side of him at forty-five degree angles, the two sets of cargo barges shone dimly from the place where he stood. Even though tens of thousands of stars glowed all around them, their combined radiance only equaled the light of a full moon on a cloudy night. He tried reading the names of the other eighteen ships, but their darkened hulls made such a task a near impossibility. "No matter," he thought. He could just as easily check with the communications operator.

Kershaw placed his hands behind his back and walked the length of the bridge. He had tried sacking out for a while in his quarters earlier, but the lumpy mattress, combined with the conversation he had with Neu, left him feeling agitated. Rather than fight the inevitable, he got up and strolled through the ship, eventually finding his way onto the bridge. The pilot, navigator and RadAR operator were all at their stations. They gave him a cursory greeting and then went back to their duties. Even the electrostatic cloud they passed by a short while ago did not offer much of a distraction. RadAR had located and tracked the interstellar phenomenon long before, and though the field generated by trillions of ionized particles did exert quite a pull, a simple course correction came and went without much fanfare. He hoped the cloud would be in its active phase, but no such luck. Few things in nature equaled the spectacular display brought about when a mass of hydrogen gas mixed with other exotic molecular compounds. The colorful electrostatic discharges delighted everyone who happened upon them at such a time. On other occasions, however, you barely knew they were there, as they appeared just like any other ordinary cloud of dust and interstellar particles. "At least my luck is consistent," he thought cynically.

The proximity alarms sounded off all around him. Kershaw jumped when the klaxon fired off three successive bursts. Climbing out of his chair, the pilot scooted over to the RadAR station. His eyes widened at the sight. He immediately summoned Tul Lan-Ro to the bridge.

Kershaw came up behind the pilot. His scope revealed a fuzzy blip at the periphery. After making another three hundred-and-sixty degree sweep of the area, the faint object appeared again, this time a little closer. Telemetry from his scans started to scroll down the side of his screen.

"Why was I summoned?" Tul Lan-Ro asked when he rushed onto the bridge.

"We've picked up something on long-range tracking," Kershaw replied, his voice sounding higher than usual.

"I am isolating the contact now," the operator said. "I can only say the unknown is maintaining a linear course."

Neu likewise came running onto the bridge. "What's going on?" he demanded. "I heard the alarms."

"We've made contact with something out there."

"Correction," the pilot interrupted in a low tone. "I am now detecting multiple contacts. They are tightly packed, and maintaining the same heading."

Kershaw's heart sank. There could only be one answer.

"The Deravans," Neu said, verbalizing what every bridge officer was probably thinking.

"Do you think they're patrolling this far out of the solar system?"

Tul Lan-Ro bent over and studied the screen. "What is the course of those contacts?"

"They are holding steady at two hundred and ten degrees along the orbital plane...wait." He made an adjustment on his panel. "They are slowing."

A different set of alarms rang out. The piercing noise pressed in on Kershaw's eardrums.

Neu looked around the bridge. "What's going on now?"

The RadAR operator changed the orientation on his display. "They are scanning the area. I am picking up a powerful beam coming this way." He cocked his head over. "Those ships are changing course."

"Right for us," Neu said in a cold tone.

"Confirmed," the RadAR operator replied. "Unidentified ships have set a course for our position. They will arrive in twenty-five tal teks."

Kershaw felt as though those blips had backed him into a corner, with no place to run or hide. Hide. If they could hide, the Dervans might miss them. But where does one hide in space?

"We need to camouflage ourselves somehow," Neu stated. "Help us blend in with the background. Is there anything in the region we can use? An asteroid, a gravity field—anything."

Scattered ideas fired off in Kershaw's head. If only he could concentrate, but those alarms blaring in his ears continued to jumble his already frazzled thoughts. He took a step back and mentally drove away every distraction. Doing so helped. "The electrostatic cloud," he declared.

Neu turned his way. He appeared annoyed. "The what? What are you talking about?"

Kershaw brushed past him and pointed at the RadAR station. "Scroll back on the screen. Remember seven or eight minutes ago, the electrostatic cloud we passed?"

The operator gave a quick nod. He accessed a data file and entered a time sequence code. His central screen changed, revealing a fuzzy image in the distance.

"Of course," Tul Lan-Ro said. "We can fly into the heart of that cloud. Those electrostatic discharges should obscure the Deravan's instruments."

"If they don't get here first. What is its location from here?"

"At this velocity, it would take just over five tal teks."

Kershaw forced his way between Neu and Tul Lan-Ro. "Shut down the thrusters, all the power systems—everything."

Neu pulled on him from behind. "Are you crazy?" he objected. "We have to get to that cloud now, not float around in space so the Deravans can swoop in and finish us off."

Kershaw pointed at the screen. "If you change course and head for the cloud under power, the Deravans will see that a hundred kilometers away."

"He is right," Tul Lan-Ro concluded. "If I recall my physics, electrostatic clouds create very powerful gravity fields. Without engine power, it would draw us into the middle of all that swirling hydrogen. If we do this right, the Deravans just might believe we are a cluster of small asteroids, caught by the cloud."

"Is there any way we can signal the other cargo barges without a radio? They'll pick up any transmissions for sure."

"We have flashers in the forward and aft sections of the ship."

"Signal them immediately. Let them know about our plan."

Sul Lan-Ro nodded at the radio operator. He in turn placed his hands on the keypad at the base of his screen. Like an old-fashioned typist, he sent the message to those ships behind them.

After a minute had passed, Neu just couldn't wait any longer. "Have they responded to our signal yet?"

"Yes, Commander. The last ship has confirmed the order. They are standing by."

"All right, cut engines one-third," Tul Lan-Ro ordered. "Make it nice and gradual." He glanced at the other systems on the operator's boards. "Prepare to neutralize main power."

"Deravan ships will come into visual range in twelve tal teks."

"We are slowing. 0.35 stellar velocity...0.25...0.15. The pull of the electrostatic cloud is increasing. 0.10 stellar velocity."

Neu checked their position on the RadAR screen. "Zero forward motion," he called out.

"We are being pulled backwards. 0.04 stellar velocity...0.05...0.06."

"Power everything down. I want zero readings."

What little light that existed on the bridge faded, immersing them in almost perfect darkness.

Tul Lan-Ro's ship floated into the outer boundary of the cloud. As though the electro-static cloud was somehow aware of their arrival, it sent an angry bolt past the forward section of the barge, briefly lighting the bridge a strong shade of blue. Neu took a step back from the windowpanes after several more bolts zipped past him in the blink of an eye.

Their barge unexpectedly slowed, as though it had collided into something behind them. A hollow banging sound echoed throughout the ship, prompting everyone to look around.

"We must have entered the densest portion of the gas cloud."

Another discharge flew past the bridge. When it became dark again, no one dared speak, fearing the Deravans would somehow hear. Something struck the ship from underneath. The barge tipped five degrees past vertical. With the stabilizing thrusters shut down, they were at the mercy of the Newtonian forces working against them.

"How long should we wait here, Subidor?" the operator whispered. "Without RadAR, how will we know where the Deravan ships are?"

"We will just sit here, quiet, and hope we can get a visual on them."

"The Deravan ships should arrive in less than one tal tek."

Neu closed his eyes. "If only we knew where they were," he said in a muffled voice.

Tul Lan-Ro stared out the windows, past the cloud. An occasional star flickered through the tempest outside. "They are there," he stated. "I can feel them."

"Subidor," the operator pointed. Off in the distance, faintly at first, outlines of the three vessels started to emerge.

No one moved. No one said a word. The long minutes rolled on, but all three ghostly apparitions remained.

Several more strong discharges struck their barge, shaking it hard. Feeling the effects of the electrostatic tides, the ship began to roll over to her starboard side. Another barge came into view. "Here it comes," Neu whispered, and then grabbed a support beam tightly. The vessels collided into each other and then tumbled away in opposite directions.

"We cannot stay in here much longer," Kershaw said after shooting a quick look at Neu. "If those bolts don't get us the other barges will."

"What other choice do we have? If we make a run for it, the Deravans will be on top of us in a second." Two more discharges struck the hapless cargo barge, causing it to list over even further. As if to add insult to injury, another barge slammed into them from behind.

"I think our options are running out, Subidor."

Tul Lan-Ro pulled himself over to the navigation station. "Prepare to activate main power," he ordered in a barely audible voice.

"But, Subidor," Neu protested, "We won't stand a chance if we leave now."

He turned around and faced him. "And we don't have much of one in here, either. If we die today, at least we will go out with a fight."

The RadAR operator pushed himself out of his chair and made his way to the power relays.

"Power up main systems on my order," he said. "Then we will—"

"Subidor," the pilot whispered," the Deravans are pulling away."

Everyone turned their heads to the spot where the ships had been for the last few insufferable minutes. Their ghostly outlines, faint at first, disappeared as they pivoted around and headed in the opposite direction. Kershaw never thought a whole lot of nothing could look so good.

"I think the plan worked," Neu concluded.

Tul Lan-Ro shook his head. "Yes," he replied. "It seems fortune has been on our side."

"How much longer do you think we should stay in here? Without RadAR, we have no way of knowing when the Deravans will leave the area."

"We will just have to hold tight a short while longer," Tul Lan-Ro said after he checked the chronometer above. "After two tal teks I will send out a single ship. If the area is clear, then we can resume our mission."

This was about as good an answer as anyone could give. The reality was, no one really knew.

S.F.S. CORONA
0231 PROXIMA MERIDIAN TIME, AUGUST 28, 2217

The green muddled disk of Neptune had been the most prominent feature on the main screen for the past several hours. When they first came into visual range, the eighth planet from the Sun was nothing more than a speck of light. Now it had grown not only in size, but also in its gravitational effect on the fleet.

"Distance to the planet?" Yamane asked from his seat.

"We are seventeen thousand, five hundred kilometers from Neptune. Orbit should be achieved in fourteen minutes, thirty seconds."

Yamane shot a quick look at the information on his data pad. They were behind schedule by ten seconds. Though the difference between the theoretical and actual was negligible, it surprised him the error had been that large.

"One minute until we enter Neptune's orbit, Commander."

"Slow the *Corona* to 0.15 stellar velocity."

The r-tech entered the command code into his console and successfully disengaged the master control program. The *Corona* was literally back in his hands again. He toggled the view of Neptune over until the Sun appeared. From that distance, it looked like a small, yellow disk. "There you are," he whispered to himself after the last remnants of his home world slipped past the curvature of the yellow, average-sized star. They had arrived at just the right time.

"The Earth is just entering its occultation phase behind Neptune," he called out to Yamane. "In seven hours and four minutes, it will move into position behind the Sun."

"Bring the fleet in, nice and steady," he replied, never taking his eyes off the screen.

When the nav-tech inputted two sets of course corrections, the *Corona* angled over for a brief moment, and then straightened out again. Coming in at a shallow angle, the stellar cruiser achieved orbit after experiencing almost no turbulence at all. The dreadnoughts followed the same trajectory and came in behind them, then the destroyers, sub-cruisers, and cargo barges.

Yamane was about to congratulate the navigator when he caught sight of a cylindrical object in the distance, coming towards them. His suspicions were aroused in an instant.

"Sir, I've got a—"

"I'm already on it," he said, cutting the r-tech off. "Alter course five degrees to the port. Let's give whatever that is a wide berth."

The *Corona* made the adjustment as her directional thrusters fired. In a mirror-like repeat of what they had just done, the device altered its course right for them. No one had to tell Yamane what this meant. He bolted out of his chair and hustled over to the navigator's station.

"The unknown object is on an intercept course—one thousand meters and closing."

Yamane wanted to avoid using their weapons this close to Earth, but time didn't permit him the luxury of thinking through another course of action. As this point, it was either them or that object. "All forward batteries, prepare to fire on the incoming object. Stand by on my mark." He tracked its forward motion. "Ready...Fire!"

A pair of plasma bursts shot out of the bow and instantly vaporized the cylinder. The metallic device flared up into a huge fireball. Overtaking the *Corona* in a matter of seconds, the resultant blast wave slammed into the ship's hull. She listed over onto her side ten degrees past vertical. Everyone held on tight until the shaking began to subside. If the stabilizers hadn't kicked in when they did, the stellar cruiser would have gone over even further.

When the vessel righted again, Yamane felt a wave of relief sweep over him. That blast could have done a whole lot of damage to the ship. If he hadn't seen it when he did, the result might have been very different. His positive feelings about surviving the explosion did not last long, however. Why was that device in Neptune's orbit anyway, and who put it there? Yamane wanted answers, and he wanted them now.

LEAD CARGO BARGE
DAIETH TIME PLUS TEN

Another fusion blast exploded off the starboard side of the lead cargo barge heading for Earth.

"Can we increase velocity?" the subidor asked in a calm voice. Before the pilot could reply, a direct hit destroyed the ship. Three Deravan vessels flew right through the ball of light that had been the cargo barge just moments before. The remaining eight vessels applied full thrust in an attempt to outrun their pursuers.

The next cargo barge in line took the point.

"Our speed is up to 1.68 stellar velocity," the pilot called out.

The subidor paced back and forth on the bridge. He stopped from time-to-time and compared their position to his. "Distance to the Deravans?"

"They are three hundred kintars behind and closing."

The subidor verified their position. "I want engine output at maximum," he ordered. "Commander Yamane's plan will not be of much value if we do not reach the Earth."

Hesitation registered on the officer's face. "But, Subidor, we are already ten percent past design limits."

He gave him a harsh glare. "Then make it twenty," he barked.

An ion cannon burst detonated a short distance away. The ensuing blast waves shook their ship for a moment before the navigational operator regained control again. "Bypass the overrides," the subidor ordered. "Set velocity for 1.70."

"But subidor—"

"Do it!"

Just as the lead barge began to pull away from their adversaries, the Deravans unleashed a second barrage. As their aft section absorbed hit after hit, their speed dropped at incremental levels, until a final, fatal hit pierced her hull.

A different alarm sounded on the bridge. The subidor paid it little notice, his attention fixed on the next row of enemy ships ahead of them.

"Subidor, power outputs for the engines are beginning to spike. Containment fields are at forty-two percent and falling."

He went over to his station. "Can you compensate?"

The operator did his best, but a look of frustration revealed the outcome. "I have tried, Subidor, but we have suffered a lot of damage. Many of the main systems do not respond."

Another Deravan vessel targeted the barge's engine nacelles, and then opened fire. A pair of fusion blasts struck them with unequaled precision. Collateral damage ruptured the already weakened engine core, causing the barge to go up into a brilliant ball of white light and vanquished dreams. The glow quickly died down until there was nothing left to indicate it had ever existed.

The next cargo barge in line took the point.

CHAPTER
26

DEK-PAR
DAIETH TIME PLUS ELEVEN

Kershaw had his men go through the procedure again. "Not good enough," he said. "You're still twenty seconds over."

He wanted them to know the operational format of the omega band receivers and power cells with their eyes closed. Since he and his team had never worked with them before, he saw to it that they spent most of their free time studying modes of power, programming procedures, transmission band wavelengths, and emergency repair scenarios for each one. Experience had taught him over the years that it was the simplest things that usually broke down when you least expected it.

Kershaw reset his timer, and then dropped his hand like a starter in a race. "Go."

A member of team A detached the access plate while their leader entered the access code in the upper left-hand corner of the control panel. The cursor scrolled through the programs in a matter of seconds. Every one of the systems was functioning within preset parameters. He then powered up the main systems. The cell was just about to come to life when Kershaw pressed a button on his data pad. The power flow indicator registered a disruption in one of the lines.

"I've got a problem here," the team leader said. Other members of his team jumped in and remedied the computer glitch. "Time?" he asked.

"Two minutes and thirteen seconds," Kershaw said in his all too familiar way. It was a tone every team member from every team had learned to dread, one that meant they would have to go through the scenario again.

LEAD CARGO BARGE
DAIETH TIME MINUS FOUR

Bridge alarms rang out again. Most of the crew, already acclimatized to constant threat of attack, barely gave them any notice.

"There are twelve Deravan ships approaching," the RadAR operator reported.

The subidor made his way over to his station. "Distance?" he asked, impatient.

"Four thousand kintars."

He was both pleased and worried by the number of vessels sent against them this time around. In their last encounter near Jupiter, they had done well enough there all right: six enemy vessels encountered, and only one cargo barge lost. Now they would be facing twelve. Perhaps Yamane's deception is working. "The increased number of ships sent against us seems to suggest the Deravans believe Earth is the destination of our fleet." The subidor stopped where he was. Perhaps he might be getting ahead of himself. They were still a long way from the Terran home world.

"They are coming in at 1.68 stellar velocity. Much faster than before."

The subidor's attention settled on the screen. "Let the games begin," he said to himself. Feeling the eyes of the bridge on him, he turned to the navigator. "Change course ninety degrees. I want as wide a berth as possible."

A different set of alarms went off. Rather than the sustained monotone noise they were accustomed to, these were intermittent, and several octaves higher.

The subidor stopped in mid-stride and returned to the RadAR station. "What is the problem this time?"

The operator did not respond at first. Instead, he inputted several commands into his console.

The stars on his screen swept to the left. A number of faint images appeared, though they were just barely in view. "Confirmed," he said aloud. "I have one...two...three...make that six ships approaching on our port side. They will intercept us in eleven tal teks."

The subidor's face shrunk. "Why were they not detected before?"

The operator shook his head. "Unknown, though our antenna array has suffered extensive damage. Perhaps there are gaps in the outgoing signal."

The subidor spun around. "Take evasive maneuvers," he ordered. He then looked at the targeting grid. "Make your course one-five-seven degrees. Speed, 1.70 stellar velocity."

The navigator inputted the commands into guidance control. Rather than changing course as expected, his ship lurched forward just a bit and then stopped, followed by a muffled explosion from the rear. The other five cargo barges shot right past them.

Feelings of anger welled up within the subidor, anger towards the Deravans, and anger towards his ship for breaking down at the worst possible moment. He pressed the com-system button near the RadAR station. "Engine room, what is going on down there? I need full power and I need it now!"

"We have lost our main engines!" a voice yelled over clanking noises in the background.

"Can we still maneuver?"

"Negative. The entire converter relay assembly is gone. No chance of repair."

The subidor placed his hands behind his back and closed both eyes. He needed to think. "Kill the alarm," he ordered. His mind went through a myriad of contingencies, but they all ended the same way. "Do you have any recommendations?"

"The directional thrusters are still operational," the engine operator replied after some thought.

"I do not think—" the subidor objected, but then stopped. As though a switch had gone off in his head, his senses heightened. He suddenly became aware of everything around him: officers at their stations, sounds of alarms blaring into his ears, even the feel of the deck under his feet. In that one instant, the intention of the engineer became clear. "Evacuate the engine room and have the crew report to the bridge," he ordered.

"Right away."

The subidor did not hesitate. He scurried past the other operators and went right for the emergency panel on the wall. Despite the frenetic activity taking place all around him, his field of view narrowed down to a black and yellow striped panel in the middle of the bulkhead. When he entered the seven-digit code, the door popped open, revealing power flow chips, crossover valves, and a data entry pad behind it. The subidor accessed the instructions on the pad and skimmed through the text. "To open the manifold," he read, "depress valves one and two, and then resequence the power regulators." It almost seemed too easy, but he followed the instructions to the letter. The subidor knew he was successful with the execute button began to blink off and on.

"Directional thrusters are armed and ready," the navigator called out from his station

The subidor turned back, a hopeful look on his face. "Distance to the Deravan ships?"

"Twelve hundred kintars."

"Signal the other cargo barges. Tell them to continue on their heading for Earth at all costs."

Muffled voices sounded in the corridor behind the bridge. The subidor turned to see the engine room crew arrive. Most had made it on their own power. A few, however, bandaged and unable to walk, had to be carried in by fellow crewmembers.

The subidor resumed his place behind the navigational operator. "Brace yourselves for a stronger than usual burst of acceleration. I have already opened the power flow regulators. Once they start their burn, there will be no way of stopping them."

Most of the crew grabbed hold of the nearest firm object while others just stood in place, a look of resolve on their faces.

"Distance to the ships?"

"Nine hundred kintars."

"Release the coolant dampers in the main engine core."

The operator pulled down both levers. "Coolant dampers released."

"Reactor core temperature is rising. Explosion is imminent."

The incoming ships positioned near the middle of the screen maintained their course and speed.

"Seven hundred and fifty kintars."

"Fire the directional thrusters," he ordered.

The operator pressed the final sequence button. At first, nothing happened. A flash of anger exploded within the subidor, much stronger than what he had experienced before. He marched over to the navigator's station, but before he could say anything, a strange moaning noise echoed throughout the barge, followed by a series of sporadic jolts. Readouts and lights on the bridge dimmed as power continued to flow directly into the thruster chambers. The ship lurched forward, stopped, and then surged ahead. The subidor's expectations rose.

"Our speed is at 0.05 stellar velocity...0.09...0.12...0.15."

"Main power is down to forty-one percent. We have enough burn for two more tal teks."

Ion fire exploded nearby. Bursts of pink light flashed in front of the bridge. "Maintain course," the subidor ordered without hesitation.

Another explosion rocked the dying ship.

The last hit brought about a surge in the number of cascading failures. "I am losing the signal lock on the engine containment fields."

The subidor spun around. "Re-route whatever power is available. We must keep the lock active." He went to the RadAR station: "Distance?"

"RadAR is no longer functioning, but I estimate about one hundred kintars."

Several blasts slammed into the weakened vessel, one hitting it in the aft section. The subidor worked his way over to the window panels. In the distance, he could see the last vestiges of their compatriots. At least they will be safe, he thought.

"Power levels are now at twenty-four percent."

"Ninety kintars to intercept."

The subidor returned to the battle. "Prepare to neutralize containment fields."

"Fifty kintars."

Amidst a sea of blasts detonating all around them, a solitary bolt of concentrated plasma energy struck the barge near the forward section. After a flash of crimson light, power on the bridge fell to zero, bathing everyone in darkness. The engineering operator ran his fingers along his console. In his mind's eye, he saw the exact location of the emergency bypass circuits. A press of a button later, power came up again.

RadAR telemetry flickered back onto the operator's screen. "Our speed is down to 0.17 stellar velocity," he read aloud.

"Channel all remaining power into the thrusters."

"Twenty kintars to the Deravan ships."

The operator gave a quick nod and then opened the flow regulators to their highest settings. The barge increased her speed at a slow but steady rate.

"Ten nil teks to impact."

The operator eyed the flashing readouts directly in front of him. His systems were starting to overload.

"Five nil teks to detonation point...four...three ..."

"Brace yourselves."

The cargo barge reached its destination, exploding into a blinding white ball of light, and then—nothing.

The next cargo barge in line took the point.

DEK-PAR
DAIETH TIME MINUS ONE

Kershaw paced back and forth on the bridge. He felt exhausted and alert, all at the same time. But with only two hours left before they arrived at Mars, he knew the matter had become academic. Who could relax now?

When he reached the furthest edge of the bridge, he stopped and turned back. This time around, the dusty orange disk of Mars caught his eye. The mottled surface of the planet stood apart from an endless sea of black all around it. They were still too far away to see the *Lexington* trapped in orbit above the inhospitable world, but his old ship was there, waiting for them.

Surrounded by the sounds made by the instruments on the bridge—RadAR, environmental controls, the engineering section, and the like—he checked their coordinates for the umpteenth time. Kershaw was pleased the mission had gone as planned so far, feeling less anxious about their chances; especially since they hadn't encountered any Deravan ships since the electro-static cloud. He wasn't certain if it was dumb luck or if the cargo barges Yamane sent ahead had drawn the enemy back to Earth. There was also the remote possibility the Deravans had abandoned his home planet, but he didn't put much stock in that scenario.

He heard someone come up from behind.

"What are you doing here, Lt. Commander Kershaw?" Tul Lan-Ro asked when he entered the bridge. "I expected you would be in your quarters getting some rest." Kershaw said nothing. "I am sorry to interrupt your solitude. I should go now."

He knew the Antaren was trying to be hospitable, but he wasn't in much of a talking mood.

"Are you all right?" the subidor asked, pressing the issue. "You seem troubled."

Kershaw shook his head. "No," he replied. "I'm all right. I ..." his words faded. He found himself staring into Tul Lan-Ro's eyes. After all these years spent with Antarens, he could never quite get over those glowing eyes. They were both absorbing and mysterious. During the war, when he stumbled across an Antaren freshly killed in battle, it took some time before the glow faded. Even then, it still felt as though he was still looking right at you with a piercing kind of deathstare into your soul. A soldier only needed to experience this once or twice before he covered the face of his fallen foes, unable to take it for very long.

Finding himself feeling unnerved by the relentless gaze, Kershaw stepped aside and put some distance between the two. His anxiety level lessened.

"Thank you for your concern, Subidor, but it won't be necessary."

"I often come here myself during the night watches to look at the stars. As you can see, the periodic sounds from the ship's instruments can be quite soothing. It gives me a chance to think about past experiences, or wonder whether I have made a difference in other people's lives."

"I suppose so," Kershaw replied, his voice distant. He found himself again drawn into the swirling tan and green storm clouds in Mars' upper atmosphere. What better place to determine the future of Mankind than the world named for the Roman god of war, he thought. It almost felt as though the fates themselves had decided long ago that such an event should take place there—like an important play staged in their honor. "I think it's time I excuse myself for a while, Subidor," Kershaw said, forcing a yawn, "Get in some bunk time before we arrive."

"I am glad we had this talk. Perhaps we will have another opportunity again."

"Perhaps," he replied, and then excused himself. Just as Kershaw reached the corridor, he turned back. The Antaren's attention had already surrendered to the view. Tul Lan-Ro stood there motionless. Kershaw wondered what he was thinking.

S.F.S. CORONA
0955 PROXIMA MERIDIAN TIME, AUGUST 28, 2217

At precisely the seventh hour, Yamane's fleet broke orbit and entered the next phase of the operation. Unlike when they arrived, however, the armada of ships left without incident. His greatest fear centered on the possibility of the Deravans stumbling onto them, but their unwanted arrival never materialized. In fact, since the encounter with the space mine, nothing out of the ordinary had taken place. He didn't know if this should make him feel better or worse. Everyone assumed the Deravans had placed the weapon in an orbit above Neptune, but no one really knew for certain. After an analysis made by the r-tech after the blast, he discovered the device registered an almost zero energy reading when they were five kilometers from it. But as the fleet approached, power levels emitted by the mine started to rise. Further analysis determined the device's kinetic energy transferred into the power systems, propelling it forward. No one had ever seen anything quite like it before. This had all the hallmarks of the Deravans. Yet, they had not come to investigate the explosion. The logic, or lack of it, he found most perplexing.

Seeing the data pad in his lap, Yamane picked it up and scrolled down the screen. He checked the astro-clock. "Commander Neu's ships should arrive at the *Lexington* any time now," he said in a hopeful tone, "assuming the other barges have drawn the Deravans away." Maybe Yamane had the answer that had so befuddled him. Maybe ...

CHAPTER 27

DEK-PAR
DAIETH TIME MINUS ELEVEN

"The *Lexington* should be in sight by now," Neu said from the bridge, his voice uneasy. He went over to the RadAR monitor, hoping it might have picked something up by now. "Still nothing." He sighed in frustration.

Moving through the field of debris and twisted wreckage, the squadron of cargo barges altered their course around scattered remains of the previous battle, caught in orbit above Mars. Because the remnants of their once-proud fleet had settled into a relatively concentrated area, determining which ship was which became difficult. Neu shuddered at the thought of the firepower it had taken to level this kind of destruction. The entire Star Force fleet destroyed in a single day. It was almost more than he could bear. His friends and family, all that he knew, were gone. He could only imagine what those poor people back on Earth were going through.

"Anything yet?" he asked the RadAR operator, growing even more impatient. "According to Commander Yamane's calculations, the *Lexington* should be here."

"Maybe he made a mistake," a disembodied voice chided him. Neu shot a look in the direction of the comment, but no one owned up to it. He stared at them for an extended period of time, but decided to let the matter go. Privately, however, he suspected the unknown crewman might be right. The *Lexington* was not where it should be. Yamane's old ship might have floated away in some unknown direction. Worse yet, she could have burned up in Mars' atmosphere. If the latter scenario were true, then they had made this journey for nothing.

"I think I have something coming up ahead," the RadAR operator called out. "A vessel is just sneaking up behind the curvature of Mars."

Neu rushed over to the RadAR station, his heart pounding. He fixed his gaze on the display, but didn't see anything. "Can you pinpoint the location?" he asked.

"With all of the other ships in the area I am having difficulty. Radiation levels are pretty high. Maybe if I tighten the incoming signal." The operator made an adjustment. He leaned closer and studied his screen. Another adjustment followed. "RadAR pulses are much stronger. There is definitely a big ship out there...about the size of a—"

"Stellar cruiser," Neu interrupted. He went over to the windows. There, straight ahead, an unmistakable outline slowly emerged from behind the red planet. The vessel was dark and difficult to see at first, but as the ship cleared Mars' upper atmosphere, catching the sun's light, a stellar cruiser appeared in the distance.

"I want a confirmation," Neu said to the operator, breathing a bit easier.

After a quick nod, he reset his scanner for the tightest beam possible. The outgoing pulse locked onto the ship, and then bounced back. A magnified image of what it had encountered materialized on his monitor. He tracked the picture to the right. Though it was difficult to see at first, a scarred and pitted hull revealed itself, until a large white "S" drifted into view.

"There it is," Neu commented. "Keep going."

An "F" came next. Moving further to the right, another "S" materialized. The operator continued panning. There, under the bridge, the ship's identity could finally be established - - S.F.S.*Lexington* appeared in tall, white letters, standing out against the dark gray hull. They had found their ship.

A contented smile formed on Neu's face.

"Fifteen tal teks before docking," the navigational operator called out. "Distance...one hundred and fifty kintars."

"Signal the other ships and have them prepare for boarding." Neu brought up his data pad. In the upper right-hand corner, the total elapsed time for the mission counted down. They were thirty-two minutes behind schedule. His thoughts flashed back to the electrostatic cloud. The delay could have been a whole lot longer if the Deravans had actually gotten in their way.

"Ten tal teks to intercept."

"Are you picking up any other signals?"

"Negative, Commander. I am only reading the *Lexington.*"

Neu returned to the windowpanes stretching the length of the bridge. There, before him, was the ship they had come all this way to meet. When the *Dek-Par* swung around in a parabolic arc, he saw her hull up close. A myriad of blast marks covered the surface, like a pox that had affected the exterior of the ship. As the barge swung around to the other side, he realized that the entire aft section was gone, along with most of her pulse cannons and communication antennas. He could only imagine how bad the fight must have been. But despite the massive damage she had suffered, the *Lexington* remained a beautiful ship, her quiet dignity still intact.

"All teams have reported in, Commander."

Neu turned back to the navigational operator. "Distance to the *Lexington?*"

"Fifteen kintars and closing."

A rhythmic pinging noise sounded after every RadAR sweep. If a pulse bumped into an object out there, it would come back at a much higher pitch. So far, none of them had.

"Five kintars to the *Lexington*."

Neu went over to the navigator's station. The time for standing and watching was over. They were there to do a job. "Slow the squadron to 0.005 stellar velocity," he ordered. "I want us brought in nice and slow."

When the navigational operator implemented the order, their cargo barge decelerated. The remaining vessels matched the maneuver with equal precision.

"We are now two kintars from the *Lexington*."

Exhilarated, Neu watched the massive ship come towards them. He noted that a gaping hole existed where the engines used to be. Cut into the hull another fifty meters, the light of the sun lit up several exposed decks. Not too bad, he thought. During the war, he had seen ships in far worse condition, restored to almost new in a couple of months. Patch up the holes, replace the engine compartment, slap on a little gray paint, and no one would ever know the difference. He wished there was a space dock around right now.

Two short beeps sounded in the cargo bay. "All right men, that's the signal," Kershaw said into his headset. "This is what we have been training for. I want team A in the front. Team B behind." He entered the final command code into the access panel just to the left of the hatch.

A large rectangular-shaped lock pulled back after the magnetic couplings disengaged. The door moved steadily outward, revealing the stellar cruiser only a stone's throw away from them.

Kershaw's respiration rate started to increase. "Check your equipment one more time. I don't want any accidents because of carelessness. It will be dangerous enough there as it is." Trying to hold his emotions in check, he added. "Team A, you've got the point."

When Kershaw stepped aside, the group shuffled over to the lip at the end of the cargo bay.

In a simultaneous show of support, all ten men and women gave a thumbs-up signal, and then fired their maneuvering jets in two short bursts.

At about the halfway point, Kershaw turned back and gave the signal. "Team B, fire up your cargo movers. The others should be in position about now."

After giving a thumbs-up signal in return, the pilots grabbed the maneuvering stick with one hand, the thruster control with the other. Moving down the line, they emerged from the cargo barge one at a time.

Kershaw jumped onto the last transport just before it took off, and held on tight. Looking up ahead, he saw his old ship looming over them like some terrible creature ready to sink its teeth into the approaching transports. He turned away, focusing his attention on the men standing on the edge of deck five. In a matter of seconds, his mover slid into the awaiting arms of his men.

Intentionally keeping his back to the ship for a couple of minutes, he approached his job like a swimmer rising to the surface after a deep ocean dive. If he rose too fast, nitrogen bubbles would form in his bloodstream, bringing about terrible anguish and death. And like that swimmer, if he took in the ship too fast, his feelings too might overwhelm him.

"How is it looking over there?" Neu asked on the radio.

The question caught Kershaw off guard. "Uh," he stammered, "the first cells are being brought to the ship as we speak."

After the pilot offloaded his cargo, he jumped back into the transport and powered it off the deck. Pivoting around one hundred and eighty degrees, he made his course for the lead barge.

Kershaw felt he could finally turn and face his ship. He drew in a deep breath and opened himself up to whatever would happen next. Images of the battle flashed in his mind. The smoke, crewmembers screaming, the panic—they all returned with frightening clarity. Kershaw closed his eyes tight and shunted those thoughts aside. When several moments passed, he opened them again. A long, dark corridor filled his field of view. He brought up his forearm and accessed the *Lexington*'s schematics. Deck five, section A3. "All right," he said with a certain forced bravado. "Let's get that first cell in place."

Their initial start into the access way had been easy enough since the ochre-colored light coming from the surface of Mars illuminated the walls and ceiling well enough, at first. But the further they ventured into the inner recesses of the ship, the darker it became. With the loss of engineering, internal power was nothing more than a distant memory. There were the backup batteries, of course, but those cells lasted just a couple of days before they too faded into a permanent state of lifelessness. In every way, the *Lexington* was a dead ship.

When both teams could no longer see ahead, they activated the portable lights mounted on their helmets. This gave the moment a surreal effect as multiple beams darted about twisted pieces of wreckage. Wherever a person looked, a shaft of light went with him, throwing strange and contorted shadows on one wall one moment, and elsewhere the next.

Kershaw went a little ahead of them. He checked the corridor for anything that might pose a problem, such as dangling wires or serrated metal edges. There were also those things he hadn't thought of, which in his mind were the most dangerous of all. The unknown almost always was. "When we reach the end, near the junction," he said on the radio, "we will enter the botany lab on the right."

Since the gravitational compensators had suffered the same fate as the other systems, the tech teams had little trouble getting the first power cell off the transport and onto the ship. It took just a couple of members of his team to keep the five hundred kilogram cube a meter above the deck. A gentle nudge here, a stronger push there, all the way down the corridor. Newton's first law of motion did the rest.

"This is the lab," Kershaw said just as they rounded the corner. As long as he kept his mind focused on the task at hand, he felt in control.

Two sliding doors were open about halfway, but not enough for the power cell to get through. Kershaw motioned for two team members to pry them apart. Grabbing both ends, they grunted and pushed with all of their might, until both doors finally gave way.

Kershaw stepped over a medical tray floating between the deck and his knee. He took a quick look around. His breaths became shallow as beads of sweat collected over his upper lip. To his relief, he didn't see anyone in the lab. Kershaw did note, however, a number of plants on a shelf, lining the wall across from him. They had died the instant the hull depressurized, instantly freezing when oxygen and heat suddenly escaped into the vacuum of space. There were also data pads, centrifuges, and medical equipment in there, but not much else. A feeling of relief washed over him. He had successfully passed over the second difficult hurdle.

The display above his right wrist gave the precise location of where they needed to place the cell. "Bring her around," Kershaw pointed. "Right there, near the wall." He examined it more closely. "We'll have to cut. A portion of the front half has to be set in the next room."

"How far?"

He checked again. "Three quarters of a meter." Kershaw signaled the team member furthest away from him to break out the laser torch. When the others pulled down their protective visors, he added, "All right, let's get started."

The tech bent down on one knee and programmed the cell's dimensions—height, length and width—into the control panel. Within seconds, thousands of luminescent yellow sparks ricocheted off the floors and walls of the botany lab. Most of Kershaw's team took a step back, hoping to avoid the stream of super-heated particles flying all around them.

Following its pre-programmed instructions, the torch climbed up the wall and then made a hard right turn. The mobile device moved horizontally for a certain distance, and then angled back down again. When it reached the deck, the torch shut itself off.

Kershaw floated over to the wall and examined the results. The cutter had done its job perfectly. He slipped his glove into the newly created gap and pulled. The cut-out portion swung down onto the deck, as through it were falling in slow motion. "Get the cell and put it down over here," he pointed.

Members of team B brought up the cube and guided it to the spot he indicated with a minimum of effort. All that hard work during their trip to Mars was beginning to pay off.

"Three more centimeters this way," he said after comparing the cell's position to the one flashing on his display. Team B gave the cell a gentle push. The oversized cube jerked over a couple of times. "Perfect," Kershaw said with his hands extended.

Two hours later, they had gotten three more cells and two omega band receivers into position.

Kershaw brought up his wrist. "One hour and twelve minutes remaining." They were right on schedule. He figured the first batch of cells and receivers shouldn't take long to get into position. According to Henthorne's instructions, he needed to place them near the aft section of the ship. Receiver number three, however, had posed a challenge. In order to bring it to the required location, his team had to cut through two decks and four walls. No matter, Kershaw thought. They would finish their work soon enough... and none of those terrible memories had returned—yet.

"Fisher's bringing the next receiver," one of the team members said when he saw Kershaw check the time. Unlike the power cells, the receivers were much smaller. They had just one function—link the cells together to create a continuous circuit. Instead of relying on inefficient copper wire, a focused magnitron beam connected the cells together. Because of the high levels of radiation in the area, these were the only receivers strong enough to pierce through the interference. The only drawback was that they needed to be in perfect alignment with each other. Just the slightest variance of a nanometer or more, and the beam might miss the receiver altogether. They were effective, but very touchy.

"Where are we in the sequence, sir?" Fisher asked.

Kershaw looked at him before accessing the information from his wrist. He appeared to be about twenty. His eyes were brown, as was his hair. Kershaw wondered if someone so young could understand just how important their job was. "We're seventh in line. It shouldn't take more than twenty minutes before the beam reaches our position." He looked down the long, dark corridor. The light from his helmet lit up the walls, deck, and bulkheads. "Here's a bit of good news, though. This receiver will be placed in the botany lab, near the first cell."

"Finally, a break," someone joked.

As he had done before, Kershaw went into the lab after his team reached the open doorway. This time, his anxieties were not so strong. From there he counted off ten paces. Just after his last step, he placed the receiver right on that spot. Another crewmember came over and bolted all three pads onto the deck. Pop, pop, pop. When Kershaw had secured the device, he went to the access panel and opened it. His thoughts blurred. Working for several hours without a break was beginning to catch up with him. He cleared his mind and entered the seven-digit code. The computer lock disengaged. He had successfully gained access into the power cell's master program.

"We're in," Kershaw said to his team. "I'll run a systems check, make sure it's functioning properly." He clumsily typed in the commands, his padded gloves reducing his dexterity to that of a two-year-old.

Every piece of data crammed into the crystalline memory chips fired off in rapid sequence. The mesmerizing blur lasted for almost a minute and then stopped. A cursor reappeared. "All systems are functioning perfectly. We can now bring the power online."

"Two minutes remaining," someone called out.

Kershaw realized they didn't have much time. But rather than hurry, he blinked a couple of times, steadying himself, and then inputted the final command sequence. Power output indicators went from zero to one hundred percent in less than a second.

"Power flows are holding strong."

Kershaw looked the unit over. "Is the receiver in position?" he asked.

Ensign Fisher bent down and peered into the targeting scope. "I'm getting it lined up now."

The device almost seemed to respond to his verbal cue. A small parabolic dish moved upward slightly on its own, and then rotated three degrees to the right. Fisher entered a rotation command into the keypad. The receiver panned just a little bit further. "That should be about right."

Kershaw knew his statement was theoretical at best. The location of the dish meant nothing until the operator two decks below them opened the containment loop and fired the beam in his direction. If they were fortunate, the mirrors, particle enhancers and refractor lenses would bend the signal just enough, and line it up with the receptor on their first try.

"Lt. Commander Kershaw," a voice said on the radio.

"Kershaw here."

"Are you in position to receive the magnitron beam?" He looked at Fisher. The ensign nodded his head a couple of times.

"Affirmative—we are in position."

Both teams in the botany lab took a few steps back from the power cell. They weren't taking any chances.

"Stand by. The magnitron beam should arrive any moment now." Just as the transmission ended, a shaft of orange light burst through wall and struck the receiver, but only in part. Luminescent and continuous in nature, the beam deflected away at an almost perfect right angle. Fisher tried to compensate. His efforts, however, only made things worse. The beam came around in the opposite direction, right where both teams had thought they were safe. Two crewmembers jumped out of the way as a third yelled, "Look out!"

Bemused, Kershaw grinned. He didn't think men in bulky EVA suits could move that fast.

A grimace appeared on Fisher's face. He brought the receiver around at incremental levels, until the beam slipped right into the magnetized receptor plates. Then it was a matter of opening the highway, as he called it, and channeling the streams of tightly packed ions into the containment loop. Success. But they didn't have time to congratulate themselves. Team number eight was next in line, and they were waiting. "Standby to receive the magnitron beam," Fisher said into his headset.

"Standing by. Any time you're ready."

He pressed the circulator button. In an instant, a bolt of orange plasma shot out of the power cell at the speed of light. He then took a reading on the beam's integrity. The look on his face said it all. "Connection complete," he said to Kershaw.

"Very good, Ensign," he replied, more than pleased. "I'll finish getting our equipment stowed away. You go back for the last receiver."

"I'll be back before you know it," Fisher promised. He disappeared into the dark.

Kershaw collected all the tools and threw them into the box in a haphazard fashion. From the outset of the operation, they had needed to stay on schedule, no matter what. But being tied to the clock drained him. Above all else, there was nothing more important than keeping his thoughts focused. Otherwise, they would drift into areas he didn't want to go. Kershaw checked the time. They were still on schedule, but not by much. That was good, but where was Fisher?

He decided to go into the corridor. Out there, alone, Kershaw felt the walls press in on him. He checked the time again. Fisher was cutting it close.

A pair of faint lights flickered in the distance. Growing stronger with each passing second, the lieutenant commander saw two EVA suits coalesce into solid form. "You guys took long enough," Kershaw complained when they arrived with the receiver.

"Couldn't do anything about it," Fisher apologized. "The cargo mover coming over from the barge experienced a computer glitch. He had to turn back and wait for another transport."

"Yeah, yeah, yeah," Kershaw said as Fisher put the receiver into his impatient hands.

They moved onto the next spot indicated by the data pad on Kershaw's wrist. Once in position, the other two techs checked the power systems, lenses, receptor, targeting scope, and containment loop. Satisfied they were working properly, Fisher moved the delicate components into position.

In the quietness of the moment, Kershaw let his attention wander. Catching sight of something just past the power cell, he found a half-opened doorway at the end of the corridor. Movement registered in the corner of his eye. "What the ...?" he said aloud.

"What is it, sir?" Fisher asked.

"I think I just saw something." His heart began pounding faster.

"I don't see anything," he replied after looking both ways in the corridor.

"It's probably nothing, but I should check anyway."

Fisher brought himself up. "I'll go with you."

Kershaw waved him away. "That won't be necessary, Ensign. I can handle this."

"But, sir, no one should ever go off by themselves. You know the regulations."

"All right," Kershaw sighed, annoyed at his insistence, "but just stay behind me."

He rose to his feet and fired a quick series of bursts. Both doors, about a half-meter apart from each other, came up on him fast. Kershaw's outstretched hand curled around one of the edges when he gently collided into the doorway. Peering inside, his helmet light illuminated the lab. Grotesque and strange-looking shadows danced before them from every corner. Other than an odd beaker floating past or some other piece of equipment tumbling away, the room appeared normal in every respect.

"The room appears empty, sir. Maybe some debris floated by the door."

Kershaw scanned the interior one more time. He needed to be sure. "I guess you're right." His frayed nerves calmed.

But just as he turned to go, something bumped into his leg. His eyes darted about. To his horror, the body of a medical tech floated past, his face frozen at the moment of death. "Help me get this door open!"

Fisher grabbed one of the edges and pulled with all his might. His door jerked a bit at first, and then finally gave way. "That's got it," he declared.

Kershaw entered the lab. Several frantic moments passed. He summoned all the strength in his possession and checked the room again. A shaft of light caught something on the other side, near a computer terminal. Moving closer, his worst fears came to fruition. The medical tech was not alone. He floated about aimlessly alongside two other frozen crewmen. His perceptions of the lab lessened as the walls pressed in on him a second time, almost to the point of suffocation. "This is my fault," he said to no one in particular.

Concerned, Fisher reached out to him. "Are you all right, sir?" he asked.

Kershaw took two steps back, as though he were moving away from something, something terrible. "It's my fault they're dead. I should have never convinced Yamane to abandon ship without looking for survivors first."

"Lt. Commander Kershaw...I think we should get back to work. Time's running short."

He looked away. "We never should have come back. How can we sacrifice these men a second time? This is a memorial to the fallen, not some science experiment."

"Sir, we haven't finished setting up the receiver. After that's done, then we can leave."

Kershaw jerked back in one sudden motion. "Keep your hands off me!" he screamed. "I am ordering all the teams off the *Lexington*—now."

The other member of their team began to take notice of the confrontation.

"I'm afraid we can't do that, sir. But I think it would be a good idea if the two of us left. We can wait for the other teams to finish by the cargo mover."

They were trespassing. This place belonged to the dead. "What are you talking about? Stow your equipment away. We are leaving immediately."

Fisher shook his head. "We can't, sir—our orders."

Off. We have to get off. "I'm giving you new orders," Kershaw said with a far-off look in his eyes.

"What's going on down there?" someone asked on the radio.

"It's Kershaw," Fisher replied while trying to hold him in place. "He's really lost it."

Fisher's assistant abandoned the receiver and beat a path right to the other two. Together, they tried to subdue him, but he resisted. "Let me go!" Kershaw screamed. I cannot let them stop me. "I'll see you court-martialed for disobeying my orders."

Commander Neu, who had been listening to exchange behind the communication operator, stepped into the fray. "What's going on over there?" he demanded

"We can't sacrifice the *Lexington*. This ship should become a memorial for those who died."

"Anybody. Come in," Neu shouted.

"This is Ensign Fisher. Something has happened to Lt. Commander Kershaw. We're trying to get him off the ship."

"Should I send out a rescue team?"

"Negative. I'm decreasing his oxygen supply. This should calm him down."

"How long before the receiver is in position?"

"I'm ready now."

"Get Kershaw out of there. You'll have to finish this on your own."

"Understood, Commander."

Fisher's assistant finally got Kershaw off his feet. Though he continued resisting, both men managed to wrestle him into the shaft. "I order you to release me," he repeated a number of times. Get away from them. "You'll all pay for this."

"This is Fisher," he said into his headset. "How long before you can send the magnitron beam?"

"Right now. We were just waiting for your signal."

"Send it over now. I'll line up everything from my end."

The crewmen trying to keep Kershaw subdued fired their maneuvering jets once he was in position. When they emerged from the interior of the ship, he saw a rescue team waiting next to a cargo mover. Kershaw saw what they were intending to do. The fear registered in his eyes. "Don't bring me back to the barge," he pleaded, "Please—you don't understand." Kershaw lunged at them, his mind fighting the lack of oxygen while his body struggled against his captors, sucking up the precious gas. His lungs couldn't keep up. Darkness faded over him. He passed out.

"What is your progress, Fisher?" Neu asked on the radio. There was no reply.

"I'm just finishing up now," he said after several moments. "The beam has been caught and I am waiting for the next team's signal. Get the other teams off the ship. I should be no more than a minute or two."

"This is Lieutenant Inouye. The last receiver is in place."

"Good. I am opening the containment loop now." Fisher entered the final command code. The magnitron pulse came through the power cell emitter, went down the corridor, and through a wall. He made sure the signal integrity held firm. "Ninety percent," he read. "Good enough."

Neu bolted over to the window panels. The few remaining cargo movers reached their respective barges. Even though the distance between them and the *Lexington* was just a couple hundred meters, to him it felt more like a million. He looked over his shoulder. "Signal the other subidors. Tell them we will be departing in five tal teks."

Neu then scurried over to the communications station. "Have all the omega band receivers been linked together?"

"Yes, Commander. My instruments indicate the circuit has been completed."

"I want a short pulse sent to them, minimal power."

Tul Lan-Ro, who was monitoring the mission from the RadAR station, turned around when he heard the order. "May I ask the purpose of sending out a pulse?" he asked. "Doing so might reveal us to the Deravans."

Neu met his question with a reassuring smile. "I haven't gone crazy, like Lt. Commander Kershaw," he replied. "This will be our only opportunity to know whether or not the power cells actually work. If they do, a small EM field should form around the ship. If not, then we stay until the problem is fixed." He looked up, mouthing something to himself. "By my estimation, a two and-a-half percent power pulse should be just enough to create a field," Neu continued, "but be undetectable beyond a range of five kilometers."

Tul Lan-Ro offered a slight bow. "A wise decision," he complimented.

Neu studied the *Lexington* one last time. "Prepare to send out the pulse."

"The command code has already been entered. Ready for transmission."

Here goes nothing. "Activate the power cells."

The operator pressed a single blinking button on his console. Power readings on his display started to rise. "Point nine percent," he read. "One and-a-half...two percent."

Neu listened to the words. So far, nothing on the surface of the ship suggested the power cells had created anything. "Come on," he said to himself like a kind of prayer. "Just a little more."

"Sir," the operator called out, "something is happening on the *Lexington*."

Neu hustled over to his station, just in time to see a ring of energy form in the middle of the ship. "The field is two hundred meters wide and expanding."

"It looks as though the system is operating perfectly," Tul Lan-Ro congratulated.

"Cut power," Neu ordered. He checked the chronometer above the window panels. "This won't mean a thing if the Deravans find us here. How long before we can depart?"

The communication operator swiveled his chair around. "All the cargo barges report their transport teams have returned from the *Lexington*. We can leave at any time."

"RadAR—anything on your scope?"

"I have made three sweeps of the area. There are no other ships in this sector."

"Good. Bring the engines online," he ordered. "Heading ..." Neu glanced at the navigator's scope. "One-eight-six. Speed, 1.04 stellar velocity."

The pilot entered the command codes into his console. The *Dek-Par* pivoted around and pulled ahead of the others. When they had gone a safe distance away, the remaining vessels executed a similar maneuver and came up from behind.

"Holding steady at one-eight-six. Speed—0.75 stellar velocity, and increasing."

Neu found himself standing in front of the windows. The *Lexington* fell away from them, moving steadily towards the rim of Mars. What had once been a ship twenty times their size devolved into a gray speck floating in a sea of black. As though a giant hand had grabbed the ship from underneath, she continued her downward descent, until the red planet blocked all proof of the stellar cruiser's existence.

A warm grin blossomed on his face. For the first time since the mission started, he felt they had a chance.

CHAPTER
18

TERRAN SECTOR
DAIETH TIME PLUS ONE

All four surviving cargo barges maintained a direct trajectory to Earth at 1.62 stellar velocity. Pursuing Deravan ships were not far behind.

Another cluster of enemy vessels ahead of them fired a concentrated volley of ion blasts in their direction. The barges took evasive maneuvers. They darted about in a random fashion, making it difficult for the Deravans to lock onto them. The lead subidor considered himself fortunate to have made it this far. Their last encounter with the enemy had reduced their strength by another ship. If they didn't do anything to slow their rate of loss, none of them would reach Earth alive.

"A squadron of enemy vessels is positioned directly ahead. Range...ten thousand kintars."

Lost in thought, the subidor stood in front of the panel of windows. A brighter-than-usual red giant captured his attention. The star looked a lot like Antares. He missed his home.

"Subidor," the navigational operator repeated.

"Time to intercept?" he asked from his place.

"Nine tal teks."

The subidor's eyes drifted down to the deck. They had their orders: reach Earth at all costs. But with the losses they had suffered, fulfilling their mission seemed more daunting after each encounter with the Deravans. "How many ships are ahead of us?"

The operator entered the query into his console. "Nine, Subidor."

They were so close, and yet, a very real possibility existed that they might be stopped just short of their goal. The Earth remained a hazy blue dot from that distance, but the planet represented so much more. Reaching the Terran home world symbolized an important victory against the Deravans. And if they didn't make it, his faith in Commander Yamane assured him their deaths would not be in vain.

He looked up. The red pinpoint of light amidst the thousands of others caught his attention again. He wondered if they would ever reach their destination.

"Deravan ships are increasing their speed to 1.65 stellar velocity. They will intercept in three tal teks."

"Can we match them?"

"Perhaps a bit more could be coaxed out of the engines," the navigational operator replied. He entered a new acceleration formula into his console. The look on his face said far more than any computer readout ever could. "I am not getting a response. Power flows are starting to degrade."

The subidor strode over to the intercom. "Engine room, this is the bridge. Can we increase our velocity?"

"We are losing the containment fields for the reactor cores," the engineer replied, his voice hurried. "I am not sure how much longer we can keep them intact."

An unexpected fusion blast glanced off the edge of their barge. The subidor pivoted around. "Take evasive maneuvers," he ordered.

S.F.S. CORONA
1412 PROXIMA MERIDIAN TIME, AUGUST 28, 2217

Yamane's armada of ships slipped past another interstellar cloud of dust. He gave it a wide berth, lest they have another bow shock incident. Pressing on, the fleet passed through the shadows of the great gas giants, Uranus and Jupiter. The r-tech monitored Saturn from a distance when they crossed through its elliptical plane, but the planet had been too far out of position for Yamane to incorporate it into his plan. Not that he minded so much. In fact, he could not have been more relieved. The memories of what they had gone through there were still fresh in his mind. He did not need a visual reminder of what humanity had lost there.

"What is the fleet's speed and heading?" Yamane asked the nav-tech.

He leaned closer and accessed the information from his screen. "We are holding steady at

0.953 stellar velocity. Maintaining course zero-one-seven, straight for Mars."

Yamane sat back in his chair. He suddenly felt alone, as though he were at the bottom of a deep, dark hole. Up above, he saw a small opening. He wished Stan were on board right now. Over the past two days, he had missed having his friend around. His quick wit and gregarious nature always helped him see the better side of life. They were very different people in most respects: he, quiet and introspective, Kershaw, outspoken and loud. Maybe that's why they had remained friends all these years. Unease settled on Yamane. He worried for Kershaw, almost as much as for the decoy barges headed for Earth. He hoped they were alive and well, but it was a murky hope at best.

"Commander," C-tech Landis called out. "I'm receiving a message from the *Bok-Nor*. The call signs indicate it is a priority one message."

Yamane swung the command chair around. "Put it on."

"I'm afraid I can't. The transmission has ceased. But the message did indicate a shuttle will arrive in the next few minutes."

"Strange. Nothing else?"

He shook his head. "No, sir."

Yamane placed his hand on his chin. He then looked at the astro-clock. "Contact the landing bay so they can prepare for the ship's arrival. Also, dispatch an honor guard so they can escort whoever this is to my quarters."

"How do you know it is only one person?" Webster asked from his station.

"I cannot say exactly, call it a feeling," Yamane replied, his eyes steady. "In the meantime, take command of the bridge until I find out what this is all about."

"Understood, Commander," he replied, though his demeanor suggested he wasn't comfortable with the idea of Yamane meeting with an Antaren—alone.

TERRAN SECTOR
DAIETH TIME PLUS TWO

The lead barge started to slip further ahead of the others heading for Earth.

"Subidor," the RadAR operator called out. "Long range scans have picked up the Deravan fleet in orbit above the Terran home world. At this range the signal is still weak, but they are definitely there."

He went over to the RadAR station. "Bring it up on your monitor. I want to see for myself."

"Yes, Subidor," the operator complied.

A fuzzy blue sphere appeared on his screen. Suspended just above the planet, the subidor saw a faint haze of gray. "There you are," he whispered. His supposition, however, would not be worth the breath he exhaled without some hard data to back it up. "I want confirmation. Track their movements. Give me a total as soon as it is available."

"Three ships coming in off our starboard side!" the RadAR operator shouted out.

The subidor's actions became more precise and fixed. "Increase speed to 1.70 stellar velocity."

A sea of explosions detonated all around them. Unrelenting blast waves violently shook the cargo barge with frightening precision. Alarms bells rang out from every corner of the bridge. As the deadly bursts dissipated, three enemy ships passed by overhead.

"What is our status?"

"Another cargo barge has been destroyed. We have sustained slight damage to our maneuvering thrusters, though they are still at ninety-five percent power levels."

Another fusion blast detonated off their starboard bow. "Take evasive maneuvers."

Power levels on the bridge fluctuated again. The subidor was about to open the intercom when the systems came back on line. He watched the velocity gauge steadily climb. "Distance to Earth?"

"Fifty kintars."

A wave of fatigue swept over the subidor. He and the crew had been going nonstop since beginning their journey. Judging by the way the mission had gone so far—a one-way journey.

He turned towards the panel of windows. The Terran world had grown a little larger.

"Forty-five kintars and closing."

Three Deravan ships swung around for another pass. Their appearance evoked an image of death in the subidor's mind. It wasn't anything he could describe or put into words, just a feeling of an insatiable hatred of all living things emanating from them.

"Forty kintars."

The Deravans fired a volley of fusion blasts. Yellow and blue flashes went off all around them, rocking the barge first to her starboard side, and then her port. Drawn into the unintended creation of beauty amidst the deadly detonations, the subidor was reminded of the lights surrounding Tel Shador at night. "Are the other three barges still with us?" he asked.

After checking his scope, the RadAR operator replied, "Negative, another one has been destroyed."

"Thirty-five kintars and closing."

He stepped back and faced the windows again. A realization came over him, as certain as the rising of their sun: they just had to make it. "What is our present speed?"

"1.12 stellar velocity and holding."

Not enough. They had to go faster. "How about the other barges?"

The RadAR operator made an adjustment on his screen. A pulse went out and then bounced back. "They have slowed somewhat, but both ships are still with us."

Just a little more. "Status report. What is the number of Deravan vessels encircling the Terran home world?"

The operator reconfigured his screen. Earth appeared in the middle. Positioned just a little higher, scores of tiny yellow dots; all locked in geo-synchronous orbit. "Scans indicate there are nine hundred and thirty ships above the Terran world."

Mission accomplished, he thought, proud of himself. The Deravans were right where they needed to be. With their assignment complete, the subidor could set a course for Mars anytime now. He, however, dismissed such a thought. Their engines were all but gone, and the enemy was pressing in on them. He figured if it ended this way they would at least go down well. The only thing the subidor had not counted on was an overwhelming desire to know the outcome of the battle, though he suspected he already did.

When the three barges were twenty kintars away, additional Deravan ships fired up their main engines and blasted out of Earth's orbit. The subidor did not have any doubts about their destination, though he wondered why the Deravans would go to all this effort just to stop them. They were three defenseless vessels against an entire fleet of warships. Perhaps, he thought, by reaching the planet, the Antarens had challenged a twisted version of pride on their part.

A muffled explosion registered from the rear of his ship.

"Ship's speed is 1.08 stellar velocity and falling," the navigational operator called out.

The Deravan ships immediately reacted and closed in on the damaged vessel.

"Our speed is now down to 1.02 stellar velocity."

The barge violently shook as another hit slammed into her hull. She tumbled over on her port side.

The subidor made his way to the navigational station. "Can you compensate?" he asked.

"I am trying."

Another explosion triggered a new series of alarms. The lights on the bridge flickered and then dimmed to about half strength.

"What is our status?" he yelled over the klaxons.

"RadAR is out and our power level has dropped below thirty percent."

"Can we still maneuver?"

"Yes, but just barely."

"Distance to Deravan ships?"

"Unknown." An explosion rocked the ship with unequaled ferocity. Smoke began to fill the bridge. The subidor looked up at the navigator's screen when another hit knocked out remaining power. The ship listed over even further. "Are the stabilizers operational?" he called out.

"Negative. My boards do not respond."

Another blast ripped through the crippled ship. Terrible explosions detonated near the aft section.

"Subidor, what should we do? Our engines are gone."

He turned to the operator. Calm surrounded the senior officer. "We die well."

Moments later, the cargo barge was gone.

All three Deravan ships flew through the fireball, and then changed course for the surviving barges heading for Earth. They, however, had waited too long. The two barges slowed just as they entered orbit. The crews, in an act of defiance, stood by at their stations awaiting the fate they all knew would come; content in the knowledge they had successfully completed their mission.

The Deravan ships, seizing their opportunity, fired their weapons one last time, and finished them off.

S.F.S. CORONA
1425 PROXIMA MERIDIAN TIME

The swish of his door announced Yamane's arrival. He looked about his cabin. Since he had no idea what the purpose of this meeting might be about, he wanted to make certain his quarters conveyed the idea that he ran a tight ship.

Faint sounds of footsteps echoed in the corridor. Judging by the number of boots clomping on the deck plates, there were six or seven people heading his way. Yamane prepared himself. He stood in the middle of the room, his hands at his side.

The sounds in the corridor ceased. His room felt quiet, still. Knock, knock, knock.

"Come in," he replied after a few seconds went by.

The door slid open. Kel Sen-Ry stood in the corridor, accompanied by an escort who appeared uncomfortable standing so near an Antaren.

"It's good to see you again," Yamane said, surprised by his appearance. He had all but been certain the unidentified occupant of the shuttle had to be Tul Lan-Ro, the Antaren fleet's commanding officer and chief strategist. He maintained a friendly demeanor, nevertheless.

Kel Sen-Ry nodded his head in an acknowledgement of the greeting. He stepped just within the boundaries of the room. The door slid closed behind him with a swoosh.

Both of them stood in place, facing each other. Yamane thought his guest might be waiting for some kind of traditional response. If this was the case, he was going to be disappointed. They just didn't have the time for it. Instead, he cleared his throat and said, "We might be more comfortable over here," he suggested, breaking the prolonged silence.

Kel Sen-Ry went over to the chair closest to him. Yamane had set them facing each other, about a meter apart. He hoped the configuration would encourage an open dialogue, but with the requisite distance expected by the Antarens.

In one single action, Kel Sen-Ry went from walking to sitting. Yamane thought he gave off a sigh when he sat in his chair.

"Commander Yamane, I am grateful for you meeting with me under these, how shall we say, unorthodox circumstances," he said, belying no emotional meaning to his words. "I am certain you must have some questions about why I am here."

"You could say I am more than a little curious," Yamane replied diplomatically, careful not to say anything against the unknown.

"Although it goes against our traditional ways of conducting an informal meeting such as this, time constraints force me to dispense with the usual observances, and get right to the point."

"I appreciate that." Kel Sen-Ry had no idea how much.

He leaned closer. "What we discuss in this room could have a profound impact on not only the success of the operation, but the future of our two peoples as well," he said almost in a whisper. "The High Council has instructed me that at the proper time I should reveal what you do not know about the Deravans. Tomorrow, we will send many of our people to their deaths. If you understand nothing else, those deaths will be for a greater purpose than you realize."

Yamane rubbed his chin. "But I thought Sul Ren-Ta told me everything. What else is there?"

"The truth."

Yamane felt an icy draft enter his room, making the hairs on the back of his neck stand on end. If felt like another presence had passed through the walls and stood in their midst. Dark and malevolent it was, as though someone or something did not want the next words spoken. Yamane came to his feet, his eyes darting about. Visibly, they were the only ones there. Fear was the surest path to defeat. If he gave in to his, then their fate was all but assured. He sat back down and focused his attention squarely on Kel Sen-Ry. The Antaren's calm made him feel safe again.

Kel Sen-Ry stared into Yamane's eyes. "That was your first lesson," he said in a cryptic manner.

Yamane cleared his throat. "What do you mean?"

"The Deravan's influence goes far beyond their physical presence, as you just witnessed."

Yamane felt the tension coursing through his body and forced himself to physically relax. He knew what Kel Sen-Ry was implying. That force—that energy that had just flooded the room—it was alive, and it was connected to the Deravans. For sanity's sake, he feared acknowledgment of such a possibility. Yamane bluffed, "You're not making any sense. Our fleet is still millions of kilometers from Mars. We haven't sighted any of their ships."

"This is not what I am saying. Perhaps, if I start from the beginning, you might understand what we are truly up against." Kel Sen-Ry paused for a second or two. Both luminescent eyes turned upwards, as though he was trying to draw inspiration from some unseen object. "Long ago, far beyond our earliest recorded history, there was a great and mighty civilization. Though they are known by a number of names, we refer to them as the Great Creators."

Yamane sat forward. "Go on."

"They revealed to us what took place in the beginning—how our world began. From what our sacred writings describe, it was once a paradise, where nothing stood between our people and the Great Creators. Can you imagine a place where there is no pain, no suffering—no death?"

Yamane could. "Something tells me the story doesn't end here."

"Unfortunately, it does not." Kel Sen-Ry's eyes dropped. "As a means of guiding many of the younger races sprinkled throughout the galaxy, the Great Creators sought the assistance of one that showed tremendous promise. At first, this race embraced their special calling with unbridled enthusiasm and zeal, but over the course of time, they began to think differently. They believed the fulfillment of their destiny could only be realized through control, not servitude." He paused, as though the next part pained him deeply. "The Prophets have given us the name of this race."

A name formed in Yamane's mind. "The Deravans," he said in a deep voice.

Kel Sen-Ry looked up to the ceiling again. "Yes, the Deravans. When they challenged the authority of the Great Creators, a war between the two ensued. The Prophets indicate the powers they unleashed went far beyond anything we could ever comprehend." Kel Sen-Ry rose from his chair and wandered over to the porthole. "The conflict went beyond our perception of reality, working its way into the realm of other dimensions. What took place there had a direct impact on our existence here. The battle raged back and forth, until the Great Creators defeated the Deravans and barred them from the dimension in which they reside. How many dimensions there are, no one can say. But the Deravans defied the outcome of the war and sought other worlds, other allies to join their side. For them, the final battle is not over, but merely postponed."

Yamane listened with rapt attention, completely spellbound by the tale. The one and only thought on his mind since the Deravans had driven them from Earth had been the liberation of his home world. For him, nothing else mattered. Now, was it possible the upcoming battle had a much deeper meaning?

"In time, this rebellion reached the shores of our planet. I am afraid to say it did not take long before we too craved an existence apart from those who had loved and done so much for us. Like the Deravans, the further we moved away from what we had known and experienced with the Great Creators, the more our perceptions of ourselves became twisted and distorted. But they did not give up on us—" Kel Sen-Ry inexplicably stopped in mid-sentence. "The Prophets tell us The Deravans believed the only way the Great Creators could be defeated is if they reshaped the galaxy, conquering it so completely, that no trace—no fingerprint—of the Great Creators is left. And so, they began their conquest of every race, every people, and every civilization."

The words were hard to hear, but Yamane found himself believing them. "If what you say is true, why do the Great Creators not stop the Deravans? So much pain and suffering might have been avoided."

The question gave Kel Sen-Ry pause. "Our writings tell us the Great Creators could have done this at a time of their own choosing, but they held back for the sake of the High Son. He is the key to everything."

Yamane furled his brow. "The High Son? I know he is important to your culture, but what role does he play in all this?"

Kel Sen-Ry spun around. Every facet of his demeanor conveyed the significance of what he would say next. "The High Son is the only link between our dimension, and that of the Great Creators. Our sacred writings reveal the folly of trying to stand against the Deravans without the Great Creators' help. Our world succumbed to their influence, as did yours. The arrival of the High Son taught us that without him intervening on our behalf, we have no chance of defeating them."

"And how, exactly, does he intervene?"

Kel Sen-Ry leaned forward, and said, almost in a whisper, "You felt it. That darkness that entered the room a moment ago. That thing—a hunter—was not from this dimension. It was sent by the Deravans from the outside. But take hope. The High Son also works from the outside, but in an opposite fashion. Where the Deravans place fear and doubt in their enemies, the High Son removes. I suspect you have felt moments of direction or encouragement when they have been most needed."

Yamane could hardly catch his breath. "All this time, and I didn't even recognize what was really going on around me."

"The Great Creators have been waiting for the day when we would be ready for their return. This was one of the purposes served by the prophets. They prepared us for your coming." He went back to his chair. "You have been sent to help usher in a new era, but it cannot be done apart from the High Son. Only through him will the paradise lost so long ago be realized."

"This is almost too fantastic to believe, but everything you've said not only fits into what has happened to humanity, it actually makes sense of it all."

Kel Sen-Ry appeared to smile, but then it faded just as quickly. "Yes, but our sacred writings also give us a dire warning. As you well understand, our ships and weapons have been prepared for the Deravan's arrival. But just as important, even more so in my estimation, are the people themselves. The Prophets have told us that we must possess unquestioned character and integrity. If the Great Creators see neither characteristic in either race, we will find ourselves on the side of the defeated. With no one else who can stop them, the Deravans will then have free reign over the galaxy."

Yamane thought about what Kel Sen-Ry said for a long time before he responded. "If what you are saying is true, then defeating the Deravans means more than saving the Earth. We are fighting for the life of every living being in the galaxy."

"As enemies of the Great Creators, the Deravans will try to crush anyone who sides against them."

Rubbing his face with both hands, Yamane replied, "I didn't realize until just now how high the stakes really were."

"What you have been given is a tremendous honor, and a tremendous burden."

"It would explain a lot," Yamane reasoned. "All those times I wondered why certain events didn't go the other way: Kalmedia, the battle for Earth, the mutiny, or your support. I often sensed an unseen hand had been guiding events all along. Seems I was more right than I knew."

"The Great Creators have been with you every step of the way, as evidenced by the appearance of their special representative, the High Son. He is the one with whom you spoke, the one who validated your calling—then and now. We were aware of what his appearance meant, but felt it prudent if nothing was said until now. You had a lot to consider and it would take time sorting out all the issues involved. But that time has passed. You must decide this day whom you will follow; the Great Creators or the Deravans. There is no other choice since you can only give your allegiance to one."

There was no debate this time, no speculation. Just the truth. "I choose the High Son and offer my allegiance to the Great Creators."

Rising to his feet again, Kel Sen-Ry smiled at him in a knowing way. "Time waits for neither of us," the Antaren declared, "and we both have important matters which require our attention. I pray the fortunes of the battle go well for us both. Until then, Commander." He offered him a long, slow bow before leaving his quarters.

The honor guard snapped to attention when Kel Sen-Ry appeared. They flanked the Antaren on both sides, and then escorted him to the lift at the end of the corridor.

When his door slid shut Yamane found himself alone, again. Unlike before, he didn't mind so much this time.

CHAPTER
29

S.F.S. CORONA
0736 PROXIMA MERIDIAN TIME, AUGUST 29, 2217

The alarm sounded. Yamane bolted up. He didn't know where he was. His eyes darted about. The familiar sight of his quarters brought a certain measure of relief. He sat on his bed, taking in the feel of the morning; though on a ship like this, morning, noon, and night all looked the same.

Swinging his legs around, both boots clomped onto the deck. He felt surprisingly refreshed after getting only five hours of sleep in the last two days. He was tempted to lie back down again, collect his thoughts; but as usual, there was no time for such indulgences. Only the future concerned him, and the future could be found in one place—the bridge. Neu's cargo barges would return soon and he felt he should be there when they did.

Yamane sat back. His quarters felt quiet, serene. He drank in the sensation like a man who had gone days without water. It was a welcome respite from the turmoil existing beyond his cabin door. The words Kel Sen-Ry had spoken to him only a few short hours ago came flooding back. Yamane was still amazed how the anxiety he associated with the unknown had dissipated so completely after embracing the truth. The presence and support offered by the Great Creators imbued him with a feeling of supreme confidence. He was not in this fight alone. Then a single, disturbing thought descended upon him. His mood turned. "How does one know if the character and integrity required of men even exists?" he asked himself. Looking out the porthole window, he knew they would find out soon enough, in battle.

"Commander on deck," Major Webster said from the command chair when Yamane arrived.

"Sir, something has just entered long range tracking," the r-tech said. "We were just going to signal you."

When Webster stepped aside, Yamane took his place in the command chair. A thousand suns glimmered on the main screen, dim in comparison with the red planet in the center. "Can you determine what the identity of the contact is?"

"No, Commander. They are still too far away."

Yamane placed his hand on his chin. The unknown contact might be anything: a rogue comet, one of the surveillance ships, or the incoming cargo barges. There was also a more obvious answer—the Deravans. He checked the time. 0747. The barges were due about now, but then again...

Yamane rose out of his chair and went to the r-tech's station. The unknown contact appeared like a fuzzy blip on his screen. Sending out an active pulse would settle the matter in a nano-second, but if the blip were the enemy, they would be found out faster than the time it took for the pulse to return. On the other hand, if Yamane didn't take any action, he might be playing right into the Deravan's hands. Either way, it was a lose-lose situation.

"What is the distance of the contact?"

"Fifty thousand kilometers." His face went white. "Wait a minute. The blip is breaking up into multiple contacts. I cannot give you an exact number at this range, but I would say about fifteen or so."

Yamane stood upright. "Signal the launch tubes. I want a squadron of fighters sent out so we can positively identify those contacts while they're still out of range of our ships."

"Understood, Commander. I'll send the order now."

With great efficiency on the part of the pilots and flight teams, five Min fighters flew out of the *Corona* less than a minute later. They made a single course adjustment, straight for the unknown contacts.

A deathly silence filled the bridge.

"The fighters should be close enough for visual confirmation by now," Webster blurted out while tracking the progress of the squadron from his station.

"Have you detected any weapons fire on your boards?" Yamane asked the r-tech.

His monitors remained the same. "Negative, Commander. Wait a minute." The r-tech pressed a couple of buttons at the base of his display. Yamane's heart skipped a beat. "They are circling back in this direction."

"Are you picking up any radio traffic?" he asked Landis.

The c-tech shook his head. "Negative, sir."

Yamane didn't know if this was good news or not.

The five fighters coming up on them quickly assumed a standard flying wing formation. One of them suddenly broke away from the others. The pilot banked his fighter over hard and set a course for the bridge. When his ship was ten kilometers away, he rolled it to the left and then the right. The pilot repeated the maneuver, and then flew out of view. Understanding the meaning of the pilot's actions, the bridge erupted into the sounds of claps and cheers.

"Okay, people, I need everyone back at their stations," Yamane said with his hands extended. "RadAR, continue to monitor the area ahead of us. Mr. Landis, signal Commander Neu the moment he re-engages the fleet. I want his barge brought on board at his earliest convenience." He paused for a moment. "I should be there when the ships arrive." He went over to the engineering station. "Mr. Webster, you have the bridge."

Yamane stepped onto the tarmac after he slid the lift gate open. Ground crews were already in position, along with emergency teams in the rear of the bay. A pungent mixture of fighter exhaust, grease and fuel hung heavy in the air.

"Landing bay. Prepare for ship's entry," a voice boomed on every loud-speaker.

A flagman stood on the tarmac, with batons in hand. He started to back up just as the transport penetrated the binary magnetic shielding.

The operator, eying an overlay of the grid on his console monitor, manipulated the field to allow for the ship's entry. Hugging the ship at the atomic level, the barrier formed a tight seal around it, preventing air and heat from escaping into space. If the operator allowed the slightest gap to form, he might jeopardize the integrity of the entire barrier.

Yamane stood to the side, watching the shuttle edge its way in. While the ship lacked any aesthetically pleasing qualities, intended primarily as a craft of functionality, the piloting skills of her cabin crew could not have impressed him more. The transport floated in gracefully, making ever-so-subtle changes in direction and speed. He almost expected to see dust blowing up from underneath the ship, but Antaren technology went far beyond the use of simple thrusters. Their anti-grav drive easily held the shuttle in place, producing almost no sound at all.

The flagman made his way to the left, both batons mirroring each step. The transport stayed right with him. When he positioned the shuttle over the three nearest stalls, he crossed his batons in an "x" configuration. The ship went down at a steady rate, until it rested on the tarmac.

Yamane ran over to the airlock the instant the engines shut down. Several other crewmembers gathered behind him.

Even before the hum from the turbines had subsided, the forward hatch clicked three times. After another series of pops and clicks, it slid open. Neu stood on the other side. He looked tired, haggard. Taking a first shaky step onto the deck, he saw Yamane. His hand went up and offered him a salute.

"Welcome home, Commander," Yamane said in a congratulatory tone. "It's good to see you again." He looked the shuttle over. "It looks as though you all made it back in one piece."

"Thank you, sir," he replied, though the response seemed more out of obligation than sincerity. Neu brought up his data pad and handed it to Yamane. "This is a detailed report of the mission. I know there's not much time, but you should get through it before we reach Mars."

"I'll get right on it," he said after a cursory glance. "And the status of your teams?"

"They were successful," he exhaled. "Every power cell and receiver is in position."

Those were the words Yamane had wanted to hear since he sent the barges to the *Lexington*. He should have been happy about the news, but a little voice in his head told him something wasn't right. Yamane thought it might have been the fatigue factor, but Neu's subdued nature seemed to go much deeper.

"Commander—Frank," Neu stammered. "There is something else you should know." Just as he was about to continue, a stretcher came out of the forward airlock. Two crewmen carrying the litter hustled past Yamane. A man lay under a wool blanket, held in place by four leather straps. "Stan," was all he could get out. Kershaw didn't speak, didn't move. His face was pale, but he was alive. Unconscious, but alive. One question burned in Yamane's head: "What happened?"

Neu scratched the side of his tired face. "I'm not quite sure," he replied, his voice sounding hoarse. "We had just finished placing the receivers when Kershaw started issuing crazy orders. He said that what we were doing wasn't right and we should leave the *Lexington*. It was all Ensign Fisher and his team could do to get him out of there." He looked past Yamane, just in time to see Kershaw placed into an awaiting hover cart. "After he had been brought back on board the cargo barge he still fought us. A shot of neurontin pretty much knocked him out for the duration of the trip."

A dark cloud formed around Yamane as his perceptions of the area around the bay lessened. The operation did not seem so important anymore. A growing awareness of his own fatigue drew Yamane down even further. But he couldn't stop, not now. He had to continue leading, one heavy step at a time. "I understand," he forced out.

"Do you have any idea why Kershaw snapped like that?" Neu asked.

"You had better get back to your ship, Commander," he replied. "There's not much time left and there are probably matters on the *Adler* which require your attention." He saluted before Neu could respond.

Yamane found himself within the confines of the lift again. He should have been pleased about the mission's outcome, but their success had come at a price. Maybe he shouldn't have put both of them together. Maybe he had asked too much from his old friend. A dark feeling welled up within Yamane. Without Kershaw to cover his back, the outcome of the battle seemed a little less certain.

"What is our ETA to the *Lexington*?" Yamane asked.

The nav-tech looked at his chronometer. "Four hours and sixteen minutes."

Not much time left, Yamane thought. All of the planning related to Operation: *Lexington* Gambit had been set. He had resigned himself to his purgatory-like existence, but didn't like it much. More waiting. How he hated the waiting.

Yamane placed his hands on his tired eyes and rubbed them. The gentle movement felt good. Repositioning himself in his chair, he became acutely aware that the atmosphere on the bridge had changed, as though it had become electric. He turned to his left before looking right. Everything appeared normal enough. Then he had a sudden feeling someone was standing behind him. He swiveled his command chair around, towards the rear of the bridge. There, in the shadows, a lone figure stood. Yamane was about to get up when the person stepped into the light.

"Stan," he gasped. "What are you doing here?" He rose to his feet. "I thought you were confined to the med-lab." The memories of Kershaw strapped down in a stretcher returned. "Have you been released?"

"Dr. Owens just signed off on my flight status," he replied, looking like a new man. Standing tall and confident, his hair neatly trimmed and combed, it looked like the pain of the past was gone, as though someone had lifted a heavy yoke off his weary shoulders. "Commander, I formally request permission to return to my post."

Yamane's initial reaction was a categorical "no". He went over the details of what happened in Neu's report. People just didn't recover from a breakdown this fast. He had even considered the possibility Kershaw might never recover from his ordeal. Yet, hours later, the person he knew before the mission had somehow returned. Such a thing couldn't be denied. In fact, he even appeared the better for it.

"I realize what I'm asking is a lot, but I know where I need to be—and that place is the engine room. You don't have to tell me how crazy this sounds, but something tells me I should be in engineering when the battle starts. I ...I just can't say it any other way."

Yamane looked him over again. "How can you know such a thing?"

"It's difficult to describe. Call it a feeling, a sixth sense flex." He took a step forward. "Please, Frank. You have to trust me."

Yamane could not deny that whatever plagued Kershaw before had seemingly disappeared. On the other hand, would he risk the lives of the crew on someone who had experienced some form of breakdown? Then something remarkable happened. A calming presence settled upon him, saying, in effect, "The outcome will be as he says." Yamane had experienced that same feeling before. Once when he opted not to go to the New Frontier, and again when he spoke with Kel Sen-Ry a few short hours ago. "Permission granted," Yamane replied, the words slipping out of his mouth before he realized it.

Kershaw smiled, offered a quick salute, and then left the bridge without another word.

"You cannot be serious," Webster protested from his station. Yamane ignored the comment. "After what took place on that mission, you're letting him go back to the engine room? How do you know he won't have another episode?"

"I don't, Major," Yamane conceded, "but I believe things will work out, just like he said."

Webster was about to object again when Yamane held up his hand. The matter, as far as he was concerned, was closed.

"The surveillance ships should transmit their signal any time now," Landis reported.

Yamane wondered how it must have been for the crews out there—all alone—each ship millions of kilometers away from the others. Had their silence been because they didn't detect any Deravan ships, or had they suffered the same probable fate as the cargo barges? There were plenty of questions. Yamane glanced up at the astro-clock. They would have their answer soon enough.

He focused his attention on the speakers atop the c-tech's console. Any moment now, he thought. But they remained frustratingly silent. Seconds passed, an eternity passed. And then, as if someone had cued them at the proper time, the speakers crackled to life. "This message is addressed to the Deravan fleet in orbit above the Earth. You have initiated an immoral attack against the inhabitants of this planet. If you do not cease all hostile activities, an armada of warships approaching the planet Mars will have no choice but to use deadly force against your ships, destroying them if necessary. You have one hour to comply."

"This should get their attention," Webster said in a sinister tone.

"They are sending the message again."

Yamane tapped his fingers on the data pad. "Turn the speaker off and signal the rest of the fleet," he ordered. "We are now on battle alert status. Have all ships regroup into attack formation." The lights on the bridge instantly changed to a muted crimson color. "RadAR, I want active sweeps of the area. If you pick up a microbe on your screen, you tell me."

"Aye, Commander."

After receiving their orders, all twelve dreadnoughts shot ahead of the *Corona*, and took up a position ten kilometers from Yamane's ship. The destroyers went next and came alongside the big ships, triggering the launch of wave after wave of skyjackets from their respective vessels. Yamane could not remember the last time he had seen such an impressive sight. Swarms of Antaren fighters darted all about—up, down, left, and right—their black and yellow motifs flying past the bridge in a blur.

When their turn came, the seven sub-cruisers flew past every Antaren ship already assembled and went into formation a thousand or so meters ahead of them.

"All ships have signaled they are now in position," Landis reported.

Yamane compared the progress of the fleet with the text on his data pad. They were right on the mark. "Good. Get me the *Drummond*."

"Moran here," the radio replied.

"This is Commander Yamane. You have the lead now, Jim. You'll earn your pay for the week if you get us to *Lexington* before the Deravans do."

"Piece of cake, Commander," he replied, his tone light. "We'll bring the fleet in, no problem. *Drummond*, out."

Taking the point, all seven sub-cruisers slotted back into a standard v-shaped formation. Three ships positioned themselves on Moran's left, and three on his right. Yamane felt the fleet was as ready as it would ever be. His feelings were confirmed when he scanned the bridge. Every officer, every tech was at his station, prepared for whatever came next. Nothing left to do but wait. Then a particular word settled into his mind. Ritual. "How could I have forgotten," he said to himself after sitting up. Just as with a patrol in his Min fighter, a ritual needed attending to first, one he had observed since his earliest days in the academy.

Yamane jumped to his feet and went to the engineering station. "Major Webster," he said softly. "You have the bridge until I get back."

A quizzical look crossed his face. "Yes, sir."

Yamane entered the lift before anyone else on the bridge saw him leave. He closed his eyes and reached for the panel. His finger found the button for deck three. Moments later, he had arrived. He peered outside, but ducked back in when three crewmembers walked past. They were having a disagreement about the fastest way to get the port sequencers back online. Their voices fell away after they went around the corner.

Stepping into a now empty corridor, he reached an intersection halfway down. He could go straight, left or right. The choice didn't matter so much, until something of interest caught his eye. Up ahead, near the bend, a technician was working at one of the access panels. Sparks flew up and over the partially opened door. Yamane approached and watched him work. He wondered what kind of a future awaited the unknown crewman.

Dimly lighting the darkened hallway, a cascading stream of yellow beads of light fell onto the deck. Yamane could not take his eyes off the sight. He reveled in the simple beauty of their short but spectacular lives.

The crewman shut off his laser torch. After taking off the safety goggles, he inspected his work. A muffled sound came from behind. He looked back over his shoulder. Yamane was gone.

Moving further down the corridor, the steady hum of the ship's power conduits filled his ears. It had been set at a lower frequency range than he recalled. Up above, he found the relays. Tucked inside velthane brackets spaced apart at regular intervals, Yamane saw a dozen pipes of varying widths stretching the length of the corridor. He stopped dead in his tracks. Were they ready for the Deravans? Would they ever be? He figured his fellow crewmembers had asked such a question a million times over.

Yamane started up again. He came across a hatch left ajar. Just as he was about to secure it, he paused when his hands wrapped around the locking mechanism. The cold, hard qualities of the metal made an impression on him. They needed to be just as hard and unfeeling. The Deravans were a formidable enemy, showing no one the slightest inkling of mercy. The only way of winning the war, he thought, was by beating them at their own game.

When he heard several other crewmen approach from around the corner, he moved into the shadows. They were joking about something. He stepped back into the light after they passed. This had been the reason why he came, to gauge the status of the crew and ship before going into battle. After all he had seen and heard, Yamane had the answer for which he sought. He was not disappointed.

Yamane went back the way he came. His lift was still there, waiting for him. He slammed the gate closed and pressed the lighted disk marked "B". The decks passed by at regular intervals, registering in his ears when they did. Clickity-clack, clickity, clack. The time for reflection had ended. Only the future mattered. Yamane checked his uniform one last time. Everything about him, his appearance, his demeanor, even his posture, had to convey the idea he was ready for the Deravans. If he believed this, then the crew would believe it too.

Yamane took his place in the command chair again. "Report."

The r-tech pressed his earpiece a little deeper into his ear canal. "RadAR is picking something up. The signal is strong and definitely heading this way."

"Is it the Deravans?" Yamane asked, fearful of the answer.

"Yes. They blasted out of Earth's orbit shortly after they received the message."

No doubt heading for Mars, Yamane thought. "How long before we reach the *Lexington*?"

"The fleet should rendezvous with the stellar cruiser in forty-seven minutes."

Soon, he thought, very soon.

CHAPTER
30

We glorify rugged wills; but the greatest things are done by timid people who who work with simple trust.

-John La Forge

S.F.S. CORONA

0102 PROXIMA MERIDIAN TIME, AUGUST 30, 2217

"I'm beginning to pick up multiple images on my monitor," the r-tech cried out.

Yamane kept his place in the command chair, not moving. "What is their speed...and how long before they reach the *Lexington?*"

The r-tech's hands fumbled for the information on his console. He turned back. "1.05 stellar velocity, commander. Their ETA is seventeen minutes."

Yamane glanced at the display on his right. To his horror, hundreds of blips had already filled the screen. He turned away, his mind reflexively avoiding what it did not want to acknowledge. The confidence he had in his plan a few short hours before ebbed into a feeling of hopelessness at the sight of so many enemy warships.

Another feeling, almost as strong as the first, hit him with near perfection. Fear? Panic? No. Irony. Yes, that was it. How else could he describe the very best the enemy had to offer, pitted against a wreck of a ship? He looked up at the main screen. The *Lexington* glistened in the distance. Sorrow tugged at Yamane. Images of abandoning ship flashed in his mind.

"The Deravans will be in range of the *Lexington* in ten minutes."

Yamane verified their position again. The blips were there, but in even greater numbers than before. "Have all sub-cruisers assume an attack posture, standby on my mark."

"Defensive computer protocols have been engaged," Landis said to Yamane. "All targeting monitors are online. Pulse cannons are at full power."

The commander leaned back in his seat and surveyed the bridge. He tried to gauge the status of his crew. Will they remember their training and do their job when both sides meet in battle? For that, Yamane did not have an answer. "Distance to the enemy ships?" he asked after glancing at the main screen.

"Sixteen thousand kilometers."

"The Deravans are redeploying their fleet," the r-tech yelled over the sounds of computer systems buzzing around him. Their overall formation, once a solid and unbroken mass of metal and machines, reorganized itself into three lesser-sized squadrons in a matter of seconds.

The efficient manner in which the Deravans executed the maneuver chilled Yamane. "Speed and heading?" he asked.

"Unchanged," the r-tech replied. "They are maintaining their heading toward Mars."

Yamane's ship sat behind and a little above the Antaren dreadnoughts. They were laid out in front of her like twelve breech-loaded shells, ready for use at a moment's notice. Located at the highest point of the stellar cruiser, sat the bridge. And in the middle of the bridge Yamane waited...and worried. The overwhelming numbers at the Deravan's disposal rattled him—and he had good reason to feel as he did. His experiences at Mars and Earth taught him they didn't have the firepower to outfight their determined enemy, but he hoped to outthink them. On this his whole plan rested.

Optimism wrestled against Yamane's fears. Perhaps we can win this fight with little difficulty after all, he thought. A nice sentiment, but it was a lie. Who was he kidding? A single fear had been haunting him from the beginning—that the Deravans could alter course at any moment and fly beyond the range of the *Lexington*. And if they did, Yamane would be right back to where he started—taking them on from a position of weakness. On the other hand, they might also hold their present heading, right into the trap he laid. The odds seemed fifty-fifty, either way.

Doubts crept into his mind. What if—? Yamane could not finish so terrible a thought. Shifting uncomfortably in his chair, he stared at their trajectory marked on the r-tech's targeting grid. The enemy armada held firm; they had not changed course. He should have been pleased, but something deep within told him they were taking too much for granted. "Time to intercept?"

"Six minutes, twenty seconds."

Every tick of the clock forced his hand into a direction he didn't want. Placing his frontline ships in the line of fire was taking a terrible risk, but keeping the enemy fleet on course had to outweigh all other considerations. Ruthless thinking, to be sure, but when the very survival of humanity was at stake, he had no other alternative.

"Signal Commander Moran," Yamane said to Landis. "Tell him to prepare for an assault on the Deravan fleet."

Landis spun around. "Sir?" he gasped, his eyes wide. "You want him to do what?"

"You heard me, Lieutenant," the commander barked back. "When the enemy armada flies within ten thousand kilometers of the sub-cruisers' position, they will fire their thrusters and make their course right for them. Then when Moran's fleet is ten kilometers away from the Deravans, they will fire a five second salvo before circling back, past the *Lexington*. We must ensure the enemy maintains its heading, even if it means risking some of our ships."

Landis shook his head in a knowing way. "Understood, Commander," he smirked. "I'll send the message now."

S.F.S. DRUMMOND
0115 PROXIMA MERIDIAN TIME, AUGUST 30, 2217

In less than a millisecond, decoding algorithms incorporated into the *Drummond*'s transceiver unscrambled Yamane's orders, flashing them across her communication console. "Sir," the c-tech called out, "I am receiving a transmission from the *Corona*. Commander Yamane is giving us the go signal for a direct assault against the Deravan fleet."

Moran brought up his data pad and scrolled down the text. "What are the two distances?"

"Ten and ten."

"Tell him we'll make ourselves nice big fat targets," he said with a broad grin.

The c-tech offered a weak smile in response and then sent Moran's answer.

Repositioning himself in the command chair, he assessed their tactical situation. There, ahead of him, were hundreds of ships, each positioned equidistant from the next. Moran leaned to his right. "What is the distance between the two fleets?" he asked his r-tech.

Beads of sweat glistened on his forehead. "Twelve thousand kilometers, Commander."

"And their heading?"

The r-tech inputted a set of commands into his console. "Unchanged. They are coming right at us, course—zero-zero-seven."

"Not long now," Moran said, almost in the form of a prayer. "Just a little bit more."

"Deravan ships are now eleven thousand kilometers away."

"Almost there," he whispered.

The distinctive sound of the proximity alarm went off. "Ten thousand kilometers."

Moran stood upright. "Now!" he yelled. "Fire up the main engines."

The c-tech signaled all seven ships waiting in line; their guns poised on those enemy vessels in the line of fire. In an act of unanticipated choreography, the thrusters of every sub-cruiser ignited at the same instant. A flash of brilliant white light demonstrated to the dreadnoughts and cargo barges just how exact their timing had been.

Moran's vessel took the point. Coming up about a thousand meters back, three ships on his starboard side and three on his port, the six other sub-cruisers, fanned out like sharpened talons, readying themselves for a quick strike.

The r-tech's attention remained fixed and resolute. Nothing existed for him except the targeting display a few centimeters away. He tracked the enemy's movements until the proximity alarm just to his left rang out a second time. "We've reached the ten kilometer mark," he shouted to the commander after turning back.

Moran's face became tight. "All batteries...commence firing!"

A blaze of red and blue plasma bursts shot across the bows of all seven sub-cruisers. Multiple flashes registered in the distance moments later, and then—nothing.

"What is their course and speed?" Moran shouted out.

The r-tech verified the results. "Unchanged, sir. Pulse blasts have had no effect."

Moran glanced at the astro-clock. They had just enough time. "Give them a second volley."

"I'm inputting the command now."

Every gunner honed in on his prey, locked on, and then fired. Dozens of energy bolts coursed through the cannon chambers, discharging a fraction of a second later. In a repeat of the first salvo, the lethal bursts slammed into the hulls of those ships ten kilometers away, detonating into dazzling fireballs. When the massive bombardment had dissipated, the truth became all too evident. Deravan shields had absorbed the full fury of what the sub-cruisers could throw at them. Without exception, every one of their vessels flew through the barrage, undeterred.

"Hard about!" Moran ordered. "One hundred and eighty degrees."

After he entered the command codes into his console, the nav-tech grabbed hold of two support struts and held on tight. The sub-cruiser's directional thrusters fired on cue. Fighting the forces throwing her forward, the million-ton vessel traveling at 0.35 stellar velocity began buckling. Bulkheads let out deep moans as they contorted under increasing pressure, while deck plates started to pop out of their holds.

"Commander, we're coming around too fast," the nav-tech yelled. "She's not going to make it."

"Hang on!" The *Drummond* suddenly lurched over. Every person on the bridge took hold of whatever was within reach as the sub-cruiser banked hard on her port side.

"Come on, baby," Moran whispered to himself, "don't let me down."

Responding in an almost intelligent way, his ship swung around in a parabolic arc, back towards the *Lexington*.

Moran clutched his data pad tight. "Are the Deravans still pursuing us?"

The r-tech wiped the perspiration from his forehead. "Affirmative, sir. They're holding steady. Course—zero-zero-seven."

S.F.S. CORONA
0119 PROXIMA MERIDIAN TIME, AUGUST 30, 2217

Commander Yamane's ship waited before the crimson disk of Mars. Despite being outgunned by a factor of fifty, he knew they had to be the victors. If not, the enemy armada would snuff out the human race without a second thought. He considered their odds for success. "Twenty to one," he whispered to himself. Too low. More like a hundred to one. He sighed deeply.

"The Deravans will be in range in thirty seconds."

Yamane checked the r-tech's monitor a third time. To his horror, enemy ships encompassed the left of the display; shattered remnants of their once-proud fleet dotted the right. His attention remained fixed on those barely recognizable derelicts floating in the distance. Would they be joining them soon? He lifted his eyes. We'll all know soon enough.

"The Deravans will be in range in twenty seconds."

Yamane swiveled around in his command chair. His face became hard. "Don't press that button until I give the word," he said to the r-tech, his voice deep.

"Aye, sir," he replied. "Ten more seconds."

Every pair of eyes settled on the main screen. "Five...four...three," the crew mouthed in unison, "two...one...zero." High-pitched alarms rang out from every corner of the bridge.

"The Deravans are now in range!"

Yamane exhaled, paused for a second and then said, "Charge up the cells."

Without even looking, Landis' finger came down on that most important of buttons, the one sequencing the final command directive. All three transceivers scrambled the compressed data streams before sending them to the omega band receivers on board the *Lexington*.

A penetrating silence filled the bridge.

"Power signal sent, Commander. The cells should charge up right about now."

The Deravan fleet, positioned at its closest proximity to the *Lexington*, flew past the stellar cruiser. Every gauge and display tied into those cells, however, remained at zero. The electro-magnetic field had not formed. Yamane waited for several moments. A feeling of dread crept up on him. Seconds passed, but still no change. Something had gone wrong.

"The signal isn't going out," Landis stammered.

Now dread and fear gripped Yamane. "Re-initiate the program and send out the signal again."

Landis inputted the sequence a second time. He looked back, his pale face glistening. One second turned into two, then four, and then eight. The c-tech's eyes darted back and forth. "I don't understand," he said in a shaky voice. "Power levels are still at zero."

Yamane rushed over to the communication console and somehow singled out that all-important button amidst a sea of knobs and switches—the one signifying the difference between life and death. Pressing down on it with the heel of his hand three, maybe four times, he then looked up at the main screen. Disaster met him there. They had not stopped the Deravans. Terrible images of what they would soon unleash against Earth flashed before his eyes.

"I've tried everything," Landis complained, "but the signal still isn't reaching the cells."

"Try again," Yamane snapped back with a distant, almost trancelike stare

Hesitation filled the c-tech's eyes. He started to speak, but inputted the directive instead. Shrill noises came from every speaker on the bridge, providing the dim answer. "The transmitters are working perfectly, but something is blocking the outgoing signal."

Walls, ceiling tiles, deck plates—they all pressed in on Yamane. He responded with slow, deliberate steps away from the main screen. In that one instant, everything seemed lost. There was no backup plan for him or for Moran. The Deravans would hit his ships first, and then attack the rest of the fleet without hesitation. Confusion reigned in his mind. He needed a solution, any solution. None came.

Yamane closed his eyes tight. He hoped it would snap him out of his stupor. It didn't work. He opened them again. The frantic scene of Landis yelling into his headset trailed off into a deep silence. Turning the other way, Yamane became acutely aware that the characteristic noises put out by the ship's instruments were also absent. An undeniable feeling of timelessness seeped over him. He found himself being drawn back by the pull of time. Then everything went dark ...

Like a lightning bolt sent down from the heavens, a wall of light struck Yamane. It had been as though he had relived a lifetime's worth of experiences within a span of a few seconds. Trying to shake off the effects of whatever had happened to him, he fell back into the command chair. "The Deravans," he thought. "We still have to generate the electro-magnetic field."

C-tech Landis turned around. "Commander, I'm picking up a low level frequency coming from one of the destroyers. It's identical to the ones I've monitored before." Yamane didn't respond. He just sat there, staring at the screen, covered with a blank expression. "Commander, did you hear me? The *Ruk-Qia* is sending out a message to the other Antaren ships in the fleet."

A pair of disrupter blasts seemed to come out of nowhere, and struck the *Corona* at her midpoint. Alarm bells rang out on the bridge. The dissonant din seemed to shake Yamane out of his stupor. "Status report," he yelled. "How badly have we been hit?"

"Minimally. Only minor damage to the outer hull," Webster replied from his station.

"Triangulate on those two hits. Find out where they came from."

"Commander," Landis shouted, "I'm picking up another transmission. It's coming from the *Ruk-Qia*."

"Can you tap into it?"

"I'll try." His receiver buzzed and hissed. He made a couple of adjustments. It helped a little, but not enough to lock onto the signal. He leaned closer, altering the frequency just a bit more.

"...opportunity of ridding ourselves of Star Force tyranny. I call on all Antaren patriots. Fight for the same cause as the Deravans. Together we can destroy the last remnants of ..." the transmission faded and hissed again—static, and then silence. Landis tried adjusting signal modulation, but the frequency had shifted into an unknown part of the band. With a nearly infinite number of places the transmission could hide, he just sat back, defeated.

"We have been betrayed," Yamane said under his breath. The crushing reality of the implications of the transmission came crashing down on him like a multi-ton weight dropped from a great height. "Without their help, we have no chance."

Another destroyer broke formation and headed for the *Ruk-Qia*. The ship fired several shots at the *Corona* as it flew by. The disrupter bursts passed over them, and into the depths of space.

The alliance between both worlds was fast falling apart. If he didn't regain control now, then every living thing on Earth was as good as dead. "RadAR," Yamane bellowed. "Are you picking up any other Antaren ships siding with the *Ruk-Qia*?"

He wiped off his sweaty fingers first before bringing up the fleet on his scopes. Dozens of yellow dots appeared, but they remained fixed, no movement. "Negative, Commander. Fleet integrity is holding firm."

The r-tech spun around, a look of guarded optimism on his face. "Sir, I've figured out why the signal isn't reaching the *Lexington*. It's being jammed...by the *Ruk-Qia*."

Yamane bolted from his chair and went over to the RadAR station. "Helm, change heading forty-six degrees...speed, 0.50 stellar velocity." He turned to Landis. "Signal the gunners. Have them fire on the destroyer when we get into range. Also, send a message to Commander Moran. His ships must keep the Deravans in place. I don't care how he does it, but we need time to destroy that vessel."

Moran acknowledged the order with his characteristic self-effacing sense of humor.

Yamane returned to the command chair. "Switch views," he called to the nav-tech. "Get a fix on the *Ruk-Qia*, and plot the most direct course to her."

The fleeing destroyer popped up on the main screen. It flew about erratically, attempting to evade pulse cannon locks.

The *Corona* pivoted around and then fired her main thrusters. "That's your course," Yamane said to the navigator. "Stay right with that ship."

The *Ruk-Qia* inexplicably began to slow. Alarm bells went off in Yamane's head. "What's she doing?" he asked himself. Then, for no reason at all, the destroyer stopped dead in space. Before he could respond, the rogue vessel turned and fired on them.

"Incoming!"

Multiple blasts struck the stellar cruiser down the length of her hull, throwing her over in the opposite direction.

Yamane used the railing for support. "Target their engines and return fire," he yelled.

"Sir, my panel is registering an energy discharge of unbelievable power; and it's coming right for us. I've never seen this kind of reading before."

Yamane turned to the r-tech. "Have any Deravan ships broken away from the main body?"

"Negative, Commander. The discharge came from Tal Win-Tu's ship, the *Bok-Nor*."

"Not him, too," Yamane said, the full force of the admission crushing him. His head dropped, bringing his empty hands into view. If the subidor in charge of the Antaren fleet had turned against him, the others would fold like a house of cards.

"The energy wave will intercept us in five seconds."

"All hands, brace for impact," the r-tech cried out.

The wave shot past the *Corona*, mildly buffeting the ship. Hitting the *Ran-Doj* ahead of them, the energy discharge dissipated shortly afterward. "What the—?" Yamane said aloud. He could only think of a handful of times an

Antaren gunner had missed his target at such close range. Despite the mutiny, he considered himself a very lucky man.

The *Ruk-Qia* changed course, right for the *Ran-Doj*. "Looks as though we get two for the price of one," Yamane thought greedily. But just as he was about to open fire, the second destroyer began to slow. It looked like they were trying the same trick as before at first, but when the hull started to buckle, he realized something else was going on.

"Sir, I'm reading a steady drop in their reactor core containment fields."

Even before the r-tech finished speaking, both ends of the vessel bent upward, folding at the point where the energy wave struck the ship. Explosions went off from one end of the hull to the other. The keel suddenly gave way, tearing the destroyer in two. When the aft section came into contact with the center of the blast point, both reactor cores ruptured. The ensuing explosion blasted shards of metallic debris into every direction, and then—nothing.

Landis looked back over his shoulder. "Sir, I'm receiving a signal from the *Bok-Nor*."

Yamane couldn't take his eyes off the screen. "Put the message on."

The screen switched over from the star field to the bridge of Tal Win-Tu's ship.

"I hope I did not alarm you too much," the Antaren said in his characteristic monotone voice, "but you were in the direct line of fire. Timing was critical, and so I did not have the opportunity to warn you about my intentions."

Yamane offered him a nervous smile. "I'd say the first use of the lambda wave would be classified as a success, although I did have my doubts about the target for a second or two."

"Again, my apologies," he replied with no discernable change in his meter of speech. "If I had known about their intentions before this, I would have already dispatched the situation quickly and efficiently."

Yamane believed him. "I'm sure you've figured out that the *Ruk-Qia* is jamming the signal to the *Lexington*. We are prepared to step aside so you can take care of them just as you did with the *Ran-Doj*."

The Antaren hesitated. He suspected Tal Win-Tu was holding back. "I am afraid not. The lambda wave generator has sustained damage, and may take some time before the repairs are completed. Since yours is the closest ship, I defer such a task to you."

The news disappointed Yamane. Another setback. "I understand. Hopefully, Moran can hold out a little longer."

The *Drummond* pivoted around and targeted the next ship in line. "All batteries fire," Moran ordered. The pulse cannons tracked the nearest ship in their sights as the sub-cruisers flew over a small group of Deravan vessels. He turned towards the main screen. Three enemy ships were trying to outflank them.

"We can't let them cut us off." Moran shot a quick look at the navigator's station. "Change course one hundred and twenty degrees. Maybe we can use this opportunity to keep the Deravans within the range of the *Lexington*."

The *Drummond* slowed and implemented the maneuver. "Give them our broadside," he ordered. "All batteries, fire at will!"

The sub-cruisers banked over on their port sides. At just the right moment, the gunners sighted their prey and unleashed a deadly barrage. Multiple blasts struck the ships closest to them. His plan worked. Those vessels making their course for the *Corona* ran into a wall of plasma energy, effectively blocking them. Undaunted, they turned back and headed for Moran's squadron. When the Deravans moved into range, their guns swung around and let loose a salvo of ion fire of their own. Caught off guard by the unexpected move, all seven sub-cruisers sustained multiple hits.

Yamane watched the *Ruk-Qia* trying to take evasive action. The destroyer went up, down, left, and right, all the while maintaining full thrust.

The commander held onto both armrests tight. "Range," he asked the r-tech.

"Fifteen kilometers and pulling away."

"Increase speed so we can overtake them. Have all pulse batteries stand-by."

The hum from the ship's engines increased as the ship accelerated. There was a slight shift in the coloration of the stars on the main screen. The destroyer took evasive action again, but the nav-tech stayed with her, matching his opponent maneuver for maneuver. They fired a couple of shots in haste, but missed by a wide margin.

"Subidor Lan Din-Ny's ship has just entered optimum firing range."

"All batteries stand by." Yamane looked at the RadAR console. The destroyer slipped right into the targeting zone. A feeling of satisfaction pulsed through his body. "Fire at will!"

Every gunner on the *Corona*'s starboard side unleashed a simultaneous barrage. The destroyer tried to maintain a minimal profile against her pursuer, but their strategy proved ineffective. Most of the energy bolts hit their intended targets with surprising precision. Blast after blast detonated in and around her engineering section.

"Now we've got them," the r-tech said, grinning like a cat that had just captured his prey. "They are slowing to 0.34 stellar velocity...0.31."

The *Ruk-Qia* fired several disrupter shots in return, but the destroyer's gunners missed by a wide margin.

"Maintain firing."

A second salvo of weapon fire detonated on the surface of the middle ship. The destroyer listed over on her port side, smoke and fire pouring out of a dozen or more sections.

"My readings show that her main engines are badly damaged."

Yamane didn't want to let this opportunity slip out of his fingers. "What is their weapon status?"

"Main power is dropping. Even if they did get off a shot, their levels are so low that disruptors should not cause any real damage."

"Is the signal still being jammed?"

Landis checked his screen. "Affirmative."

Several blasts struck the *Corona*, rocking the stellar cruiser unexpectedly.

Yamane swiveled the command chair around. "Someone is taking pot-shots at us. Is another Antaren ship siding with them?"

"Affirmative. The *Nok-Pon* circled about and came up from behind." He paused. "Wait a minute...they are charging weapons again."

"What are your orders, Commander?" the nav-tech asked.

"Target Lan Din-Ny's ship first. When she goes, the EM field should generate. Then we'll take care of the *Nok-Pon*."

The nav-tech entered the course change. When the directional thrusters fired, the *Corona* pitched over five degrees past vertical. The heavily damaged destroyer fell out of view for a second, but then reappeared after the *Corona* came upright again.

Just as Yamane was going to give the order to fire, two more blasts struck the *Corona* from behind. "Hold her steady," he said under his breath, ignoring everything else around him. "Just a few more seconds."

The wounded vessel fired off a couple of feeble shots, but with the same results as before.

"All batteries—fire!"

Both sets of pulse cannons easily hit their targets at such close range. Shot after shot tore through the hull of the ship. Devastating explosions sliced through the interior, tearing up decks at will. The weakened containment fields finally gave way.

"My instruments indicate the ship will blow at any time."

Yamane jumped to his feet. "Get us out of here," he yelled. "Flank speed."

Even before he finished speaking, the destroyer went up in a brilliant white ball of light, vaporizing her in an instant. The *Nok-Pon* tried to pull away, but her crew did not react quickly enough. The blast wave struck the ship at nearly point blank range. In a moment, she too was gone.

"Brace for impact," Yamane yelled as the leading edge of the shock wave struck the stellar cruiser. A hail of metallic fragments and compressed energy pockets pounded the ship from stem to stern. The buffeting subsided only after the nav-tech managed to change their course into the detonation zone, the same he would do for a bow shock.

Breathing heavy, Yamane tried to collect his wits. "How badly were we hit?" he asked.

Landis appeared distracted, as though others were talking to someone else at the same time. "I'm getting reports from all over the ship," he replied after taking out his earpiece, "but no one is reporting any significant damage. Mostly radiation burns and system overloads. We got lucky."

"Is the signal still being jammed?"

The r-tech reformatted his screen and made a sweep of the area. The results popped onto his screen. "All scans show negative," he replied. "I think we got the one that counted."

Daring to embrace his hopes again, Yamane gave his uniform a quick tug. "Change course one hundred and eighty degrees." He turned to Landis. "Signal the rest of the fleet. Tell them to prepare for attack. It's time we unveiled our little surprise."

S.F.S. CORONA
0148 PROXIMA MERIDIAN TIME, AUGUST 30, 2217

"Will our signal be strong enough to activate the cells at this distance?" Yamane asked.

"I cannot say for certain with all of the surrounding interference, but I believe so."

"There is only one way to find out," he said under his breath. He got out of the command chair and came up next to Landis. "Charge up the cells."

The c-tech inputted the command sequence. Every pair of eyes on the bridge found the *Lexington*.

Time itself seemed to slow as the seconds clicked off, one after the other. The stellar cruiser sat out there, dead. Yamane's fears started to rise. Just as he was about to give the order again, the ship's hull started to glow.

"My instruments indicate the cells have accepted the command code. They are charging up."

Filled with a deep-seated sense of validation, Yamane watched indicator number one go from zero to a hundred percent power output reading, as the magnitron beam passed through the omega band receiver. The next indicator lit up moments later, followed by number three. When the beam reached all twenty-seven, a viable circuit formed.

The *Lexington*'s dark gray exterior changed. Becoming lighter in tone, the hull gave off a dull red color, then turned to a bright orange. But what happened next even took Yamane by surprise. A ring of white light emerged at the far end of the stellar cruiser. As though the ship had somehow captured a continuous lightning storm and forced it into the shape of a circle, the discharges made their way down the length of the hull; transforming it into brilliant luminance. The *Lexington* blazed with the intensity of the Sun. It was the most magnificent thing Yamane had ever seen.

"Commander," the r-tech called out, "those ships nearest the *Lexington* are starting to slow."

"Confirmed," Webster yelled from his station. "The cells are at full power. My instruments indicate the EM field has achieved a range of just over eighty-five thousand kilometers."

Yamane swiveled the commander chair around, his hopes buoyed. "Have all ships regroup and prepare for a direct assault against the enemy fleet," he said to Landis. "Are the cargo barges in position?"

"Affirmative, Commander. They have just signaled and are awaiting your go-ahead."

He sat upright in his chair. "Tell them—Godspeed."

All seventeen rows of cargo barges, eleven strong, fired their thrusters at the same moment. Blasting away in unison, they flew past the *Corona* as a single entity, like a squadron of fighters performing for the crowds at an air show.

"Contact in thirty seconds." The r-tech bent closer. "The cargo barges will reach their jettison coordinates in five...four...three...two...one...now."

Yamane strained to see the bridges flying off in different directions. Faint glows of exhaust revealed which way they all went. The scene reminded him of a fireworks display on some long-ago Fourth of July celebration. In his mind's eye, he could see the rockets rising higher and higher in the summer sky—all hurtling toward their inevitable outcome. But as impressive as the display might be for a boy of ten, it was nothing compared to what followed next. When the first wave of cargo barges slammed into a wall of Deravan ships, a series of dazzling explosions erupted, one after the other. Flashes of greens, pinks, reds, and blues went off in rapid succession, bathing the bridge in short-lived hues of light. Most of the crew clapped and cheered as they saw ship after ship struck down by the onslaught directed against them.

The next wave struck moments later, and the next, and the next one after that, until every ship had hit its intended target.

"Have the destroyers move into position so they can pick up survivors," Yamane ordered. "Signal the rest of the fleet. Give them the final go code. Now it's our turn."

The seven sub-cruisers led by Commander Moran fell back into a flying wing formation. His ship, the *Drummond*, positioned itself in the middle, with three sub-cruisers on one side, and three on the other. A row of enemy vessels came into view. Because of the EM field, none of them could maneuver, nor could they defend themselves. The gunners sighted their prey and took aim. When the computer got a target, they fired. Bolt after bolt struck the exposed hulls all waiting in line. The blasts easily tore into the ships, detonating deep within. An enemy vessel exploded, followed by two more. A fourth disappeared in a flash of yellow light.

Circling around for another pass, the squadron of tightly packed ships registered even more kills the second time around. Without defensive screens protecting them, the Deravans had been reduced to nothing more than a paper tiger: fearsome in appearance on the outside, hollow on the inside.

Moran sat in the command chair, thoughtful. "How many did we get?" he asked the r-tech.

He punched up the information on his console. "Thirty-seven ships destroyed, seventeen damaged, Commander."

"Change heading one hundred degrees. Bring us around again."

The nav-tech inputted the course correction. Banking over hard on her starboard side, the *Drummond* came out of her parabolic arc and took aim. When the nearest Deravan ships came into range again, Moran unleashed the full fury of what he could throw at them.

"Turn the ship about thirty-seven degrees," Yamane ordered. The *Corona* pivoted around on her axis and applied full thrust. They just barely avoided the dying embers of what had been a Deravan ship only moments before. Three skyjackets darted around the debris and then targeted the next one in line.

"How long before the cells expire?" Yamane asked; his attention fixed squarely on the main screen.

The r-tech craned his neck over. "Four minutes, thirty seconds."

"Bring us in nice and straight," he said. "I don't want to miss a single ship."

Gunners on both sides of the stellar cruiser focused on a cluster of vessels in their sights. After taking aim, they fired in rapid succession. Countless numbers of plasma discharges flew across the vacuum of space in the blink of an eye. Concentrated and tightly packed, those bundles of energy cut through decks and bulkheads, causing a catastrophic amount of destruction along the way. Multiple blasts ripped through the hapless vessels. The first Deravan ship in line went, then the next. Others joined them soon after.

The *Corona* jerked over, and then slowed.

Yamane spun the command chair into the direction of the engineering station. "Ship's status." he yelled above the noise around him. "Why are we slowing?"

"Unknown, Commander," Webster replied. "Power levels are fluctuating."

"Engine room to the bridge," a voice said on the intercom. The sounds of men and women yelling in the background made it difficult for him to differentiate one voice from another.

Yamane wanted answers, and he wanted them now. "This is the bridge.

What's going on down there?"

"I need to shut down the primary generators. They've been damaged by flying debris from our last attack run."

He recoiled at such a thought. How could they stop now? "What about the secondaries?"

"They're around ninety percent, but they won't hold up for long if we—"

"Understood. Do whatever you can but keep those engines going. Bridge, out." Yamane swung his chair around. "How much longer before the electro-magnetic field is lost?"

The r-tech brought up the information on his board. "Less than one minute, Commander."

Yamane glanced at the data pad in his lap. "One minute," he mumbled to himself and then went over the RadAR station. "How many Deravan ships have we destroyed?"

The r-tech looked up. "One moment, Commander," he replied before making a sweep of the area. The screen went dark and then came up again. Little yellow dots popped up in groups of tens and twenties. On the right of his display, a counter ticked off the numbers. "My scope shows three hundred and forty-one enemy ships still remaining."

"Time?" he asked after their numbers sunk in.

"Forty-five seconds."

Yamane went back to the command chair, but didn't sit in it. "Just enough time for one more attack run." He looked over at the nav-tech. "Helm, make your course one-one-eight, right for those ships off our starboard bow. Have every gunner take as many shots as he can before power levels can no longer sustain the EM field."

"Yes, Commander. We'll see how many more of them we can take out."

The *Drummond* flew over three Deravan vessels. All of them were hit by weapons fire, but the damage they inflicted on them was minimal at best. "We let those three slip through our fingers," Moran carped as he stood behind the nav-tech. He shot a quick look at astro-clock. Not much longer. He hurried over to the command chair. "Engine room. What is our repair status?"

"No, the other way!" a voice said, yelling at someone in the background. "Hold on a second." There was a prolonged pause before he returned. "No changes, Commander. The main generators are still down."

"When can you bring them up again?"

"I'm not sure. Maybe ..." his voice became subdued. Moran heard the sounds of a muffled conversation. "I'm sorry Commander, but things are pretty busy down here. I'll signal you again when we can fire them up again.

Engine room, out."

"Commander, power levels on board the *Lexington* are dropping off," the r-tech said after he had verified the information displayed on his screen.

Yamane brought up his data pad. He accessed the last two paragraphs of his operation. "How much time before the entire field collapses?"

"It's almost gone now. Probably in the next twenty seconds."

"Signal the fleet," he said to Landis. "Have them fall back to our position. We'll regroup and then face the Deravans head-on."

The r-tech reformatted his central display. They had run out of time. "Too late, Commander. I'm getting some readings from the Deravan ships furthest away from the *Lexington*."

"Clarify."

"Their internal energy levels are starting to rise. Power outputs are also climbing. They should be operational again in a matter of seconds."

Three Deravan ships broke free from the force that had immobilized them. Firing their thrusters in one sudden burst, they pulled away from the others. Then another ship, a little bit closer to the *Lexington*, overcame the same force holding it as well. Soon, whole clusters of Deravan vessels had regrouped.

Yamane had never been more proud of his old girl. She had performed above and beyond the call of duty. He wanted to see her one last time, while she still carried a quiet dignity and grace about her. "Navigator, switch to the rear view," he ordered. "Bring up the *Lexington*. I want to see her before she goes."

In an instant, a view of the stellar cruiser replaced the image of the Deravans slowly rising from their prolonged slumber. The brilliant glow, which had emanated from the stellar cruiser for the past half hour, quickly subsided, until nothing of its former glory remained. Once again, the *Lexington* had become a dead ship.

"I have six enemy vessels heading right for her. Intercept in fifteen seconds."

Yamane looked away from the screen. "Maintain your course and speed," he forced himself to say.

"But, Commander?" the nav-tech challenged. "Aren't we going to—?"

"There's nothing to save," he snapped back. "I will not risk the loss of a single vessel for something with no strategic value."

Those words pained him to the core, but the truth, no matter how brutal, could not be minimized. Yet, by saying them, he had signed the death warrant of his former ship.

When Yamane brought up his eyes again, he witnessed Deravan vessels fire into the *Lexington* with ion cannons and fusion blasters at nearly point-blank range. The deadly bolts struck the helpless vessel in the midsection. Three others came up from behind and added their firepower to the orgy of death. In every case, they blasted away chunks of the hull with a casual indifference, exposing multiple decks underneath. Their combined firepower cut through the decks like a laser scalpel in the hands of an expert surgeon.

Yamane could only watch from a distance, powerless to do anything about it. Every blow inflicted against her was like a kick in the gut. The *Lexington*, however, had served her crews well; and this was, as he saw it, a fitting end for any ship of war—giving her life for the sake of others.

The fatal blow finally came when all six Deravan vessels fired in unison, slicing the stellar cruiser cleanly in half. Caught in the gravity well of Mars, both sides tumbled away from each other, to their eventual deaths.

Yamane summoned all the strength within him, and said, "Prepare to attack on my mark."

CHAPTER
32

BOK-NOR
DAIETH TIME PLUS SEVEN

Enemy fire struck the *Bok-Nor*. Tal Win-Tu kept his place, unmoved.

"The last hit came close to the lambda wave generator," the communications operator said to him in forced tones. "Containment fields are losing their cohesiveness."

The subidor returned to his station. Around him, forming two concentric rings in the middle of the bridge, operators monitored the course of the battle. Off on the side, near the rear, sat the redundancy officer. "Is there any way we can stabilize them?"

"Affirmative, but it will take time."

Tal Win-Tu looked up. "Bring us about, two-one-five degrees. Speed, 0.47 stellar velocity. Get us out of range of those ships."

Three Deravan vessels swung around from the rear and fired again. Their reinforced neutronium plating repelled the ion blasts, for now.

Tal Win-Tu figured out what they were attempting. A noble effort, but wasted. "New course, zero-four-zero degrees, maximum thrust."

"We cannot, Subidor. The Deravans have boxed us in."

They have not gotten the best of me yet. "What about the disrupters? Can they be fired?"

"Not at this time. Main power is still channeled into the lambda wave generators."

He went to the weapons station. "Fire on the lead ship and then plot a course between the other two. We can slip through before they know we are gone."

The weapons operator looked up at the subidor. "I do not believe this will—"

Tal Win-Tu glared back. "Do it," he ordered.

Shrinking back in his chair, the operator inputted the command code. Three loosely connected lambda wave streams struck the nearest Deravan ship at her midsection, and then dissipated. The vessel began to slow. Her smooth, angled lines, so flawless, abruptly changed. The point where the streams struck the ship started to collapse upon itself. When the hull finally buckled, multiple flashes of light pierced through the breaches.

"Reverse course, maximum thrust," Tal Win-Tu ordered. "Put as much distance between us and that vessel."

When the engine core fell into the effect, containment fields dropped to zero. A sudden release of energy engulfed the entire vessel. Moments later, it was gone.

Tal Win-Tu returned to his station, satisfied. "Charge up the generators," he said to his engineering operator. "Bring us about and target the next ship on your display."

S.F.S. CORONA
0238 PROXIMA MERIDIAN TIME, AUGUST 30, 2217

Several hits echoed throughout the *Corona*. "Is there any way we can increase power levels to the pulse cannons?" Yamane asked in a state of profound frustration.

"They are already at five percent above maximum. If we push them any higher, their components will burn out." Another ten-kiloton ion blast detonated on their hull. A number of lights dimmed before coming up again.

"Three enemy vessels have crossed our targeting plane," the nav-tech yelled out, his voice sounding grave.

Yamane swung the command chair around. "Hard about," he ordered. "Target those ships and fire when they're in range."

The *Corona* made an abrupt course change and locked onto the Deravan vessels a short distance away. Reacting to Yamane's aggressive move, they veered towards their left, and then cut to the right like a gazelle doing anything it could to escape a lion closing in for the kill. The nav-tech stayed with them.

"Commander, the lead vessel has just entered optimum range."

Yamane wiped the sweat from his forehead. The back of his hand glistened in the dull red light. "Signal the gunners. Have them fire at will."

A flurry of plasma bolts pounded the hull of the enemy vessel five kilometers away.

The central Deravan ship began to waver. Dropping back somewhat, the other two tried to provide cover. Their ploy didn't work. A second volley from the *Corona*'s gunners slipped through the narrow gap and slammed into the vessel. Defensive screens absorbed the initial damage inflicted against it, but as multiple blasts struck the weakened hull, the Deravan ship slowed.

"Sir, I'm picking up some power fluctuations coming from their location. It looks like they're trying to bolster their reserves."

A triumphant expression appeared on Yamane's face. "Continue firing."

Additional plasma bursts detonated on the surface of the enemy ship, until their defensive screens finally gave way. The next hit slipped through a wide gap that had formed on the hull, and the vessel transformed into a ball of crimson light. "Gotcha!" Yamane yelled with his fist clenched in front of him. "Not so strong, after all."

The two surviving ships swung around and fired on the *Corona*. Concentrated bundles of photonic energy pierced her outer hull. Alarm bells rang out on the bridge. "Commander," Webster yelled, "I have breaches on decks seven through nine."

Yamane opened the intercom. "Damage control, initiate emergency procedures on decks seven, eight and nine." He repositioned himself in his chair, only faintly aware of the smoke wafting up from the lower decks. "Target those ships. Keep firing until their defensive shields buckle. That's their weakness. They can deflect our weapons, but only for a short while."

The Deravans pivoted around and came at the *Corona* a third time. "Enemy ships approaching on our port side!" the r-tech cried out. Yamane clung to both armrests. Four ion bursts detonated at strategic points along the surface of the stellar cruiser, causing the vessel to roll onto her starboard side.

"Return fire and don't let up until they're destroyed," Yamane ordered with fiery eyes.

Scores of plasma blasts struck both ships circling back for a fourth pass.

The Derevans retaliated with a barrage of weapons fire of their own. Hit after hit went down the *Corona*, stopping just short of the bridge.

Landis spun around in his chair. "Sir, their last run severely damaged the port landing bay. Numerous fires are raging out of control."

The demands of command were beginning to wear him down. Deravans were pounding him from every side, with no end in sight, and crew members expected him to know what to do about it. "Send whatever repair teams are available."

Commander Neu brought his ship alongside the *Drummond*. The latter could still maneuver, but just barely. She had suffered a tremendous amount of damage at the hands of the Deravans. Main power had dropped below fifty percent, half her guns no longer operated, and the primary generators were shot. If the secondaries went, they would be dead in the water.

"Commander Moran, fall back to coordinates zero-seven-one," Neu suggested after he checked the nav-tech's scope. "We'll regroup there so the Deravans cannot outflank us."

"Our engines are a bit sluggish, but we'll do our best."

Neu took the point, the *Drummond* not far behind. Three Deravan vessels off their port bow pivoted around and set a course right for them. Three others on her starboard side did the same. He had been so intent on protecting Moran's ship that he had missed their strategy altogether, until the proximity alarm sounded.

"Commander, I have one...five...eight...twelve enemy vessels on an intercept course."

Neu jumped out of his chair and went to the nav-tech's station. "Plot a heading out of here," he ordered. "I don't care where, just get us moving."

The navigator looked up, fear registering in his eyes. "I can't. They've cut us off."

Neu slammed the console with his hand. "How could I have been so stupid?" He turned to his c-tech. "Signal the *Drummond*. Have them concentrate their guns on enemy ships closest to us. If we're lucky we can take a couple out and create an opening."

He shook his head in a languid manner. "Aye, Commander, I'll send the message now."

Deravan ships drew even closer, tightening their chokehold on the encircled sub-cruisers. Both trapped vessels fired back, but it was a feeble attempt at best. Blue, white and red bolts all found their target, but enemy screens held.

Just as the *Adler*'s gunners prepared themselves for another volley, the Deravans pivoted their guns around and unleashed a vicious response. Numerous explosions registered along the hull of Neu's ship. The sub-cruiser shuddered after each ten-megaton blast detonated on her surface, throwing the bridge crew from their stations. Most of the lights on the bridge went dark. Neu waited for them to come up again, but they didn't. He crawled back to the command chair. Just as he pulled himself up, the emergency lights kicked in.

"We need main power restored," he yelled above the noise around him, "or the Deravans will finish us off for sure."

"I'm trying," the e-tech snapped back. "Just give me a minute." He found his portable light and shined it on the console. Bringing up a schematic of their semitronic systems, he tried to get a reading on the main plasma cables. Three of them did not register any power at all. "My boards indicate four lines are still intact."

Neu hurried over. "Can you bypass, get power restored up here?"

"Patience...patience," the e-tech commented to himself as he inputted a series of commands into his console. Plasma energy shot past the damaged area, and then became reintegrated with the main cable at the next junction. "I think that's it," he said in an optimistic tone.

Lights came up first, followed by navigation, communications, engineering, and RadAR.

Neu returned to the command chair. "What is our weapons status?"

"Only half of our pulse cannons are operational. As far as I can tell, they are hovering at seventy percent power levels."

"Commander, I'm getting damage reports from all over the ship," the c-tech called out.

Turning back, he replied, "Have emergency teams initiate rescue protocols."

An intense flash of bright light flooded the bridge. Even with a barely functional screen, he could clearly see the source of the explosion.

"I can't be sure, but I think that was the *Dykstra*," the r-tech concluded. "She had been in that general area before the explosion."

Neu didn't have the time to acknowledge their loss. The *Adler* was outnumbered and outgunned. If he didn't come up with a way out of this fast, they would join the sub-cruiser soon.

"Target the nearest ship. Make sure—"

The Deravans fired first. Neu grabbed the command chair and held on tight. Lights on the bridge dimmed as two blasts struck them hard. "Helm, get us out of here," he yelled. "I don't care if you have to ram those ships, just get us out of here."

The nav-tech spun around. "What about the *Drummond*? We can't just leave her behind."

Another blast slammed into their side. A portion of the outer hull gave way. "Commander, I have hull breaches on deck eight."

Anger flashed on Neu's face. The Deravans were pounding his ship right out of existence, one painful hit at a time. He, however, had come too far to just roll over and die. "Seal it off," he replied in a sharp tone.

Two more hits struck the wounded vessel. The bridge went dark again for a brief moment.

"If we don't get out of this turkey shoot soon, they'll tear us to pieces."

"Power levels are dropping. I don't think we can last much longer."

Eruptions of light filled the main screen a second time. Neu prepared himself for the end. But then, as if a miracle had taken place, multiple blasts struck the Deravan ships surrounding them. They fired in return, but were met with a ferocious response.

A dreadnought, two destroyers and fourteen skyjackets flew over the *Adler*. The tightly packed squadron fired again. A Deravan ship went up in the ball of light, engulfing two other vessels on either side. In a matter of seconds, all three of them were gone.

A darkened silhouette flew out of the shadows and finished off another enemy ship directly ahead. The Sun crested past the rim of Mars, bathing the ship in its light. Tall white letters—*S.F.S. CORONA*—stood out against her dark gray hull.

A wave of fatigue washed over Yamane. He had been going non-stop since the battle had begun. Deciding on which heading, speed, target, and course of action again and again during the course of the battle had taken its toll on him. He was spent. After rubbing his eyes, he turned back towards Webster's station. "What is the status of the Deravan fleet? How many ships do they have left?"

"I count one ninety-seven in all," the major replied.

The news buoyed Yamane's spirits. His plan was working. Though tempting, he didn't want to get too confident too soon. *Pride goes before a fall.* "This is a good start, but we're not out of this yet."

The r-tech stiffened. "Commander, I have multiple targets zeroing in on our position," the sound of surprise in his voice. "I count twelve in all."

Yamane turned around. "Back us out of here. We can't make it a fight if we're boxed in."

The r-tech made an adjustment on his scope. "Correction. Another nine enemy vessels have come up from behind. There is no way out."

Anger registered on Yamane's face. "They set the bait and we took it," he said with both hands tightly balled, disappointed in himself.

Two hits rocked the *Corona*. "Return fire. Try to keep them at bay."

Before Landis could issue his orders, the Deravans retaliated with another barrage. Hit after hit blasted the stellar cruiser, tearing away chunks from the outer hull.

"Commander, I am receiving damage reports from all over the ship." He stopped and bent closer. "Emergency teams have already been dispatched."

Another series of hits rocked the stellar cruiser. Lights flickered off and then came up again, though not as strong as before. Even more smoke from below found its way onto the bridge.

Yamane swiveled his chair around. "Is there any way we can hold them back?"

"I don't think so, sir. There are just too many Deravan vessels out there."

Think. Think. Yamane caught sight of his data pad. He brought it up and quickly scanned through the operation, but none of his contingency plans even remotely covered this scenario. His hand fell back down into his lap. He felt as though they had failed... then an idea came to him. Yamane went over to the r-tech. "Our only choice is to break out. Plot the most direct course out of this cocoon they've formed around us." He turned to Landis. "Send a general distress call. See if there are any nearby ships. Maybe they can thin the enemy out a bit."

The c-tech bobbed his head up and down in a knowing way. "Yes, sir."

When Yamane resumed his place in the command chair, he opened the intercom. "Engine room," he said in an urgent tone. "This is the bridge."

"Go ahead, bridge." Kershaw replied without a hint of surprise in his voice, as though he had been expecting his signal.

"We're in a bit of trouble and we'll need your engines now like we've never needed them before."

Not to worry," he reassured him. Yamane felt himself comforted by Kershaw's confidence. "I've been monitoring the progress of the battle, and I'm already set up for emergency acceleration. You'll get all the power you need."

"I knew you wouldn't let me down," he said warmly. "Yamane, out."

Three Deravan ships fired on them again. All three blasts hit their marks, shaking the bridge with unequaled ferocity. The assurance about their chances for victory Yamane experienced only moments before ebbed away, leaving nothing but an empty hole of uncertainty and doubt. He hated the Deravans for that.

Yamane cursed himself for letting the enemy get to him like that. He refocused his attention back on the main screen. "Make your course, one-six-four. Standby on my mark."

The enemy came around from behind and made a course right for the *Corona*.

"I think they're planning on ramming us. Contact in seven seconds."

Let's see who has trapped whom. "Now!" he ordered. "Maximum thrust."

The *Corona* shot forward in a burst of acceleration. Caught off-guard by the unexpected maneuver, the Deravans began to fall behind.

"RadAR shows the Deravan ships in our flight path are holding steady."

Yamane leaned forward. "They're drawing a line in the sand," he said to himself.

"Twenty kilometers and closing."

"Signal pulse batteries. Have them lay down a suppressive fire directly in front of us. I don't care if their barrels melt, they have to continue firing at all costs."

"But, Commander?" Landis objected. "If they miss just one ship, we'll be destroyed in the collision."

"Fifteen kilometers."

"We don't have much of a choice. It's this or nothing."

A look of resignation settled on Landis' face.

A wall of multi-colored plasma bursts detonated in the distance. Blooming into enormous fireballs, Deravan ships in the area fell behind the curtain of light.

"Have we created an opening yet?" Yamane yelled.

The r-tech flipped a couple of switches. "I can't tell," he replied after checking his scopes. "Plasma discharges have rendered RadAR useless."

"Contact in five seconds."

Yamane cleared his throat and sat upright in the command chair. "All hands, brace for impact." Even before the words had dissipated in the smoky bridge, the *Corona* lurched downward with tremendous force. The nav-tech tried to compensate, but the multiple explosions going off around them became too much for the ship's stabilizers. Another series of blasts pushed the vessel over several degrees past vertical.

"We have hull breaches on decks two, four, and seven," Landis yelled above the noise.

Yamane looked ahead, hoping he could see stars shining through the melee. The main screen, however, revealed a continuous wall of fire, marked by shadowy outlines of Deravan vessels right behind. It was an awe-inspiring sight of color and devastation that both delighted and terrified at the same time.

"Our speed has dropped to 0.62 stellar velocity."

Yamane braced himself. "Hang on."

Another blast slammed into the *Corona*.

"We are now at 0.47 stellar velocity."

"Commander!"

The stars, which the energy discharges had blotted out for what seemed like an eternity, re-emerged. The buffeting subsided as soon as the stellar cruiser cleared the Deravans' line of fire.

Yamane swung his command chair around. He drew in a couple of breaths. "What is the status of our fleet?" he asked the r-tech in an even tone.

"Just a minute, sir." After flipping a couple of switches, the requested information scrolled down the left side of his screen. "There are seven dreadnoughts, twenty-two destroyers, fifty-one skyjackets, and ..." A smile appeared on his face. "I don't know how they've done it, but all five Min fighters are still with us."

"And the Deravans? How many ships do they have remaining?"

"Fifty-two vessels in all."

Yamane turned towards the engineering station. "What about our ship?"

Major Webster inexplicably rose from his console and went right over to him. "Only twenty-seven pulse cannons are still operational," he said in a low whisper. "Power levels are hovering just above sixty-eight percent. Most of the RadAR antennas have been blasted away, reducing our effective range to five hundred kilometers."

Enemy fire struck the *Corona* again. As had happened so many times before, the bridge went dark for a second or two, before the lights kicked back in.

"Three Deravan ships are coming up on us fast."

When Yamane brought the command chair around, they fired their weapons a second time. "Get us out of here," he ordered.

The nav-tech inputted a course correction. The stellar cruiser didn't respond. He tried again, but the results were the same. "Something's wrong. I'm not getting a response." Two more hits rocked the *Corona*.

Subidor Tal Win-Tu's ship, the *Bok-Nor*, took the point. Two other dreadnoughts sat further back. Accompanying destroyers and skyjackets took up a position behind them and provided cover. Twenty kintars away, a squadron of Deravan ships waited. Neither side moved. Neither side blinked.

Tal Win-Tu studied his cunning foe. Though they outnumbered them by a ratio of ten to one, he did not consider their superior numbers much of an advantage. The loss of four dreadnoughts early in the battle had gotten his attention soon enough. With the implementation of the lambda wave, the tide had turned in their favor somewhat, especially since the Deravans did not seem to have a defense against the weapon. The one thing he hadn't factored in was the problem of wave instability. Not only did they have difficulty keeping the generator from imploding, but the focused beams of energy sometimes veered away in unexpected directions. Several clean misses resulted before a team of engineers figured out a way to correct the problem. The weapon was online again, though the solution required longer charge times between uses.

"The generator is set and ready for firing," the communications operator said to Tal Win-Tu.

"We will have to make every shot count on this run. What is the range of enemy ships?"

"They are holding steady at twenty-one hundred kintars."

Tal Win-Tu drew in a deep breath and then exhaled. "Signal the other two dreadnoughts. Form up and keep tight. Have them fire on my mark."

The once darkened vessels became brightly lit as focused streams of energy flew out of lambda wave dischargers. Crossing the gap in less than a nil tek, they hit their targets with unparalleled precision. Soon after, enemy ships started to implode.

"How long before the generators—"

"Subidor!" the RadAR operator called out in a high voice. "I read another nine vessels heading right for us."

Tal Win-Tu went to his station. "Where did they come from?" he asked.

"I do not know. They appeared out of nowhere."

He went to his weapons officer. "How long before the generator is recharged?"

The operator checked his boards. "Another two tal teks."

The subidor turned and faced the main screen. "That is why those ships did not take evasive action," he commented to himself. "They sacrificed themselves, knowing our weapon took time to get set up again." He went back to his station. "Communications, signal the other ships. I want the destroyers and skyjackets to form up into three tightly packed bundles. Each group will fire a sustained burst against every enemy vessel. We will attack on my—"

"Subidor, I am getting some unusual readings from the *Tok-Von*," the operator interrupted. "Their wave generator is destabilizing."

"Can you get them on the radio?"

"Too late. The field has collapsed."

A small explosion erupted in the mid-section of the dreadnought. For once, the subidor hoped it had been from a Deravan hit. But what followed dispelled any hopes he may have embraced. The ship began to twist and contort, acting as though she could resist the inevitable. Both her bow and aft sections began to tilt upwards, until the vessel succumbed to the forces working against her. Metal plates creased and then ruptured against the tremendous pressures focused on the increasingly shrinking area. Tal Win-Tu could only imagine what those poor souls trapped on board were experiencing.

"Have all ships pull back," he ordered. "Try and get as much room as possible between us."

The dreadnought broke apart in several places, causing a series of lesser explosions to go off along her hull. When the engine section came into contact with the effect, the entire vessel became luminescent for a moment, and then vanished inside a ball of light. Moments later, the *Tok-Von* was gone.

Tal Win-Tu leaned back against the railing. He felt weak, but not defeated. "Helm, set your course for those ships. We attack at once."

Another explosion echoed throughout the *Corona*. The smoke on the bridge made it difficult for Yamane to see. "Can we increase power to the pulse cannons?"

"I'll try, Commander, but a number of systems are no longer responding."

"Do what you can."

"Commander. I can't raise the engine room. Internal communications have been knocked out."

Two more blasts pierced the ship's weakened hull. The *Corona* listed over even further. What had been a minor nuisance now became a major concern.

"Get a message to Lt. Commander Kershaw. I don't care what it takes. He must get the engines up and running again."

"Yes, Commander." The officer saluted and then hurried off the bridge.

Yamane made his way over to the communications console. Every breath of putrid smoke burned his lungs just a little bit more. "Are you certain our message was sent out?" he choked.

"The distress signal is definitely going out. It repeats every fifteen seconds."

"Then why hasn't anyone come to our aid?" Yamane asked. Despite feeling an intense frustration that bordered on anger, he fought for control, knowing he couldn't afford to let it cloud his thinking.

"Commander, a ship has just entered my scope. It is heading in our direction."

Yamane glanced at the RadAR console. His heart sank. The Deravans were coming in for the kill, and there was absolutely nothing he could do about it. Rather than surrender, he focused his gaze at the main screen and accepted whatever fate befell him and his crew. But as the ship circled around and made their course for them, Yamane noted something familiar about the outline. It wasn't a Deravan ship at all. "That's a dreadnought," he said, visibly relieved.

"Their call sign indicates it's the *Bok-Nor.*"

Tal Win-Tu popped onto the screen. "Sorry we took so long," he said in his typically stoic manner, "but we had a little problem to contend with."

"Better late than never."

The screen switched back. The Antaren vessel swooped in and took aim at six enemy ships making another attack run against the *Corona.* Without any warning, their weapons fired. A number of hits registered against their hulls, punctuated by small flashes of light detonating on the surface of each ship.

"Full reverse," Yamane ordered. "Try and get us out of here while the Deravans are occupied with the *Bok-Nor.*"

The nav-tech punched the information into his console. Nothing happened. He tried again, but with the same results. His chair spun around. "Commander, we've just lost the secondaries."

"What about weapons? Can we still defend ourselves?"

"Power levels have dropped below thirty percent. Even if they do score a hit, the Deravans' shields will easily repel the blasts."

Yamane fell back into his chair. It felt like someone had lowered a heavy weight onto him, steadily crushing the life out of his already drained body and mind. Sooner or later, the Deravans would recognize just how vulnerable they were, and come in and finish them off. He looked down and stared at his empty hands. Yamane felt as though he had failed his crew. *Not a fitting end at all*, he thought, *not at all.*

CHAPTER
33

The choice between life and death is ever recurrent. In varying forms it appears whenever a new adaptation is needed or a new potential is ready to be born.
-Frances G. Wickes

S.F.S. CORONA
0449 PROXIMA MERIDIAN TIME, AUGUST 30, 2217

A warm, gentle breeze blew onto the bridge. Lost in his thoughts, Yamane paid it little attention. Then he heard the faint sounds of speaker static; a small miracle, considering the amount of noise swirling around him. Lifting his head a bit, Kershaw's unmistakable voice came from his chair's right armrest. Just then, the consoles around him started to come alive. RadAR popped up first, then communications, navigation, engineering, life support, weapons, until every system seemed to be operational. Crewmembers watched in stunned silence.

Though he was pleased, it didn't make any sense to Yamane. He knew how good an engineer Kershaw was, but this feat surpassed even his skills as a magic maker.

"Engine room to Commander Yamane," Kershaw called out a second time. "Please respond."

"This is the bridge," he replied after making a quick scan of the stations nearest him. "I don't know how you did it, Stan, but we are at full power up here."

"Verified, Commander," Webster said, jumping in. "Weapons, RadAR, directional thrusters, main engines—I could go on. They have all been fully restored."

Yamane shook his head in response. "How did you manage such a feat?"

Kershaw did not respond at first. "Well...I...I'm not sure how I should answer your question...maybe we can ..."

He was right. Now was not the time. "Understood," Yamane replied. "Bridge, out." He rose to his feet. "Weapons status."

"Fully charged and ready for action."

"Hard about, one hundred and eighty degrees. Signal the rest of the fleet. Have them rendezvous at our position."

"Yes, Commander," Landis replied. "Right away."

Yamane pivoted in his chair around. "Deravan ships," he said to the r-tech, "How many, and where are they?"

"I'll check, sir." A host of small yellow blips appeared on his screen after a simple flip of a switch. "I have them on my boards. They are located ahead of us, in groups of threes and sixes."

"How many of them are left?"

He seemed to do the math in his head. "Twenty-five."

Yamane leaned forward, never taking his eyes off the main screen. "And on our side?"

"Not including the *Corona*, we have seven dreadnoughts, twenty-one destroyers, fifty skyjackets, seven sub-cruisers, and five Min fighters." His response was efficient and to the point, but with a tinge of optimism coloring each word.

Thinking about the ratios helped. "I would say the odds have finally swung in our favor, though I wouldn't count the Deravans out just yet." He went to Landis' station. It was time to finally end this thing. "Signal the fleet. Have them form up on our position."

"Sir?"

Yamane's attention remained fixed on the twenty-five enemy vessels lined up against him twelve thousand kilometers away. "No subtlety, no tricks," he said under his breath, "just out-and-out brutal force against brutal force."

"Yes, sir," Landis replied in a soft voice. "I'll send the message."

Yamane resumed his place in the command chair. Nestled between the armrest and his leg, his data pad caught his eye. He picked up the small semitronic device and turned the screen towards him. Text streamed past the small display, stopping only when he reached the last line of the operation. He read the words aloud. "Victory will only be achieved if you keep your resolve to the end—no matter the cost." Yamane wasn't quite sure why he had finished his plan with that particular sentiment, but after what they had gone through, it seemed a fitting way to bring the battle to a conclusion.

He rose to his feet. Taking in the bridge, he realized he had never felt more proud of his crew than at this moment. "Signal the fleet. We will commence our attack on my mark." He drew in a deep breath, paused for a second, and then said, "Make your heading zero-zero-one—right down the Deravans' throats."

Every ship under his command fired up their main thrusters.

Yamane clenched both hands together into fists and summoned up the last little bit of his waning strength. In the background, faintly at first, he heard the r-tech call out the distance between them and the Deravans. "Ten thousand meters...nine thousand...eight...seven."

"We will enter their firing range in five seconds."

"Maintain course and speed."

"Six thousand meters."

Small bursts of light went off in the distance. They looked like the flashes of a camera at a dignitary's press conference. The experience gave the moment a surreal quality. But then the reality of their situation hit him with unquestioned ferocity. Blast after Deravan blast detonated all around them, briefly lighting up the bridge after each explosion.

Yamane held firm. "Return fire as soon as we are in range."

A second wave of explosions detonated in front of them. The *Corona* took evasive action, before straightening out again.

The proximity alarm went off. "The Deravan ships are now in optimum range."

"All batteries—fire at will!"

Having already sighted and locked onto the enemy ships, every gunner opened fired on their prey. Dozens of plasma bursts and disrupter bolts crossed the distance between them in a fraction of a second. Hit after hit slammed into each targeted vessel. With no hint of movement or acquiescence, as though this was some kind of test of wills, they just sat there, taking it.

The attack had a devastating effect on them. One of their ships went, then another, until all six were gone.

Six more enemy vessels moved forward, taking the place of the ones they lost. They, however, suffered the same fate as before. The next six took their place, and like their predecessors, they just sat there, holding their ground.

Yamane sat in stunned silence. He couldn't understand why the Deravans weren't defending themselves. "What is our range?" he asked the r-tech.

"Two thousand meters and closing, Commander."

Yamane's fleet of ships passed over the seven remaining enemy vessels, held in place as though some unseen force prevented them from acting. The seven sub-cruisers bringing up the rear targeted the ships coming up on them fast. The Deravans struck first, vaporizing two skyjackets right away, and then striking the *Rostov* in her aft sections. Plumes of black smoke started billowing out of her hull.

Now Yamane understood their strategy. "Break off attack," he ordered. "All ships pull up."

He did not give the order in time. Deravan gun emplacements swung around and fired on the *Chadwell*, hitting her bridge in the first volley. Three more hits into the ship's engineering section quickly ended her existence.

"Deravan ship coming over our port bow," the r-tech called out.

"Evasive maneuvers," Yamane ordered. "Heading—one-seven-eight."

The *Corona* fired her thrusters, bringing her parallel to the enemy vessel passing in the opposite direction. Seizing their opportunity, both vessels fired at each other at point blank range.

The *Corona* violently shook after each blast detonated on her hull, but she gave as good as she got. Repeated hits overwhelmed the Deravan ship's defensive screens, exposing it to plasma fire. The next bolt tore through the hull. A pair of other blasts finished them off.

Yamane wiped his sweaty hands on his pant legs, his heart pounding in his chest. "How many ships do they have left?" he yelled out.

"My scope indicates there are only four remaining."

"Four. Let's be careful on our next run," he warned. "You never know with them."

The r-tech bent closer to his screen. After making a couple of adjustments, he said, "The Deravans are changing course—heading right for us."

"I knew it. Back us away from them, flank speed!"

The *Corona*'s engines hesitated at first, but then kicked in and started to pull away.

"Time to impact?"

"Twenty seconds."

"We only need a clean shot," Yamane whispered to himself.

"Fifteen seconds to impact."

A torrent of thoughts filled his mind. After they had come so close, now it appeared the Deravans had gained the upper hand against them.

"Ten seconds."

The lead Deravan ship exploded. Yamane looked up. The one next to it followed soon after. "What the—"

Before he got another word out, the *Bok-Nor* flew overhead. Pivoting around on her axis, she took aim and fired on the two remaining ships. Yamane rose out of his chair. "Target the same ship," he ordered, relief punctuating each word.

The gunners locked onto the nearest vessel and fired. Tal Win-Tu's vessel did the same. Moments later, it was gone.

Flying through the waning fireball, Yamane expected to see the lone Deravan ship on the other side. It was nowhere to be found. He figured the blast took care of their problem for them, until the r-tech got his attention. "Commander, my scope shows the enemy pulling away." He then cocked his head over. "If these readings are right, they are only traveling at 0.01 stellar velocity. It's almost as if they want us to catch them."

"Or maybe they suffered damage in the blast." He turned his chair towards Landis. "Signal the other ships and have them close in. I don't want our prize to slip through our fingers."

The c-tech turned back and offered a quick nod.

"You've done it, Commander," Webster congratulated from his station. "We've beaten them." A number of other officers verbalized similar sentiments.

Yamane didn't respond. Instead, he looked up at the ceiling and slowly exhaled, wearing an expression of satisfaction. He wanted to celebrate with the crew, but the Deravans hadn't been defeated just yet. Only when that ship surrendered would he permit himself the luxury of acknowledging their victory. "What is their status?" he asked the r-tech.

"The Deravan vessel is one thousand meters off our quarter panel, boxed in by three Antaren dreadnoughts. It's not going anywhere."

Yamane pivoted around in his chair. "Are the Deravans sending out a distress call," he asked Landis, "or offering their surrender? Anything?"

Both eyes darted back and forth. "No, Commander. They are just sitting there."

"Strange." He pushed out of the command chair and went over to the navigator's station. Something about this whole thing felt wrong. "Bring us in nice and slow. I want to get a better look at what's going on."

The *Corona* fired several short burst from her thrusters. The stellar cruiser drifted towards the enemy ship at a slow but steady rate.

"All engines stop," Yamane ordered after they had come within five hundred meters.

"All stop," the nav-tech replied.

Yamane went before the main screen. He studied their once-formidable enemy for several moments. What they had up their sleeve, he couldn't even begin to guess. "Do your instruments reveal anything?"

"Negative, Commander. Every scan has come up negative."

"Some things never change," he commented to himself.

"Wait a minute." The r-tech pressed the receiver in his ear a little closer. "I am picking up a power buildup." He paused. "I don't think it's their weapons, however. The signature is different."

Yamane took two steps back. "Are you certain?"

"Confirmed. I ran a second scan. The results are the same."

"Maybe they have something else in mind." He paused and gave the Deravan ship a good, long look. Studying the opaque, triangular-shaped vessel before him, he hit upon an idea. "Set the transmitter to 1998 megahertz."

"Sir?" the c-tech asked. "I'm not sure I understand."

"You have your orders, Lieutenant. 1998 megahertz."

Landis was about to object again, when he gave an affirming nod, and entered the frequency change into his console. "The channel is open, Commander."

"This is Commander Yamane to the Deravan ship. Please respond." The receiver replied with static. "I repeat. This is Commander Yamane. Do you read me?"

The main screen switched over to a view of something else. A lone figure materialized out of nothing. Yamane felt the hair on the back of his neck stand on end. Shadowy in appearance, the Deravan seemed to be in a state of flux, becoming translucent for a brief period of time and then turning solid again, as though he drifted in an out of their dimensional plane. Behind him—a wall of black—radiating out into a seemingly endless realm of darkness. In the middle of what looked like a head were two red eyes. They glowed with a fiery intensity of hate and rage. A person could not look upon them and not feel a chill right down to the bone. No; it went much deeper, darker. He could not help but believe they were the essence of pure evil. What the figure embodied went far beyond the physical, into a realm no one understood. How far, Yamane did not dare wonder.

"Your fate has been decided," the otherworldly voice said in a slow and deliberate manner. The screen immediately switched back to the previous view.

Silence filled the bridge. Yamane understood the meaning of the words, but how they applied here, he could not say.

Without any warning, the ship exploded into a fireball of white brilliance. The ensuing blast wave passed over them, and into the infinite void of space. *A final act of defiance*, Yamane thought soberly. He sat back in his command chair. Looking into the face of a Deravan was not something he would soon forget, if at all.

But all this paled when a mixture of relief and satisfaction filled him from within. He finally permitted himself the luxury of acknowledging their victory.

Some quiet congratulations were offered from one officer to another. Others simply sat at their stations, lost in their own thoughts. Yamane gave them every second they needed. He owed the crew that much.

When the time felt right, he got their attention by calling out the nav-tech's name. "Mr. Dunagan," he said softly, "it's time to go home."

EPILOGUE

S.F.S. CORONA
0700 PROXIMA MERIDIAN TIME, AUGUST 30, 2217

The distant blue planet sat in the middle of the main screen. How long it had been there, Yamane did not know. In fact, he wasn't certain just how much time had passed before he realized his thoughts had led him elsewhere. He tried not drifting off during the journey back, but the temptation proved too strong. The memories of his time in the academy, his first time in a Min fighter, getting married to Liana, and so many other things came through the transom of his mind. But no matter how much he longed to escape into the safety of the past, the present always intruded at the most inopportune times. Much of his anxiety stemmed from a fear of what they would find on Earth. This reason more than any other was why he sought escape into himself. But each tick of the clock brought them closer to their final destination.

The mood on the bridge changed. Yamane felt the difference the instant it happened. A vague memory settled upon him. The sensation felt the same as...he slowly rotated the command chair. Standing at the rear of the bridge, as he had done before, Kershaw waited near the entrance, half in the shadows.

Yamane's spirits rose. "How are the repairs going down in engineering?" he asked.

A small smile appeared. "The same. You know, some things never change." He approached the commander with hesitant steps.

"Well, now that you're here, maybe you can answer something for me."

Kershaw's eyes dropped. He seemed to have already figured out what the question was going to be. "You want to know how I restored major systems all over the ship in the middle of the battle."

Yamane's demeanor became more serious. "Yes, that's right. There was no possible way you could have done what you did, and yet, you did it."

A pained look settled on Kershaw as he took a step back. The railing prevented him from going any further. "I'm not sure how I should say this, and so I'll just give it to you straight." He paused, collected his thoughts and then continued. "We were in a bad spot. The ship was getting hit on every side, power steadily failing, and the reactor cores were on the verge of losing containment. I didn't know how we would get out of it alive. Then, in the midst of all the chaos, a sense of peace enveloped me. . The experience was similar to the one I had on Antara, when you went through that test of theirs. Remember the voice? The Antarens called him the High Son. Well, in a moment of desperation, I asked him to save us. It was at this point that all the systems came up again. I don't know how else to describe what happened." Kershaw looked away.

Yamane knew his friend too well. His manner of speech, the searching way in which he talked, suggested this was only half the story. "What else?" he asked. "I know there's more."

"This...wasn't...the...first time I experienced this," he replied with slow, tentative words. "I sensed the same thing when I was lying in my hospital bed after returning from the mission. I had almost fallen asleep when a presence entered the room. I looked around, but no one was there. Then I heard a strange voice tell me I had a decision to make. Frank, it was the High Son, I swear it. . He was there too. I know this sounds crazy, but he was there. He let me know he could help me, but only if I let go of the past and embrace the future. And that's exactly what I did. All the anger and guilt I had been carrying around for years was gone. I felt I had finally been freed from the past. Then I had an overwhelming desire to return to duty. I knew if I weren't in the engine room when the battle started, something terrible would happen. That's when I reported to you on the bridge."

Yamane didn't know what he should say. There was, however, one thing he couldn't easily sweep aside—Kershaw was a changed man. He had sensed it then. He sensed it now. Yamane looked him over a second time and offered a reassuring smile. "When an opportunity presents itself, maybe we can talk more about this later; try and figure it all out. Right now, we have a great deal of work to do, and yours is in the engine room." He extended his hand towards the corridor.

Snapping to attention, he replied. "Of course, Commander. Thank you, sir." He spun around and left the bridge.

Yamane pivoted the chair, back towards the front of the bridge. Warm memories of his old friend still filled his thoughts. "How long before we enter Earth's orbit?"

"Twelve minutes, Commander."

He had drifted off longer than he realized. "No matter." They would soon be home.

A solitary blue sphere filled the screen. Yamane took in the wondrous sight. From this distance, the planet appeared unscathed, as though the attack against Earth never took place. He figured his optimistic appraisal probably stemmed from unusually large pockets of cloud cover at present over most of North America. The systems, however, were somewhat darker than he remembered them being. Perhaps they were simply rain-laden thunderclouds, he thought. Perhaps it was something else—like the effects of a sustained bombardment suffered at the hands of the Deravans.

Growing impatient, Yamane just couldn't wait anymore. "Are you picking up *any* transmissions?" he asked.

Landis retuned his receiver. "All the bands are clear. I'm not reading anything."

"We will reach the Earth in one minute, Commander."

He gripped the armrests of his command chair tight. Time would tell soon enough.

The *Corona* slowed when it was about one hundred miles above the planet. When it brushed up against Earth's upper atmosphere, several sharp jolts shook the vessel, followed by a series of lesser ones. But when her stabilizers kicked in, the growing numbers of vibrations ceased almost immediately. Two directional thruster bursts fired at just the right moment leveled the stellar cruiser out. She came in and assumed a low orbit.

Yamane swiveled his chair around. "Anything yet?" he asked Landis. The c-tech shook his head. The commander turned the other way. "How about RadAR? What do your boards show?"

"There's a lot of interference down there. I've boosted the signal three times already, but I still can't get an accurate reading." He jerked forward. "Hold on...a number of large cities have just appeared on my scope. They are intact, but power levels are at near zero. I'm also picking up enormous craters covering the northern continent. There must be thousands of them down there."

Yamane looked up and stared past the main screen. *How could anyone have survived such a terrible ordeal? Maybe we arrived too late.*

"Wait a minute," the r-tech said. "I've just picked something up." He leaned closer. "I can't be sure, but I think a small vessel is coming up from the surface."

Yamane's breathing became shallow. "Could a Deravan ship have slipped through?" he asked.

The r-tech reconfigured the display. "I don't think so. It's much smaller... about the size of a private shuttle."

Yamane jumped to his feet. He wasn't going to take any chances now that they were so close to their goal. "Send out two of our fighters," he said to Landis. "I want a visual confirmation before that vessel gets too close." Locked and loaded into the launch tubes, a pair of Min fighters shot out of the *Corona* like high-caliber bullets, straight and fast. The unknown popped onto their targeting grids. The pilots angled their ships down and flew over the slow moving vessel in a matter of minutes.

"We have a visual," the lead pilot said. "It looks to be a shuttle of some kind. We are coming around for a second look."

Yamane's attention remained fixed on the speaker imbedded in the command chair armrest. "Unidentified craft, please identify yourself." Static. "I repeat, unidentified craft, please—"

"This is Gulf Wing A11KMB," an unknown voice replied. "John Bredeson piloting. You don't know how good it is to hear from you."

The bridge breathed a collective sigh of relief.

"This is Commander Yamane from the *S.F.S. Corona*. Is anyone else with you?"

"Just my co-pilot. We're heading for your position. We should reach you in about three minutes."

The r-tech turned back towards Yamane. "Confirmed, sir."

"We have you on our scopes. Maintain heading and touch down in landing bay beta when you arrive."

"Understood. A11KMB, out."

Both fighters escorted the shuttle all the way up. When they leveled out, the *Corona*'s homing beacon brought them in. The shuttle landed first, followed by her two escorts.

The flagman met the shuttle just as it came to a stop about halfway down the runway. He used his batons to guide the small ship into the nearest parking stall. When all three wheels were more or less within the double yellow lines, he signaled an engine shutdown.

When the forward safety hatch flipped open, Bredeson and his co-pilot peered out first before jumping onto the tarmac. Both men were tall, but thin. A subtle look of shock registered on their faces. They took a good long look around the cavernous bay, their mouths hanging open in disbelief.

When a clattering sound clanked and banged behind them, both Bredson and his co-pilot spun around; startled by the unexpected noise. A pair of MP's emerged from the lift and approached the shuttle.

"My name's Lieutenant Kaur," he offered after stopping a short distance away. "This is corporal Tomlinson. Welcome aboard the *Corona*. If you would follow me, I will bring you to the bridge." Both he and the corporal turned and headed back the way he came before the two could say otherwise. The lift banged to a stop at the top of the shaft. When Tomlinson pulled the gate back, Kaur stepped out ahead of them. "This way, please," he motioned.

As the four headed down the darkened corridor, the pungent aroma of smoke and burnt plastic hung heavy in the air. Kaur made an abrupt right and marched onto the bridge. He circled around Yamane sitting in the command chair and snapped to attention. "Here are the two men you wanted to see," he said in short, precise words.

Yamane rose from the command chair and offered his hand. "You don't know how pleased I am you are here." Neither man responded. Their generally disheveled appearance, three-week old beards, and withdrawn gaze told Yamane that they had endured something more than they could ever recount. "Welcome aboard," he added.

Bredeson wandered past the commander, transfixed by a view of Earth on the main screen. A noticeable pause followed. "When the Deravans encircled the planet," he said to no one in particular, a deep level of pain permeating each word, "we thought no one would survive the bombardment." Yamane came alongside. Bredeson gave no indication he saw him. "I'm all right," he said. "It's just hard to believe that we were on the brink of extinction, and now ..."

"What was it like down there?" Yamane asked as sensitively as possible.

Bredeson continued looking at the main screen with a distant kind of stare. "When the stellar cruisers were all destroyed," he stopped and looked around the bridge, "at least we thought they were, planetary defenses tried to hold them back. The Deravans took them out in the first wave. Those lucky enough to get on board a ship thought they might get through, but we don't know if any of them made it out. Then the worst came. The Deravans rained death and destruction down on us twenty-four hours a day. They incinerated military installations, power stations, cities, towns, roads, and who knows what else. No place was safe."

"How did the two of you survive?"

"Dave and I were part of the Deepcore Mining Company outside of Winnipeg. We shuttled executives back and forth between the operation and their offices in Vancouver. When the Deravans attacked the city, we held out for a while. But they never stopped. And so the two of us decided we would take our chances and make a break for the mines."

Yamane noticed Bredeson ringing his hands. "How long were you there?"

"Until today, we hid in the deepest shafts. When you're five kilometers underground, you can still hear those muffled explosions blasting the cities out of existence."

Bredeson caught himself, "And then the bombardment ceased. We waited a short while before Dave and I returned to the surface. Using the ship's scanners, we discovered the Deravans had left. Three hours later, we picked up your fleet. We powered the shuttle up and, well...you know the rest."

"When was the last time the two of you had a shower and a hot meal?" Yamane asked.

Bredeson looked around the bridge again. "A long while," he sighed.

"I'll have you escorted to the med-lab first and get checked out. Then you can sack out for a bit. I'm sure you can both use a good night's sleep on a soft, comfortable bed."

A smile appeared for the first time. "Thank you. You don't know how much we appreciate your kindness."

"In a while, when you're rested and fed, we can talk some more. There are other questions I would like to ask. Maybe I can answer some of yours along the way."

"Of course, Commander."

When Lt. Kaur escorted them off the bridge, Yamane resumed his place in the command chair. Staring at the image of Earth on the main screen, an intense feeling of satisfaction filled his soul. Despite the overwhelming odds stacked against them, both he and his crew had overcome every one, without fail.

Yamane sat deeper in his chair and thought about what his next action should be. As he gazed at the big blue world on the main screen, only then did he realize just how big a job awaited them all. Yet, Yamane felt hopeful about the future. He had moved heaven and Earth to get back home. Now, he stood on the precipice of seeing his charge completed. His first order of business, locate the pockets of survivors down below. His second order of business, begin rebuilding their broken world. *How does one start such a massive effort?*

Yamane's attention drew back into the bridge. There, in front of him, was his crew. They were the reason the human race could claim victory this day. He thought about it some more, and realized this wasn't quite true. Then a powerful realization overtook him, and everything all fell into place. Their world could be made new again, but only through the efforts of the High Son. Yes, with the help of the High Son, they would find a way together.

Also available from Silver Leaf Books:

CLIFFORD B. BOWYER

The Imperium Saga

Fall of the Imperium Trilogy

An evil tyrant weaves a tapestry of deception as he plots to conquer the Imperium. Only a few heroes are brave enough to uncover the mystery and face Zoldex directly. Follow the adventures of the heroes of the realm as they try to preserve the Imperium and confront Zoldex's forces. Their hearts are true and their intentions noble, but will that be enough to overcome such overwhelming odds? Find out in the *Fall of the Imperium Trilogy*.

The Impending Storm, 0974435449, $27.95
The Changing Tides, 0974435457, $27.95
The Siege of Zoldex, 0974435465, $29.95

The Adventures of Kyria

In a time of great darkness, when evil sweeps the land, a prophecy fore-tells the coming of a savior, a child that will defeat the forces of evil and save the world. She is Kyria, the Chosen One.

From the pages of the Imperium Saga, *The Adventures of Kyria* fol-lows the child destined to save the world as she tries to live up to her destiny.

The Child of Prophecy, 0974435406, $5.99
The Awakening, 0974435414, $5.99
The Mage's Council, 0974435422, $5.99
The Shard of Time, 0974435430, $5.99
Trapped in Time, 0974435473, $5.99
Quest for the Shard, 0974435481, $5.99
The Spread of Darkness, 0978778219, $5.99
The Apprentice of Zoldex, 0978778227, $5.99
The Darkness Within, 0978778243, $5.99
The Rescue of Nezbith, 0978778251, $5.99
and more to come!

ILFANTI

Known as an adventurer, the dwarven Council of Elders member Ilfanti is one of the most famous Mages in the realm. Everyone knows his name, and others flock around his charisma. But even Ilfanti is at a loss for why the Mage's Council is ignoring the fact that Zoldex has returned and none are safe as his plans go unchallenged.

The Empress has been kidnapped while in the midst of trying to unite the races. Her true whereabouts are unknown, but her return is vital to the survival of the Seven Kingdoms. The Mages are doing nothing, and Ilfanti can no longer condone avoiding the obvious signs that are plaguing the realm.

Follow Ilfanti as he returns to a life of an adventurer and battles against time to save the Imperium. Experience the adventure and learn if the charismatic adventurer can complete one last mission in time to save the realm.

Ilfanti and the Orb of Prophecy, 0978778278, $18.95
and more to come!

CLIFFORD B. BOWYER
CONTINUING THE PASSION

Continuing the Passion follows the story of Connor Edmond Blake, a best-selling novelist who, after suffering the tragic and unexpected loss of his father decides that the best way to honor the memory of his father is by carrying on the legacy that his father left behind.

Connor's father, William Edward Blake, a Hall of Fame High School Baseball Coach had led his team to numerous state championships. Most of Connor's memories and moments he shared with his father have something to do with and revolve around the sport of baseball. As a former coach himself, of a men's softball team, Connor decides to at least make the attempt to coach a High School team in attempt to honor his father.

Continuing the Passion is seen through the eyes of Connor Blake as he experiences the tragedy of the loss of his father, and his pursuit to help his family find a way to overcome the loss.

Continuing the Passion, 097877826X, $18.95

STUART CLARK
PROJECT U·L·F

Imprisoned for a crime of passion, Wyatt Dorren is given a second chance at life on the Criminal Rehabilitation Program. Dorren becomes the rarest of breeds: an ex-convict who has become a productive member of society, trapping U.L.F.'s—Unidentified Life Forms—from newly discovered planets and returning with them for exhibition at the Interplanetary Zoo. Dorren inspires loyalty and courage in his team members, but nothing from his dark past, or his years trapping dangerous aliens, can prepare him for what's in store now.

Project U.L.F., 0978778200, $27.95
and more to come!

MIKE LYNCH & BRANDON BARR
SKY CHRONICLES

Since the dawn of time, an ancient evil has sought complete and unquestioned dominion over the galaxy, and they have found...us.

The year is 2217 and a fleet of stellar cruisers led by Commander Frank Yamane are about to come face to face with humanity's greatest threat—the Deravan armada. Outnumbered, outclassed, and outgunned, Yamane's plan for stopping them fails; leaving all of humanity at the mercy of an enemy that has shown them none.

Follow the adventures of Commander Frank Yamane and his crew as they struggle to determine whether this will be Earth's finest hour, or the destruction of us all.

Sky Chronicles: When the Sky Fell, 0978778235, $18.95

ABOUT THE AUTHORS

Mike Lynch currently resides in San Jose, California with his wife, Kathleen, and two children. He graduated from San Jose State University in 1986 with a B.A. in History, and San Jose Christian College with a B.A. in Bible and Theology in 1994. *Sky Chronicles: When the Sky Fell*, is Mike's first novel. Mike has also published short stories, and was awarded 'Best of Show' in the Residential Aliens 2007 flash fiction contest for one of his entries. Mike also will appear in the upcoming Silver Leaf Books anthology: *The Imperium Saga: Tales of the Council of Elders*, as the author of *Pierce's Tale*.

Photo by Adam Kazmierski

Brandon J. Barr was born and raised in Redlands , California where he still lives today with his wife, Amanda. A graduate from California Baptist University, he received a B.A. in English in 2004. Brandon has enjoyed reading and writing from a young age, and began writing his own fiction in 2003. Brandon also will appear in the upcoming Silver Leaf Books anthology: *The Imperium Saga: Tales of the Council of Elders*, as the author of *Cinzia's Tale*. Brandon's most beloved genres are science fiction, fantasy, and inspiration.